Crescent City Carnage

An Alex Boyd Thriller

Mel Harrison

AHA Publishers

Dedication

Crescent City Carnage is dedicated to my friend, Sharon Perlis, a native of New Orleans, and an accomplished lawyer. My wife and I first met Sharon in the mid-1980s at the World Trade Center of New Orleans, and stayed friends over the decades.

Just before I started the first chapter of this book, I called Sharon to ask her advice on the basic story and development of the African American Creole community in New Orleans. We spoke for hours, and she gave me some excellent recommendations. She also directed me to numerous locations for research, which I found extremely helpful.

Then, unexpectedly, she passed away.

We miss her friendship and sage advice and hope she would have been pleased with how her support helped this novel turn out. May she rest in peace.

Characters and Acronyms

U.S. State Department

    DS - Diplomatic Security Service, U.S. Department of State

    RSO - Regional Security Officer, Diplomatic Security

    Alex Boyd - Special Agent, Diplomatic Security Service Regional Security Officer U.S. Embassy, London

    Rachel Smith - Political Counselor U.S. Embassy, London

    Simone Ardoin - Office of Italian Affairs, U.S. Department of State, Washington, D.C.

    Susan Witt - Special Agent/Agent-in-Charge of DS Resident Agency New Orleans

    Scott Fellows - DS Special Agent, New Orleans

    Pete Fong - DS Special Agent, New Orleans

    Isabelle Lewis - DS Special Agent, Houston Field Office

    Jim Riley - Director, Diplomatic Security, Washington, D.C.

    Tommy Rogers - RSO US Embassy Port-au-Prince, Haiti

    Luis Torres - DS Special Agent, New Orleans

    Burt Warner - DS Special Agent, Houston Field Office

New Orleans

NOPD - New Orleans Police Dept.

DEA - Drug Enforcement Administration, US Government

Edouard "Papa Ed" Ardoin - Simone's father and founder of his law firm

Camille Ardoin - Medical doctor, Simone's mother and wife of Papa Ed

Jules Baptiste - Haitian born gang leader living in New Orleans

Vern Bordelon - Regional Director, New Orleans Drug Enforcement Agency (DEA)

Destiny - Girlfriend of Baptiste

Detective "Fast Tim" Kelly - Detective, New Orleans Police Department (NOPD)

Janet "Moon Glow" Ross - Local resident, tattoo artist, and partner of Billy Whiteman

Claude Toussaint - Criminal, works for Baptiste

Captain Jim Wells - New Orleans Police Dept. (NOPD); friend of Papa Ed Ardoin

Sgt. John Washington - NOPD detective

Bill Westbrook - FBI Special Agent in Charge of New Orleans office

Billy Whiteman - Local resident, graphic artist, boyfriend of Moon Glow

Northshore, New Orleans

Billy Landry - Sheriff, St. Tammany Parish

Vinnie Fiore - Deputy, St. Tammany Parish

Prologue

Death arrives in many ways. Sometimes, it's slow and agonizing. Other times, it's violent and without warning, a shock to the senses, inflicting painful sorrow upon family . . . and friends.

All too familiar with the latter, Alex Boyd and Rachel Smith hadn't expected it to happen again, so soon. Certain losses were sad. Other losses called for revenge. This was one of those times.

Rachel bent over to tie her shoe, showing an impressive length of leg from behind; her tiny shorts topped an extension of shapely thighs that ran down to curved, well-muscled calves sharply honed from years of running.

Alex was muscular, tall, ruggedly handsome, a compliment to Rachel. He rocked back and forth slightly, warming his muscles while waiting for her. Well-matched, they made a striking pair.

The warm August sun crept above the city skyline a little before 6:30 a.m. and cast a pale glow over the French Quarter, slow to waken; it brought the possibility of a new day of excitement and exploration.

Street-cleaning vehicles scattered sprays of soapy water from swirling brushes toward the concrete, wiping accumulated detritus from the previous evening. Shopkeepers began coming out using garden hoses to wash away debris from sidewalks in front of their establishments.

More than a decade after Hurricane Katrina, New Orleans was still a city on the mend, a city where lifelong residents and business owners still took pride living there. Most were determined to maintain the culture, hospitality, and vitality of their beloved city.

Yet, a dark, criminal element also inhabited the city, one that didn't give a damn about anyone's welfare, including tourists. Such easy targets to rob, perhaps even kill.

Chapter 1

Welcome to New Orleans

The Crescent City

Stretching long limbs in the lobby of the Royal Sonesta Hotel, Alex Boyd and Rachel Smith flexed hamstrings, knees, and ankles, then bolted out the double glass front doors of their hotel. After jogging down Bourbon Street toward Esplanade Avenue, they turned right onto Conti Street a block later, then left onto Royal Street. The hotel concierge had said more high end shops and buildings were on Royal rather than on Bourbon Street; it was also one-way, and better for seeing oncoming vehicles. He was right.

Yesterday's flight from London, through Atlanta, and on to New Orleans' Louis Armstrong Airport had left them stiff, in need of exercise to rejuvenate their bodies. A time zone difference of six hours between London and New Orleans meant they had awakened at 3:30 a.m. since their body rhythms were still on London time. But that was much too early to leave their room and do something useful. So, to kill time until sunrise, they looked at their emails, read news stories on their laptops, and engaged in limited sexual foreplay before putting on their running shorts and t-shirts.

Delighted to be visiting the crescent city on the famed Mississippi River for the first time, Alex and Rachel had jumped at the chance when Simone Ardoin, Rachel's former deputy in the Office of Italian Affairs in the State Department, had suggested they join her for a week's vacation in her hometown. The sad truth was that Alex and Rachel were workaholics, and since their marriage in Rome a few years back, they hadn't taken as many long vacations as planned during their euphoric honeymoon when the future stretched before them. So, this week was an attempt to make up for that failing.

Now, jogging in the street, they avoided sidewalks full of cracked concrete slabs and potholes that could cause serious injury. Every block also had sections where homeless people were sleeping under cardboard, their personal junk piled next to them. *What? No shelters*, Alex wondered. *Guess the city admin is too indifferent, or incompetent to find a solution.*

From the hotel, they covered ten blocks to Esplanade Avenue, a wide tree-lined street, divided by a center median, called "neutral ground" in New Orleans, before turning left toward City Park.

"Jesus, it's humid down here," Rachel said at a little under the two-mile mark, her words broke with each step. "Maybe our plan to run five miles was a little ambitious?" They separated from running side-by-side as a vehicle approached, then came back alongside each other after it passed.

"You're right, I'm sweating like a pig. This humidity sucks," Alex replied.

She gave him a thumbs up. "Let me know when you want to turn around."

"How about if we up our game? Let's sprint for the next two blocks, then stop?"

"You're on." Rachel broke stride and accelerated away from him, her brown ponytail flipping out the back of her Dodgers baseball cap as she ran.

"Hey, that's cheating!"

"Catch me if you can." Her words were nearly lost in the air.

Alex kicked into overdrive and started rapidly closing the gap. *Damn, she's competitive,* he thought with a smile.

They both knew Alex was faster, but it was the journey, not the result, that tingled their senses. Ever since attending separate colleges, both on athletic scholarships, they loved to compete against each other, whether in the gym, in routine humorous conversation, or in the bedroom. It was the glue that held their relationship . . . well, partly. Another was a healthy sexual appetite for each other, as well as their mutual respect for each other's professional abilities.

He was almost up to her, knowing he could easily pass, but hung back a tad to watch her long legs powering her forward. He loved the view and watched her well-defined arms pumping with each stride. A smile crossed his lips. *Maybe tonight . . .*

Just ahead, he saw the intersection and a car turning the corner, heading in their direction. It wasn't in his nature to let her win, nor would she want it that way, but the approaching car made his decision easy. He passed her as the car whizzed by.

Rather fast, buddy, Alex thought. By habit, he took note of the color and plate.

Both had stopped running and were bent over, breathing in the heavy, humid air with an occasional groan. Then they held each other. Sweat dripped down their bodies. Across the neutral ground, a dark blue Camry slowly drove by at maybe ten miles per hour. Alex made eye contact with one of the four guys inside. Then the vehicle picked up speed and went on, but Alex filed it away in his memory. *Hmmm, a lot of street activity this morning,* he thought.

"Shall we take it easy on the way back?" Alex asked.

"Sounds like a plan to me."

They jogged back on Esplanade Avenue toward the Mississippi River, crossed over Rampart Street, on the edge of the French Quarter, and decided to walk three blocks to Bourbon Street for the last stretch.

Alex loved the neighborhood. Tall, leafy trees on both sides of the street with a wide center neutral ground where a few people were walking their dogs. The houses had a variety of older genteel styles, some constructed of wood, others of brick or finished off with stucco. Balconies and front porches were in abundance, along with potted flowers dotting everything with color. As they drew within a block of Bourbon Street, the same beat-up dark blue Camry Alex had seen earlier, passed by, again, still filled with four guys. But this time, it drove close enough that he noticed the hideous tattoos on the arm of one man as it hung out the window; one was the head of a dragon. All were young, in their twenties, and tough-looking. Two of them stared at Rachel.

"Alex?"

"I know, Rach. Let's keep an eye on them."

The Camry pulled over and parked just ahead of the couple. Alex grabbed Rachel's sweaty bicep, pulling her to a stop. Three men exited the car; all wore tattered blue jeans resting well below their waist, sleeveless sweat-stained t-shirts, and expensive looking sneakers.

"Rach, cross the street."

The men walked faster and caught them in the center of the neutral ground, surrounding Alex and Rachel.

"If you want to rob us, you can see we've been running," Alex said. "We don't have any money on us." His voice was firm, confident, as he stared into the eyes of the man directly in front of him. The man's left eye was twitching slightly; a scar ran from that eye halfway down his face.

"Shut the fuck up," the thug yelled. "Gimme your sneakers. Gimme your watch, too," he pointed to Alex's Casio G-shock, inexpensive compared to his Jaeger-LeCoultre back at the hotel. The thug looked at Rachel. "The same with you, tall girl. Sneakers and watch . . . *now!*"

The punk lifted his shirt a tad so Alex could see the pistol stuffed in the front of his waistband to show he meant business.

"Okay, here's my watch," Alex said as he took a step forward, pretending to undo his watchband. Within striking distance, he used the full force of his two-hundred and ten pounds, pivoting his hips into the strike, and slammed the heel of his right palm into the man's jawbone. "Twitch-eye" collapsed on the ground.

Reaching down, Alex grabbed the pistol from the unconscious man's waistband and pulled the slide back, chambering a new round, ejecting the old one.

At the same time as Alex's strike, Rachel edged closer to her nearest guy. When Alex struck, so did Rachel. Lashing out with a straight front kick into the man's left knee, she nailed him with full force. He fell to the ground with a cry of agony.

"You bitch! You busted my kneecap . . . you *dead, bitch!*"

He grabbed for the gun in his pocket, but Rachel kicked him in the face . . . hard. The gun flew from his hand as he sprawled flat on his back, motionless. Her eyes burned with anger and she gave a second kick to his head.

"Who's the bitch, *now*?" she snarled. Alex's eyes widened in surprise at her vicious reaction, knowing the man was already out cold.

The third attacker ran to the Camry and leapt into the back seat. The driver floored it. Tires squealed as they raced off.

Alex and Rachel stood there, breathing heavier than normal.

"What, now?" she asked.

"I called da cops!" an old woman yelled out from the porch of a nearby house. "I seen it all! I'm glad you wasn't hurt."

"Does this happen around here often?" Rachel asked.

"Sometimes. You was amazin', honey."

Rachel smiled and yelled back to her. "Thanks. I watch a lot of movies!"

Holding the thug's pistol in one hand, Alex waved a "thanks" to the old woman just as sirens filled the air. Alex estimated the cops were about two blocks away.

"Rach, let's wait for the cavalry." She nodded. Then, as the sirens got louder, he placed the pistol on the ground.

"I'll tell them what I seen!" the old woman shouted from across the street.

"We'd be grateful! Thank you," Rachel replied.

Alex put his arm around Rachel as the marked car pulled up; it jumped onto the neutral ground.

"You okay?" he whispered to her.

"Yeah. The guy was a punk." She spit her words out with fury. Alex stared at her without expression. "What? Am I not supposed to say that?"

"I'm smiling because I love who you are. If you were a guy, I'd say you've got a real set of balls."

"Hmm. I *think* that was a complement," she said. "You guys can't have *all* the fun. Women like to kick ass sometimes, too, ya' know."

"Whew. Better that guy than me." He pointed to the unconscious thug on the ground, but silently, he wondered if he should say something about her vicious kick to the guy's head after he was unconscious. *Considering who she kicked, however, maybe her reaction wasn't that over-the-top,* he decided.

"Don't worry, Hunk Man, I've got your back." They both laughed.

The cops got out of the patrol car as Alex and Rachel waved to them, hoping it showed they were the good guys. Alex identified himself as a special agent with Diplomatic Security and described what happened. Within a minute two other police cars arrived.

When two of the men on the ground groaned, it was obvious they were starting to come around. The police handcuffed them and put them into the back of a black and white cruiser.

Alex overheard the old woman give a full description of the action from her porch as one cop took notes.

"Mr. Boyd, since you remembered the license number of the Camry, we hope to track down the other two soon, even though the car was probably stolen," one cop said. "We've been after this four-man gang for weeks. After you and your wife clean up back at the hotel, please go to Royal Street police station and make a formal statement. I'll tell the station to expect you.

Although neither cop was familiar with Diplomatic Security when he mentioned his position, they seemed impressed that he was a federal special agent.

Well, that was a great start in the Big Easy, Alex thought as they walked back to the hotel. *If that's what happens before breakfast on our first day here, I can hardly wait for lunch.*

Chapter 2

Lunch with Simone Ardoin

Hours later, Alex and Rachel pushed open the double front doors of the Royal Sonesta Hotel on Bourbon Street again and were engulfed in the heavy summertime humidity of this unique city on the Mississippi River. Unpleasant smells of the French Quarter assaulted their nostrils; smells wafting from unemptied trash bins mixed with stale beer spilled on sidewalks since the last cleaning. Nevertheless, it was thrilling to be in this three-hundred-year-old enclave of the old American south.

Working for the U.S. Embassy in London for the last eighteen months had been rewarding, and yes, stressful, so this one-week vacation in New Orleans was too good an invitation to pass up. Their good friend and colleague, Simone Ardoin, had seen to it that they would enjoy this time away from their daily lives. Joining her for lunch now was their only agenda.

As they stepped onto the sidewalk in front of the hotel, Alex smiled at Rachel, clasped her hand and kissed her on the cheek.

Wearing high heels, her brilliant green eyes were level with his own brown ones. She smiled back at him.

"What's up with the kiss?" she asked.

"I'm just happy to be here with you."

"That's sweet." A half smile formed on her lips; her face lit up looking at him.

On yesterday's journey from Heathrow, Alex had felt the tension within him begin to dissipate. But this morning's attempted robbery reminded him that danger was never far away. But now, it was time to enjoy amazing food, marvel at local architecture, and listen to some mellow jazz.

As a trained special agent with the State Department's Diplomatic Security Service, Alex was always attuned to his surroundings. Noticing people as they walked by, visually checking whether they were concealing a weapon or firearm, was second nature. He also observed parked cars, checking if someone was inside watching them. Facial expressions on passersby, such as eyes staring at them, a clenched jaw, or rapid tongue movements to moisten lips, all might signal panic, fear, danger, or more than simply a natural curiosity. It took mere seconds, but Alex considered his pseudo-paranoia as just taking routine precautions.

Of course, someone might be just staring at Rachel, he thought, *who wouldn't find her gorgeousness intoxicating.* Standing a little over six feet tall in heels, she had luxurious, long, wavy brown hair. Her face glowed with a healthy outdoor complexion from years of playing competitive tennis and other sports. Her determined jaw line exuded a natural challenge to any serious athlete noticing her. Someone would have to look very closely to spot two small scars on her cheekbones inflicted upon her five years earlier by a terrorist when she fought him hand-to-hand in Islamabad, Pakistan, to save her own life.

Alex, himself, was rugged and handsome, with a full head of thick dark brown hair. His height and physique gave him a presence that people noted. He had been a jock all his life and, now, at forty years old, could still hold his own against any competitor. Their combination of looks and athletic bodies always seemed to draw attention, so as usual, Alex had to sort out any odd-ball behavior from real danger. In the French Quarter, the former was abundant. So far, everything seemed normal as they stood in the afternoon heat. He took a deep breath, confident for the moment, they could enjoy the French Quarter without concern.

"It's almost two o'clock," Rachel said. "We'd better get a move on."

"Don't worry, I see Galatoire's from here. It's a block away. I'm glad we ran this morning because we're going to pack on calories at lunch."

"To say the least. But I don't think you're starving. We had a good meal at breakfast."

"Sure, but that was hours ago," he said. " My Eggs Benedict with crawfish was mostly protein. Besides, look who's talking, big girl. You *devoured* all your omelet with andouille sausage in that heavy cream sauce. I don't suppose *that* was some type of 'low-cal' sauce, now, was it?"

"I just want to fit into the local culture," she laughed. "Simone told me that New Orleanians will eat anything that moves, as long as it has plenty of sauce on it."

He loved her clever comeback, and laughed.

SIMONE WAS SEATED IN GALATOIRE'S WHEN THEY ARRIVED. THE room was much deeper than wide, with a few windows at the front. In the rear was the waiter's station and entrance to the kitchen. The walls on both sides had rectangular mirrors running the length of the room with green wallpaper above them. The floor had small geometric pattern of black tiles mixed in with larger white ones. Lighting was provided by overhead fixtures of lamp clusters attached to brass fans, as well as wall-mounted lights also on brass fixtures. If he had not known he was in New Orleans, he might have assumed they'd wandered into a bistro in Paris.

Alex wore a blue blazer and pleated grey slacks from a French clothing designer while Rachel wore a sleek, knee-length dress from a haut-couture designer in Paris. They both looked amazing. Alex liked the narrow waist on Rachel's dress which accented her figure and showed off her exquisite calves. Seeing them approaching, Simone stood-up to greet them and they all embraced in greetings.

"Welcome to my favorite restaurant," Simone said as they sat down.

"I can see why," Rachel replied.

"Can I get a burger and fries here?" Alex asked with a sly grin.

Simone laughed. "You most certainly cannot!"

He liked Simone Ardoin. Two years ago, as Rachel's deputy in the Office of Italian Affairs in the State Department in Washington, DC, Simone had proven to be smart and a good writer. And just as he and Rachel had served in Rome for a few years, so had Simone, although it had been earlier in her career. Currently, Simone was still assigned to Washington.

Before she could say anything else, Simone looked up and

smiled at the waiter in a black tuxedo who had walked over to their table.

"Rachel and Alex, let me introduce you to Casey, our waiter, and my friend. I've known Casey for twenty years. Moreover, his father was a waiter here before him." They both greeted him.

"It's good to see you again, Miss Simone," Casey said.

"And the same to you, Casey."

"Can I get anyone a cocktail?"

Simone looked at her guests. "How about if we just share a bottle of wine?" Alex asked. Simone nodded, and she suggested a white since they were all having fish.

"Casey, we'll have a bottle of Pouilly Fuisse," Alex requested.

"Very nice selection," Casey replied. "I'll return in a moment along with French bread."

While he was gone, they looked at the long menu until he returned bringing the wine, bread, and creamy butter they had ordered.

As soon as Casey left, Simone wasted no time. "I need to tell you something important. Yesterday evening, I ran into a man who I recognized from years ago when I worked in the American Consular section in Haiti. His name is Jules Baptiste."

"Is that good news?" Rachel asked.

"No, not at all. He's a criminal and used to run a visa fraud gang with links to New Orleans. I didn't speak to him yesterday, but I followed him to see what he was doing in the French Quarter. I can't *imagine* how he got here because he *never* would have qualified for a legitimate visa. By the way, in case you were wondering, he didn't see me." Her eyes raced between Rachel and Alex, looking for a reaction. Then she continued, "It's okay, don't worry; I know my way around the Quarter."

Alex shot a quick glance at Rachel whose body had backed

away from the table, her mouth now open. *Simone played with fire, and put herself in a dangerous situation,* he thought. "Why did you follow him?" Alex asked.

"I don't understand what you mean. The guy's a crook," Simone replied.

Rachel leaned forward, her arms resting on the table. "That's Alex's point. This guy could be very dangerous. In fact, you said he's *head* of a Haitian gang with ties here in the city."

"Yes, he is. When I ran the non-immigrant visa section at the U.S. Embassy in Port-au-Prince, we always knew he was at the top of a large fraud ring. But the cops in Haiti were paid to the look the other way, so we could never nail him. And believe me, we tried hard."

"Simone, now that you've discovered Jules Baptiste is here," Alex said, "let's have my Diplomatic Security colleagues in the New Orleans office work with the local cops to make a case against him."

She was about to answer when Casey brought the first course of lunch; they stopped talking. After he presented each plate of food and wished them *bon appetite,* Casey left. Simone looked at Alex and Rachel, again.

"Let's change subjects. You'll love this meal," she said. "Rachel, Galatoire's is famous for the turtle soup you ordered. And Alex, your *shrimp remoulade* is a classic New Orleans appetizer, although Arnaud's Restaurant is credited with inventing the famous sauce."

Everyone tried their dishes. "Oh, my god," Alex said. "This is *great*. I love the tanginess of the sauce." Rachel also praised her turtle soup, which she had never had before.

"My parents have eaten in Galatoire's since before I was born," Simone smiled. "In fact, we have this corner table every time." There was a lull in conversation as the threesome enjoyed their meals.

"Look, I'm sorry if you think I took a risk by following Jules Baptiste into a couple of bars, but I wanted to find out if he lives here now, or if it was just business in the French Quarter."

"How many bars did you follow him into?" Alex asked.

"Three. He seemed to have collected money at each of them. Probably to supply illegal Haitian workers as cleaners or cooks. Or maybe to deal drugs."

"Did you do anything else?" Alex asked, He took another bite of his exquisite shrimp remoulade while his eyes never left Simone.

"No, I didn't have time. I just wanted to see where he went."

"Okay, that's good," Alex said, swallowing the last morsel of his appetizer. Simone looked down and pushed her food around her plate. Alex figured she had held something back and guessed Rachel thought the same.

"Simone, is there something else you want to tell us?" Rachel asked. The pause seemed without end.

"Yes, I went back to each of the bars after I lost Baptiste in the crowd, and asked a few questions."

"*Jesus*, Simone!" Rachel said. "If these bars are working with Jules Baptiste, then you've *exposed* yourself to unwanted scrutiny." Simone lowered her eyes and fidgeted with her silverware.

I've seen this behavior before while working at U.S. embassies abroad, Alex thought. *A well-meaning and hard charging young officer tries to do the right thing without first thinking through the consequences.*

"Simone, since you know this guy is a crook, I can appreciate your efforts to bring him to justice," he said. "But let's approach this as a team effort from now on. My experience as a special agent and a regional security officer has taught me that a criminal case requires preparation, documentary evidence, and witnesses. This can take a lot of time. Following Baptiste into bars by yourself isn't enough, and it was dangerous. Will you agree not to do that again?"

"Okay, I'm sorry, I promise I won't," she said as a slightly pink tinge crept onto her lovely dark skin. That Rachel had been Simone's former boss in Washington only seemed to reinforce her embarrassment.

"We're worried about your safety," Alex replied. "I'll contact Susan Witt, our senior DS resident agent here, and let her know about this guy. She can follow up with the rest of New Orleans law enforcement and figure out how to proceed."

"That's great, I would feel much better about it all. Thanks, Alex. I appreciate it."

Wanting to emphasize how dangerous New Orleans could be, Alex told her about their attempted robbery earlier in the day. Simone was appalled and understood his point that even well-trained people could run into trouble. Again, she reassured them she would be cautious from that moment on.

"By the way, I'm delighted you both agreed to visit New Orleans. Tomorrow, you can meet my mom and dad. We'll have Sunday dinner with them at their house in Uptown. It's the same house where I grew up."

"How long has your family lived here?" Rachel asked.

"Well, my family came to New Orleans from Haiti in the early 1800s as 'free people of color,' to use the old phrase from back then. But we've lived in the current house since the late 1960s. My parents were one of the first to integrate the neighborhood."

"I have your parent's address, but how exactly would we find it?" Alex asked. He held up a printed paper from an email Simone had sent him earlier.

"If you're driving from the French Quarter, it's a few miles up St. Charles Avenue, just past Audubon Park, and Tulane University. The street is on the left, heading toward the river."

"*You* went to Tulane, didn't you?" Rachel asked.

"Yes, I did. Both undergraduate and law school."

"But you didn't want to *practice* law?" Rachel asked.

"Much to my dad's chagrin, no, I didn't," she said. "He wanted me to follow in his footsteps and join his law firm. But I wanted the Foreign Service instead. Besides, I'd had enough of Mardi Gras parades, debutante balls, charity galas, and the social scene here."

"That doesn't sound so bad," Alex said.

"I guess not, but once you get locked into that lifestyle, you tend to lose perspective on what's important in the larger world."

Casey arrived with their main courses. When the order was placed before Alex, he smiled in anticipation of the first taste. On Casey's recommendation, he had ordered the *sole meuniere* cooked in a lemon-butter sauce, topped with lump crab meat and fresh asparagus on the side and crowned with a dollop of hollandaise sauce.

Before he could even take his first bite, Rachel had already begun savoring her sautéed Redfish with Crabmeat Yvonne, loaded with jumbo lump crabmeat, artichokes, green onions, and mushrooms in a *meuniere* sauce. *That's my girl*, he thought, smiling.

Simone had also ordered the sole, but without crabmeat. All smiling as they ate, they enjoyed every morsel. The bottle of

Pouilly Fuisse, shared among the three of them completely enhanced the memorable meal.

Lost in thought, Alex reflected on his own upbringing. It had been quite different from this unique local culture. Because his parents had both worked for the CIA, he had grown up abroad and moved every few years. Never regretting having to make new friends, his childhood in Paris and Cairo gave him language skills, toughness, and an independence not found in most children.

Even Rachel grew up in a culture different from this one, he thought, *she's a California girl, whatever that means culturally. But she's the smartest woman I've ever known, and a terrific athlete, too.*

However, the only problem Rachel seemed to have, in his mind, was that she had become intolerant of people who didn't put in enough effort to meet her expectations. *Perhaps her own increasing responsibilities and rank in the State Department have contributed to that,* he thought. *She really pushes herself to excel and can't understand why others don't.* Over time, Alex had watched her attitude toward subordinates change, and even upon occasion, had delicately suggested she might try to communicate her expectations to her minions, before hitting them over the head with a sledgehammer. It hadn't always gone too well.

Later, when Casey offered dessert, Simone selected a piece of warm pecan pie with vanilla ice cream. Alex and Rachel each had warm bread pudding, a classic baked concoction with milk, sugar, and eggs.

After the meal, Alex picked up the tab. "I think I've gained an inch on my waistline," he said to the women's appreciative laughter. Leaving the restaurant, they stood on the sidewalk of Bourbon Street absorbing the full ambience of the unique

Quarter's architecture and all its overhanging wrought-iron balconies decorated with colorful flowers. As they watched people passing by, their eyes were drawn to some interesting souvenir shops. *The French Quarter looks more like a charming Caribbean town than a major U.S. city,* he thought.

"Simone, Rachel and I want to stop at this nearby Walgreens to buy a New Orleans Times-Picayune newspaper," he said. "Then, we're going to walk by the river and around the French Quarter. Want to join us?"

"No, thanks, I need to spend time with my parents. I want to catch up with them before I return to Washington. But I'll see you tomorrow at their house for dinner."

They all embraced with goodbyes and kisses on the cheeks. Then Simone walked away from them toward the Royal Sonesta hotel; she planned to catch a taxi.

Alex and Rachel headed toward the great Mississippi River to explore. This Saturday afternoon in the French Quarter had seemed idyllic. But life has a way of surprising you.

Chapter 3

Playing with Fire

One block from the restaurant, as Simone approached the hotel, she froze in mid-stride. Jules Baptiste, and two other men were about to cross her path on Bienville Street. She looked for Alex and Rachel, but they were too far away. She could have called them on her cellphone, but Baptiste was already walking away from her with long strides. She decided to catch up to him as best she could, by herself.

Even though Simone had promised Alex and Rachel she wouldn't act alone, this opportunity had presented itself, and she decided to take the risk.

She followed Baptiste into the same bar where she had followed him the day before. But he seemed to have disappeared into the crowd of clientele, and she lost him. Nevertheless, she spoke to the bartender, and a few customers, leaving her business card with each of them, describing who she was looking to find.

"Are you sure you didn't see a tall, black man come in here a minute ago?" Simone asked the bartender.

"Hey, I'm busy mixing drinks. Sorry, I didn't see anyone like that."

"Well, I just saw him come in here. Look, if he comes back, I'd appreciate a call. My number is on the card. I'm staying in Uptown at my parent's house for a few days. I want to talk to him about visa fraud."

"Sure. You know, now that you mention it, I think I've seen a guy like that around here."

"The guy that I'm looking for is Jules Baptiste. He's from Haiti and he shouldn't even be in this country."

"You say his name is Baptiste?" the bartender asked. "I heard he works with a guy named Claude Toussaint, who isn't happy with him. Maybe Claude will talk to you."

"Yeah? That would be great. Ask him to call me."

Simone walked out of the bar, satisfied with the little progress she thought she had made. At first, she considered contacting Alex and Rachel to tell them what had occurred, but on second thought, she didn't want to incur their disapproval and decided to wait.

That evening, Simone was at her parent's house late at night when her cell phone rang. She didn't recognize the number, but saw it had a New Orleans area code, so she answered.

"Hello, is this Simone?" a deep male voice asked.

"Yes, who is this?"

"My name be Claude Toussaint. I hear you want to talk to me, yes?"

"That's right. I understand you're not happy working with

23

Jules Baptiste. I'm interested in him and some gang activities connected to visa fraud."

"I might be able to help . . . but not over the phone."

"Okay, can we meet . . . *tomorrow*?" Simone asked. There was a long pause.

"No, I'm leaving town . . . but I can see you . . . *tonight*."

Simone looked at her watch, it was already 9:40 pm. Should she meet him? She hesitated and ran a hand through her thick black hair, trying to think. Her heart was pounding. Sweat pooled on her upper lip. She'd been cautioned by Alex and Rachel *not* to do anything without checking with them first.

But this is my opportunity to move things forward, and I don't want to miss it! After all, Claude is my one lead to find Batiste. "Okay, Claude. Where can I meet you?"

"Do you know NOMA? You know, the art museum in City Park?"

She thought about the danger of meeting at night, before committing, then reached for glory: "Yes, of course I know it."

"Okay, park off to the right of the museum. There's a school across a small bridge. I'll meet you there at 10:30." Without another word, Claude hung up.

Simone's stomach did a back-flip. She dialed Alex's cell phone, then Rachel's cell, but neither picked up. *Shit! I'll wait five minutes and try again,* she thought. But both calls went to voice mail. *They could be in a loud bar in the French Quarter,* she thought, *but I can't wait.*

Simone was sweating and her hands were trembling. The phone call had shaken her. Yet, it meant she would be able to talk with someone willing to rat out the Haitian visa fraudsters. She hadn't expected Claude to call her directly. She had expected a tipoff from the barman about where he could be found. But instead, the new development was off the charts. She was delighted her plan had worked out, exceeding her expectations. Simone had made a decision on the spur of the moment and, for better or worse, it was time to go, time to roll the dice. It was time to take a risk that she had been warned against taking. She was gambling with her life.

She walked down the beautiful center staircase in her parent's home, the home where she had been raised. Although she hadn't lived here in years, whenever she visited Uptown New Orleans, she considered it her home as well.

"Don't tell me you're going out at *this* hour," her mother, Camille, said when Simone walked into the living room holding car keys in her hand.

"I have to meet someone; it's business."

"Business? At *this* time of night?" her father, Papa Ed, asked.

"Let me come with you; it will be safer that way."

"I'm thirty-two years old, Dad. I'm a Foreign Service Officer; I've lived around the *world*. I know what I'm doing."

As one of the best criminal defense lawyers in New Orleans, Edouard "Papa Ed" Ardoin's firm had represented some of the richest clients in the city, but his firm had also represented some of its violent scumbags, as well, and he knew how dangerous life could be in New Orleans. He didn't like Simone going out at all.

"Honey, it's been raining most of the evening, why don't you meet this person tomorrow?" Papa Ed said. "If it's about that visa fraud problem, you mentioned, I counsel you to call your friend, that Special Agent from Diplomatic Security . . . Alex Boyd, before you go off to meet anyone."

"I'm sorry, Dad, but if I don't act now, this opportunity might slip through my fingers. I already tried Alex's number, as well as his wife, Rachel's, but my calls went to voicemail. I promise to try again."

Simone looked at her recent call list, found Alex's number, and called. But the phone rang five times before going to voicemail, again. This time, she left a message.

"Hello, Alex, it's Simone. After lunch at Galatoire's I saw Jules Baptiste and followed him, but not for long. I lost him, but just got a call from a Claude Toussiant, who works for Baptiste. He's willing to meet tonight to tell me about the Haitian fraud ring in New Orleans. Call me back when you get this message."

Her parents listened as she left her voice message. But, still extremely worried, her mother said, "I think you should stay home, Simone."

Simone thought for a moment, then said, "Look, the guy I'm meeting is leaving town tomorrow. It's now or never."

"It's never, '*never*,' honey," Papa Ed said. "Someone can follow up with him another time. Where are you meeting him?"

'By NOMA in City Park."

"At night? Honey, I *insist* you not go to this meeting, now."

Simone kissed them both on their cheeks. "Thanks for your concern, but I'll be fine." She left the living room and grabbed her rain jacket in the hallway, then headed out to her rendezvous.

PAPA ED IMMEDIATELY CALLED CAPTAIN JIM WELLS, HIS CLOSE friend in the police department, and asked if they would dispatch a police cruiser to NOMA at City Park. His friend assured him that he would take care of it. Papa Ed expressed his thanks. Inwardly, he wished he would have pressed his daughter harder about staying home.

SIMONE MADE A LEFT TURN OUT OF HER PARENT'S CIRCULAR driveway, leaving the 19th century white columned house in Uptown quickly behind, and headed toward St. Charles Avenue. Earlier, an intense rain had soaked the streets; now steam rose from the roadway because of the humid eighty degrees, even at this late hour. She turned her windshield wipers on once, just to clear off accumulated water.

At the neutral ground, where streetcars ran, she turned right onto St. Charles Avenue. The road ran under a canopy of old oak trees; stylish ante-bellum homes were on either side. A black BMW began following her rental car toward the central business district. She didn't notice it.

TEN MINUTES LATER, STILL DRIVING TOWARD CITY PARK, SWEAT began appearing on her face. She shivered, perhaps from the car's air conditioner blasting on her now wet skin, or perhaps, from anxiety about the meeting she was anticipating.

What am I thinking? I don't have to do this alone? Within seconds, she felt like a fool, yet, she drove on.

Simone snaked her way through the fringe streets of the Central Business District and onto the ramp connecting to I-10 west. Fewer cars were on the road at this time of night. Within a short while, she exited onto South Carrollton Street, heading for City Park. At Esplanade Avenue, she took the circle to the left and drove into the park. The museum was in front of her, and she veered to the right, crossing the mini bridge by the school.

She had been reviewing her action steps while she drove and intended to record her conversation with Toussaint on her cell phone. She needed the names of the fraud operators in New Orleans, other than Baptiste. She would turn this information over to Diplomatic Security, then return to her Foreign Service job in Washington, D.C.

Simone parked next to the curb under a streetlamp. She tapped the steering wheel with her fingers as a nervous gesture. *Damn, I better take some deep breaths to calm down*, she thought, recognizing her own anxiety.

Rolling down her side window, she smelled the fresh air after a rain, an earthy aroma of grass and trees. After a minute, the lights of a car coming up behind her shone brightly in her rearview mirror. She pressed the audio button on her cell phone to start recording, then put it in the inside beast pocket of her lightweight blue rain jacket. Her watch indicated it was 10:30 pm. When the car stopped behind her, she exited her vehicle.

"Is that you, Claude? Can you turn off your lights?" Simone called out. Staring into the headlights, she was unable to see anything. The other car turned on its brights.

"Hey! I asked you to turn *off* your lights!"

Simone wasn't a big woman and fighting off an attacker wasn't something she had ever considered. *Besides*, she thought, *Claude wanted this meeting*. She caught the silhouette of a man getting out the passenger side and approaching her from his side of the vehicle; when he walked in front of the car, its headlights blinded her.

"Claude? Is that *you*?" she called out again. The man extended his arm toward her, and Simone felt safe enough to relax her knotted shoulder muscles, thinking he wanted a handshake.

It wasn't a handshake.

Chapter 4

Hiding in the Grass

In total darkness, Billy Whiteman and Janet Ross, known as "Moon Glow" to her friends, lay on a blanket under one of City Park's large oak trees. They kissed and explored the soft curves of each other's bodies.

Then, about a hundred feet away, someone parked next to the curb. They looked up. While the broad base of the tree they lay under hid them from sight, they heard the sound of a woman's voice. It was the urgency in it that caught their attention, and they both slid over a little on their blanket to see more. They continued watching as a second car pulled up and parked behind the first one, then turned on its bright lights.

The woman called out: "Claude, is that *you?*"

They heard the woman yell something else. Then watched as another figure, this one tall, male . . . got out of the second car.

Billy tightened his grip on Moon Glow's arm and drew her closer. "What do you think is going on?" she whispered.

"I don't know, but it's got to be something covert," he said.

She smiled. Billy always used special words, like "covert." It was one thing she liked about him.

They watched as the woman shielded her eyes from the bright headlights. In the illumination, they could clearly see her, and from their angle, they also saw a tall man walking toward her, one arm outstretched. A second later, they heard two shots ring out and saw flames shoot from the gun's barrel. The woman crumpled to the ground.

Billy opened his mouth, but Moon Glow put her tattooed hand over it to silence him. Instinctively, they flattened their bodies onto the ground. The gunman approached the fallen woman and fired two more shots into her head. Again, they saw the muzzle flashes and heard the weapon's report. Then they watched the killer get back into the second car and drive off.

Nothing moved. The night was silent again.

Stunned, Billy and Moon Glow lay on the blanket for another thirty seconds without words. Then Billy said, "Let's get the hell *outta* here!"

Not giving a damn about their blanket, the young couple ran toward their apartment building as heavy rain began pouring down. From the park, they ran across Carrollton Avenue and reached their own place within minutes.

"Maybe we should call the cops," Billy said while pacing inside their rented living room, yet his voice held little conviction.

"No way! *You* saw what happened," Moon Glow protested. "That guy's *a killer*! Who's gonna protect *us* if we tell?"

"I think I recognized the shooter," Billy said, eyes wide, looking into her face.

"Me, too. I've seen him around the Quarter. He's *really* scary."

"What are we going to do?"

"Nothing. It's none of our business." Moon Glow walked into the bathroom, hands shaking. She had never seen anyone killed before, although she once saw a dead guy outside the tattoo parlor where she worked in the French Quarter. *The cops said he died from an overdose,* she thought, remembering the scene. *This was a lot different.*

Moon Glow thought back to when she had moved to New Orleans from Philly. She'd been cautioned that New Orleans could be dangerous. But, until tonight, she hadn't found that to be the case. Sure, there were bums, street peddlers, and drug users, but she figured New Orleans wasn't that different from other major cities. No one had bothered her since her arrival, although she had been busted twice for possession of marijuana. It was a minor offense, and the cops had left her alone since then. All she wanted to do was to live in harmony with her surroundings, and add to the number of tattoos adorning her arms, hands, and neck.

Billy Whiteman was book smart, although Moon Glow felt she had better street smarts. She brushed her multi-colored hair out of her face, pushing the purple, green, and gold strands off to the side. About to sneeze, she pinched her nose with her fingers, although her nose-ring got in the way.

YEAH, SHE THOUGHT, STAYING OUT OF THIS MURDER SCENE IS WHAT *we should do. As long as I carry on with my life, and Billy stays focused on his computer graphic arts business, we'll be fine. Yeah.*

FIFTEEN MINUTES BEFORE THE SHOOTING, SGT. JAMES AND Patrolman Grayson were drinking coffee together in the police station nearest to City Park. They looked up as their supervisor, Lt. Robinson, came into the squad room looking concerned.

"Okay, guys, I want you to go to NOMA and look out for the daughter of Ed Ardoin," Robinson said. He explained the call he had just received from Captain Jim Wells, a friend of Ardoin's. "Wells said the girl was meeting a questionable character tonight and might need protection."

"Ardoin? The criminal defense lawyer?" Sgt. James asked.

"Yeah, that's him."

"Shit, that guy's always busting our chops when we make a *clean* arrest."

"I know," Robinson replied. "But he's a friend of the captain. So, get your ass over there, and look around."

"Okay, Lieutenant. Will do." Robinson left the room.

Patrolman Grayson started to stand up, but Sgt. James grabbed his arm. "Hold on a minute, I want to finish my coffee."

They sat another ten minutes before James went to take a piss, wasting more precious time. Finally, they got into their police cruiser and drove to the park.

———

BY THE TIME THE TWO COPS ARRIVED AT THE FRONT OF NOMA, they could see no one was around. The museum was closed at this hour. As the wipers dutifully swiped back and forth, clearing the windshield of heavy rain, they slowly drove around the building, then headed across the mini bridge.

"Hey, James! Is that a *body*?" Grayson yelled out.. He pointed to something lying in the road next to a parked car. James maneuvered their patrol car to block the road before both officers got out with their Glock's drawn. As far as they could tell, nobody else was around. James approached the woman's body, knelt next to her, and felt for a pulse.

"Nothing. She's dead," he said. "Call it in," he directed Grayson.

"Dispatch from Unit 285," Grayson spoke into the two-way. "We have a dead female between the New Orleans Museum of Art and the Christian Brothers school in City Park. Victim has been shot multiple times. Send backup units, a forensic team, and the body wagon."

"Copy that, unit 285. Support is on the way."

James scanned the immediate surrounding area as the rain increased intensity. *Hmm, no bullet casings on the ground, and no discarded items that I can see,* he thought and holstered his weapon. Then, reaching for a pair of latex gloves, he put them on and reached inside the parked car for the woman's purse on the passenger seat. He took out her wallet and looked at the Virginia state driver's license.

Oh, geez, Simone Ardoin, the daughter of Ed Ardoin. James blew out some air. *The shit is about to hit the fan.*

Chapter 5

Notification

B y the time backup and forensics arrived, there was an all-out downpour. Regardless, the New Orleans Police Department did its job; but even if there *had been* any evidence, it was washing away with each passing moment. Sgt. James and Patrolman Grayson, now wearing NOPD issued raincoats, saluted Captain Wells as he arrived at the scene.

Although Wells knew Simone Ardoin personally, he hadn't seen her in years. Now, looking down at the body lying next to the car, he had trouble recognizing her because of the two gunshot wounds to her face. He noted two more bullet wounds to her chest. In the end, however, there could be little doubt the victim was Simone Ardoin.

Wells shook his head; he was furious. He had personally told Papa Ed that dispatched officers would protect Simone, his daughter. Now, Wells looked around and caught Sgt. James in his line of fire.

"So, James, after I spoke to Lt. Robinson on the phone, how *long* did it take you to get here?"

"We left the precinct right after we spoke with Lt. Robinson," James lied.

Captain Wells turned his head and glared at Patrolman Grayson.

"That's right Captain, *immediately*!" Grayson concurred.

'Simone Ardoin had to drive all the way from Uptown to get here," Wells said. "You were a lot *fucking* closer. Why weren't you here *first*?"

"To be honest, sir, we left as *soon* as we were ordered," James lied again.

Captain Wells gave him a long look as he pulled the collar of his jacket tighter to stop water from running down his back. "Detective Sgt. Tim Kelly will be here soon to take charge of the case. Brief him when he arrives," Wells ordered gruffly.

"Yes, *sir*," James replied, nodding curtly.

Wells walked back to his police cruiser and sat behind the wheel for five minutes. Wanting to be the one who broke the news to Papa Ed Ardoin, he was at a loss for words to console him. Not knowing the full story of *why* Simone was in City Park this late at night, he thought, *I hate this part of the job.* Then pounded the steering wheel. "Son of *bitch*!"

Wells put his cruiser in gear. He would drive to Uptown where he would tell his friend of thirty years that his only child had been murdered. Sometimes, life just sucked.

CAPTAIN WELLS STOOD BEFORE THE FRONT DOOR OF PAPA ED Ardoin's large home. He glanced at his watch. *Hmm. past midnight.* He hesitated ringing the doorbell. Wells knew he would have to be strong to help Papa Ed and Camille through the next few moments. Amid the constant downpour and the grief now engulfing him, he reached out, at last, and pressed the buzzer.

When Papa Ed opened the door, Wells saw his expression change from welcoming to grief. It was as if a window shade had been pulled down. His lower lip quivered; Papa Ed blinked his eyes rapidly, and tears formed. As they locked eyes, Papa Ed's hand went to his mouth, then he cleared his throat.

"Tell me she's . . . only *injured.*"

Wells was silent for half a second. "I can't."

A long moment passed before he could say more. Both men wrestled with their emotions. "I'm sorry, my old friend, she's gone." Papa Ed's legs wobbled, and Wells grabbed his arm to steady the older man. He moved them both forward and inside to the foyer.

Camille's voice carried from the kitchen. "Is that Simone?" The petite woman hurried into the foyer and saw both men facing each other with heads down, eyes closed, and complete sorrow marking their faces. She screamed, and dropped to her knees. Papa Ed rushed to her side, knelt beside her, and took her in his arms. Wells took out a wrinkled handkerchief, and wiped his own eyes. Finally, Simone's father looked up, and with pleading eyes, asked, "What happened?"

"She was shot."

"Shot? How?"

Wells paused, took in a long, deep breath, and swallowed hard. "I'm afraid to say, but . . . several times."

Camille howled and collapsed against her husband's

shoulder. The two of them stayed frozen in grief for more than a minute. Then Papa Ed asked, "Did your officers see who did it?"

"No, they arrived after she was shot. No one else was around. I'm *so* sorry. Tell me, who was she meeting?"

"I don't know his name. No, wait, I heard her leaving a voicemail for her friend, Alex. She said she was meeting a 'Claude Toussaint.' It was somehow connected with her work at the State Department."

"The *U.S.* State Department?"

"Yeah, something to do with visa fraud. Ever hear of a guy named Claude Toussaint?"

"No, but we'll find the people responsible. I *promise* you that."

Papa Ed nodded. He gently lifted Camille up off the floor, then hugged her tightly as she sobbed a mother's sorrow.

This is the worst night of their lives, Wells thought. *It won't be any better tomorrow.*

An hour later, Captain Wells left the Ardoin home to seek out Detective Kelly. *This effort will be an all-hands-on deck operation,* he promised himself. *I can't change the past, but I damn well will influence the future of this investigation.* He was determined to keep *this* promise to his old friend.

When the rain stopped around midnight, Alex and Rachel hailed a taxi to take them back to the Royal Sonesta Hotel from the jazz club in Faubourg Marigny, adjacent to the French Quarter. The music had been outstanding, but so loud in the confined space that they both had turned off their phones just after the musicians began playing; it would have been useless hearing any calls coming in, much less be able to talk. Now back in their hotel room, they turned the phones back on, and saw they had messages. Each listened to their voicemails from Simone.

"Oh, my god, Alex, we'd better call her right away!"

"Absolutely." He tried Simone's number, but it went right to voicemail after a few rings. Rachel tried on her phone, but got the same result.

"What should we do, Alex?"

"Let's try again in fifteen minutes." The results were the same.

"Do you have the phone number for her parent's house?" Alex asked.

"I do, but it's after midnight. Should we call?"

"I think we'd better. She might need advice. I wouldn't want her to do something impetuous."

Rachel dialed the number, and waited while it rang several times. Unbeknownst to her, Papa Ed had decided against answering any calls on their land line. Wells had his cell phone number, if there was a break in the case.

"Let's try again first thing in the morning," Alex said.

"I guess that's all we can do."

But neither slept well. Alex knew she had disregarded their advice and probably jumped into the lion's den. *I just hope she hasn't gotten in over her head.*

Chapter 6

Condolences

The following morning, Rachel waited until 8:00 a.m. to call Simone. Again, it went to voicemail, so she tried calling Simone's mother at home. Since it was Sunday, she wasn't sure if the Ardoin family might be at church at such an early hour but still decided to try. She assumed Simone had returned home late last night, and even hoped she would be up, and ready to explain about what happened yesterday. Rachel put her cell phone on speaker and waited while it rang nearly ten times before Camille answered.

"Hello . . . this is . . . Camille."

Rachel noticed how she dragged out each word in a monotone.

"Camille? Hi, it's Rachel Smith, a friend of your daughter. My husband and I are visiting from London. Simone left me a voicemail last night, but when I returned the call, she didn't pick up. Is she home?"

There was a long pause and Rachel heard crying on the line.

"Camille?" Then Rachel heard Papa Ed come on the line. She also noticed Alex come closer so he could hear.

"Rachel, this is Ed. I'm sorry to tell you that . . .that Simone didn't come home last night because . . . because someone killed her."

"What?! Oh, *no-o-o*! Ed, I'm s-o-o-o sorry," Rachel felt as if a dagger had been thrust into her heart. She couldn't take a breath deep enough and it took a few seconds to clear her throat.

"How do you *know*?" Rachel dropped down on the bed and Alex put his arm around her shoulder.

"Last night, the police came by and told us," Papa Ed said.

"I'm *so* sorry, Ed," Rachel repeated.

"I believe Simone talked to you two about the man she was meeting. Am I right?"

"Kind of," she glanced over at Alex. "May Alex and I come over to your house to discuss it?"

"We would appreciate it," Papa Ed said. "The police may be here, too. Perhaps, we can all compare notes."

"Okay, we'll see you in about an hour."

ALEX SPENT THE NEXT TWENTY MINUTES CONSOLING RACHEL BEFORE they got dressed. He hugged her, massaged the back of her neck, and kissed her gently on the forehead. Despite all they had been through in the past, Alex had never seen her so distraught; she had cried, thrown herself onto the bed, and cried some more. Seeing her so upset made him fight back tears of his own. Afterward, they picked up their rental car from the hotel valet and drove down St. Charles Avenue toward Papa Ed and Camille's house in Uptown. Under normal conditions, they would have talked non-stop about the beautiful antebellum homes along the route and commented about the wonderful tall oak trees. But not this morning. They were both engrossed in fleeting images of the last time they were with Simone.

"Oh, Alex, Simone was such a terrific foreign service officer and such a good friend. She was smart, funny, and her skills were first class. This is so tragic."

"Yeah, I know." There wasn't much more Alex could say. *Maybe if we hadn't gone to the jazz club*, he thought, *then we wouldn't have had our cellphones turned off. We could have reasoned with Simone and maybe she'd still be alive.*

WHEN THEY PULLED UP TO THE HOUSE, THERE WAS A MARKED NOPD car in the driveway and a late model black Ford sedan parked by the curb. Papa Ed met them at the door where they all shook hands, then he led them into the living room where they met Camille, Captain Jim Wells, and Detective Sgt. Tim Kelly. The room was large and elegant, with crown molding and tall sets of French doors that led out to a narrow veranda. A beautiful room, usually bright, it now seemed subdued with a veil of sadness.

Although they had never met Simone's parents, Rachel embraced Camille, who returned the hug, holding her close for a longer than normal first time. It was almost as if by hugging Rachel, Camille could still feel her daughter through their friendship.

"I'd like to talk to you about my daughter . . . and her work," Camille said. "You were her boss in Washington, is that right?"

"Yes, I was."

"Camille always said you were a good person . . . her best friend at work."

Remembering Simone with those words made Rachel tear up again. "I'd be delighted to tell you *anything* you want to know about Simone," Rachel sniffled again. "Shall we sit over here?" She pointed to a sofa and two chairs in the corner of the spacious living room. As they sat, Rachel noted several antique pieces of mahogany furniture spread around the room, as well as a few oriental carpets.

Papa Ed was talking quietly to Alex and the two cops. "Gentlemen, I'd like to speak with you in my study." They followed him down a short hallway into a large room with a beautifully buffed antique desk and two comfortable-looking dark brown leather chairs and matching sofa. Two large windows had white planation shutters partially open. A long built-in bookcase covering one wall was completely filled. Two other walls were covered with photos of prominent-looking people, and well-known politicians. Alex knew from talking with Simone that her father was a significant political player in the city, and based upon the photo collection, Papa Ed was much more than that.

Many photos showed Papa Ed posing with well-known national civil rights leaders, an assortment of New Orleans mayors and Louisiana governors, and even one of Ed standing with former U.S. Presidents Jimmy Carter and Bill Clinton. There was a cluster of diplomas including what appeared to be an undergraduate degree from Xavier University of New Orleans, and another from Loyola of New Orleans Law School. A set of framed certificates hung on the wall which Alex didn't understand; one was from the Martinet Legal Society, and the other from the Original

Illinois Club. On the book shelves were additional photos of Simone and Camille throughout the years. It was a pleasant setting.

"Detective Kelly, I understand you've been assigned to investigate who murdered my daughter. If there is anything . . . *anything*, I can do to help you find the killers, just ask," Papa Ed said. "She was our whole world."

"Thank you, Mr. Ardoin. We'll do our best; you have my word."

"Detective, are you aware of the voicemail that she left for Alex Boyd and his wife?"

"No," Kelly replied. He turned to Alex. "Who *are* you exactly?"

"I'm a special agent with the Diplomatic Security Service. Simone worked for my wife at the State Department in Washington. She invited us to visit New Orleans. That's why we're here, at her invitation." There was no meaningful reaction from Detective Kelly.

Alex looked at the man. *What gives with this guy? Doesn't he have any natural curiosity? Or is he just thick between the ears?*

Then Alex relayed how Simone had seen Jules Baptiste in the French Quarter and had later arranged to meet Claude Toussaint at NOMA the night she was killed. He played the voicemail Simone had left on his phone for everyone to hear. Captain Wells focused on the message, Papa Ed wiped tears from his eyes, and Detective Kelly took notes.

"So, this is all related to a visa scam artist from Haiti who Miss Ardoin encountered during her posting there?" Sgt. Kelly asked.

"Yes," Alex replied. "But he's *more* than a scam artist. This Baptiste heads a gang. I'll contact the U.S. Embassy in Haiti and get you more information about this gang and anything else I can dig up."

"Thank you, that would be helpful," Kelly said.

"Papa Ed, our families have known each other for decades," Captain Wells said. "While we're often on opposite sides of the fence in court, you have always been a straight-shooter and treated our officers with dignity, unless, of course, they deserved to be called out for some infraction, or poor judgment. NOPD is standing with you in this tragedy."

"I know it, Jim. And I appreciate that."

"If anything further shows up, you know where to find us," Captain Wells said. They all stood up to leave. But Papa Ed held back.

"Alex, will you stay a moment?"

"Of course."

Captain Wells and Detective Kelly took their leave as Papa Ed and Alex sat down again.

To Alex, Papa Ed was an impressive man. In his late sixties, he carried a few extra pounds on his six-foot frame, but still looked fit. His short hair had turned grey at the temples, while his deep voice commanded attention. As the founder of his own law firm, Alex figured Ed had to be very smart.

"I assume my daughter was murdered by this Haitian gang lord, or on his orders."

"That's my assumption as well." Alex remained silent only a second. "How good is the New Orleans police department?"

Papa Ed sighed. "They're a mixed bag. But to be fair, Alex, I haven't gone to trial against them in a few years. My junior associates handle that type of work now. I spend most of my time with municipal and corporate clients, and represent some unions. I'm speaking of utility companies, the transit authority, and the Longshoremen's union. "Simone told me that you and Rachel warned her off about following the Haitian. For that bit of caution, I thank you. I just wish she'd taken your advice."

"I'm sorry we failed, Ed, but what she tried to do took a *lot* of guts."

Papa Ed took a handkerchief from his pocket and blew his nose, then rested his head in both hands, while his elbows were on the chair's armrests. He was silent.

Alex couldn't imagine his anguish; his only child murdered by a savage. Then Papa Ed looked up.

"Listen, Alex, Simone told us about your exploits, about what you and Rachel have done overseas in places like Pakistan and Italy. I was impressed. Is it possible for you to stay longer in New Orleans, and work with the police? Find her killers?"

"I'll call Washington and London to make that request, Ed. I'm sure they'll agree."

"Thank you . . . and please, call me *Papa* Ed. It's the nickname my *friends* use."

"I'd be honored, *Papa* Ed."

"I saw you noticed my certificate from the Original Illinois Club. . . on the wall."

"Yes, what is that?"

"It's the oldest African-American Mardi Gras club in North America; it's based here, founded in 1895. We don't have a parade like the other clubs, but we *do* have a Mardi Gras ball. We also have a debutante ball and all the hoop-la that goes with the whole debutante season. Simone was Queen one year." He paused and blew his nose again. "That was a long time ago."

Then, as Alex watched, Papa Ed's body started shaking; he sobbed a few times, head hanging low in the room now silent as a tomb. Alex sat quietly, allowing the man his private grief; honoring a father whose life has changed forever. Finally, Papa Ed's composure returned.

"This is the worst time of my life. I don't see a way forward. What's the point?"

"Papa Ed, I'll have the Diplomatic Security office here in the city work with the NOPD. Since Simone was a commissioned officer in the Foreign Service, I'll bet other federal agencies will want to support the investigation. I'll try to ensure it happens."

"Thank you, Alex. Camille and I need your help more than you know."

Chapter 7

Support

On the drive back to their hotel, Rachel told Alex about her conversation with Camille. "The poor woman is devastated. At least, she said she can count on her closest friends to help her deal with the tragedy. Oh, Alex, I'm not sure how Camille is going to get through this. She and Simone were very close. She was their only child."

"I know what you mean, Simone's father said the same even though he seems to be pretty strong. When we get back to the hotel, I'm going to call Susan Witt to get the ball rolling with Diplomatic Security. She can support the NOPD in the murder investigation."

Susan Witt, now Resident Agent-in-Charge of the New Orleans office for Diplomatic Security, had worked for Alex years before at the U.S. Embassy in Islamabad, Pakistan. They had remained in touch and were good friends.

ALEX STOOD JUST INSIDE THE HOTEL ROOM'S FRENCH DOORS, looking out at the swimming pool in the center courtyard. He had dialed Susan Witt and was waiting for her to answer. When she finally did, he smiled.

"Hey, Alex, is this you?"

"It is, Susan. I know we're locked on for breakfast tomorrow morning, but there's a change of plans; something important has happened."

"Well, if you can't make breakfast, I understand."

"No, it's more than that, Susan. Sadly, the woman we were visiting here in New Orleans, Simone Ardoin, was murdered last night."

"Oh my *god*, Alex. What *happened*?"

"I'll tell you details later, but in brief, she spotted a visa fraudster in the French Quarter who she had known about since her assignment in Haiti. Simone went on her own and tried to gather info. But last night she was fatally shot. I think the fraudster must have killed her. Since it's both a visa fraud case *and* a murder, Diplomatic Security can take the lead at the federal level, and partner with NOPD. That's unless the FBI wants to jump in and take over, because Simone was also a federal employee." Alex took a breath. "After I call Washington and London to get permission to stay here for the investigation, I'd like to work with your office on the case."

"Of course, Alex. We can also raise the matter with the city's crime task force and get their support."

"Excellent. Regardless of who ends up in charge, I just want these killers caught."

"Can we meet this morning about the murder?" Susan asked.

"Rachel and I would like that, thanks."

"Great. You know where the DS office is located in the Canal Place office tower, right? Let's meet there in an hour."

"Perfect. See you then, Susan."

As soon as he hung up, Alex called Jim Riley, Director of Diplomatic Security in Washington for approval to stay in New Orleans for at least another week or two.

At the same time, Rachel called the American Embassy in London and Deputy Chief of Mission Bainbridge Wellington to report the news of Simone's murder.

"We'd like to stay at least through the funeral," she said, then listened. "Thank you," she replied.

With that accomplished, Alex and Rachel walked down Iberville Street to the DS office to meet Susan Witt.

SUSAN WITT WAS ALREADY AT THE OFFICE BY THE TIME ALEX AND Rachel arrived. They found the front door unlocked and Susan waiting in the reception area. The three of them embraced; it had been a few years since they had seen each other, although they had exchanged emails from time to time.

"How's your arm?" Alex asked. During their last assignment together when terrorists had stormed the U.S. Ambassador's residence in Islamabad, she had sustained a gunshot injury.

"It's fine. Not even uncomfortable anymore. What about your side from getting shot in Cairo? Is it healed?"

"I'm good," he replied.

She turned to Rachel. "This must be emotionally tough for you, Rachel. I know Simone Ardoin worked for you, right?"

"Yeah, she did. She was also a good friend."

"So, tell me all about it, and we'll devise a strategy to move forward."

Alex and Rachel took turns providing background that led up to the murder. At the end, Susan said, "Since you've met Tim Kelly, lead detective from NOPD, let's contact him later this afternoon and find out what's happening with his investigation. He may have developed some leads by then."

"Good plan, Susan," Alex replied. "What should we do in the meantime?"

"Let's go to my apartment. I'll make some coffee and throw some lunch together for us."

THEY LEFT THE OFFICE AND DROVE ABOUT TEN MINUTES DOWN ST. Charles Avenue to a tall building, a mix of condos and rental apartments. Susan's apartment overlooked the streetcar line on St. Charles Avenue, a major parade route for Mardi Gras.

The décor inside her two-bedroom apartment reflected Susan's personality - spartan. She had all the usual furniture but a very limited number of knick-knacks, far fewer than most people in the Foreign Service accumulated.

"Nice apartment," Rachel said. "But where's your overseas stuff?"

"Well, I only served one permanent tour in Pakistan until I was wounded. That didn't give me much time to get the usual rugs or brass things at bazaars. And during my previous time in combat zones as a U.S. Army Captain, I really didn't have the time, or interest, to go shopping." She started toward the kitchen. "Give me a few minutes; I'll be right back."

When Alex and Rachel heard utensil noises, they joined her

and helped prepare the meal. As they sat eating lunch, Susan looked at the couple.

"Thanks for briefing me about Simone's voicemail. We need to find this Claude Toussaint or Jules Baptiste. They'll know who killed Simone, that's if they didn't do it themselves."

"Exactly right," Alex replied. "By the way, these tuna fish sandwiches are *stupendous*." Rachel laughed while Susan looked back and forth between the two and chuckled.

"Okay, you guys know I'm a cowgirl from Oklahoma. Steak and potatoes are still my favorite foods, so give me a break here."

"Sorry, I couldn't resist," Alex said. "It was nice of you to provide lunch, and we haven't had tuna fish sandwiches in forever." Then he glanced at his watch and saw the time. "Why don't we call Detective Kelly and find out what's happening with the case."

"Okay. Do you have his number?" Susan asked.

Alex gave her Kelly's business card; she dialed the number and put the cell phone on speaker. A sergeant answered and Susan identified herself as a Special Agent with Diplomatic Security.

"Sorry, Fast Tim isn't in now."

"Fast Tim?" Susan responded. Alex and Rachel both raised their eyebrows.

"Yeah, his nickname. I think he's taking a few hours off."

"When will he be back?"

"Not sure. Could be an all-day gig, or just for the afternoon."

"I don't understand. What do you mean, 'an all-day gig'?"

"A private detail."

"Is anyone else working on the Ardoin murder case, now?"

"Not sure, my shift just began."

"Okay, thanks. Please leave a message that I called and say that Alex Boyd and I will see Detective Kelly tomorrow morning." She hung up and Alex noticed she was pissed off.

"What the hell was *that* about?" Alex asked.

"The NOPD lets its officers work secondary jobs to top up their poor salaries." Alex and Rachel stared at each other and shook their heads in disbelief.

Rachel couldn't hold back. "Is this *America,* or are we in a third world country?"

ELSEWHERE, MOON GLOW ROSS AND BILLY WHITEMAN WERE AT their apartment located close to where they had seen Simone Ardoin murdered in the park. They were contemplating their precarious situation as witnesses while Billy scarfed down a spam sandwich with mustard. Moon Glow sipped from a bowl of Ramen noodles.

"I still think we need to tell the cops what we saw," Billy said.

"Absolutely not. We'll get killed long before the guy can even go to trial," she replied.

"So, you're saying, that's it? We do nothing?"

"Listen Billy, we can't protect ourselves. We'd be sitting ducks once the killers find out we spoke to the police."

Moon Glow was terrified and beginning to contemplate leaving New Orleans.

Chapter 8

Trying to Make Progress

The next morning, Alex, Rachel, and Susan had breakfast at the Royal Sonesta. Then, while Rachel stayed in the hotel room to do on-line searches about crime in New Orleans and the history of Haitian Creoles immigrating to the city, Alex and Susan drove to meet Detective Sergeant Tim Kelly at the police station.

Entering the detectives' area, they saw it abuzz with officers making phone calls, writing reports, or talking among themselves. Tim Kelly was in a corner of the room behind a metal desk; beside him was a woman wearing a loose dark jacket and pants. Both were laughing and amicably chatting. As they approached, the woman glanced up, then stopped talking, got up and left. Alex noticed a police badge attached to her belt.

"Hey, good to see you again, Mr. Boyd," Kelly said. "And you must be Special Agent Witt. I just got your message yesterday. I've been out of the office."

"Yes, I'm Agent-in-Charge of the Diplomatic Security office in New Orleans." Susan reached out and shook his hand.

"Right. I met your predecessor a few years ago."

"So, Detective, did you develop any leads from yesterday afternoon?" Alex asked.

"Sorry, I was off duty doing something else. But we're on it this morning."

"You were *off*?" Alex's voice was piqued with annoyance. "Why is *that*? Doesn't NOPD work *around the clock* on the murder of a *government official*?" His face showed anger.

"Hey, hey! Fuck *you*, man. You're way out of line! I had an approved detail yesterday to handle!"

"What does *that* mean? An *approved* detail?" Alex demanded.

"We all support private events with off-duty cops. None of us gets paid enough from our city salaries to support our families. So, yesterday I was in the Garden District providing security for a wedding reception. It lasted five hours."

"So, you were at a *garden* party." Alex said, nearly speechless. *I've never heard of such bullshit.* Of course, he'd never been a cop in New Orleans. But he didn't know of *anyone* in Diplomatic Security, or even the Foreign Service, who had a secondary job.

"You don't think these private details are a conflict of interest?" Alex asked.

"No, I don't. It comes with the turf," Kelly defended himself.

Alex paused and considered his position. He needed the help of NOPD, but the culture was very different from what he was used to. *I'd better drop it for now,* he decided cautiously. *But I'm damn mad!*

"All right, how about if we start over. I assume Simone Ardoin's body is at the morgue."

"Yes, it is. But we have her clothes and belongings here. Do you want to see them?"

"Yes, I do. Thanks," Alex replied less heatedly.

They walked into another room and Detective Kelly grabbed a large box from a shelf. "She was shot four times, twice in the head, and twice in the chest."

Alex and Susan both put on latex gloves, but it was Alex who picked Simone's dress out of the box. Two bullet holes had torn the dress where her heart would have been. He carefully laid the blood-soaked dress on an adjoining table, then reached into the box again, pulling out Simone's cell phone.

"Has this been examined?" Alex asked.

"We tried, but it's dead."

"Maybe someone in your office has a charger. Can we ask around?"

And no one had the initiative to charge the phone yesterday? Alex thought, trying to check his anger the best he could. But he was wrestling with a desire to lash out at the incompetence again.

"Sure," Kelly replied. He put on a glove, himself and took the phone from Alex. They walked back into the squad room together where Kelly called out: "Anybody got a cell phone charge cord?"

Within seconds, someone volunteered a charger matching Simone Ardoin's phone. Kelly gave it ten minutes, then turned it on.

"Mind if I take a look?" Susan Witt asked. Kelly handed it to her while the charger was still connected. Susan went to Simone's call list, scrolled down, and copied some numbers. A few of the more recent ones were identified as belonging to Alex or Rachel, but there was an unidentified local call that had come in about 40 minutes before she died. Alex figured it might have come from Claude Toussaint about their meeting. An outgoing call was to an international number.

"That country code belongs to Haiti," Susan said.

Kelly and Alex watched Susan manipulate the phone. She scrolled through Simone's recent photos but said nothing. Then went to her voice recordings. The last one matched the approximate time of Simone's death. She wrote the time down before putting the cell on speaker. By the time she pushed the playback button, a small crowd of detectives were surrounding her.

Simone's voice was clear and distinctive on the recording: "Can you turn off your lights?" A few seconds separated her next words: "Claude, is that *you*?" A moment later, she said, "Hey, I asked you to turn *off* your lights." Then a brief pause, followed by two gunshots, a body hitting the ground, and Simone groaning. It took another ten-seconds for the next sound to playback - two additional gun shots. Finally, there was the noise of a car driving off.

The room was silent. Susan blinked her eyes; Alex cleared his throat. He looked around at the faces, glad they were showing interest, but wondered if they were merely watching Susan's skills. *Or did this tragedy finally register with them,* he wondered.

Susan handed the phone back to Kelly and sat on the edge of the nearest desk. They had just heard the final moment of Simone's life. It was a stunning discovery.

"We can now confirm that Simone thought she was meeting Claude," Alex stated. "Whether it really *was* Claude has yet to be established. Can you clone her phone to produce a copy of her data?"

"No, we can't," Kelly replied. "Not here."

"I have a guy in my office who is a wiz with cellphones,"

Susan said. "He can do it. You can keep the original phone as evidence, and we'll take the copy. That okay?"

"Sure."

Susan took out her own cell phone and called Special Agent Scott Fellows. When he answered, she explained the situation. He confirmed coming to the police station with equipment needed to clone the phone.

She let Kelly know the time Fellows would arrive. Then Alex had an idea.

"Kelly, do you remember when we spoke yesterday at Papa Ed Ardoin's house," Alex said, "I played her voicemail where Simone said she had followed Jules Baptiste near Galatoires after lunch?"

"Yeah, I recall," Kelly replied.

"I've noticed security cameras in the French Quarter," Alex said. "Would NOPD have usable video footage archived for the areas around Galatoires, and maybe the Royal Sonesta Hotel? I'm thinking we might be able to spot Simone following Baptiste."

"I haven't done that yet," Kelly responded, "but I can. Our tech should be in the office tomorrow; I'll have her look at it first thing." Alex and Susan stole a quick glance at each other.

"That will be very helpful," Alex said.

NOT LONG AFTER, SPECIAL AGENT FELLOWS ARRIVED AND CLONED Simone's phone. When he finished, Alex, Susan, and Fellows went outside and sat in Susan's car.

"That Detective is a piss-poor example of law enforcement," Alex complained.

"I know," Susan replied. "He takes no initiative at all. By the way, when I knew we were going to see him today, I looked through my predecessor's notes on NOPD contacts. Do you know why Detective Kelly's nickname is 'Fast Tim'?" She didn't wait for Alex to guess. "It's because he works so *slowly*. The guy is a piece of shit. I also heard when Katrina hit the city, he went AWOL for at least a week."

"That figures," Alex replied. "Look, Papa Ed is tight with a man named 'Captain Wells.' I'll mention this problem to Ed and maybe he can do something to improve NOPD's response. Susan, I'll keep your name out of the conversation because you still have to work with these guys after the case is over. I'll also give him an update."

"Great, I'll call that overseas number from Simone's cell phone. If it *is* in Haiti, it might tie in with the murder," Susan said. "By the way, what are you and Rachel doing for dinner?"

"We haven't planned anything. Why, are you offering more tuna sandwiches?"

Susan laughed. "Damn it! Stop with that already. No, since you're staying in the Quarter, I thought we could go a restaurant that serves great barbequed shrimp."

"You mean like . . . on a grill?"

"No, this is really *amazing*. It's a whole bowl of shrimp with tons of butter, olive oil, some garlic, lemon juice, basil, paprika, cayenne pepper, rosemary, oregano, and Tabasco sauce."

Alex opened his eyes wide. "How in the world do you *know* this? No offense, but that doesn't seem to be your MO." She smiled; he knew her so well.

"I read the recipe on a box at the food store," she said. "You'll love it. Tell Rachel to dress very casually; the meal will be sloppy. You use your fingers to peel the shrimp. I'll be at your hotel at 6:00 pm. We can walk to the restaurant," she said. "Scott, care to join us?"

"No thanks, I'm eating at home with my family tonight."

"Thanks, again, for coming and helping out," Susan said. She drove Scott Fellows over to his parked car, then drove Alex back to his hotel.

Up in their hotel room, Alex dialed the phone number for Papa Ed.

Chapter 9

Asking for Help

Rachel was in their hotel room when Alex returned; on her laptop, she was browsing the history of Haitian Creoles in New Orleans.

Alex was wrestling with a moral dilemma. He wanted to share everything with Papa Ed and Camille, yet he couldn't bring himself to tell them he had heard Simone's last words, her actual last breath on her cellphone recording. Nor did he want to say that he had heard the very shots that had killed her. Her death had completely shattered them already, so he decided to hold off mentioning this new information. . . for now.

He dialed the home number and Papa Ed answered immediately.

"Hello, Papa Ed, it's Alex."

"Hello, Alex, what's happening?"

"I've just met with Susan Witt, the agent-in-charge from our local DS office, and Detective Tim Kelly. We've retrieved some data from Simone's cell phone which includes her last few calls and are checking them out now. We believe one call she received may have been from Claude Toussaint just before she died. There's another earlier call that Simone made to Haiti."

"Okay, at least that's something to follow-up on." His voice was somber.

"Also, because her phone message said she'd seen Jules Baptiste, and followed him, I asked NOPD to retrieve CCTV footage in the French Quarter. It may give us additional leads, if we see anything on the video. I'll also ask the cops to review any earlier coverage of the Quarter around the time Simone first spotted Baptiste. Right now, I don't know precisely when that was."

"I do; Simone told me exactly when and where." Papa Ed gave Alex the precise time and location.

"Excellent! Thank you, Papa Ed." Alex waited a few seconds. "I have to tell you about a problem, and I'm asking your advice."

"What is it?"

"The detective, Tim Kelly, seems . . . unmotivated. Frankly, he's very *un*impressive. For example, yesterday afternoon he took off, and worked a private detail instead of developing leads in Simone's case. Since you're friends with Captain Wells, do you think Wells can put a fire under Kelly's ass?" There was a pause.

"I didn't say anything yesterday at our house, Alex, but I remember Kelly from some previous cases when I represented criminal defendants in court. Kelly is one lazy, sloppy s.o.b. with his work. I'll take care of it. Thanks for letting me know."

"Sorry I had to mention this."

"Nonsense, I'm glad you did." He cleared his throat before speaking again. "And I have a request for *you*. This may seem strange in our time of mourning, but on Tuesdays, Camille and I always have lunch with friends at a restaurant called Dooky Chase in Treme. Have you heard of it?"

"No, I haven't."

"Well, this group we've eaten with for decades insists we meet with them because they want to express their condolences in person. To tell the truth, we're not up for it. But every one of them *knew* Simone, in fact, when she was younger, she would come with us to the restaurant when school was out of session. Can I ask you and Rachel to accompany us? I believe the group would like to hear how Simone evolved into an accomplished young woman at the State Department. It would mean a lot to Camille and me."

"We'd be honored."

"Thank you. It will be important for our memory of Simone."

Alex agreed and they ended their call. Alex wasn't always a soft and sensitive guy, but Papa Ed and Camille's pain had gotten to him. He pulled out his handkerchief, wiped his eyes, and blew his nose. Alex had seen death many times and had witnessed those who grieved for their loved ones. But the sadness of Papa Ed and Camile seemed deeper than most. Their feelings clutched at his soul and dragged him down. He felt as if he was in an underworld of endless grief.

AFTER ALEX BRIEFED RACHEL ON WHAT HAPPENED AT THE POLICE station, he asked her what she had discovered on the internet.

"Nothing of specific help for the case, but I do have a better understanding of the Haitian and Creole communities here. First, the term 'Creole' is confusing because it can apply to a broad group of people, some born in Louisiana, some born in the Caribbean, and even at different periods of time. But mostly, people with a mix of French, Spanish, and African heritage are what we think of as Creole.

"In any event, my guess is that unlike many Creoles, Jules Baptiste's family didn't move to Louisiana after the slave rebellion against the French in Haiti in the early 1800s, because Simone said she knew of him in Port-au-Prince. As for Claude Toussaint, I haven't got a clue. There are a lot of Toussaints in Louisiana, and, in fact, there was a General Toussaint Louverture who was a leader in the Haitian revolution. So, Claude's people might not have immigrated here early, if at all. As I said, nothing of help to this murder case."

"Nevertheless, impressive research on your part, Honey Bunch."

Rachel smiled. "You haven't called me 'honey bunch' in a while."

"Then, I guess that proves it," Alex said.

"Proves what?"

"That you're a legit brunette with smarts from California, and not a secret blonde."

He had been sitting on the edge of the bed. Now she jumped off the chair and dove on top of him as he cracked up laughing. Rachel smothered him with kisses and laughed between breaths. Then they lay quietly side by side. They usually had sex several times a week, but in this circumstance, it didn't feel right. They were mourning Simone's death.

I assume Rachel feels the same way, he thought. They took a brief nap, arms entwined, until it was time to meet Susan Witt for dinner.

DEANIE'S WAS LOCATED ON IBERVILLE STREET IN THE FRENCH Quarter, a few blocks from Bourbon Street. Susan met them at their hotel and all three walked to the restaurant. They entered and saw a hostess station on the left. A large u-shaped bar was straight ahead, crowded with patrons eating raw oysters and waiting for tables to open. Additional high-top tables were off to the side. The main restaurant floor with multiple tables set for patrons was beyond the hostess station on the left. Since Susan had called ahead, they were seated right away.

The menu showed a variety of fried seafood plates. Alex looked around and noticed some of the more obese patrons with enormous platters piled high with towers of fried foods. *Hmmm. I wonder if the restaurant has a special arrangement with the cardiac unit of the closest hospital.* He smiled at his own joke.

"As I mentioned earlier, I recommend we all have their barbecued shrimp," Susan said.

"That's fine with me," Rachel replied.

"I'm game," Alex said.

The restaurant was quite large with lots of tables seating four people, and a few for larger groups. On one wall was a plaque displaying the record of past New Orleans Saints seasons. Lots of failures until the era of Coach Jim Mora. The Saints had been so bad in the early days, that fans wore paper bags over their heads and called themselves, "The Aint's." Yet, the fans were loyal, and the stadium had always been full.

Someone walked by their table wearing a T-shirt quoting Tennessee Williams. It read: "America has only three cities: New York, San Francisco, and New Orleans. Everywhere else is Cleveland."

The patrons appeared to be a mix of out-of-town tourists, at least judging by their logoed baseball caps and colorful tees. Racially, the diners were a healthy combination of blacks and whites; everyone was having a good time.

The waitress brought three Abita Amber beers from a brewery across Lake Pontchartrain in St. Tammany Parish. Rachel raised her glass. "I'd like to propose a toast to Simone." Alex and Susan raised theirs, too. "Here's to Simone Ardoin, a great friend . . . rest in peace," Rachel said. They all took swallows while thoughts were on the lovely woman they had known. Alex looked at Rachel and saw a choked expression; he put one hand on her arm in consolation. They all remained quiet for a moment.

"Let me tell you what I found out this afternoon," Susan said when they resumed their conversation. "I called the number in Haiti from Simone's recent call list. I was put through to a guy who is an American consular officer in Port-Au-Prince. Apparently, Simone had called him to check on Jules Baptiste. This guy confirmed to me that the Consulate never gave Baptiste a visa, so he must be here illegally. Also, they know Baptiste *does* run a visa fraud ring, and he's into the drug trade."

"Okay, we suspected drugs," Alex said.

"Simone told the consular officer the same story she mentioned to you, that she had followed Baptiste into several bars," Susan said, "but during her call to Haiti, she actually *mentioned* the names of the bars."

"Excellent. We can pass that info on to the cops tomorrow," Alex said, as he saw the waiter bringing their orders.

The waiter also brought bibs and presented each with a large bowl of barbequed shrimp smothered in butter-lemon sauce and a lot of delicious debris at the bottom of the bowl. This was accompanied by baguettes of French bread and small mixed side salads. On a separate, larger plate for them all to share were small red potatoes boiled in the same spicy seasoning as the shrimp.

After tying on their splatter bibs, they peeled the hot, sauce-drenched shrimp and enjoyed a taste of pure heaven. In no time, their fingers were covered in buttery barbeque sauce which also tasted delicious as they licked their fingers. Then, dipping pieces of French bread into the buttery sauce, and savoring its flavor, was almost an orgasmic experience.

"Susan, what happened?" Alex asked. "I thought you were a steak and potatoes girl."

She laughed in response. "Even *I* can appreciate *this* cuisine. I'm convinced that Deanie's barbequed shrimp is a basic food group that I must eat on a regular basis."

Well, enjoy tonight, Alex thought, *because tomorrow is another day working with 'Fast Tim' Kelly . . . if he's still speaking to me.*

Chapter 10

Detective John Washington

At exactly 9:00 a.m. the following morning, Alex, Rachel, and Susan arrived at the NOPD station and asked for Detective Sgt. "Fast Tim" Kelly. *Just the thought of working with this guy pisses me off,* Alex thought as he scanned the room. A guy about Alex's height approached them.

Hmm, I'm guessing mid-thirties, light-brown complexion, close-cropped black hair. Looks fit.

"Are you looking for 'Fast Tim?'"

"Yes, we are," Alex replied.

"Well, I'm Detective John Washington. I've replaced him on the Ardoin murder case." He extended a hand and all three shook it in turn.

Whoa, this guy's grip is strong, Alex thought, then realized John Washington was bigger than he first thought. *Shoulders are broad, physique muscular.* Alex stared at him a few seconds. "Didn't you play football for LSU?"

Washington smiled. "Yes, I did, but that was over a decade

ago. You have a good memory, and you're not from around here."

"LSU is on television a lot, so I recalled your name," Alex said. "What happened to Tim Kelly?" he asked. *Not that I give a crap,* he thought.

"I think you can figure that out," Washington replied. Alex nodded. Rachel coughed to get their attention.

"Oh, sorry," Washington responded, "Let's use the small conference room down the hall." They followed him.

As they walked, Rachel whispered to Alex, "Talk about instant 'bromances'!"

"What?"

"The look on your face was positively *adoring,*" she whispered back.

"So, I like football . . . besides, this guy was *great.*"

They reached the room, and everyone took a seat. Then Washington began summarizing details. "Let me state what we do and do not know:

"First, the cell phone number for Claude Toussaint must be a burner because there's no account connected to it.

"Second, he's a small-time hood with a few arrests on his record. We know he works for Baptiste from time to time.

"Third, we don't have Toussaint's current address, nor do we have an address for Jules Baptiste, although we do know Baptiste moves around the metro area a lot.

"Fourth, Baptiste has been convicted of drug possession, assault, and he's suspected of being involved in five murders. But we can't prove the murder charges in court."

"With a rap sheet like *that,* why wasn't he deported after serving time, assuming he *did* serve time?" Susan asked.

"Exactly the point," Washington said. "The drug charge was

considered a misdemeanor; the assault conviction was reduced at trial to 'time served.' So, since *you* guys are Feds, you tell *me* why he wasn't deported."

"Good question," Susan replied. "Must have been politics." Washington nodded, then continued.

"Right now, I have sources looking for both Toussaint *and* Baptiste. Somebody is going find them. If they didn't kill Simone Ardoin, maybe one of their associates did, and we'll make the connection."

From that point, Susan told Washington about her call to the American Consulate in Port-au-Prince, Haiti, and other details. He listened while she described what the consul had said about Simone's earlier call to him, and links between Baptiste and the drug trade. Susan named the bars where Simone had followed Baptiste and Alex confirmed the date and times.

"Okay, that's great news," Washington said. "I've asked for our tech to come in and work overtime to examine the CCTV tapes from the Quarter. Now I can tell her where to focus her attention. Thanks for that info. I'll also ask her to pull up private establishment tapes if there are any available."

"When we're done here," Susan said, "I'll contact Vern Bordelon at DEA and ask if he can tell us anything about either Baptiste or Toussaint since drugs may be involved. Do you know Bordelon?"

"I do," Washington replied. "He's a good man."

"Is there a city crime task force we can ask for support?" Rachel asked.

"Yes, there is," Susan replied. "That's a good idea. Since we don't know where Baptiste and Toussaint are hanging out, we should make sure everyone in law enforcement is aware of our concern."

"Let's stay in touch and find these assholes who killed Ms. Ardoin," Washington said. He handed his business card to each of them and they did the same in return.

ONCE BACK IN THE DIPLOMATIC SECURITY OFFICE, SUSAN CALLED Vern Bordelon, the DEA agent in charge. Being in his office, he invited them over for a meeting.

The three of them piled into Susan's official car and drove to Metairie, where DEA had its regional headquarters for a four-state region. The office was on Causeway Blvd., just before the bridge that traveled across Lake Pontchartrain.

They arrived within the hour and Susan made introductions.

"It's good to see you again, Susan," Bordelon said. He turned to Alex and Rachel. "Susan's told me all about her time in Pakistan with you guys. Sounded exciting."

"It was," Rachel replied. "But I wouldn't want to try it again. Once was enough."

"Hey, do you guys know Sam Combs?"

"Yeah," Alex replied, "he was in the DEA office in Karachi."

"That's right. We joined DEA at the same time. In any event, what can I do for you?"

"Are you aware that a State Department officer named Simone Ardoin was just murdered here in New Orleans?" Alex asked.

"Yes, I am; I read about it in the paper."

"We think she was killed by either Jules Baptiste or Claude Toussaint."

"Baptiste is a bad motherfucker," Bordelon replied. "But I didn't know he was linked with that murder. He's involved in

71

the cocaine trade, although his action is much smaller than the Colombians. I don't know this other guy . . . Claude Toussaint."

"Toussaint works for Baptiste. Also, Baptiste is running an illegal visa scam in Haiti," Susan said.

"I didn't know that. Hold on a minute while I log into my computer." When it was up and running, he said, "Baptiste doesn't have a fixed address, although he has operated throughout the area, including across the lake in St. Tammany Parish. My guess is his links run even farther afield than we've documented."

"Is he on the radar of other federal agencies?" Alex asked.

"On the radar, yes. But I'm not certain how much info the other Feds might have on him. I could ask the joint crime taskforce and see what pops."

"Who's on the taskforce?" Rachel asked.

"The FBI has the lead, then its DEA, DS, Homeland Security, NOPD, the Louisiana State Police, Alcohol, Tobacco and Firearms, Coast Guard, and then Jefferson Parish Sheriff's Office. By the way, you're in Jefferson Parish now. I'll make an inquiry to the taskforce and let you know."

"Thanks," Susan said. "That may close some loops. Since it's almost lunch time, care to join us?"

"No thanks, I've got paperwork to finish. Maybe next time."

AFTER LEAVING VERN BORDELON AND THE DEA OFFICES, SUSAN drove them to Veterans Blvd. for Japanese food at the Shogun Restaurant. Alex and Rachel devoured sushi, while Susan opted for a crispy tempura, and other cooked items.

Momentarily between bites, Alex thought about their

meeting and was pleased with the day's progress. *With Washington in charge of the investigation for NOPD, and the Feds now involved, maybe we're headed in the right direction,* he thought. One aspect of deep concern, however, was that Baptiste was a badass. *This might not end without more violence.*

Chapter 11

A Celebration of Life

Neither Alex nor Rachel felt comfortable intruding on the private life of Simone's parents, but Papa Ed and Camille had insisted they come to lunch and talk to family and friends about Simone's work with the State Department. It was a way to celebrate her life and her many accomplishments with people who knew little about the Foreign Service and cared even less, for that matter, about the world outside of Louisiana.

So just before noon on the next day, Alex and Rachel drove their rental car out of the French Quarter and headed toward Dooky Chase's Restaurant in Treme. The grand matron and chef of the restaurant was the elderly Leah Chase, known as the Queen of Creole Cuisine. Both she, and her restaurant, were legends in the city.

Alex found a parking space near the corner of Miro and Orleans Streets. The area appeared to be a low-middle income residential neighborhood with one or two-story wooden houses, not unlike much of the city, other than the posh Uptown and Garden District areas that had much larger homes, indeed, mansions in some cases. Unlike the surrounding buildings, Dooky Chase's Restaurant was made of brick, with a small set of steps leading up to the front door. A sign outside announced it had been in business since 1941.

Alex took his suit jacket from where he had placed it on the back seat and slipped it on, then followed Rachel up the steps and through the front door.

"Wow, this is not what I expected from the outside," Rachel said surveying the room as they entered and stood next to a hostess podium off to the right. Behind them was a narrow room painted with dark green walls which contained a bar. The large room they were facing, however, had red walls with a few white columns scattered around the room. The carpet was also red, blended with a swirled cream pattern. The dining chairs were a very elegant red and white striped.

"We're joining the Ardoin gathering," Alex said to the smiling, attractive hostess.

"Follow me, please." She led them to the left and into a private medium-sized room with gold painted walls and attractive local artwork. Papa Ed and Camille greeted them.

"Welcome, and thank you for coming," Camille said, while embracing Rachel, then Alex. She led them over to join a large group of friends who stood nearby. Predominantly African American, the group also included several white people, one of which was NOPD Captain Wells. In the main room, Alex noticed the overall clientele was a balanced mixture of races including one group of local Catholic school girls wearing plaid uniform skirts and white blouses.

"Let me introduce you to our friends," Papa Ed said,

shepherding them across the room and over to a cluster of about twenty well-dressed people. Papa Ed was keen for Alex and Rachel to know with whom they were speaking, so he mentioned a few details of each person as they shook hands.

First up was the mayor of New Orleans. Then there were a few judges, both federal and local; several city council men and women; a few union officials, lawyers, the chief of police, and assorted businessmen and women who ran impressive sounding charities or social organizations.

Alex's head was swirling with the list of VIPs, and he realized it would be difficult to keep their names and positions straight. Rachel, however, was doing an excellent job of chatting and already had answered questions about Simone Ardoin's work for her in Washington. Then he found himself standing next to Captain Wells whom he had meet at the Ardoin home the day after the shooting.

"Captain, you mentioned that you've known Papa Ed for almost thirty years. How did you originally meet?"

Wells sucked in some air, as if he was about to jump into the deep end of a pool. "Since you're here to help us, I'll tell you the *abbreviated* story. I was a young patrolman at the time Papa Ed was a young defense attorney. One night, a home robbery occurred, and three members of the family were shot and killed. I was one of the responding officers. Later, detectives arrested a gangbanger for the murders and Papa Ed was his defense council. Although the gangbanger was definitely a bad dude with a criminal record, for reasons I won't go into now, I somehow wasn't convinced he had done it. As the kid's trial began, I arrested someone else on different charges by total coincidence. But the guy had a handgun on him, and our lab matched the gun to the murders in the gangbanger case. Eventually, the guy I arrested admitted he had done the family killings. So charges against Papa Ed's client were dismissed. That's the short version, and we've been friends ever since."

Alex was intrigued and wanted to hear more, but Papa Ed had begun to address the group. "Why don't we take our seats," Papa Ed said to everyone. He ushered Alex and Rachel to chairs in the middle of a long table with chairs on both sides. Once seated, Papa Ed spoke.

"I want to thank everyone for being here to remember our Simone. Most of you can remember when she was a darling, little girl, and over the years, you watched her grow up into a fine woman of accomplishment." He paused to dab his eyes with a napkin.

"Joining us today are two of her friends who now work in London, Alex Boyd and Rachel Smith. They came to New Orleans to be with Simone for the weekend. But their visit was cut short . . ." Papa Ed had to stop again and catch his breath. "Rachel was Simone's boss at the State Department in Washington. I know from my chats with Simone that Rachel was also one of her closest friends and mentors. Rachel's husband, Alex, is a Special Agent with the State Department and has agreed to work with the NOPD to help find Simone's killers."

Again, he paused, his chin quivering, eyes glassy. Camille reached over and placed her hand on his. "Once we've all ordered, I'd like Rachel to tell you about Simone's work and about who she became in the Foreign Service," Camille said.

As if on cue, waiters brought menus and the group made their selections. Over the next fifteen minutes, Rachel told the group about Simone's sterling performance as a Foreign Service

Officer. She described Simone's earlier assignments in Milan and Rome as a consular officer, then her work in Haiti as the chief of the non-immigrant visa section.

When someone asked if Simone's work was related to her death, Rachel said the case was under investigation and she couldn't say more about it. Alex noted the judges and lawyers in the room nod in agreement with her.

Then the meals arrived. Alex and Rachel had both ordered unsweetened iced tea. Then Alex started with a cup of Creole Gumbo before his entrée of the restaurant's famous fried chicken with a side of stewed okra. Rachel had Shrimp Creole along with a mystery vegetable she had never heard of called *mirliton*, a New Orleans specialty; she said it reminded her of eggplant.

Forty-five minutes later, Alex thought the meal was over, but the waiters brought individual portions of bread pudding for everyone. Apparently, this was a group tradition. The dish was covered with an incredible creamy praline sauce garnished with butter, cinnamon, nutmeg, raisons, eggs brown sugar, vanilla extract, and bourbon.

"Good thing this is another low-cal recipe," he whispered to Rachel.

"Yeah, I'll meet you in the gym later this afternoon."

Over coffee, Alex and Rachel learned that Camille was a medical doctor with far reaching connections in the New Orleans social scene. She had gone to Tulane for her undergraduate degree, then worked as an aide to a city councilman for a few years before going on to medical school where she became an internal medicine specialist. She was currently active in a number of charities and community events.

After the meal ended, everyone exchanged goodbyes; Papa Ed escorted Alex and Rachel to the restaurant door, then said he wanted to mention something they might consider important.

"My law practice has defended a lot of questionable characters. I've considered calling a few of those I've gotten off just to see what they might know about Simone's killing. Of course, they've got friends in low places, and since New Orleans isn't that big, I thought, perhaps, they might have heard of Claude Toussaint or Jules Baptiste. I just want you to know what I plan to do."

"Papa Ed, I don't think that's a good idea," Alex replied. "Why not give Captain Wells the names of your former clients, and let NOPD do the work?"

"I hear you, Alex. Nevertheless, I need to take a more active role."

"I understand how you feel, Papa Ed, but that would be a mistake. I know you have great contacts and everyone is on your side, but let the cops do their job."

"Your counsel is wise, Alex. But this is *personal*. You know what I mean."

Alex had a feeling the grieving man wouldn't listen to any more advice. But as they shook hands, Papa Ed surprised him with one more question.

"I understand that Detective Washington replaced Kelly as the lead investigator on Simone's case. How is that working out?"

"It's like night and day. Thanks for making it happen."

"As I said, Alex, this is personal. I know Detective John Washington is the best."

"I'll let you know when we have a break in the case," Alex

said. He smiled as he gave the older man one more re-affirming shake of the hand. Then he and Rachel walked to their car.

Then Alex drove to the police station to see if John Washington had any new leads. Afterward he called Susan Witt with the same query. He had hoped for something fast to turn up. On the agenda for tomorrow was Simone's funeral.

Chapter 12

The Funeral

The pews of St. Augustine's Catholic Church in Faubourg, Treme, were full of people paying their respects to Simone Ardoin. Worshippers represented both the elite and non-elite of the city drawn from all walks of life: black, white, and Creole. In a city famous for the importance of family ties and life-long friendships, those in attendance represented values far above politics, race, or wealth.

St. Augustine was a pretty, white-washed building that traced its heritage back to the 1840s for "free people of color." Some of the original members of the church had even bought pews for their slaves, a first in the history of slavery in the United States. Alex counted ten stained glass windows in the large interior; someone had told him the windows had been brought to New Orleans all the way from France. The main altar, centuries old, was made from Italian marble.

He held Rachel's hand during the sermon and watched as a tear ran down the side of her face. She dabbed it dry with her handkerchief. Some of the people whom they had met earlier at Dooky Chase's Restaurant went to the pulpit one at a time to share precious memories of Simone and speak of her past to the assembled mourners. As Alex looked at the pulpit, it took a moment to figure out even that object was unique, it appeared to be a hand-carved tree stump.

Then it was time for Rachel to speak. She had been reluctant to accept the honor and told Camille and Papa Ed that only lifetime friends and family should do so. But Camille wanted Rachel to close out the service by telling everyone how Simone's life had culminated in success in the Foreign Service. So Rachel agreed and spoke for ten minutes. She highlighted Simone's mastery of the Italian and French languages, her work as an American Consular Officer in Milan and Rome, and of her promotion as the young head of the non-immigrant visa section at the American Embassy in Port-au-Prince, Haiti. Rachel recapped the awards Simone had won for her superior performance over the years, then closed with the following tribute:

"In the time I worked with Simone Ardoin in the Office of Italian Affairs in the State Department of the United States, I can unequivocally state that her understanding of Italian politics was unmatched, and her analytical skills were among the best I have ever seen. But more important than her work, she was a good person, a compassionate person, and someone who Camille and Papa Ed could be proud of having raised as a daughter. She had high standards and the courage to do what she thought was the right thing. I valued Simone's friendship, and I'll miss her smile, her humor, and her laugh. She was an extraordinary person, and she was my friend."

Rachel walked back to her pew and slumped beside Alex. He

wrapped his arm around her shoulder as she leaned against him. The bishop ended the service with a prayer, then everyone walked to the front doors of the church to see Simone's casket loaded into the hearse.

Thank God it's a sunny day, Alex thought, because in every other regard, the mood was very dark.

ALEX AND RACHEL JOINED THE PROCESSION TO THE CEMETERY. Unlike other cities, where the dead were buried below ground, the water table in New Orleans dictated that people were buried above ground, in stone tombs. The designs and stone carvings on many family tombs were intricate and attractive. Even cemeteries in New Orleans reminded visitors that this city was unique, its culture apart from the rest, and its heritage unmatched in America.

They stood near the back of the gathering to allow family and longtime friends to pay their respects. When Alex glanced around at many of the other tombs, he noticed a couple keeping their distance. They were not dressed like the others and didn't appear to fit in. The girl was wearing grungy grey jeans with tears in the pants some thought fashionable. She wore a short sleeve shirt revealing an abundance of colorful tattoos on her arms. Her male companion was dressed in a similar manner, inappropriate to the occasion.

Alex pulled out his iPhone and discreetly snapped a few photos of the couple. He wasn't sure why he did it, but their presence was so completely out of place that his instincts told him the photos might have some meaning later.

As the funeral ended, he and Rachel returned to their car. He took a minute to send his photos of the bizarre couple to Detective John Washington along with a question asking whether the couple was familiar to him. When he typed the text, he also asked to see the crime scene where Simone had been shot. Washington texted back that he would check out the photos, then asked if Alex would meet him at the police station so they could visit the crime scene together. Alex responded he would, then dropped Rachel off at their hotel. The funeral had been emotionally draining for her and she wanted to rest.

WHEN THE SERVICE ENDED, MOON GLOW GRABBED BILLY'S ARM and pulled him away from the others at the cemetery. They walked rapidly toward a nearby bus stop on City Park Boulevard that was on a direct line back to their apartment.

"Hey, hey, what's the rush?" he asked.

"I read that killers sometimes go to their victim's funerals," Moon Glow replied. "We need to leave before we're spotted."

Waiting at the bus stop, Moon Glow's eyes continually scanned passing cars, hoping no one would notice them. Her paranoia was growing each day.

"I ASSUME THE CRIME SCENE WAS SEARCHED," ALEX ASKED AS HE and Detective Washington were driving in an unmarked Ford up Esplanade Avenue toward City Park and NOMA.

"I assume so," Washington replied. "As you know, I wasn't brought into the case until a few days later. But I can tell you that it poured rain on the night of the murder. If there was any evidence, the rain washed everything away. So we can assume the crime scene is contaminated now. Still, it will be useful for you to see it."

Earlier, after Alex had dropped Rachel at the hotel, he had called Susan Witt. She had agreed to meet the two men next to the museum. Since Alex and John had another five minutes before they would arrive at NOMA, Alex asked Washington about his football background at LSU.

"So, you were a defensive back, right?"

"Yeah, I played cornerback."

"I believe I saw you on TV make an interception in a bowl game."

"Good memory. Yes, I did."

"Did you get drafted by an NFL team?"

"No, but I had a tryout here with the Saints."

"What happened?"

"I made the team but sat on the bench for a year. That's when I discovered how much faster and quicker receivers are at the pro level. Listen Alex, I have to confess that I googled you and found out some good stuff about your awards in Diplomatic Security. I also saw you played basketball for the University of Virginia."

"Yeah, that's true. We even went to the Final Four when I played."

"Did you start?"

"Not often. I played point guard, but as a back-up."

"Ever tryout for the NBA?"

"Are you kidding, John? Maybe you haven't noticed, but I'm a *white* guy, and I *can't jump*. And, yeah, I'm not as quick as those NBA players. Although I once beat a turtle in a race."

Washington laughed so hard he nearly drove into a parked

car. "That's good, Alex, very good." They made a fist bump, then drove over the mini bridge on the side of NOMA and saw Susan's car was already there. Washington drove to the exact spot where Simone was killed and parked. It was directly under a streetlight.

"The forensic techs searched the roadway and the adjacent area around here," Washington said. Alex looked around and figured it still might have been possible to miss a key piece of evidence in a heavy rain, especially since Detective "Fast Tim" Kelly had been in charge of the investigation. Alex had also read the police report which stated the streetlight directly over Simone's car had been working on the night of the shooting. Therefore, the men had some light for their search.

"When I was a bomb tech in the Army," Susan said, "we always searched for evidence a hundred to four hundred yards away from the blast. I know Simone wasn't blown up, but maybe we should expand our search area."

"Fine by me. Let's divide up the area," Washington said. Susan pulled out two sets of evidence gloves for Alex and herself. They split up and Alex headed for a group of trees about 100 feet away. As he approached, he saw a blanket spread out on the ground. There were food scraps and an empty bottle of wine laying on it. He stopped and took photos of the blanket and the surrounding area with his iPhone. Walking closer, he noted one end of the blanket was folded over on itself. He carefully lifted a corner and saw a Louisiana driver's license and snapped a photo of it.

"John, Susan, come here. I found something!" he yelled out. When they joined him, he pointed to the license on the ground. Washington put on a latex glove and picked it up. It was in the name of "Janet Ross" and the address was nearby, in fact, at the edge of the park. He used his cell phone to call the station and run a record check. A minute later the station called back and told him that Janet Ross had a short rap sheet for minor drug possession.

"She's very young, according to her birthdate on the license," Alex said. "And her face resembles the girl I saw at the funeral. She was loaded with tattoos and looked grungy. Because of the blanket, wine, and food, maybe she was here with a friend."

"Hell, she might be a witness," Washington said. "Let's go to her apartment and interview her." They drove both cars to the Esplanade Apartments where the receptionist confirmed that Janet Ross lived in the building with her boyfriend, Billy Whiteman.

Alex, Washington, and Susan went up to her unit and knocked on the door, but no one was home. "I'll follow up on this later," Washington said.

"Yeah, that's all we can do," Alex replied. He turned to Susan, "Can you give me a ride back to the hotel?"

"Sure."

"John, I'll see you tomorrow. Call me if anything develops."

Chapter 13

The Raid

Early the next morning, Alex was with Susan in her office talking about the Ardoin case with two other DS special agents who worked for Susan. One agent, Pete Fong, was Chinese American on his second assignment in Diplomatic Security; the other was Luis Torres a Mexican American agent on his first tour of duty. Susan's third agent, Scott Fellows, was in New York helping on a protective detail for a senior member of the British royal family visiting the states.

"Pete, since your surname is Chinese, do you speak the language?" Alex asked.

"Only a little; I'm fourth generation American. We didn't speak it much at home."

"I only asked because my wife, Rachel, speaks Chinese from her tours in Hong Kong and Beijing."

"Did she enjoy the assignments?"

"She did, and the State Department's Asian Bureau would

like her to take another tour in China." Alex's cell phone rang. He glanced at the screen and saw Detective Washington's name before answering.

"Good morning, John, what's up? Were you able to contact Janet Ross?"

"No, but I have news. We have a lead on where Claude Toussaint lives."

Alex sat up straight and put his cell phone on speaker. "Where is he, and what's the plan?"

"Toussaint lives in Chalmette. That's in St. Bernard Parish." Susan gave a thumbs up indicating she knew the location.

"We need to coordinate with the deputies in St. Bernard, but we plan on raiding Toussaint's house as soon as possible. I've already got a warrant for his arrest and to search the house. I'd like you and Susan to accompany us."

Alex noticed the enthusiastic looks from Special Agents Pete Fong and Luis Torres. "Is it okay if we bring along two more of our agents?"

"Sure. But since the location is in St. Bernard, *they* have jurisdiction and will want to make the raid themselves. You can observe."

"We understand. Where do we meet you, and when?" Alex asked.

"Join us at my office; we'll drive to Chalmette as a group. I'll get back to you with the time." As the call ended, Alex looked at Fong and Torres.

"Have you guys participated in a raid before?"

"No," Fong said. Torres shook his head.

"Okay, follow Susan's lead and be patient. Remember, the sheriff's deputies are in charge of this one." Then Alex looked at

Susan. "Since I travelled here for vacation, I didn't bring my gun. Do you have an extra one in the office?"

"Sure. Follow me." She walked across the room to a heavy steel door of a walk-in armored room and dialed in the combination. Alex looked over the hardware and selected a Glock Model 19 and three magazines. After sliding his belt through the holster, he secured it on his right hip, then put two magazines on his left side inside a leather magazine holder. The third magazine, he put into the Glock, chambered a round, and holstered the weapon.

"Since you're a London embassy guy now, Alex, when was the last time you qualified at the range?" Susan asked.

"Hey, give me a break. I qualified last month."

"Really? You hit anything?" she asked with a smile.

"You know me . . . I got a perfect score."

Fong looked Torres. "Is that for real?"

"It is for real, Pete," Alex replied. "But here's the secret: When someone is shooting at you, your own shots won't be so accurate. Expect that. With bullets whizzing past your head, it tends to bother most people when aiming a gun. Go figure . . . so practice, practice, practice."

Alex's phone rang; it was Detective Washington again. "Alex, can you guys meet us now? The St. Bernard Parish Sheriff's Office is prepared to raid as soon as possible."

"Okay, John, see you in twenty minutes."

Before they left the DS office, Susan called Vern Bordelon from DEA to update him and ask if he had any operations in Chalmette. He didn't. Then she called the local FBI office and spoke to the special-agent-in-charge. The result was the same.

Good thinking, Alex thought. *She was probably concerned about disrupting any undercover operation.*

Before they left the garage located below the DS office, Pete Fong and Luis Torres placed four M-4 carbines into the rear of the large black Chevy suburban they would drive to Chalmette. Then, as an extra precaution, each agent put on a DS tactical vest which held four extra magazines for the M-4. Alex doubted they would need this much firepower since the sheriff's deputies would take the lead, but he was fond of the saying: "You can never have too many guns, nor too much ammo."

After joining Detective Washington, it took the group some forty minutes to drive to the rendezvous point where they would meet the St. Bernard SWAT team. Alex had never been to this area, but saw a few signs mentioning the town of Arabi, which they drove through. He also saw some commercial signs about various local businesses. The area was flat and whenever he glimpsed housing, he had a sense this parish was less affluent than Orleans Parish. After a while, they pulled into a strip-mall parking lot for the rendezvous.

Lt. Broussard was a fifty-year-old white guy with an extended gut, and a large USMC tattoo on his right forearm. "Okay y'all, when we done talking here, we gonna hit this house over here." He pointed to it on a map.

"Do you know anything about this house, or about Claude Toussaint?" Detective Washington asked.

"Negative," replied Broussard. "I checked our database before coming, though. The house and Toussaint have been under the radar."

"What about general crime on the block?" Washington asked.

"Oh yeah, we made some drug busts before."

"Lt. Broussard, I'm as anxious as anyone to find Toussaint and his boss, Jules Baptiste," Alex said, "but I wonder if it would be a good idea to surveil the house for a while before busting right in? What do you think?"

"I think you ain't from here," Broussard replied. "You see, our guys can't blend in good into that neighborhood. I'd rather have the element of *su'prise* on my side."

Susan Witt jumped into the conversation. "Are you going to use any drug dogs or bomb sniffers once you bust in?"

"We'll bring 'em in later," Broussard said.

Alex realized their suggestions weren't going anywhere. *I figure Broussard is just a good old boy who rose through the ranks by seniority rather than expertise. But now isn't the time to argue with someone out of his depth.* He and the DS team would have to make the best of the mediocre planning.

"Okay, let me thank you in advance for your cooperation. We'll be with you, but as back-up while your team makes the raid," Washington said.

"Exactly right, this is *our* show," Lt. Broussard confirmed. "Let's go."

EVERYONE GOT BACK INTO THEIR VEHICLES AND DROVE TO Toussaint's house. Washington had brought three other NOPD cops with him all riding in one marked police SUV. Lt. Broussard drove his own marked police sedan, and had eight cops from the St. Bernard Parish SWAT team loaded into two black tactical vehicles, essentially large SUVs which appeared to be armored.

On their final approach, Alex could see it was a poor

neighborhood of run-down one and two-story homes with several vacant lots between existing structures; gargantuan weeds and high grass grew wild in the open spaces. Streets were littered with plastic bags, empty soda cans, and assorted rubbish. All existing houses had peeling paint, some with broken windows, and even the yards of occupied houses were full of weeds and dead grass.

I wonder if Hurricane Katrina decimated the houses on these vacant lots, he thought.

The squalor appalled him, but he had seen enough of the world to know that poverty existed everywhere and was even worse abroad.

Fixing problems like this is complicated and long-term, he continued to think. *It really requires stable family life with two parent households to guide children; better schools with the latest technology; community leaders who actually care about their neighbors rather than amassing clout, notoriety, and wealth; and finally, a government to develop incentive programs fostering hard work and real opportunities, not policies making people dependent on handouts.*

The thought of it all pissed Alex off. *Damn! Generations of these kids are heading in the wrong direction based on somebody's personal and socially wrong-headed decisions.*

The five-car team pulled up in front of the suspect's house and the eight St. Bernard SWAT members divided into three groups: four ran to assault the front door using a battering ram; two of the eight sprinted to the rear of the house; and the remaining two stayed outside the front door to provide security for the assault group.

Pete Fong had driven the DS Suburban and parked it last in line behind the others; all four DS agents got out. Susan and Pete grabbed their M-4 carbines from the back of the SUV and walked over to Detective Washington. All eyes were on the four officers at the house door.

"St. Bernard Parish Sheriff's Office! Open up!" yelled the lead SWAT cop. He waited five seconds, then motioned a second cop to use the battering ram against the lock. The door smashed open. All four cops ran into the house looking for Claude Toussaint.

Alex saw the three uniformed NOPD cops outside their cars, ready to lend support. Up and down the street, residents were coming outside and standing on their front porches, watching the action. He assumed they had all seen this kind of action before and were merely curious.

With crossed arms, Alex leaned against the suburban while the SWAT team carried out their raid. It was a pretty quiet one, unlike past DS raids in which he'd taken part. Here, there was little communication between units. Then he heard someone inside call out: "Clear!" The call was repeated several times as they found each room empty of threats.

Then, without warning, the slow pace of the raid was shattered from inside the house as the loud sound from semi-automatic rifle fire pierced the air; it sounded like AK-47 fire to Alex. The SWAT team returned fire using M-4 carbines.

Without hesitation, Alex and Torres drew their Glock pistols and ran toward the house, entering just behind the two SWAT officers who had been posted outside the front door. Alex could see two cops at the top of the stairs firing loud bursts down a hallway on the second floor. The smell of cordite drifted to the bottom of the stairs.

But even before Alex and Luis could climb the steps, the raid was over. Two gunmen lay dead, killed by the St. Bernard deputies. *Probably drug dealers,* Alex thought. One cop came down from the second floor and passed him.

"Was Claude Toussaint upstairs?" Alex asked.

"Negative."

Disappointed, Alex and Luis were about to leave the house when gunfire erupted from an adjacent house. By the time Alex and Luis reached the wooden front porch, one NOPD officer was lying in the street, clutching a leg wound. Another NOPD officer was just reaching him when rifle fire erupted again from the upper floor of the second house. Bullets ricocheted off the pavement hitting the second NOPD officer in his leg as well.

"Luis, follow me!" Alex said.

He and Luis ran down the porch stairs into the street to improve their shooting angle and aimed their Glock pistols at an open window. Alex felt his heart race as he exposed himself to the killing zone. But it had to be done. He stopped abruptly and assumed a balanced stance, legs spread, knees slightly bent. He swiftly shot six rounds at the gunman firing into the street. Alex's grip on his weapon was firm; the site picture of the gunman was clear, although the distance to the target, about forty yards away, was not ideal for a pistol.

Alex and Luis peppered the open window; return gunfire ceased. But a second later, new gunfire erupted from an adjacent window. Now Alex could see muzzle flashes from the rifles of two gunmen. He heard bullets whizzing by at high velocity and saw a few shots ricochet off the street close by.

Susan Witt and Pete Fong chambered rounds into their M-4s and let loose with bursts of accurate fire into the house's open window. Alex fired another four rounds with his pistol at this new target. Having fired a total of ten rounds of ammunition, with five rounds still left in his gun, he ejected his magazine and loaded a fresh magazine of fifteen rounds. As he stopped firing to assess whether the gunmen were still at the window, out of the corner of his eye he saw a determined Detective Washington rushing toward the house, joined by two St. Bernard Parish SWAT officers from around back of the first house. All three of them rushed through the front door; Alex heard yelling and shots fired. Then silence. The next moment was eerily quiet . . . until he heard the local cops calling for ambulances.

A few seconds later, Detective Washington walked out of the house while holstering his handgun; he wiped sweat from his forehead and headed back to his patrol car to make a report over the radio to NOPD headquarters. As he walked, Washington left bloody footprints in the street.

Lt. Broussard was also on his radio contacting his parish's chain of command. Alex turned to give medical aid to the two wounded NOPD officers lying in the street, but they were already being attended by men from the SWAT team.

An uninjured Luis walked up to Alex just as he spotted Susan and Fong standing about ten yards away. Alex holstered his Glock and shook Luis' hand.

"You did well, Luis, thanks."

"It was my first time under fire," Luis said. "Do you feel as strange as I do?"

"Of course. You never get used to it. Hopefully, you'll learn from the experience. Just reflect upon what you did right today. That will help."

"What now, Alex?"

"Just listen," Alex replied. "You'll pick up on things being said." Then, he called out to Susan, "I better let Director Riley and Rachel know what happened."

He took out his cell phone, and only then, realized he was

drenched in sweat; his heartbeat still seemed fast. Taking some deep breaths, he looked at his hands. *At least they seem steady,* he thought. *Interesting . . . training and experience have trumped my adrenalin rush.* He dialed Rachel's number.

"Hey, Rachel, I'm calling to let you know I'm okay."

"You're better than just *okay*. You're the *best*."

"No, I'm serious. Susan's office supported the St, Bernard Parish Sheriff's Office and the NOPD in a raid at a Chalmette house to find Claude Toussaint. I'm sure there will be a news story later today since two policemen were wounded. Everything developed at the last minute, but now you're up to speed."

"Let me guess . . . you were in the raid as well."

"Naturally. But as I said, I'm fine." They spoke another minute, then Alex called Director Riley to give him a heads-up before he heard about it on the news.

Done with his calls to Rachel and Riley, Alex looked up and down the street; people were still watching from their porches. He had a sense they had seen this before because no one appeared excited.

How sad, he thought, *this has become routine for them.* He heard sirens from approaching ambulances and saw police cars about a block away racing to the scene.

Holy shit, he sighed. *It was a set up. The gunmen were waiting for us and coordinated their attack from both houses. I wonder if someone in NOPD or St. Bernard Parish Sheriff's Office is a rat. Or maybe the original NOPD source on Claude Toussaint is the culprit. Either way . . . we were screwed.*

Chapter 14

Liaison with the FBI

U nlike a Hollywood movie, where cops just move from one shootout to the next in pursuit of bad guys, in the real world, every law enforcement officer who uses their firearm has to make a detailed statement of everything that occurred. It's not as easy as it sounds because officers are under massive stress and fear during the incident.

Later, when writing a statement, timelines can get confused, and what *actually* happened may differ from what the officer *thought* happened. Everyone handles danger differently; some are composed while others may be psychologically near the breaking point.

Since the raid on the St. Bernard Parish house involved two different police departments and one federal agency, the process was more complicated than usual. Susan Witt took the DS team back to her office to write up their statements. Copies would be provided to NOPD and St. Bernard Sheriff, and in return, DS would receive reports from those two departments.

Seated at separate desks in the DS office, Alex finished his statement and looked over at the two young officers to see how they were doing. Pete Fong was literally wringing his hands and appeared to be editing his work a few times. Luis Torres kept drinking water and was sweating, otherwise he seemed focused on the computer screen. Susan had also finished her statement and was now staring at a blank wall. Alex hoped she was merely considering what the bosses in Washington would want to know.

Within an hour of having returned to the DS office, Susan got a call from the DS Director of Investigations, informing her that he and another senior officer from the DS Office of Professional Responsibility would travel to New Orleans to ensure proper procedures had been carried out during the raid. Alex, Luis, and Pete stood outside her office listening in on the conversation. Susan clarified to the Director of Investigations that the St. Bernard Parish sheriff had been in charge, with DS and NOPD only there acting in support. Alex knew from experience that one incorrect statement by Susan could spell trouble down the road. Her description of events, however, was precise and accurate.

After the call ended, Alex told Fong and Torres to be truthful in describing what happened to the Washington guys when they arrived.

"Is it normal for an internal investigation to occur after an incident?" Pete Fong asked.

"Yes, it is, and it should be," Alex said. "Think of it as a form of quality control. At least all the officers in our Office of Professional Responsibility are special agents, themselves, and are experienced. When I was the RSO in Islamabad, we even had a State Department Accountability Review Board come out after the terrorist attack. So, if you've done your job right, you should be okay, as long as you stick to the facts when you explain whatever happened."

While Alex deliberately painted a proper picture of what *should* occur to these two men, in the real world things could be more complicated. For example, after the terrorist attack on the US Embassy in Pakistan years before, when Alex had been in charge of the Marines, the subsequent Accountability Review Board sent from Washington had an excellent and experienced chairman. There had also been two security professionals on the board, one retired from DS and the other a corporate security director. However, two other board members had been trouble from the start.

He remembered the first one had been a retired State Department economics officer who had served in small embassies where little or no threats had ever occurred. She had never been in any chain of command defending an embassy and was completely out of her depth in assessing the lead up to their attack, or the necessary actions needed once battle was joined. She had felt obligated to defend the senior political officer who had tried to override Alex's orders to the Marines back then. The other troublesome board member was a mid-grade management officer who was supposed to be the board's logistical officer. But he had tried to insert himself into the debate on whether Alex had exceeded his authority in defending the embassy.

Thank god the experienced officers on the board had ruled the day, Alex thought, *only in large part because the ambassador and deputy chief of mission had supported me.*

For Alex, it was a cautionary tale of how doing the right thing in life and death situations could sometimes backfire if *incompetent* people were later assigned to review the incident. It had made him skeptical of quickly trusting any Foreign Service officers until he had sufficient time to judge them.

Pete looked satisfied with Alex's answer, so Alex turned his attention to Susan. "How are you going to distribute our statements to the cops?"

"I thought I'd drive over to NOPD headquarters and drop them off myself so I can pick up their statements. I'll do the same thing with St. Bernard Parish. Do you want to tag along?"

"No, I going to hook up with Rachel. What are you doing for lunch?"

At that moment, Susan's cell phone rang, and she answered. After ten minutes of conversation, she hung up. "That was Bill Westbrook, he's the Special-Agent-in-Charge of the FBI office here in New Orleans. He's been briefed by NOPD about the raid, and he'd like to get our views as well."

"Is he a good guy?" Alex asked.

"That's hard to say. He doesn't share much info, lacks a sense of humor, and isn't all that friendly. Maybe he knows his job, but I can't evaluate that yet. On the other hand, maybe he's another cautious FBI agent who just follows orders from the political bigwigs in FBI headquarters. In any event, he's heard about Simone Ardoin's murder, and he wants to know more. I asked him to meet us for lunch and he suggested Mother's."

"*Mother's*? What's that? A convent?"

Susan laughed. "No, it's a hole in the wall place on Poydras Street that has amazing food. The rear room is big enough and noisy enough that we can talk with some modest privacy."

"Is Poydras Street near the FBI office?"

"Oh, no. The restaurant is downtown in the Central Business District. The FBI office is near the small Lakefront Airport which is a wasteland for restaurants."

"Can I bring Rachel?"

"That would be a good idea since she knew Simone Ardoin better than any of us. Meet me at Mother's at 1:30 p.m. Any taxi driver will know where it is."

WHEN ALEX RETURNED TO THEIR ROOM IN THE ROYAL SONESTA, Rachel was ending a phone call with Assistant Secretary of State for European Affairs Archibald Watson. He was a close friend who was about to transfer to Brussels as the US Ambassador to NATO.

"That's great Archie," Alex overheard Rachel say. "I can't tell you how much I appreciate being able to stay in New Orleans a little longer. The police believe they know who ordered her murder, but it's a matter of finding the actual hitmen." She waved to Alex as he entered the hotel room.

There was a pause in her conversation as she listened to Archibald Watson on the other end, then replied: "Yes, Simone's parents have taken her death very hard. I've never seen two people so distraught . . . Yeah, that's a good idea. The Ardoins would appreciate a call from you. By the way, I'm seeing Camille tomorrow or the next day to reinforce how special Simone was to all of us. Alex has stayed in touch with Simone's Dad."

Again, Alex noted a pause.

"Okay, just email me any work that I should see. If it's classified, you can send it to Susan Witt, the agent-in-charge of the DS office in New Orleans. I'll return to London as soon as possible. Thanks, Archie. Goodbye."

She took a deep breath and blew out some air, sighing at the end. Alex sat next to her and put his arm around her waist, squeezing her as she rested her head against his shoulder.

"You heard half the conversion," Rachel said. "Archie said I can stay here for a while."

"That's wonderful, Rach."

"So, tell me about this morning. Did Baptiste's people try to kill the cops?" Alex recapped the entire drama. She listened quietly, waiting until he finished before she spoke.

"So, it was just another day at the office," she said.

Is she being sarcastic? He wondered, *Is she becoming psychologically hardened and too accepting of our recurring bouts of danger? She has always been courageous and determined, but I hope she hasn't become too callous about life's unfair and violent side.*

He paused for a moment and reflected upon his own mindset. *As if I can talk! It wasn't so long ago that I stared at a dead hitman on a street in Paris who I had just killed, and I felt no emotion at all, just part of the job.*

They locked eyes, then embraced tighter. He held her for half a minute. "We're having lunch at 1:30 with Susan and the special-agent-in-charge of the New Orleans FBI office."

"Are they taking over the case?"

"Good question. I don't know, yet. I think he's just gathering information for Washington to make that decision." She nodded in understanding.

"Is this a fancy place for lunch? I have to decide what to wear."

"Susan said it's a hole in the wall with great food. Why don't you wear your slinky black dress that you brought, or your bikini and high heels?"

"You're no help at all," Rachel chuckled. "Not to mention you're sexist."

"I'm not sexist. If I were, I also would have asked Susan to wear *her* bikini. But okay, if you insist, you should wear loose fitting pants, grungy tennis shoes, a lumberjack shirt, and thick glasses." He smiled.

"You do a great impression of being a dork. I'm going to disregard your advice and wear something casual."

"I knew you could work it out. After-all, your Mensa IQ is off the charts."

She shook her head in mock despair. "You'll have to do better than that, Hunk Man." Rachel walked into the bathroom to touch up her make-up. He saw her smile in the mirror and knew that deep down, Rachel was pleased he valued both her intellect as well as her incredible physique.

———

THEY EXITED THE TAXI AND HE LOOKED AT MOTHER'S RESTAURANT from the sidewalk. *How can something so famous look so ordinary?* He puzzled, looking at the unimpressive front of the one-story red brick building. *Susan called it a hole-in-the-wall . . . but still.*

There was a ramp to help the handicapped get up to the door, and a sign to the side confirming that it was, indeed, Mother's. Poydras Street was very wide and filled with tall, modern office buildings and hotels. At the far end of the street, away from the Mississippi River, was the Superdome.

"Okay, I guess this is the place," Alex said.

Rachel was wearing designer blue jeans with modest heels, and a loose-fitting cream-colored silk blouse. Her wavy brown hair draped onto her shoulders. Alex thought she looked like a million dollars but also knew she would look just as good in a lumberjack shirt and thick glasses.

He wore casual khaki slacks, a button-down collared blue shirt, and a lightweight grey herringbone sports jacket, the latter because he was armed with his Glock pistol and needed to cover it up. They opened the front door and found Susan waiting inside for them.

"Okay guys, take a look at the hand printed menu on the wall behind the food station," Susan said. "Here, you make your order while you're standing in line. You can see what they're serving in the large trays behind the glass display. Then we move down to the cashier and order a drink. I have a corner table for us in the next room on the left."

"What's good to eat?" Rachel asked.

"Everything. If you like roast beef, order the Debris sandwich on French bread. You can also try their amazing red beans and rice or the crawfish étouffée. The other choices are good as well."

"What's *étouffée*?" Rachel asked.

"It's like a stew type of thing. I think you make a roux and add onion, celery, bell peppers, garlic, and hot sauce," Susan replied.

What the hell is a 'roux'? Alex wondered. He almost asked, but decided it was too much information for him. As Susan left for the larger dining room, he looked over the array of selections.

"I'll have the roast beef Debris sandwich," he told the woman behind the counter.

"Do you want it dressed?" she asked.

"What?"

"Dressed . . . you know, with shredded cabbage."

"Yes, I'll take it dressed." He whispered to Rachel, "Of *course*, I want it dressed. Who would eat a *naked* sandwich?"

Rachel smirked and ordered the crawfish étouffée. They each

got a bottle of Barq's root beer, a local favorite. After paying and collecting their food, they left the small room which looked more like a diner than a well-known restaurant and entered an enormous room with very high ceilings and overhead fans. It had an industrial feel.

Sitting next to Susan on her right was Bill Westbrook from the FBI and on her left was Detective John Washington from NOPD. After shaking hands, Alex and Rachel sat in vacant chairs at the round table.

"Susan was just telling us that the three of you served together in Pakistan," Westbrook said.

"That's right, Bill. Someone had to enjoy the posh life," Alex replied with a small smirk. Westbrook didn't smile, either he'd missed the joke, or had completely left his sense of humor at home this morning. He was about fifty years old and had brown hair mixed with grey, a square jaw, and seemed very uptight. *I can't put my finger on it,* he thought, *but I don't trust the man.*

"Rachel, was it difficult for you and Susan to work in that environment?" Westbrook asked.

"No, not at all," Rachel replied. She looked at Susan who nodded in agreement. "The Pakistanis didn't expect us to dress in burkas, just so long as we dressed conservatively, which meant a pants suit or loose-fitting dress with long sleeves," she continued. "It was a matter of respecting their culture and using common sense."

"Weren't you and Alex in Rome when the American ambassador was kidnapped?" Westbrook asked.

Alex hesitated for a moment. *Is this guy going to be trouble?* "Yes, that's correct," he said out loud. "I was the senior regional security officer and Rachel was the embassy press officer." He stared at Westbrook, his jaw tightened, ready to defend his past actions against the incompetence of the FBI.

"I'm not a close friend of John Reynolds, but I knew him," Westbrook said with a deadpan expression. "He rubbed a lot of agents the wrong way." Westbrook was referring to the senior FBI agent, John Reynolds, who had flown to Rome to help secure the Ambassador's release, but in reality, Reynolds had been out of his depth .. and a liar.

"How did he rub *you*?" Alex asked.

"We got along as best we could."

Alex hadn't thought about senior FBI Agent Reynolds in years, although he couldn't forget that asshole who had tried to deep-six him after the ambassador had been kidnapped.

With a glance at both Alex and Rachel, Westbrook had another question. "Can you share the concern Simone Ardoin had about Jules Baptiste and Claude Toussaint?"

Alex took half a minute to think about how best to describe the situation. Then, he took the lead to talk about Simone's knowledge of Baptiste's criminal activities from her prior assignment in Haiti. At the end of the briefing, Westbrook commented.

"Thank you for bringing me up to speed. Just before lunch, I spoke with headquarters," Westbrook said. "Some think we should assume responsibility for the case since Ardoin was a commissioned officer in the U.S. government, and perhaps, killed by a foreign citizen. But I'm comfortable with NOPD in the lead, especially since Detective Washington is in charge of the case. Now that I know Diplomatic Security is involved, as well, I'll tell headquarters that we should just monitor things, and provide whatever advice we can."

"Thank you for your support, Bill," Alex replied. "We'll keep you updated as the case progresses."

"Yes, we will," John Washington confirmed. "Now, how about we sink our teeth into our meals."

Alex bit into his roast beef sandwich. Gravy and small bits of shredded beef oozed out the sides of the flaky French bread and fell onto his plate. "Oh, my God! This is the best sandwich I've *ever* had. This chopped cabbage on top is *great*! I may order a second sandwich."

Judging from the speed with which Rachel was devouring her plate of crawfish étouffée, he assumed she loved it and watched as she shook a few more drops of Tabasco sauce on top of her food, then savored every bite.

Bill Westbrook looked at Detective John Washington. "Well, John, it appears that New Orleans has just found two more converts to its cuisine."

"Happens every time, Bill."

Susan was keeping up, too, just as her cell phone rang. "It's a call from our embassy in Haiti," she told the group. Then she listened to the caller for ten minutes, spoke a few times, and finally said a thank you before hanging up.

"That was Tommie Rogers, our regional security officer at our embassy in Port-au-Prince. He sent me an email I need to look at; said the local cops have a break in Simone's case, but he just gave me the condensed version during our call. You're going to be surprised."

Chapter 15

Break in the Case

As the meal ended at Mother's Restaurant, Susan Witt gave an abbreviated version of her phone call with Tommie Rogers, embassy RSO in Port-au-Prince, Haiti. Westbrook, Washington, Alex, and Rachel all decided to accompany Susan back to her DS office and read his complete email detailing the break in the Ardoin case.

Seated at her computer, Susan printed out copies for all four of them. "The Haitian police unit which gave the RSO this info has been trained by the DS Anti-Terrorism Assistance Program," Susan said. "That's why they're so cooperative with the embassy. As you can see from the email, a Port-au-Prince local thug named Emmanuel Thibault has frequent contact with Jules Baptiste because they're in the visa fraud and drug smuggling business together."

She turned to Bill Westbrook. "Bill, you recall that Baptiste is the boss of Claude Toussaint, the one who called Simone Ardoin for the meeting in City Park, right?" Westbrook nodded. "Well, from Haiti, Thibault phoned Baptiste several times at a number in Mandeville, St. Tammany Parish. The number is listed in the email. The RSO doesn't know if the Haitian cops are monitoring Thibault's phone calls, or if they have an inside source in his operation in Port-au-Prince."

"I can get the Mandeville address for this number," Westbrook said.

"So can I. Hold on a minute," Susan replied, quickly searching on the computer, then printing out the address in Mandeville. "Since this may involve drug smuggling, I better let Vern Bordelon at DEA know about it."

"I know both the sheriff in St. Tammany Parish, and the chief of police for the City of Mandeville," Westbrook said. "You want me to call them and say that you want to meet about the case? I won't be able to see them, myself, in the next day or two but I can call to set up a meeting for you."

"Yes, thank you, Bill," Susan replied. "John, how about if we pay a visit to the sheriff in St. Tammany Parish. We should ask Vern Bordelon if he wants to come with us." John agreed.

"Alex and Rachel, do you want join us?" Susan asked. Alex looked at Rachel.

"You bet we do," he replied.

"Okay then. Let's plan on tomorrow morning after Bill confirms the appointment with the sheriff."

HAVING THEIR LATE AFTERNOON AND EVENING FREE, ALEX AND Rachel felt it was time to speak with the Ardoins and give them an update on their daughter's murder case. But when they called Papa Ed to set up a meeting, he told them Camille was tied up with patients at the hospital, however, he would be available at his office in the Central Business District.

Arriving at Papa Ed's office building, Alex looked up at a modern glass and steel high rise. After checking in with the law firm's receptionist, they were escorted to Papa Ed's office, passing a fair number of occupied offices in the long corridor.

I'm guessing Papa Ed must have at least twenty associates, maybe double that, Alex thought.

The view from his upper floor office was spectacular; you could see the great Mississippi River in the distance, as well as the Central Business District and French Quarter closer by. One wall of his office was filled with law books, neatly placed in a massive mahogany bookcase. Papa Ed's desk was large and looked antique, or at least was an excellent reproduction. At one end of the room was a conference table surrounded by six comfortable-looking leather chairs; next to that setting was a plush upholstered sofa and two matching chairs with a coffee table in between.

"It's so good to see you, again," Papa Ed said. He walked from behind his desk and shook their hands.

"I hope we aren't keeping you from business," Alex said.

"Not at all. I'm just here to sign off on some completed work. I really can't focus on any new cases yet. My mind just isn't ready."

"We understand," Rachel said. "We thought you'd like an update on Simone's case."

"Thank you. Let's have a seat over here." He led the way over to the sofa and chairs across the thickly carpeted room. After they were seated, Alex began.

"Have you heard about this morning's shootout in Chalmette?"

"Yes, I caught it on the midday TV news. Was that related to Simone's murder?"

"It was," Alex replied. "But we didn't find Claude Toussaint or Jules Baptiste there. Nevertheless, we're pursuing another solid lead outside of Orleans Parish."

"I see." Papa Ed stared out the window for a few seconds before returning his gaze to Alex. "Maybe I should contact some of my former clients and see what they can find out."

"I think we've discussed this a few days ago, Papa Ed. Collecting information is one thing, but let's make sure this is coordinated with the cops."

"Naturally." Papa Ed sounded sincere, but Alex wasn't buying it. Ardoin was one of several powerbrokers in the city, and Alex was more certain than ever that Papa Ed wasn't used to biding his time while others took action.

Alex stared into the older man's eyes, then leaned forward in his chair and said, "I can see you're a man of tremendous analytical skill. Please don't let your emotional side cause you to make an error in judgment in pursuing Simone's murderers. In the end, they *will* be caught or killed by the cops."

Returning Alex's stare, Papa Ed waited a few moments before replying. "As I said once before, you're a wise man, Alex. But things play out differently here in New Orleans. I *trust* you and Rachel. But let's just say that not *everyone* I deal with in the city plays by the same rules, including law enforcement. Sometimes you have to shake the tree to make coconuts fall to the ground."

"I understand, Papa Ed. But, please, be careful."

"I'm going to call Camille to see when she's free," Rachel said. "I think she'll want to chat more about Simone." Papa Ed smiled.

"You're right. She *would* like to talk with you some more. Thank you, Rachel."

PAPA ED ARDOIN CLOSED HIS OFFICE DOOR JUST AFTER ALEX AND Rachel said their goodbyes and left for the hotel. As he settled back behind his desk, he picked up his cell and punched in the numbers for Leon Johnson. It rang three times before Leon picked up.

"Hey, Mr. Ardoin, I ain't talked to you in a couple of months. Nice to hear from you."

"The same here, Leon. How's life going for you?"

"Not bad. I be working at an auto repair shop, and I'm staying *real* clean."

"That's great, Leon. Now, I have a favor to ask."

"Anything you want, Mr. Ardoin. If it wasn't for you and your people, I be spending my days in Angola." Leon referred to the Angola State Penitentiary north of Baton Rouge, one of the toughest prisons in America, filled with hardcore, violent criminals.

"I just did my job, Leon."

"You did a *hell* of a lot more than that. I owe you *big* time."

"Thank you, Leon. Tell me, have you heard about my daughter being murdered in City Park?" As he spoke, Papa Ed took out his handkerchief and wiped his eyes, then cleared his throat.

"No! Mr. Ardoin! I mean, I done heard there was a murder in the park, but I ain't heard it was *your daughter*. I be so sorry, Mr. Ardoin."

"Thank you, Leon. The police are making inquiries, but I

think I need to push the process along faster. Plus, you know as well as anyone that justice in New Orleans is never certain. Guilt or innocence is dependent upon a lot of things."

"You ain't kiddin', Mr. Ardoin. I understand. You want me to ask around and find out who did it?"

"Yes, thank you, Leon. I can compensate you for it."

"Don't even think about it, Mr. Ardoin. I'll call some of da boys and we'll get the job done."

Papa Ed reflected upon Leon's last statement and took some comfort: *We'll get the job done.* It was less than subtle code meaning, "we'll find them and kill them for you." Ardoin knew that Leon was not a man to be messed with. He stood six feet four inches tall and was solid muscle; he had more tattoos than any man he'd ever seen. Leon had already spent a decade in prison, and would have gone back again, had Ardoin not won his case in court.

"Thank you, Leon. Let me know if you need anything . . . anything at all."

"We're good, Mr. Ardoin. I'll call you later, one way or the other."

———

THAT EVENING, ALEX AND RACHEL WALKED OVER TO JACKSON Square to take in the sights and feel the ambiance of the city. It was 8:30 p.m. and neither was hungry after the lunch at Mother's. They strolled hand-in-hand, pausing to listen to jazz musicians in front of the St. Louis Cathedral, then walked to one side of the square along the fence surrounding the park to look at the artists' work hanging on the fence.

People were posing for portraits and artists were churning

them out in charcoal within thirty minutes, or so. "Some of these guys are really good," Rachel said as they watched one artist at work with a client.

"I agree."

"Let's go to Moonwalk," Rachel said, referring to the raised concrete area across Decatur Street that had been erected by former Mayor "Moon" Landrieu. Arriving shortly, they looked back in awe at the cathedral lit up at night. On either side were matching 18th century stone buildings called the Cabildo and the Presbytère. Each had nine high archways on the ground floor, then another nine arched windows a level above, and finally nine smaller windows on the third floor adorning the mansard roof. The total effect was gorgeous.

"I read the Presbytère, was designed in 1791 to match the Cabildo on the other side of the cathedral," she said, "but it wasn't finished until 1813. It's built on the same site where Capuchin friars had their presbytery or rectory. But it was never used for religious services. Unlike the main structure in the middle that we call the St. Louis Cathedral. That's the oldest cathedral in continuous use in the U.S. This New Orleans cathedral was dedicated to King Louis of France."

"When was that? And which King Louis?"

"Well, I think the first one was built in 1718 but burned down; a second one also burned down, then this third one replaced it in 1789 and has been remodeled since," Rachel replied. "But I don't know which King Louis."

"I bet you didn't think I knew there *was* more than one King Louis."

She chuckled. "You're right, I didn't."

"It was dedicated under King Louis IX," Alex stated with a small grin.

"Well, well, aren't *you* the showoff?" She kissed him on the cheek.

Alex smiled. "Actually, there's a plaque on the ground behind you with that information."

Rachel laughed. "I should have guessed." They meandered along the riverfront walkway and sat on a bench. A few large ocean-going freighters or tankers meandered past them, going up the Mississippi River in the direction of Baton Rouge.

"I bet there are grain silos upriver and maybe bulk terminals, too," Alex said.

Rachel looked at him and smirked. "You're really showing off tonight. I'm impressed with your deductive powers and your knowledge of the area."

He returned the smile. "You can just call me Mr. Mensa."

"More like Mr. Internet."

He laughed and planted a long kiss on her lips. The moonlight played on her hair. "What do think it would be like to live here?" he asked, kissing her again, lightly this time.

"I think after a period of sightseeing and learning about the city, we'd get bored. Remember what Simone said about the culture focusing on Mardi Gras, debutante balls, charity galas, and long-time social contacts. Who would want to interact with the same crowd over and over? And besides, we're not from here, so we'd probably be excluded."

"You're right, Rach."

"Besides, we'd each weigh 250 lbs. with this food."

"That's for sure."

"On a more serious note, Alex, do you think we'll find Baptiste or Toussaint soon?"

"I do. I believe their days are numbered. The question is how many other people will die before we catch them."

Chapter 16

On the Hunt

After Leon Johnson had spoken on the phone with Papa Ed, he immediately called two of his best buddies, Big Bill Ledoux, and Speedy Vermillion. Both were hardened criminals and beneficiaries of Papa Ed's legal defense expertise. As the sun was setting, they met Leon at his apartment in the Algiers neighborhood of the West bank of New Orleans.

"Thanks for coming here so fast," Leon said. All sat in Leon's living room and while they talked they downed their second beers of the early evening.

"Hey, if Mr. Ardoin needs help, we be always ready," replied Big Bill. Speedy Vermillion nodded in agreement.

"Okay then, here's da deal. He believes that a guy named Jules Baptiste is responsible for killing his daughter. She was supposed to meet one of Baptiste's men named Claude Toussaint. So far, the police don't know where to find them. So let's reach out and get it done."

"Baptiste is a bad mother-fucker," Big Bill said. "I never met him, but I heard he scare the shit out of most people."

Leon paused to consider this. "He can't be tougher than you."

Big Bill replied, "It ain't about being tough. I hear he crazy and likes violence."

"Okay, got it. Let's get to work."

Without further instruction, Big Bill and Speedy stood up and walked into other rooms. Each pulled out their call phones and started calling local criminals they knew in the hope that someone would have useful information.

Over an hour passed, and their contacts were drying up, when Speedy finally hit pay dirt. He returned to the living room and said to Leon and Big Bill, "You guys know Ruthy Jones, right?"

"Oh yeah, she runs that whore house in Gretna," Leon replied. Gretna was adjacent to Algiers.

"Yeah, dat be her," Speedy said. "She said dat one of her clients told one of her hookers dat Baptiste personally greased that girl in the park."

"Why would he say that?" Leon asked.

"Ruthy say he was trying to impress the whore with his inside knowledge, like he be a big gang member himself."

Leon leaned back in his chair and thought about this for a moment. There were a lot of want-a-bees around, so maybe this guy was bullshitting.

"Okay," replied Leon. What else did he say?"

"He say Baptiste worried he brought too much heat on himself and he be moving around the area so he don't get caught."

"Does she know where he at now?" Leon asked.

"She not sure, but knows he has a place right here in Algiers."

"Really? She have an address?"

"She sure did and she gave it to me," replied Speedy.

THE ADDRESS FOR BAPTISTE'S HIDEOUT THAT RUTHY HAD GIVEN Speedy was only about ten blocks away from Leon's apartment, but they decided to wait until closer to midnight to find out if Baptiste was at that address. In the meantime, that walked to a nearby fast food place, ate some burgers and fried chicken, and then returned to Leon's place for more beers.

At ten o'clock, Leon opened a secret wall compartment he had in his bedroom closet and took out three handguns. Two were 9mm Beretta's and one was a Colt .45 model 1911. They loaded up the available magazines and waited over an hour before making the short drive to Baptiste's place. Their goal was simple---kill Baptiste and anyone else there. It would not be their first killing, nor their second, nor even their third.

It was much too hot to put on ski masks, but each donned a baseball cap and sunglasses in case NOPD had cameras in the area. Leon drove his ten year old Buick and parked about a block away from Baptiste's small house. They sat and waited, hoping to see someone going into or out of the house. After waiting a while, Leon looked at his watch, it was 11:45 pm, and then he spotted a car pull up into the driveway of the house. Leon, Speedy, and Big Bill watched as two figures got out of the car and walked to the front door. Someone opened it and they entered.

"Do you think dat was Baptiste," Big Bill asked?

Leon rubbed his chin and replied, "I'm not sure. One of the men was tall and skinny. Maybe it was Baptiste."

"Let's wait another hour and see what happens," Speedy said.

"I agree," Leon replied. So they remained in the Buick and watched and waited. Every ten minutes or so a car passed by, but none stopped. Then Leon made the decision.

"Okay, let's do it," he said.

They all got out of the car and were jogging toward Baptiste's house when three Ford F-250's came screaming from both directions on the road. They slammed on their brakes and stopped, surrounding Leon's team. Nine men jumped out of the three vehicles, some armed with shotguns or semi-automatic rifles, others with handguns.

Leon was scared shitless. He raised his hands high in the air and told Speedy and Big Bill to do the same. They were immediately disarmed and marched into Baptiste's house. All were pushed down onto their knees and flex cuffs locked on their wrists. Before them stood Jules Baptiste and Claude Toussaint.

Sweat poured off of Leon's muscular body, his heart raced, and his hands shook. Baptiste sneered down at them.

"I hear you're trying to kill me," Baptiste said ominously.

"No, no, we're just trying to find out where you been hiding," replied Leon.

"And why would you want to know that?"

"A friend wants to know," Leon said.

"I'll bet that friend is the father of the girl I killed in the park. Or else it's the cops who want to know."

Speedy yelled out," We never talk to da cops."

"What's your name?" asked Baptiste loudly.

"It's Speedy Vermillion." His voice shook so badly he could barely spit out the words.

"Speedy, hmm. You made a big mistake when you spoke to Ruthy."

Speedy was no pansy, he was tough, but the realization that Baptiste knew he had spoken to Ruthy meant she was part of Baptiste's network, and that thought sent chills through his body.

Baptiste and Toussaint walked into the next room to talk. His gunmen stayed behind, their weapons pointed at Leon, Speedy, and Big Bill.

Five minutes later, Baptiste and Toussaint returned. They stared at the three on their knees, then Baptiste spoke to his men.

"Take them out of here. Leave them by the side of the road a few miles away. One of his men tilted his head, not sure precisely what he was supposed to do. So Baptiste pointed his index finger at Leon and used his thumb to act as the hammer of a pistol. He snapped it down on the finger to simulate firing a shot.

"You got it boss."

Chapter 17

Trouble on the Horizon

The next morning, over breakfast at the hotel's Desire Oyster Bar, Alex read the New Orleans Times-Picayune sports pages while Rachel read international news on her computer tablet. But after a quick glance, he put the sports section aside since it was mid-summer and neither basketball nor football were in season. The sports coverage he really wanted to read was minimal. The front page, however, was chock full of violent stories. He read a few articles before looking up at Rachel.

"Jesus, New Orleans seems to have more murders than Beirut. I thought things had improved after Katrina."

"Camille told me once people returned to the city, crime was down for a few years," she said. "But now it's back to previous levels of nightly killings. Camille said the violence has even made its way into the posh Uptown area, but the cops and papers are both reluctant to push those stories."

"My guess is there's pressure to keep property values up.

The more people know about crime in posh areas, the more they'll move across Lake Pontchartrain to St. Tammany Parish." Rachel didn't comment and he returned to the front-page stories.

One article in particular caught Alex's eye involving three black guys who were all shot and killed in the same spot. The story said the cops thought it was an execution-style murder.

"Rach, do you know where the Algiers area is located in New Orleans?"

"I think it's across the river. Why?"

"Just curious. Three guys were shot in the back of their heads in Algiers. I guess that's too far away for us to be concerned about our safety."

"I suppose so, but Camille said there have been lots of shootouts on Bourbon Street. They occur in the wee hours of the morning and usually involve drunk people who get into arguments in bars."

"That figures." Alex continued reading more stories. When Rachel finally closed her computer tablet to eat her Eggs Sardou, Alex said, "I get the impression the cops are overwhelmed with crime in the city. I know the New Orleans police are a mixed bag of competence, and there's corruption, but their numbers are well below capacity. I'll bet the court dockets are overflowing."

Rachel nodded. "I recall reading when Katrina was about to hit the city in 2005, a lot of cops just fled with their families. Afterward, some wanted their jobs back, but others never returned."

"That's true. I can't imagine people in the Foreign Service bugging out when a situation turns dangerous, especially not special agents in Diplomatic Security at some overseas embassy. In fact, our agents in the New Orleans office all stayed during

Katrina to help rescue people and support the law enforcement officers who remained on the job."

Rachel put another drop of Tabasco on her dish of eggs, then asked, "Do you still have the gun Susan Witt gave you for the raid?"

"Yes, I locked it in the room safe before we came down for breakfast. Do you think we'll be attacked by the Eggs Sardou or the Pain Perdu?"

Rachel laughed. "Of course, not. I was just wondering if you'll be able to protect me when we're out and about."

"You can always count on me, sweet cakes. No one but *me* will ever get near your body. You might say I'm . . . 'on top' of the situation." She shook her head at his dopey humor.

"You do have a way with words, big man."

AT THE ESPLANADE APARTMENT BUILDING BY CITY PARK, MOON Glow and Billy were finishing their breakfast of muesli and fresh fruit. Moon Glow hadn't been talkative for the last day, but now she had to tell Billy about her feelings.

"Billy, I'm really worried about us seeing the killing of that girl in the park.

"I know," he replied. "We just have to be low-key, not say anything to anyone, and hope it all blows over."

"Easy to say, but I can't sleep. I don't want to *die*, Billy. Do you think we should leave town?"

He thought for a moment and pushed his cereal around in the bowl. "Let's consider that later. Right now, we should just continue what we normally do, but watch out for trouble, at all times."

Moon Glow reached across the table and held his hand. A tear dribbled down her cheek. "Okay, Billy. We'll stay for now, but if I get too scared, I'm out of here."

At 10:00 A.M., when Alex and Rachel arrived at Susan's office, Alex received a call from Detective Sgt. John Washington which he put on speaker.

"I want to let you know," Washington said, "we have an appointment with the St. Tammany Parish sheriff's office today at 11:15. The sheriff will tell us something about the local telephone number Thibault was using from Haiti to phone Baptiste in Mandeville. It might lead us to Baptiste and Toussaint's location here. I assume you and Susan Witt are still coming with us."

"You bet."

"Great. I assume Susan knows where the sheriff's headquarters is." Alex looked at Susan who nodded.

"She knows," Alex said.

"Okay, I'll meet you there," Washington replied. Then, Washington dropped a bombshell on them.

"By the way, did you see the news today about three guys killed in Algiers?"

"Yeah, I did," Alex said. "The paper said they were executed."

"That's right. All three had rap sheets and served time in prison. More interesting, though, is the one thing they all had in common: the last time each one went to trial, they were all defended by Papa Ed Ardoin, *and* each one was found *not* guilty. You don't suppose Papa Ed was calling in favors and trying to find Baptiste and Toussaint on his own, do you?" Washington's question hung in the air.

Alex and Rachel exchanged glances. Finally, Alex said, "That's a possibility, John, but I cautioned him just yesterday against doing anything like that. Papa Ed said he understood. But 'to understand' and 'to agree' are not the same."

"After we see the sheriff, I'll have a word with him," Washington said. They ended the call.

Susan stared at Alex. Then she shook her head while a look of sadness covered her face. "Can you blame him for wanting to find the killers of his daughter?"

No I can't. Alex thought. *I'd probably take matters into my own hands as well.*

"We should probably leave if we want to get to the sheriff's office by 11:15," Susan said. Everyone was quiet in their own thoughts as they went out the door.

THE THREE PILED INTO THE OFFICE'S BLACK SUBURBAN AND SUSAN took the I-10 Interstate to the Causeway exit, then headed north across the 24-mile long causeway bridge. It was the second longest causeway over a body of water in the entire world since China claimed to have a longer one.

They all rode in silence other than listening to Susan's preference for country-western music. Alex dwelt on the facts of what Papa Ed had probably done. He faulted him for impetuous action but could hardly blame the man for wanting instant revenge. But if the three murdered victims, all former hardened criminals, were really helping Papa Ed – and were killed themselves - then what did that say about the level of violence Simone's killers were prepared to inflict?

About an hour later, they pulled into the parking lot of the St. Tammany Parish sheriff's headquarters off I-12. A deputy waited for them in the lobby and escorted the three to Sheriff Billy Landry's office. Detective Washington was already there.

Landry stood a little under six feet tall and wore aviator style metal framed glasses. His hair was blond, sporting an old-fashioned crew cut. Everyone shook hands and took seats. Then, after chit-chatting for a short time, Alex's instincts told him Landry was a man who would be helpful.

"We've traced the phone number that's been called several times from Port-au-Prince," Landry said. "It's located in a middle-class neighborhood of Mandeville, but the house itself looks rundown. We've checked property records and found it belongs to a Louise Daigle. She's sixty-three and has lived in the parish her whole life. Daigle resides at another address now, so my guess is that she's renting out the property. We haven't spoken to her yet. We thought we should discuss this with you before doing anything further."

"Thank you for holding off," Washington said. "Anything else we should know?"

"I've got two of our detectives sitting in an unmarked car down the street from the house. They've just reported they don't see anyone around the house, and no vehicles are parked in the driveway."

Alex turned to Susan. "When you spoke to Tommie Rogers, the US Embassy's regional security officer in Haiti, did he happen to mention if there was a pattern to the calls made to the Mandeville house?"

"You mean like same time of day, or day of the week?" Susan asked.

"Yes."

She opened a notebook she had been carrying in the right pocket of her cargo pants, flipped past a few pages, then said, "Yes, he did. Most were in the evening, but a few were in late afternoon."

"Interesting," Sheriff Landry said. "Perhaps I'm wasting time posting my men to watch the house in the morning."

"That seems reasonable," replied John Washington. "I know that NOPD is short of funds, and I'll bet St. Tammany isn't flush with money, either. Maybe you'd like to deploy those officers elsewhere."

"You got that right," Landry said. "If it's okay with you, I'll pull my men off surveillance and repost another unit tonight. We know what Baptiste looks like since he has a rap sheet, but not this . . . this other guy, Toussaint." If we spot Baptiste, do you want him arrested? And on what charge?" Washington looked at Alex.

"Take him in for questioning and get a search warrant for the house," Alex said. "We're looking for passports, either Haitian or American. Of course, seize drugs of any kind, and weapons. Seize any papers or documents related to international travel. Also, I'd like to be clear, let's not wait for Baptiste to show up. If anyone enters the house, I'd like you to detain them for questioning."

"Will do. What about Fed participation?" Sheriff Landry asked.

Susan Witt handed Landry her business card. "At present, I've got two special agents in our New Orleans office. If you detain anyone, at any time, call my cell phone number on the card and I'll see that one of us drives out here to help with the questioning. If we can prove passport or visa fraud, the penalty can be up to ten years in a federal penitentiary and up to a $250,000 fine. Of course, we want to find the guy who murdered Simone Ardoin, so maybe someone will get the death penalty."

Rachel had been quiet the entire time. But now she spoke. "Would it be possible to drive by this property just to see what it looks like from the outside? I don't want to draw attention to ourselves but it would nice to have an idea of the area."

Landry turned to Susan. "Since you said most of the calls were made at night, or late afternoon, I guess it would be all right to just drive by the house since its unlikely someone will be there at this hour." Everyone agreed. "I'll tell my two deputies they can leave now. Here's the address." He wrote it down on a piece of paper and handed it to John Washington.

"We'll be in touch." Everyone stood and shook hands.

Once outside, Washington said, "After we drive by, are you guys interested in some lunch here on the Northshore? There's a great seafood place in Madisonville, just down the road from Mandeville."

"Sure," everyone said.

"Okay, I'll take my car and you can follow. After we pass the house, let's pull over a few blocks away and discuss anything important. Then we'll go to a restaurant called Morton's, off Highway 22. It's at the Tchefuncte River bridge."

No one realized they were about to make the biggest mistake since the Chalmette raid.

Chapter 18

Surveillance

They took I-12 back to Causeway Boulevard, then drove south toward Lake Pontchartrain for a few exits until getting off, and heading into the heart of Mandeville. As they passed small shopping centers, restaurants, and entrances to residential communities, Alex thought the area looked prosperous.

"Looks pretty nice, doesn't it," Susan said as she drove.

"I read that the Northshore was a sleepy, relatively unpopulated area until the 1960s when 'white flight' started from New Orleans," Rachel said. "When Katrina flooded most of New Orleans in 2005, making the city uninhabitable for a while, there was another rush to move across the lake to newly built homes and apartments."

"I grew up in major cities," Alex said, "but I can see the appeal of the suburbs or even rural areas if you can get away from crime and have better schools for your kids. It wouldn't be hard with the internet today, since you can buy anything you want online. And it's easy to live anywhere since many people work remotely."

"After Katrina," Susan said, "some of the best restaurants in New Orleans opened second places out here. They're still here and business is good, just like in New Orleans where there are more restaurants than ever."

Alex wondered if the age of big cities in America was drawing to a close. *Sure, cities still have the best museums and a variety of activities, but with businesses and middle-class residents fleeing insane taxation and progressive criminal justice policies, that's changing,* he thought. *The future of cities seems bleak unless new politicians are voted into office who want to fix crucial issues that seem to favor criminals over victims, not to mention failing school systems.*

Just ahead of them, Sgt. Washington pulled his car into a service station and stopped. Susan followed. He got out and walked back to the Suburban. "I just want to emphasize that we're only driving by the house that's receiving calls from Haiti. You have the address, so you'll know which one as we approach it. The house is about five minutes from here. Afterward, I'll drive on for about three blocks, then we'll pull over to discuss any questions you have."

"Okay, got it," Susan replied.

Alex was uncomfortable with this idea of driving passed the house; he even regretted that he hadn't spoken up earlier. This drive-by wasn't necessary, and although they were in a civilian Chevy Suburban with no police markings, he would have preferred not to do it. But it had been Rachel's suggestion, and he hadn't had a solid reason to veto it.

When Washington returned to his car, they drove off. Alex noted that a number of homes in the neighborhood were raised off the ground, some just a few feet, although others were up on stilts. "There are a lot of raised homes," Alex commented. "You'd think we were at a beachfront community."

"That's because when we get storms, Lake Ponchatrain floods over the seawall. It doesn't even have to be a hurricane; this part of town will still be under three to six feet of water," Susan said.

As they drove on, Washington slowed for a moment in the middle of the block and flicked on his right turn signal. Alex understood he meant the house was on the right. Then Washington accelerated away.

The house in question was a rundown one-story home, not raised at all. The patchy grass needed to be mowed, and the paint on the wooden siding was peeling. *The rent must be dirt cheap, a perfect property to be used as a front for a drug and human trafficking operation,* Alex thought.

Washington made a left turn at the end of the block, then another at the next block. He pulled over to the curb and everyone exited their vehicles.

"Okay, that's the big tour. What do you think?" he asked.

"What a dump," Alex replied. "I guess the owner is happy enough to get rent."

"Let's just review what's going to happen," Susan said. "Later this afternoon, or tonight, Sheriff Landry will put surveillance back on the house. If he sees Baptiste, they'll conduct a raid. If he sees anyone else in the house *other* than Baptiste, he may still conduct a raid."

"That's the way I read it," Washington said. Alex and Rachel agreed.

"So, anything thing else, guys?" Washington asked. Since no one had further questions, he said, "Let's go to lunch."

HALF A BLOCK AWAY, A DARK BLUE FORD EXPLORER CREPT THROUGH the intersection and pulled over. The two occupants had a clear view of Alex and the team just before Washington and the others got back into their vehicles.

"*Merde.* Aren't those two guys and the short woman the ones from the raid in Chalmette?" James Augustin asked his companion.

"*Je le pense,*" responded Michel Barthelemy.

"*Fuck!* You think so! What are they doing here?" Augustin asked. "They must know we've been using the house around the corner."

"I better call Baptiste," Barthelemy said. He placed the call on his mobile.

"What?" Baptiste demanded as he answered.

"We think the cops know about Mandeville!" His voice became high pitched, and his breathing was rapid.

"Calm down, my friend. Why do you say this?"

"Because three guys from the raid on the house in Chalmette are talking right now on the street two blocks away from our place. We're watching them now. They're about to drive off."

"Are you sure about these guys?"

"Yes, Augustin and I both agree. We saw them in Chalmette. Back then, we were about to go to Toussaint's place just as the raid started. When we saw all the cops, we stopped a block away and watched the shootout."

"And they're driving off now?"

"Yes."

"Okay, follow them, and I'll tell you what to do in a few minutes." Both hung up.

Augustin pulled his blue Ford into a driveway and turned around. He watched as both vehicles driven by Washington and Susan drove passed on the cross street. Fortunately, another car also drove close behind them, and Augustin pulled his blue Ford into the road behind the third car, but not too close, so tailing wouldn't look too obvious.

Traffic was heavy enough at this time of day to mask surveillance. Augustin and Barthelemy followed them onto Route 22, a single lane road from Mandeville into Madisonville. The two law enforcement vehicles crossed a small bridge over the Tchefuncte River and turned into parking spaces at Morton's Seafood Restaurant and Bar on Water Street. Augustin also turned, but drove past the restaurant, and parked down the street. Then his mobile rang.

"It's Baptiste. Where are you now?"

"In front of a seafood restaurant in Madisonville."

"Okay. I'm going to abandon our operation in Mandeville. So don't go back to the house. When those cops are done eating and leave the restaurant, I want you to erase them. Do you understand?"

"Yes, boss."

THE RESTAURANT HAD A CHARMING OUTDOOR SIDE PORCH. INSIDE the front door, off to the right, was a long U shaped bar. There were tables and chairs opposite the bar and business looked good, yet a few tables were still available. The casual, long room had dark wooden walls with dark wood flooring, and ceiling fans. Washington spoke to the staff at the entrance, and they were taken to an enclosed air conditioned side porch to the left of the main room. It had a wall of windows. There was a view of the Tchefuncte River with small boats docked against the bulkhead.

"This is great," Rachel said.

"You won't believe the food here," Washington replied.

A waitress arrived and passed out menus. Alex looked at other patrons. Most were in shorts and t-shirts, although a few men wore long sleeve shirts with ties, their jackets draped over the backs of chairs, probably just coming from work. He spotted a few guys in casual clothes wearing LSU or Saints baseball caps. It was his kind of place.

"What should we order?" Alex asked.

Washington suggested starting with she-crab soup, or gumbo, then sharing orders of boiled crawfish, steamed crabs, and boiled shrimp. The latter two items were cooked in Old Bay seasoning that provided a powerful flavor. Alex and Rachel agreed, but Susan wasn't as enthusiastic. She reserved the right to order "normal food" that she might find in the Midwest, even though she agreed to try everything. The others chuckled.

Washington, Alex, and Susan all ordered unsweetened iced tea because they were packing heat under their loose-fitting shirts. Drinking on duty while carrying a firearm was a clear no-no. Rachel ordered a draft Abita Amber beer.

When their orders began arriving, the group wasted no time diving into their meals. Alex's she-crab soup was out-of-this-world delicious, as was Rachel's *andouille* sausage gumbo. When the main courses were served, they looked massive as they were placed on the table, yet all four had little trouble polishing off the communal platters of crawfish, crabs, and shrimp. Even Susan did a good job devouring her share. It was the best seafood meal any of them had ever eaten.

They all passed on dessert, but shared the bill, before walking out to their vehicles. Washington said he'd stay on the Northshore to see an old friend and shook hands with the others.

As the small group split up, Augustin and Barthelemy drew their pistols. Then, just as they were about to exit their Explorer to open fire, two police cruisers pulled into parking spaces in front of the restaurant. Four cops got out, and two of them recognized Washington; they stopped to talk.

Augustin grabbed Barthelemy's arm, "Don't get out. We're out-gunned."

After five minutes of chit-chat, the four cops entered the restaurant and Washington drove off as Alex, Rachel and Susan left in their Suburban.

"Let's follow the three in the Suburban." Augustin said to Barthelemy. They needed a better place for the perfect ambush.

Chapter 19

Extreme Road Rage

Augustin watched as the three targets piled into the Suburban. The shorter woman slid behind the wheel; the man sat in the front passenger seat, and the tall woman climbed into the rear seat.

"Here we go," Augustin said to Barthelemy.

He backed their car out of the parking space and followed a short distance behind the Suburban. Both assassins had 9mm pistols under their shirts; Barthelemy also had a pump-action shotgun at his feet. It had a short pistol grip rather than a shoulder stock, which made the reduced length easier to wield inside the vehicle.

After a while, Augustin correctly guessed the Suburban was headed for the Causeway Bridge. As they approached the toll booth, he watched the Suburban roll though without stopping.

"Shit, they must have an electronic payment tag," he cursed. He stopped and paid the attendant, then realized this was even better because it helped hide his pursuit.

"Do you want to attack them on the bridge?" Barthelemy asked.

"You bet. They'll have nowhere to run. Let's wait until we are at least halfway across. Hardly any cops patrol the bridge, so by the time they respond, we'll be long gone into Orleans Parish. Besides, I'm counting on confusion by the Causeway police force. They'll think it's just another accident, until they find the bodies with bullets in them."

SUSAN, ALEX, AND RACHEL CHATTED AS THEY DROVE BACK TO NEW Orleans. Most of the conversation involved the incredible meal they had just eaten at Morton's. Alex then raised a few issues about the case.

"I forgot to ask Washington if he was able to track down the two residents in the Esplanade apartment building who might have witnessed Simone's murder," Alex said.

"Tell me about that again," Susan said.

"Since we found a girl's driver's license on a blanket in the park, we think they were there the night Simone was shot," Alex said. "They may have witnessed it. We need to talk to them. I also want to know what the police are going to do about the possible link of Papa Ed to the three murdered guys in Algiers. They had all used Papa Ed as their defense attorney. The coincidence is too convenient not to be connected."

Rachel leaned forward from the back seat. "Do you believe Papa Ed hired them to find Simone's killer?"

"I'm not sure if they were technically 'hired' by him, but what are the odds of all three being murdered together, and all three having used Papa Ed to get them off prior charges?" he said. Rachel leaned back to consider the possibilities.

"Wow, is that the New Orleans skyline?" Alex asked as he looked through the windshield.

"It sure is," Susan replied. "If you look at the middle part of the skyline, you can see the white top of the Superdome."

"How far are we from New Orleans now?" Rachel asked.

"I guess we're about halfway over the bridge," Susan replied. "So, about ten to twelve miles."

They were traveling at 65 mph in the right lane. Traffic was light with only a few cars behind them now, but later at rush-hour, it would be congested. As Alex looked over at Susan, he noticed a black SUV pull up next to them, matching their speed. The passenger lowered his window and raised a shotgun, starting to point it at Susan.

"Gun to your left! Alex screamed as his special agent training kicked in.

Without looking left, Susan slammed on the brakes, bringing the Suburban to a jolting halt, just as Barthelemy fired. The nine double-00 buck pellets from the shotgun shell had no time to spread out at such close range. The blast broke through Susan's window, then shattered Alex's glass, as the pellets missed them by inches. Both, however, were covered with broken glass, and Susan's face was cut and bleeding.

Augustin accelerated to get ahead of Susan, then skidded to a stop on an angle, blocking both lanes. Barthelemy leaped out of the Explorer from the passenger's side and stood in front of his door, pointing the shotgun directly at Susan.

"Rachel, get down!!" Alex yelled as he and Susan ducked below the dashboard. The shotgun blast completely destroyed the windshield and rear window.

Now, both Susan and Alex popped back up. Alex had his gun in hand, but Susan wasn't waiting. Screaming: "You son of a bitch!" at the shooter, she floored the accelerator. Alex saw the man's eyes bulge and terror on his face as his mouth formed a grimace; Barthelemy's stare was fixated at the front grill of the Suburban rushing toward him.

Within seconds, the heavy, powerful SUV crashed into the attacker, crushing him against his own vehicle. Alex heard the man's scream over the crunching sound of metal as the heavy and powerful Suburban smashed into the side of the attacker's own SUV.

Then, Susan backed the vehicle up a few feet as pain filled the man's face, his mouth agape, blood spewing from his mouth. He slid down onto the ground, motionless. Then the driver of the Explorer, now leaning across the hood of his vehicle, opened up, firing at Alex and Susan with his pistol. Alex heard two bullets wiz by his left ear and fired four quick shots through their shattered windshield. But with his adrenalin surging and no time to aim, he completely missed his target.

Putting the Suburban back into drive, Susan pointed it at the Explorer, just behind the rear tire, and floored it again. Her heavy vehicle leaped forward, crashing into the big dark blue Explorer, pivoting it out of the way. The driver fled, firing a few wild shots back at the Suburban as Susan chased after him. She was about to run him over when he jinked to the right and jumped over the four-foot-high guard rail, falling into Lake Ponchartrain.

Susan braked and took short rapid breaths; sweat and blood was dripping from her forehead; her hands trembled slightly. She pulled out her pistol and joined Alex and Rachel who had gotten out of the vehicle and were looking over the guard rail. The man had disappeared into the murky waters below.

He could be under the bridge or maybe he drowned, Alex thought. He estimated the distance from the bridge to the water from this point somewhere between twenty to forty feet. *The question is whether he's a good swimmer.*

Susan used her cell phone to call 911. She identified herself as a DS special agent and told the police operator what happened and where they were. The dispatcher said a response unit would be there ASAP. Then Susan called the direct numbers of both Sheriff Billy Landry and John Washington. Landry said he would coordinate with the Causeway and Orleans Parish police departments to control traffic and he would get cops there as soon as possible.

Traffic was already backed up, so Alex walked to the nearest car behind them, flashed his badge, and asked the driver what he had seen. The driver had witnessed the entire attack and seemed to be in shock, himself, so Alex calmed the man down.

"Can you show me your driver's license?" he asked. When the man produced it, Alex wrote down details and told him to wait until uniformed police arrived. Then he walked back to Rachel.

"How are you doing, Rach?" He hugged her, glad to hold her and protect her in his arms.

"I'm not hurt, but it scared the *shit* out of me. That was just like the State Department counterterrorism driving course I went through. I can't believe it happened."

Susan joined them next to the Suburban. "That was great driving, Susan," Alex said as he reached out and put a reassuring hand on her shoulder. "You were decisive and did the right thing. You better get those facial cuts taken care of when the paramedics show up."

"Thanks," Susan replied. "My guess is we'll be here for a while before the cops arrive. They'll block traffic so their cruisers can get to the scene. Somebody's going to interview us; I'm just not sure who'll take jurisdiction."

"You mean you haven't done this before?" Alex asked with a deadpan look.

"Yeah, yeah, very funny," Susan replied. "Shit, can you imagine the *paperwork* I'm going to have to deal with? Running over a guy . . . crashing the Suburban into another car. *God dammit!*" Alex smiled. It was typical agent humor in the face of adversity.

"I think you better call D.C. and report what happened," he said.

"You're right." She walked to the back of the Suburban to get the emergency medical kit for her wounds, then dialed the number for DS Field Office Management.

"Rachel, why don't you just wait in the Suburban," Alex said. "I'll join you a few minutes."

While Susan talked to her chain of command, a few drivers stacked up behind them started blowing their horns. Alex walked back to the body lying on the ground and stared down at the dead man for a moment.

He must have died from crushed internal organs and broken bones. His life ended in great pain, Alex thought. It was more of a clinical assessment rather than because he gave a damn. The guy had tried to kill them. As far as Alex was concerned, *He got what he deserved.* Alex then called Director Jim Riley. Both he and Susan talked to their respective headquarters until the first police car arrived. As he ended his call, Alex's experience told him this wasn't the end of his battle with Jean Baptiste's gang.

Not by a long shot.

Chapter 20

Jules Baptiste

J ules Baptiste hadn't heard from James Augustin or Michel Barthelemy since mid-day. He was becoming nervous that something had gone wrong with the assassination he had ordered. *It's unlike these men to leave me in the dark*, he thought anxiously. Baptiste was even depressed that his decision to kill the cops might have been counterproductive, maybe not well thought out.

He sat in a decrepit ground floor apartment in New Orleans East that had once been flooded by Katrina. Sweat dripped off his body because the air conditioner was broken. The entire neighborhood was a mixture of dilapidated old apartments and homes, sprinkled with a bit of new construction. As for landscaping, there wasn't any.

Baptiste checked the time again and realized the evening news was about to begin. He turned on the television, hoping to see a story about the death of the cops just as the newscaster opened the show. "A major shootout on the Causeway today resulted in the death of at least one person," Eyewitness News began. Baptiste smiled, assuming a cop had died. Then the driver's license photo of Michel Barthelemy filled the screen. Baptiste stopped smiling.

"An assailant named Michel Barthelemy has died after being crushed by a car driven by a federal agent. Another unknown assailant jumped into Lake Ponchatrain and a search is underway for his body. None of the federal officers sustained serious injuries."

Baptiste was stunned. He leaned back in his chair. *What the hell is going on?* he thought. *First, the cops raid my drug operation in Chalmette. If my source hadn't tipped me off, Toussaint would be in jail now. Then they find my house in Mandeville, and now my best men fail to kill these damn Feds!* Anger began rising inside the man.

Two of his local thugs joined him in the living room. One of them gave Baptiste a Dixie beer, which he guzzled down. Then, he ran one hand over his shaved head, wiping sweat away. His sleeveless undershirt was soaked and stained with perspiration; Baptiste put the empty beer can down on the end table next to his loaded Colt .45 semi-automatic pistol.

"What we goin' do boss?" one man asked in the local *patois.*

"I'm not sure, Bobby."

"I heard da newsman . . . he say da Feds was in da shootout with our men."

"Yeah. But *which* Feds? Ahh, forget that, it doesn't matter. *Any* Feds are bad news for us."

Baptiste stood up. At six feet, five inches tall, he towered over the much shorter Bobby. Baptiste was also leaner and more muscular.

"Here's what I want you to do, Bobby. Spread the word

among our people to report any time the cops ask questions about me, or about our drug and visa fraud operations. I want to know as soon as possible, what and who we're dealing with."

"I on it, boss." Bobby left the house and drove off to their network of bars and restaurants in the French Quarter.

Five minutes later, a car pulled up outside the apartment. Baptiste heard the car door slam shut. He picked up his .45, cocked it, and rushed to the window. But it was Claude Toussaint returning from an errand. Baptiste relaxed and flipped the safety on the .45 before tucking it into his waistband. A moment later, Toussaint knocked on the door and Baptiste unlocked it. They fist-bumped.

"Did you hear about the killing on the Causeway?" Baptiste asked.

"I heard it on the car radio. I can't believe they killed Michel. The man was a *legend*, a natural born killer." Toussaint shook his head and pursed his lips. He had known Barthelemy for several years; they were friends and had worked together many times.

"Yeah, I know. Michel was the best. I'll miss him a lot. Since the Feds were involved, I bet it's linked to that Simone Ardoin girl I killed."

He paused and focused his penetrating stare on Toussaint. Baptiste sneered, revealing his tobacco-stained teeth. "When I get back to Haiti, I'm going to kill some American Embassy people to even the score for Michel." He punched the palm of his left hand with his right fist. The sound echoed through the room.

"Take it easy, boss. We'll retaliate somehow. But in the meantime, how do we protect our operation?"

"Yeah, yeah. That's what I need to figure out."

"Maybe we should wait and see what happens. Another

drug shipment isn't due for a week, so we have some time. I think we should put the visa operation on hold until we're certain the coast is clear."

"That's good advice, Claude. But if I get a chance, I want to avenge the deaths of James and Michel soon . . . *now*."

"James? Did they say that *James* is dead? I didn't hear that on the radio."

"You're right. I assumed it."

A tall, lovely African American girl, about seventeen years old, walked out of the bedroom. Her eyes were glassy, a dazed look filled her eyes. Maybe she had just taken a nap . . . or taken a hit of something. Her skin was flawless, her figure slender, even model-like. She stood next to Baptiste and put her hand on his shoulder.

"Is everything okay, baby?" she asked.

"Yeah, Destiny. Just a little wrinkle. We've dealt with things before, we'll do it again." She smiled and walked into the kitchen to pour herself a glass of white wine. Baptiste watched her hips sway as she walked, smitten with her. Although she still used drugs on occasion, he had told her that if they were going to stay lovers, she would need to control her habit.

"Let's go into the bedroom to talk, Suga," he said. She smiled and glided past Toussaint. Baptiste followed. Once inside the small room, he wrapped his strong arms around her waist and brought her against his body. Destiny reminded him of his deceased wife who had perished in an earthquake in Haiti a few years before. His young son had died that day, too, crushed underneath his home's ceiling when it collapsed. He not only wanted Destiny to be in his life, he *needed* her.

"Things may be getting too dangerous in New Orleans now to continue business as usual," he said.

"I'm sure you can handle it, baby."

"Sure, maybe I can, but maybe not. So I've been thinking . . . taking a vacation away from here might be a good idea."

"Vacation? I like that idea. Where?"

"Haiti?"

"Haiti! That's not a vacation. How about Barbados, Jamaica, even Miami?"

"Yeah, that's possible too. But I have people in Haiti who can keep us safe. Later, we can return to New Orleans."

"I ain't got no one here to return to, baby, you know that. My mama's in jail for drugs, and I don't know a daddy. Besides, all I care about is you, Jules . . . just you."

Baptiste squeezed her again. Before he had met her, it seemed all he thought about was making money, building up scams, and killing people who got in his way. But with Destiny in his life, things had changed. He hadn't felt like this is several years.

———

AT THE SAME TIME, MILES AWAY AT AN NOPD OFFICE, SUSAN, Alex, and Rachel were giving statements about what happened on the causeway. The group included a Louisiana State Police investigator, the assistant district attorney for Orleans Parish, and an assistant U.S. attorney from the Justice Department, all of whom asked questions. Sgt, John Washington also sat in the room to monitor the conversation. Since he hadn't been at the scene when the shootout had occurred, he just listened unless he was asked a question about what had transpired earlier in the day.

When questioning had started an hour earlier, Alex briefly

wondered if he should have an attorney present. He had grilled enough suspects to know how things could turn to shit with a slip of the tongue. However, in this case, the evidence of an assault by Michel Barthelemy and the other unknown attacker, was overwhelmingly clear. For example, there was the eyewitness account from the guy in the car behind Susan who had observed everything and Susan's damaged government Suburban, peppered with shotgun pellets. That evidence, plus the shotgun itself used by Barthelemy and the spent shell casings from both the shotgun and the unknown assailant's 9 mm handgun substantiated their story.

Since the questions were never accusatory, Alex decided against demanding legal counsel. Then, after about forty-five minutes, an NOPD detective entered the conference room and interrupted. He said the U.S. Coast Guard had pulled the other assailant out of Lake Ponchatrain . . . alive.

"Calls himself James Augustin. He has a long rap sheet for petty crimes," the detective informed the group. "He's already squealed that he would implicate others if the prosecutors went light on their sentencing recommendation against him. He's a real piece of work."

Although he had yet to write a formal statement, Augustin had also ratted on Jules Baptiste about ordering the killing of "the cops" in the Suburban. But the best part was when he said Baptiste had *personally* killed Simone Ardoin.

THE QUESTIONING OF ALEX, SUSAN, AND RACHEL LASTED ANOTHER thirty minutes. The Assistant U.S. Attorney requested the three of them make written statements to use in court against James

Augustin and Jules Baptiste, yet he agreed to postpone the process until the next day since Susan needed to go to the hospital to have her minor facial injuries treated.

The EMT's who had arrived at the scene on the Causeway had already picked glass out of her wounds, applied antibiotics to the injured areas, and bandaged her up. And even though she felt fine, she now agreed to go to the ER for follow-up care. Susan's DS deputies, Pete Fong and Luis Torres, had arrived at the NOPD building during the interview process and now drove Susan to the hospital. Alex and Rachel went along. While Susan was being checked out in the ER, Alex called Papa Ed to give him an update on the accusations against Jules Baptiste.

Afterward, he called Jim Riley in D.C. who surprised him by saying he wanted to send a team of agents to New Orleans to protect him, Susan, and Rachel.

"I appreciate the thought, Jim," Alex said. "But it's not necessary. We really can take care of ourselves. Yet I wouldn't mind a few DS agents here to help the cops hunt for Baptiste. The New Orleans DS office only has four agents. Let me think about the manpower needs and get back to you."

An hour later, Susan returned from her follow-up care, adorned in small, fresh bandages.

"Hey, you don't look so bad, Susan," Alex said. "I figured you would look more like *The Mummy*."

She smiled. "I've been through worse."

As they left the hospital, Alex wondered if tomorrow would bring more danger. Although he couldn't predict the future, he knew being complacent was a good way to get killed.

Chapter 21

Billy and Moon Glow

The next morning at eight o'clock, Billy Whiteman and Janet "Moon Glow" Ross were in their apartment on Esplanade Ave. when Detective John Washington and another officer knocked on their door. Letting the officers in, Moon Glow was delighted to get her driver's license back, but they were reluctant to talk about what they had seen the night of the shooting.

Washington told them about Simone Ardoin, who she was, how she had contributed to America's foreign policy, and how important it was for her family and community to get justice for her killing. Reluctantly, Billy and Moon Glow reconsidered, then agreed to tell the officer what they had seen.

"We'll drive you to the police station," Washington said. "That's where you'll make your statements."

Not long after, the pair was seated at an interview table. Washington turned on a tape recorder and the formal interview

151

began. He mentioned for the record who was present and noted the time. Then said, "In your own words, what did you see in City Park near the New Orleans Museum of Art on the night of August 15?"

"We were making out on our blanket when we heard a car drive up and stop near the school," Moon Glow said.

"Did anyone get out of the vehicle?" Washington asked.

"Yeah, a black woman did," Billy said.

"How far away were you from her?"

"I'm not sure. Maybe a hundred feet."

"What was she wearing?"

"A blue colored jacket and dark slacks," Moon Glow answered.

"How could you see it was blue?"

"She was standing under a streetlamp. That's why we saw the killer's face."

Washington kept his voice calm, but inside, his excitement had just exploded because they could identify the killer. "Okay, let's go on," Detective Washington said.

"So, like really soon after she arrived, another car pulled up behind her. It was a dark BMW," Billy said.

"Sedan or SUV?"

"Definitely a sedan," he replied.

" Okay, please continue."

"The woman called out," Moon Glow said, "asking if it was 'Claude.' But the guy didn't answer. He just walked up to her and shot her two times. It was horrible."

"Yeah, he shot her twice, then he walks over and looks down on her body and fires twice more," Billy confirmed, remembering the scene. He looked down at the table. His body shuttered once, and he took a deep breath.

"Tell me about the shooter. Can you describe him?" Washington asked calmly.

"He's Jules Baptiste," Moon Glow said; her hands began to shake.

In that moment, Washington's heart rate increased, and every muscle in his body tensed as he strained to keep his composure. He pressed his hands down on the tabletop. "How can you be *sure* he was the shooter?"

"Because I seen him in the French Quarter a lot of times," Moon Glow replied. "He's always trying to get his Haitians jobs and stuff."

"Billy?"

"Yeah, I agree, it was Jules Baptiste." He reached over and held Moon Glow's hand. His eyes darted several times between Washington and Moon Glow as he licked his lips non-stop.

"Both of you are *sure* about this?"

"Yeah, Moon Glow just *told* you. He stood under the streetlamp. We saw his face." Billy said.

"Describe him, please."

"The guy's like six and half feet tall and has a good body. Kind of slender. And he's bald," she said.

"Yeah, that's right," Billy agreed.

"Are we going to have to testify in court?" Moon Glow asked.

"I'm afraid so," Washington replied. "But we'll give you protection."

"Yeah, *right*," Moon Glow said sarcastically. "I hear *lots* of witnesses get knocked off before trials even begin while you're still *protecting* them."

"Sometimes, but Simone Ardoin was a federal government employee, and the feds will also help us protect you."

Washington wasn't exactly sure about this, but he didn't want the two to retract their statements.

They spoke a few more minutes before Washington slid two yellow pads across the table and asked them to write it all down and sign their statements. He left the room while they each began writing.

Outside in the hallway, he glanced at his watch. It was ten o'clock just as his cell phone rang; it was Alex Boyd.

"Hey, Alex, you and Susan should come to the station. I've just taken statements from two eyewitnesses to the killing of Simone Ardoin. I would have called you earlier, but I didn't expect the witnesses to actually identify the shooter. They're certain it was Jules Baptiste, and they're willing to testify."

"Jesus Christ! That's *great*, John. We'll be down in a few minutes. Keep them there until we speak to them?"

"Sure. See you soon."

———

Susan and Alex took turns asking some of the same questions Detective Washington had asked. In the end, they were certain Baptiste had pulled the trigger and killed Simone.

"What about protection?" Moon Glow asked.

"We'll put officers at your home and where you work," Washington said, "Right now, no one knows you've come forward. So, we have a little time before Baptiste could find out."

"We'll talk to the State Department today and see what else they can do to help," Alex said. "The problem is that a trial might not occur for a while, even up to a year, so that's a long time to have dedicated bodyguards. But we'll push the matter and get back to you."

"That's *no damn good!*" Moon Glow complained.

"But it's the truth," Alex replied.

"Isn't the State Department just full of . . . you know . . . guys in suits who just *talk* all the time?" Billy asked.

"That's a fair question," Alex replied. "We do have a lot of guys in suits who just talk. But not in Diplomatic Security. We're law enforcement professionals and many of us have military backgrounds. We carry weapons for a living, and we *can* keep you safe."

"We'll arrange something," Susan said.

BILLY AND MOON GLOW WERE DRIVEN BACK TO THEIR APARTMENT, while Alex, Susan, and John Washington tossed around ideas before coming up with a plan of action.

AFTER ALEX SPOKE WITH HIM, DIRECTOR JIM RILEY NEEDED LITTLE convincing to have additional DS Special Agents travel to New Orleans and help protect Billy and Moon Glow. Riley had agreed to share protective responsibilities with the NOPD because all efforts were on behalf of a slain Foreign Service Officer.

"I'll ask the U.S. Marshall's Service to assist since DS has a long-standing agreement for mutual support," Riley told Alex. "Can you or Susan speak with both the U.S. Attorney's office in New Orleans, and NOPD to help coordinate?"

Alex knew the clock was ticking. He and Rachel couldn't stay away from London indefinitely. The question was, what could they do to flush Baptiste out of hiding? How could they be proactive?

He sat for ten minutes concocting a plan before hitting upon an idea. It was dangerous, it was bold . . . and Rachel wouldn't like it one bit.

Chapter 22

The Trap

Rachel entered the office just as Alex began to explain his idea to John Washington and Susan Witt. Coming from the hotel, she had called Deputy Chief of Mission Bainbridge Wellington in London and convinced him to extend their stay in New Orleans a few extra days. Now, she took a seat and listened to Alex.

"As I was saying, unless the NOPD gets a new report from a snitch, we won't know where to find Baptiste," Alex said. "So, we need to initiate action and draw him out, or at least find and arrest someone from his gang."

"Makes sense," Washington said. "What do you have in mind?"

"We know about three bars in the French Quarter where Simone Ardoin followed Baptiste. After she talked to people there, she was targeted. So, someone in the bars knows how to contact Baptiste."

"Do you suggest we bring in bartenders and staff for interrogation?" Susan asked. "I don't think they'll cooperate."

"I agree with you, they won't," Alex replied. "Furthermore, while we could plant undercover assets in the bars to observe, I think that would take a long time and we'd have to get lucky."

"Let me guess," Rachel said, "You want to provoke them."

"I do. Let's send the same person into each bar, telling bartenders he's looking for Baptiste to settle a score because Simone Ardoin was a friend of his. The guy has to convince them that he is naïve enough to think he can settle the score by himself. My guess is that someone will contact Baptiste to warn him, and Baptiste will want him to disappear. But we'll protect our undercover operator and arrest the hitmen before they strike. Then we can squeeze them for info on Baptiste's location."

Detective Washington leaned back in his chair, rubbing the back of his neck with his right hand. "Your plan's not bad, but dangerous. Even so, I *could* run it up the chain of command to get authority for this sting operation."

"How long will that take?" Alex asked.

"Probably just a day to get approval, but if we bring a cop in from another unit to play the undercover, we'd need to brief them about the situation, and about Simone Ardoin. So, that might add another day."

Alex looked at Rachel. Her jaw was clenched, and her eyes were sending lightning bolts in his direction almost signaling him not to speak. She'd had enough experience with his penchant for risk-taking to grasp what he was thinking. She knew how his mind worked.

Yet, he turned his attention back to Washington. "I propose that…"

Rachel interrupted. "No! Alex, I know what you're going to say, and I don't like that idea. If you walk into bars asking about Baptiste, it would obviously be to spring a trap. They already *know* who you are."

"She has a point," Washington said. "Plus, you don't look naïve or like a man who is an easy target. They'll figure it out."

Alex sat there with his arms crossed, looking a trifle dejected. "But if you like the *plan*, then who can we pick?" Alex asked.

Susan's mobile rang. The caller ID showed her deputy, Pete Fong.

"Yes, Pete, what's up?" She listened for a minute. "You're kidding; that's great! Let me know when they arrive. I'll get back to the office soon. See you then." Susan looked at Alex. "Well, it seems your talk with Riley worked miracles," she said. "Pete just got a call from our Houston Field Office. Riley ordered them to send two agents ASAP to New Orleans to help protect Billy Whiteman and that 'Moon Glow' girl. They're driving and should be here in about five or six hours. Then later today, two more agents will fly down here from D.C."

"Damn, I'm going to have to reassess my judgment on the efficiency of the Feds," Washington said. "Let's put off our discussion on who should play the undercover role at the bars for now. I need to talk to NOPD headquarters about protecting Billy and Moon Glow. Susan, will you give the US Marshals Service's local office a heads-up on our joint request for additional assets?"

"You got it."

"Where will you guys be?" he asked Alex and Rachel.

"I guess back at the DS office, or at out hotel."

"Okay. Let's talk later."

BY HALF PAST FOUR, TWO SPECIAL AGENTS FROM HOUSTON Diplomatic Security rolled into New Orleans and arrived at Susan's office. The first through the door was Isabelle Lewis, followed by Burt Warner.

Quick introductions were made. "Welcome and thanks for coming," Susan said as they all shook hands.

"Glad we could help," replied Isabelle. "We were told this is a low-key protective detail, so we brought casual clothes. Is that okay?"

"You bet. And the good news is that we're getting support from the Marshal's Service, too; they're providing two more agents. So, combined with two DS agents arriving from DC in about two hours, plus whoever NOPD can provide, we'll have enough people for twenty-four coverage."

"Fantastic," Isabelle said.

"Where are you staying?"

"The Houston Field Office booked us into the Marriott on Canal Street."

"Great, that's about a block from here."

The door opened and Alex and Rachel walked in. Alex extended his hand to Isabelle. "I'm Alex Boyd and you must be Isabelle Lewis. I understand you'll be in-charge of the protective team."

"Yes, I will, as long as Susan Witt agrees, but, how do you know?"

"I spoke with your SAIC," Alex said, referring to the special-agent-in-charge of the Houston field office. She blinked twice; a slight look of surprise registered on her face. She had never met

Alex before but had heard about him and his extraordinary reputation.

'Your SAIC and I were in the same entering class of agents; we're old friends."

"I see. In any event, do you know how long we'll be here? No one told us." Alex looked over at Susan and both shrugged.

"Okay, never mind," Isabelle said.

"Were the two of you briefed on the Ardoin murder and why you're here?" Rachel asked.

"Yes, actually, we were," Isabelle replied, "In addition, when Simone Ardoin was assigned to Haiti a few years ago, I was also assigned there as a temporary regional security officer. I knew Simon and liked and respected her. I also worked with the Haitian police on the visa scam problem."

"Then you know just how important this case is. Where have you guys served?" Alex asked, even though his curiosity was mainly focused on Isabelle. Burt Warner said he'd started in the Boston field office, then was an assistant RSO in Panama, and now in Houston.

Isabelle said, "I began in the Office of Protective Intelligence and Investigations in D.C.; then was assistant RSO in Caracas, RSO in Quito, and now Houston."

"When you were in D.C. did you do undercover work?" Alex asked.

"Sure, that was a basic part of the job."

"Please tell me more about yourself," Alex asked. He already had a mission in mind for her.

"What would you like to know?" Isabelle asked.

"How long were you in Haiti with Simone Ardoin?" Alex asked.

"About two months. There was a gap between RSOs, and

since I had completed my first overseas tour in Caracas, DS asked me to cover the gap in Haiti."

"You said you worked with the Haitian police on the Baptiste visa fraud problem." Alex said.

"Yes, I did. Not that I could always trust them, but the liaison work was exciting."

"Did they speak English?"

"Oh, no. But I speak French. I learned it when I was a kid in Morocco where my dad had been the assistant defense attaché in the embassy."

"That's interesting. How much undercover work did you do with Protective Intelligence and Investigations?"

"I guess in the two years I was in the unit, I assumed fake identities on cases maybe four or five times for a few weeks each time. Also, when we travelled to augment protection for the Secretary of State, there would be undercover events lasting a few hours on every trip."

Alex looked at Susan and smiled. "I think we've just solved our undercover problem about going into bars in the French Quarter."

Rachel was also interested in Isabelle's experience. "Did anyone ever pull a gun or a knife on you when you were undercover?"

"Just twice."

Rachel raised her eyebrows. "What happened?"

"I disarmed them."

Alex tried to assess Isabelle Lewis' physical capabilities to put her comments in perspective. She was around 5'7" tall, perhaps 140 lbs., and appeared fit. Her shoulders were broad, and she seemed to have a solid physique. However, he couldn't judge her quickness without seeing her in action.

She's a trained special agent, he thought, *but still...*

Isabelle continued, "Before joining DS, I was a lieutenant in the Army. I'm not a *great* warrior, but use what I've been taught. I have a knack for fighting."

"All right then," Susan said. "Thanks for your bio. Let me describe the situation: I know you're here to protect the two eyewitnesses who saw Simone's murder, but we may be able to use your skills in another way, too. First, I need to talk with Detective Washington at NOPD. Alex, could you brief Isabelle and Burt on what we have in mind for the undercover job?"

As Susan walked into her own office to call NOPD, Alex and Rachel stayed with Isabelle and Burt in the main open area and went over the plan.

"You say this agent is good?" Detective John Washington asked Susan over the phone.

"Alex and I believe she is. We haven't seen her in action, but she has undercover experience."

"Okay. Let's meet to talk about the operation in detail."

"Your place or mine?" Susan asked.

"Bring her to NOPD. That way, she can meet the other cops who'll be watching her back."

"Great. How about in an hour?"

"Sure, see ya' then."

Susan walked into the main part of the office and relayed her phone conversation. Isabelle nodded at the end of her explanation.

"I think my story should be the truth, that Simone and I were friends and worked together in Haiti. Now, I'm here looking to find out who killed her," Isabelle said.

"What will you say if they ask what your job was in Haiti?" Rachel asked.

"Consular, same as Simone. That will explain why I know about Jules Baptiste, if it comes up."

"Do you want to carry something more concealable than your Glock 19?" Susan asked.

Isabelle paused and thought for a moment. "Yeah, what do you have that's smaller?"

"The office has a few 9mm Glock 26 models and two .38 caliber Ruger five-shot revolvers."

"I'll take the Glock model 26 since it has ten rounds plus one in the chamber."

"Okay. I'll take it out of the vault." Susan walked toward the vault room, but paused when she heard the front door open. Agents Pete Fong and Luis Torres entered. With them were the two DC based special agents they had picked up at the airport. Introductions were made all around.

Then Rachel motioned to Alex, and they walked to a corner of the office. In a quiet voice, she said. "I'm glad you're not doing the undercover job."

"Are you implying that I'm not sneaky enough?" he asked. "Or that I'm so hunky I might scare the bad guys away?"

Rachel smiled. "You know what I mean. You're always taking risks and it worries me. Share the burden. Besides, you're the senior DS agent on the scene. You can delegate once-in-a-while."

He kissed her on the cheek. "Thanks for your concern, Rach."

"*Merci,* big guy."

Chapter 23

Undercover Planning

The DS team arrived at Detective Washington's office. Awaiting them were four other NOPD officers dressed in jeans, tennis shoes, and untucked loose-fitting shirts which concealed their firearms.

An hour later, the plan was settled: The next day, after lunch, Isabelle Lewis would go into each of the three bars at about the same time that Simone Ardoin had done when she was originally following Baptiste. She would ask for info about who killed Simone, implying that Simone had spoken to her before she was killed and had mentioned the names of Jules Baptiste and Claude Toussaint. She would also say that now she wanted to talk to both men. As an added piece of information she would leave behind, Isabelle would mention that she was staying at the Marriott on Canal Street.

At the same time, the protective team, both NOPD and DS, dressed in casual clothes, would spread out on the street to react if anyone started to follow or attack her. NOPD would also post two plainclothes officers at her hotel throughout the evening.

Because Susan, Alex, Rachel, and Washington might be known to others in the gang, they couldn't be anywhere near Isabelle.

During discussion of the operation, Alex watched Isabelle closely. She appeared confident, spoke with the voice of experience, and posed good questions. He felt they had made the right decision about her. Alex also believed the four NOPD guys who consistently worked undercover and knew the city would do a good job of protecting Isabelle's back. Plus, with Burt Warner and the two new DS arrivals from D.C., this team of seven seemed more than enough to handle the situation. That was it.

The meeting ended and the evening was free. Alex and Susan decided that Isabelle should remain apart from them for tonight. The two D.C. agents could hang out with Burt, but they had to avoid a cluster which would include Isabelle, just in case Baptiste's gang had tentacles extending into more bars and restaurants than the ones they were aware of. No one could know she was part of a team.

***

ALEX AND RACHEL DECIDED TO SKIP DINNER SINCE THEY HAD EATEN ample servings of crawfish, crabs, creamy sauces, biscuits with gravy, French breads, and assorted high calorie desserts during the past few days. The concierge at the Royal Sonesta Hotel told them about the New Orleans Athletic Club on Rampart Street which granted temporary memberships. The club was the second oldest athletic club in America and was in a huge multi-story building full of weight-lifting equipment, treadmills, a boxing ring, racquetball courts, and a swimming pool.

They arrived at the gym, paid for a temporary membership, changed clothes in the locker rooms, and hit the treadmills first. They ran for three miles at a good pace, then moved to the weight machines and free weights. Between reps on the bench press, military press, leg curl, squats, and dumbbells, they also talked.

"You know pressure is mounting for us to return to London," Alex said.

"I know. I got a text this afternoon from Bainbridge Wellington reminding me that the annual conferences for both the British Conservative and Labour parties are coming up. He hoped I would return to cover both those political events."

"Not too subtle."

"Yeah. What about you?"

"Riley told me they could send a temporary senior officer to fill my slot if I needed to stay here. But he emphasized that was *only* if I thought the NOPD and Susan couldn't handle things."

"Not too subtle either."

"Let's hope the undercover operation develops something," Alex said. "Oh, yeah, something else came up. Riley spoke with the Secretary of State earlier today. He authorized the use of the Rewards for Justice Program for any tips leading to the arrest of Baptiste. DS will put ads in the New Orleans Times-Picayune and on TV."

"How much?"

"Fifty grand."

"That's a lot for New Orleans."

"I agree." Alex paused, looking around at the equipment in the gym. "Okay, what's next? I guess we're almost done."

"How about the leg press machine?" Rachel asked.

"Good idea."

"Do you want to compete?" she asked.

"You're kidding, right? You *know* I can out-lift you."

"How about we each select our max lifting weight, or near enough, and then compete for the number of reps?"

"Big girl, you're such an aggressive jock."

"I didn't hear your answer, hunk man," she smiled. "Are you afraid of being beaten by 'a girl'?"

"You're also a con woman. You know that, right? How do I know you'll select your real max lifting weight?"

"Okay, you're smarter than I thought. How about we each lift three times our own body weight, and go for as many repetitions as possible?"

"Three times our weight! Are you sure?"

"Absolutely. Unless you're worried that I might embarrass you?"

"*As if!*"

Alex weighed two hundred pounds, or at least that's what he told Rachel. He first racked 400 pounds on the leg press machine to warm up, then added more weight for a total of 600 pound. When he was done lifting for maximum reps, he was sweating profusely, his heart was racing, and his legs were as wobbly as jelly.

"Your turn, Rach. How much do you weigh?"

"One hundred-sixty pounds. So, I'll lift 480 pounds for max reps, but I'll warm up with 250 pounds."

Alex looked at her magnificent muscular quads. "Hold on a minute. Are you sure you weigh just one hundred-sixty?"

Rachel's mouth gaped open in mock shock and offense. "You *doubt* my word? Do I look overweight to you?"

"It's just that you're gigantically tall, almost six feet, and you're sporting some powerful thighs. I wonder if you've added some attractive muscle-weight lately."

"You'll have to trust me."

"Of course. I never doubted you . . . not for a moment."

She turned toward the leg press machine with a sly smile on her face and powered through the first warmup set at 250 pounds, then added more weight, for a total of 480 pounds.

Halfway through her repetitive lifts, her face began turning red with noticeable veins beginning to pulsate in her neck. Her entire body strained as her thick, ripped thigh muscles bulged with each push. Yet, she didn't allow herself to stop. She groaned with each new push. Like Alex, she had been a jock all her life and had lifted weights starting in high school.

He knew the idea of quitting was unthinkable to her. As he watched her lift, Alex's mind was distracted, and he lost count of her reps. He didn't care if she out-performed him. The vision of her muscular thighs and calves powering the weight back and forth focused his mind on something else. It was a guy thing, and the fantasy was erotic.

Chapter 24

The Sting

Before sunrise the next morning, Alex lay in bed staring at Rachel's face while she slept. He saw the two small scars on her cheeks from her vicious fight years ago in Islamabad with the terrorist. Nevertheless, he felt her face was extraordinary; in fact, the scars added character to her beautiful features. Nor would anyone call her a "delicate flower" or "a porcelain vase." No, she looked like a very fit athlete with a strong jaw line, high cheek bones, and healthy outdoor complexion. Her appearance screamed, "warrior princess."

As she lay on her side, facing him, a wide grin spread across his face and he couldn't resist placing his hand on her thigh. In response, her eyelids fluttered open and her brilliant green eyes focused on him. An electric smile spread across her face.

"Oh my God, you were a beast in bed last night," she said. "I'm serious. The best you've ever been!"

It was indeed high praise coming from a woman who loved

sex and treated it like a competition for maximum pleasure and dominance.

"You turned me on at the gym," Alex said.

"Hmm, I thought so. I hope I didn't 'weigh too much' for you last night. After all, you did express concern before our leg press competition."

"Are you kidding? You're the perfect size." He slid his hand between her legs and squeezed one of her muscular quads. She flexed her leg muscles in response because it always aroused him.

"You were unbelievable yourself last night," Alex said. "You move with the grace and fluidity of a ballroom dancer, and your thighs are off-the-chart powerful. I love every inch of you . . . every inch!"

Rachel raised the pitch of her voice, as if she were the stereotypical California dumb blond with limited intellectual ability. "I hope I didn't *hurt* you last night when I squeezed my legs around your ribs. But like, now that I think about it, I thought . . . like . . .I heard a *crunching* sound. But gosh, I wasn't sure at the time. It wasn't, as if, you know, you were *complaining*."

Alex laughed, ran his hand further up her thigh. "Don't worry. I believe my ribs will recover . . . for tonight."

Her voice returned to its normal lower, sultry level. "I'm glad you'll be able to handle 'Round Two'. . . this evening, then?"

"Let me be clear," he said. With gentle pressure he pushed her legs apart and slid his body on top of hers. They laughed, and he rubbed against her body a few moments, then as sensually as possible, he kissed her on the side of her neck a few times, nibbled her ear, and moved on to her mouth. Their arms encircled each other in a tight embrace. She brought her legs up and wrapped her thigh muscles around his waist, locking her ankles behind his back, and squeezed with increasing pressure as she had done many times the night before.

He knew she was using only a fraction of her strength, but even that was erotic. In his mind, Alex relived last night, recalling that whenever she had been approaching orgasm, her squeezing power was barely under control. At other times, they had tested their upper body strength. She had sometimes succeeded in rolling him over to get on top. Those were some of their most exciting times, and they never tired of their physical game.

Back in the moment, as she lay on her back, she planted her feet on the mattress, then lifted her hips up with Alex on top. *Holy shit*, he thought, *how many women can do this? To hell with waiting for this evening.* He released his grip around her upper body and gently put himself inside her.

A giant grin spread across her face. "I knew you'd figure it out," she said, and they laughed. Round Two had begun earlier than expected.

LATER, WHILE HE WAS SHOWERING, RACHEL RELAXED IN BED reflecting upon both Alex's love-making skills, and his acceptance of who she was, what her needs were, and his ability to satisfy her. *God, I'm lucky*, she thought. Now in her mid-thirties, she had often been on an unsatisfying road until she had met Alex. As a young teenager, like many girls, she had grown more quickly and taller than the boys. Some kids had made fun of her because of her size; it had hurt her emotionally. She was a better athlete than many, but her dominance had only reinforced their criticism. Then in high school, she had discovered weightlifting. It had enhanced her skills in tennis, basketball, and track. But rather than getting praise for her performances, schoolmates had become jealous and made fun of her. The girls were the worst, giving her names like the "Jolly Green Giant," and often excluded her from their inner social circle. She had hated it. She had hated them.

In college things had become better, although few could match her combined physical and intellectual abilities. The young men seemed afraid of her strength, confidence, and maturity. Later, she accepted it would be difficult to fit into a traditional relationship. It wasn't in her personality to be submissive, to hide her intelligence, or to mask her physical needs and abilities. Rachel had figured that few men would meet her standards.

Over time, her attitude had evolved, bordering on arrogance. Still, she didn't stop looking and testing the field. But in the end, she had decided, if necessary, she would go it alone through life. Then along came Alex.

Now, she closed her eyes and let tears of joy run down her face. *Alex is a competitor like me. He's both intellectual and street smart. He's tough, yet funny. Despite his silly jokes, his maturity and self-confidence are so high that he wants me to be fulfilled before satisfying himself. He understands my passion to challenge a man, and he's not afraid of me getting the upper hand, at least for a moment. I've never met anyone like him. I don't think I ever will, either.*

Interrupting her thoughts, Alex called out from the bathroom, "The shower is all yours, Rach."

"I'm coming." The double-entendre made her laugh.

THE REST OF THE MORNING PASSED SLOWLY AS EVERYONE WAITED for the sting operation to begin after lunch. Susan and Sgt. Washington joined Alex and Rachel in the lobby of the Royal Sonesta Hotel which was centrally located in relation to the bars that Isabelle would enter.

The NOPD and DS surveillance teams paired up. One pair would enter the bar ahead of Isabelle and stay for a while after she left, observing how the bartender and cliental reacted. Then they would leave and form part of a perimeter around Isabelle for her next stop while another pair of protectors would be waiting at the third bar, all to keep her safe.

Finally, with the operation underway, Isabelle hit all three bars that Simone Ardoin had mentioned. The protection teams worked flawlessly.

At the hotel, Alex's group used discrete earpieces and monitored undercover radio chatter among the cops, prepared to lend support if it was needed. Everyone agreed it was unlikely that Baptiste could organize an attack on Isabelle *during* her bar visits, but they anticipated the need to identify one or two gang members possibly trailing her *after* the first bar stop.

"My guys have reported that Isabelle is doing great," Washington told his group in the hotel lobby. "She's not only smoothly talking with them, but even shedding a tear to convince them of her close friendship with Simone Ardoin."

Nevertheless, none of the teams spotted any Haitian or New Orleanian gangsters trailing her after she completed her third bar visit and walked back to her hotel. Rather than arresting someone trying to assault her, as they had hoped, the operation seemed to be a bust.

Alex was deeply disappointed. The plan had been his idea, but not one gangster had been spotted.

"Let's go to Isabelle's room at the Marriott, and talk," Alex said.

Joining Alex's group heading toward Isabelle's room were Burt Warner and Sgt. Guidry, the lead NOPD surveillance operator. The rest of the teams spread out in the lobby of the Marriott awaiting further instructions.

"HOW DO YOU THINK IT WENT?" ALEX ASKED ISABELLE.

"I feel I sold my cover well enough. But the bartender at the second place seemed extra sleazy. I got bad vibes off him."

"I saw him call someone right after you left," Sgt. Guidry said. "John, I think we should ask for a trace on that call. It was made at 2:45pm."

"I'm on it," Detective John Washington replied.

"At least *that's* something to follow-up on," Alex said. He looked at Washington. "You're still going to post two plainclothes officers on this floor, right?"

"Yeah. Susan already gave us the funding citation to charge a room to DS. The officers will be here from 6:00 pm to 8:00 am."

"Is there anything else we need to discuss?" Isabelle asked.

"I can't think of anything, but I'll let you know about the trace on the bartender's call," Washington said. Soon after, he and Sgt. Guidry left the room.

"I'm starving," Isabelle said. "Where's a good place to eat?"

"I think we should leave the French Quarter, just in case one of Baptiste's gangsters happens to spot Isabelle with us," Susan said. "If we leave the area, I doubt that will happen."

Everyone agreed, so she suggested Joey K's on Magazine Street. It had a great menu of *poboys*, other Louisiana specialties, and some comfort food. About to leave the room, Susan's cell phone rang. It was the DS Protective Intelligence and Investigations (PPII) Office in DC.

"Special Agent Susan Witt speaking."

"Hey, Susan, it's Randy Horowitz."

"Hi, Randy. What's up?"

"I want to give you a heads-up that Director Riley approved placing a Rewards for Justice advertisement in the New Orleans Times-Picayune for a 50K reward leading to the arrest of Jules Baptiste or Claude Toussaint. It will appear in tomorrow morning's paper. Also, WDSU television in New Orleans will interview Director Riley tonight about the murder of Simone Ardoin, and the reward."

"Thanks for letting me know. Who should the public contact?"

"Your office or NOPD. The cops gave us their hotline number. Riley will give out your number this evening during the interview and, of course, it will be listed in the newspaper ad."

"Okay, I'll have Fong or Torres man our office during the day. After-hours, we'll refer callers to the NOPD hotline."

"Great. Give my regards to Isabelle."

"Will do, thanks."

They talked another minute before Susan hung up and brought the group up to speed. Then she called Pete Fong and told him that he and Torres would have to take turns the following day covering the phones.

The good news is that I'm getting Scott Fellows back from New

York, where his protection detail on the British Royals has just ended, she thought. Then she said to the group, "Let's eat!"

There was an adage in DS that you should eat whenever you could, because you never knew when a new emergency would arise that could test your endurance. This was one of those times.

Chapter 25

Food and Advice

S usan called Fong again to ask if he and Torres wanted to join them for an early dinner, but they had already grabbed lunch. Detective Washington also declined and returned to NOPD. So, using two cars, Susan, Alex, Rachel, Burt, Isabelle, and the two DC agents went to Joey K's Restaurant and Bar.

As they drove down Magazine Street, they passed antique stores, clothing boutiques, restaurants, and old expensive multi-story homes decorated with intricately designed balconies with wrought iron railings. Some balconies had colorful flowers, while others had banners or flags supporting Tulane, Loyola, or LSU. On occasion, there was a Gay Pride flag with rainbow colors. Most homes had large porches and Greek style columns to support the balcony above. Some had see-through iron fences at the property line while others did not. The favorite house color was a shade of white, although occasionally, there were one or two pink or blue homes visible.

They parked on the street near Joey K's. As they exited their cars, Susan called out, "Watch where you're walking. New Orleans has the worst streets in America."

Alex looked around. *Whoa! She's damn right*, he thought. There were broken curbs and sidewalks everywhere, and the street itself had buckled in more spots than he could count. Repair work had started on the cross street, but no one was working to fill the massive potholes. He wasn't sure if they were still in the Garden District or if they had transitioned to the area called 'Uptown.' In either case, judging by the homes, there was substantial money in the neighborhood, yet the streets were still shitty.

"When I heard I was being assigned to New Orleans," Susan said, "I renewed my passport, because people said Louisiana was a 'third world country.' I know that's unkind, but..."

Due to the hour, there wasn't any line to que in, so the group entered quickly and divided among two tables. Alex and Rachel each took separate tables because the younger agents wanted to ask questions about the Foreign Service and it seemed best to maximize their opportunity by dividing up. Alex speculated that the three male agents who sat with Rachel just wanted to look at her up-close for as long as they could. He couldn't blame them.

The restaurant was in an old two-story wood framed building with a balcony on the second story. The exterior sported tan or light green wood slats. It was hard to make out the exact color since they were discolored with peeling paint. Inside, there were multiple dining rooms adorned with colorful local artwork on the walls. The furniture was basic with dark wood table tops and lighter brown wooden chairs, nothing fancy. The floor was gray tile. Judging by how people at one table spoke to those at other tables, Alex assumed this was a neighborhood restaurant, rather than a tourist joint.

He started with a cup of seafood gumbo, followed by a fried oyster *poboy* and a side of onion rings. Isabelle ordered Eggplant Napoleon pasta while Susan had fried chicken. At the other table, he heard one DC agent order Creole *jambalaya* and his traveling partner ordered Trout *Tchoupitoules*, although he mispronounced the second word. Rachel had broiled catfish.

As they ate, Isabelle pumped Alex for advice on selecting overseas assignments. She had already served in Caracas and Quito, which Alex said was fine for starter tours of duty. But now it was time to decide what she really wanted from her career.

"Here's what I tell others at your grade. If you want more rapid promotion, go to the embassies or consulates with the highest threat level or places that are very busy. Go to locations that stretch your abilities and give you a unique chance to shine. You want your boss to be able to write you up in a way that makes you stand out above the crowd.

"In order for you to do that, you have to be in a place where shit happens. These types of spots vary from decade to decade; sometimes it's Central America, others times its Africa, and it's *always* the Middle East, or South Asia. Occasionally, it can even be a European post like Greece or Turkey. Sometimes, you'll need a break from the tension in those risky places, so look for follow-on assignments that you consider will be like heaven.

"That will depend upon what you like, of course. For some, it's Latin America, for others, its Asia, and there is always Europe. But again, try to select posts that will challenge you. Shy away from the places that are just 'nice', but not 'outstanding' for living and culture. Try to avoid places where work is routine, and not very important to Washington.

"Again, I'm speaking in terms of promotional opportunities. I'm sad to say that in the mediocre category there are so many embassies that are just 'okay' culturally, and they're also not active enough to put you on the radar of the promotion panels. Many good officers have been assigned to those kinds of posts and their promotion rates have been slower than they would want.

"In reality, you have a limited say in where you are assigned. And DS management never thinks in terms of a career for any of us. So, you'll have to be aggressive in seeking out assignments that will fulfill whatever it is you want."

Isabelle waited half a second, considering all he said, then spoke. "I appreciate that, I really do," she replied. "When I was in the Army, people were asked their opinion about where they wanted to go next, but equally important, the Army seemed to have a general career path for people at each grade level. But I guess that's not the case in the Foreign Service."

"You hit the nail on the head," Alex said. "A wise embassy management counselor once told me that there are two assignment systems in the Foreign Service. The first is for people who don't know anyone in a decision-making capacity. So, they get whatever assignment some faceless bureaucrat in HR decides for them. The second is for people who *do* know someone who can make a difference. Make sure you're in the latter group.

"Oh, I almost forgot to mention," he continued. "At any post, you can run into fantastic or terrible ambassadors, and even deputy chiefs of mission. It's almost a crap shoot. When you think you want to pursue a specific overseas assignment, find people you can trust and respect and who have already worked with your potential new bosses. Get their opinion about your potential assignment. It could make a world of difference."

"I agree 100 percent with Alex," Susan said. "When I requested Islamabad, it was in part because I had heard that Alex and Jim Riley were great RSOs. I wanted to learn from them. And, of course, Pakistan was, and still is, the place to serve if you want to be challenged with critical threats. As Alex said, shit happens. It's best to be there when it does."

"I heard you got shot in Islamabad," Isabelle asked Susan. "Is that true?"

"Yeah, but anyone can have a bad day," Susan replied.

Alex almost spit out his coffee when Susan said that; Isabelle cracked up.

———

AT THE ADJOINING TABLE, RACHEL WAS HOLDING COURT WITH THE three young male DS agents. Among the three, only Burt had served overseas, a two-year tour as an assistant RSO in Panama. The two others were brand new to the service and asked a lot of questions about life in an embassy. Since Rachel was now serving at her fifth embassy, she just gave some sound advice based upon her experiences.

"Which post was your favorite?" Burt asked.

"Oh, man, that would be impossible to say. Hong Kong and Beijing were fascinating, Rome had the best food, and best overall lifestyle, but Islamabad had the most challenging work and the best chain of command. As for London, Alex and I have only been there for about a year. I love the place, but it's too early to evaluate how it stacks up against the others."

Burt hesitated before saying, "I heard on the QT that you and Alex received Valor Awards for fighting and killing Russian assassins outside London in the last year."

'*What?*" The other two DC agents said loudly in unison.

Rachel put her finger on her lips. "The Department would prefer we don't talk about that incident. It's not a secret per se, but we don't advertise what happened. But, yes, what Burt said is true."

"Hold on a minute," one of the DC agents said. "During our basic agent training, we read an official report of that terrorist attack on the embassy in Islamabad. You and Alex were *there* at the time?"

"Yeah. But you should talk to Alex about that event," Rachel said. "He was leading the Marines inside the embassy. The fighting was vicious and hand-to-hand at one point."

The guy remained quiet, but Rachel could sense gears moving in his brain, trying to recall what he had read. She never liked discussing her own personal fight with one of the terrorists, it brought back bad memories on how close she came to death that day. Now, she hoped he wouldn't press the matter.

"Let's change subjects," Burt said, noticing her expression. "Has it been tough being a single woman in the Foreign Service? I'm thinking of the cultural differences between America and places like the Far East and Middle East."

"It's a challenge," she said. "Other cultures expect their women to behave in ways that don't always work for American women, especially *professional* women. But I knew that when I joined." She hesitated a nanosecond. "And to be honest, I don't think I'd ever have found someone like Alex anywhere else."

The meal came to an end, and without consulting the other, Alex and Rachel each picked up checks for their tables. Susan led the way back to the office where everyone chatted for a while. Then they agreed to meet the next morning at ten unless something arose in the interim.

They were almost out of options to find Baptiste or Toussaint. It appeared the sting operation earlier this afternoon had failed to bait the killers into revealing themselves. At least, it seemed that way.

Maybe the reward offer in the media will develop something, Alex thought. *The evening is still young.*

———

BACK IN THE FRENCH QUARTER, MOON GLOW WAS COMPLETING her last tattoo for the day. The masterpiece for the guy buying the work of art consisted of a dragon breathing fire, placed on his upper right arm.

"I'll see you tomorrow morning," Moon Glow told the shop owner after the guy paid his bill. Then she left by the front door to catch the bus a few blocks away on Esplanade Avenue back to her apartment.

However, only one block later, she stopped walking after noticing a big guy across the street staring at her. The fact that he was black was usually unimportant, but since Jules Baptiste's gang was all comprised of either Haitians or African Americans, this guy staring made her pause.

Am I in danger? she wondered. Everything made her nervous now.

She started walking again, noticing the guy strolling in her same direction, still staring, although he had not crossed the street yet. Moon Glow's heart began to race. She turned around and quickly went back to the tattoo parlor.

"Billy, you've got to come pick me up," she called on her cell phone. Ten minutes later, he arrived in his car. As they drove off, she directed Billy to go in the direction she had been walking. But the guy who had made her nervous was now gone.

Chapter 26

Another Death

t mid-afternoon that same day, the phone rang four times elsewhere in the city before Jules Baptiste answered.

"Who's this?" Jules barked into the phone.

"It's Louie," the bartender said. "I got something important to tell you.

"I'm listening."

"Okay, a woman just came into my bar asking about you and Claude."

"What, asking about me by name?"

"Yeah, Jules, you heard me right. She said she was a personal friend of that girl who died in the park. She said they worked together in Haiti. She said that girl told her she visited my bar trying to follow you."

"What else did she say?"

"She knew your *name*, man. She also asked about Claude.

186

Wanted to know how to contact him. She asked me if you were responsible for killing that girl in City Park."

"Was she a cop?"

"I can't say for sure. She didn't act like a cop. She didn't look like one neither. I think she was just a civilian."

"I appreciate the heads-up. We have to stop her before it goes any further. What did she look like?"

"Maybe early thirties, white, medium length brown hair, average height and weight. She was dressed kind of nice."

"What do you mean?"

"She wore pants, dark blouse, and a jacket, black, I think."

"What's she doing wearing a jacket in summer? Maybe she was hiding something."

"How should I know? Every place is freezing inside. Maybe she was just cold."

Baptiste thought about the possibility for a moment. *Why is this bitch sticking her nose into my business, just like that Ardoin girl was doing?*

"Okay, my friend. If she comes back, let me know. I want my guys to see her."

"Will do, Jules. Oh, I almost forgot. She said she was staying at the Marriott on Canal Street."

"*Shit*, why didn't you say so before?"

"I just did."

"Okay, okay . . . you did *real* good. Thanks, buddy."

Baptiste immediately called two of his gangsters. *Damn, I miss having Jimmy and Michel on my team. They were the best, but now they're gone. Still, my new guys, Eddie and Joseph will get the job done.*

Eddie Jefferson was born and raised in a public housing project in New Orleans. A tough guy from a tough

187

neighborhood, he liked to fight. He had dropped out of school at age sixteen and been in jail as much as he was out of it. He had killed or maimed a lot of people over the years. As for Joseph Ricard, Baptiste had known this gangbanger since they were teenagers together in Port-Au-Prince, Haiti. Extortion, enforcement, and general mayhem were his specialties.

Over the phone, Baptiste gave them Isabelle's description and told them to hang out at the Marriott. If they spotted her, they were to kill her as quietly as possible.

AFTER THEIR MEAL AT JOEY KS HAD ENDED, THE DS GROUP WENT back to Susan's office to wrap up their plans for the next day. Then Isabelle decided to walk back to the Marriott, which was only a block or two away. Since she had deliberately revealed herself at the bars to Baptiste's people, Burt Warner, and the two DC agents would escort her back to the hotel where all four of them were actually staying, But they would also stay far enough away from her to disguise their connection.

Canal Street had gotten sleazy over the decades. Once a prime shopping area in the 1960s, it had gone downhill with major store closures. Isabelle kept her head on a swivel as she passed a few panhandlers, luggage stores, a Popeye's Fried Chicken place, an electronics shop, and an interesting looking Chinese restaurant. Burt walked ahead of Isabelle by about ten paces and the two others trailed in line about ten paces apart.

As Burt entered the hotel lobby first, he walked to the concierge desk and pretended to browse some tourist brochures. Isabelle walked through the front doors and headed directly for the elevators. The two trailing DC agents stopped in the lobby, then headed in different directions: one went to the coffee bar area, the other pretended to browse newspapers at the reception desk. None of them noticed anything suspicious.

MEANWHILE, TO MINIMIZE THEIR PRESENCE, BAPTISTE'S MEN, EDDIE Jefferson and Joseph Ricard, had earlier agreed to take turns either sitting in the lobby or roaming outside the hotel.

Joseph was coming out of the coffee shop when he spotted a woman matching Isabelle's description. Isabelle was still wearing the same clothes she had worn earlier in the day when she had visited the three bars looking for Baptiste.

Glad Baptiste told us to dress up, so me and Jefferson are less obvious, Joseph thought. His blue blazer and gray slacks allowed him to pass by the DS agents without a second look.

He quietly strolled behind Isabelle into the elevator. As she got off on the twelfth floor and walked down the hall to her room, Ricard remained in the elevator. When she reached her room, she briefly looked back at the elevator at the end of the hall; Joseph smiled politely as the door silently closed. But he had counted the number of rooms she had passed. It would be foolish to attack her by himself without a plan, so he returned to the lobby and left the hotel in search of his fellow criminal, Eddie Jefferson.

INSIDE HER ROOM, ISABELLE BEGAN CHANGING INTO SOMETHING more casual. She felt bloated from her late-afternoon meal of Eggplant Napoleon pasta at Joey K's, and decided to use the hotel's gym. As she changed, she placed her gun into her gym bag and headed out the door. At the half-open door across the hall, she stopped briefly to talk to the two NOPD cops on duty. She introduced herself and thanked them for their protection. Both cops were in civilian dress, either jeans or khaki pants and polo shirts. Their dark blue windbreakers hung over chairs inside the room.

But it was the appearance of the female cop that shocked Isabelle. She was of average height but must have weighed more than 220 lbs. Rolls of fat hung over her belt.

There's no way this officer could pass a fitness test. . . impossible, thought Isabelle. She knew NOPD had never been known for its fitness. It was, after-all, New Orleans, the city of fried food and massive portions. She was also aware that before Katrina had slammed into the city, many cops had fled with their families rather than remain in place to help with recovery and to fight crime. Those cops who didn't get their jobs back afterwards created a shortage of officers.

But still, couldn't NOPD maintain some level of basic fitness for the current force? Isabelle wondered. *At least her male cop partner looks in better shape.*

"I'm going to the hotel gym," Isabelle said. "I've got my gun.'" That was probably the reason they all decided it was okay for the cops to wait in their room until she returned.

An hour later, she was back at her room and told the cops she was turning in for the night; she walked across the hall to her room. After a shower, she laid in bed reading until bedtime.

THE CLOCK READ TWO IN THE MORNING WHEN NICOLE, THE FAT cop, told her NOPD partner, Sammy, that she was going down to the lobby to grab a cup of coffee and a pastry.

As she sat in the lobby, devouring her second pastry, Eddie Jefferson and Joseph Ricard entered the hotel and walked to the elevator. It was how they were now dressed, shabbily and wearing baseball hats and dark glasses, that raised Nicole's concern. Yet, it took her a minute to get out of her seat. By then, the two thugs had entered the elevator before she even got up.

"Sammy, Sammy," she called over her police radio. "There are two suspicious guys taking the elevator upstairs." There was no answer.

"Sammy, Sammy! Do you read me?"

Sammy had nodded off, but Nicole's second transmission woke him. "What's up, Nicole?"

"Two men just got in the elevator . . . they look suspicious. Stay alert." She shuffled to a second elevator, got in, and pressed the button for the twelfth floor.

———

AS THE TWO HITMEN RODE UP IN THE ELEVATOR, EDDIE JEFFERSON drew his 9mm pistol, and from a pocket, he took out a suppressor, screwing it onto the barrel. Joseph Ricard pulled out a .45 caliber semi-automatic. Neither of them knew Sammy was across the hall from Isabelle.

When the elevator door opened on the twelfth floor, Sammy, the cop, was standing in the hallway just outside his room, gun still holstered. But as he spotted the metal in the hands of both Jefferson and Ricard, he drew his own gun.

Jefferson was faster and fired his suppressed 9mm weapon

first. The quiet round hit the doorframe just above Sammy as he jumped back into the room. Then he leaned forward into the hallway again and quickly fired off two shots from his 9mm police pistol. It sounded like a cannon going off.

One of his shots hit Ricard in the thigh and he collapsed on the floor, screaming. Jefferson fired a second suppressed bullet which hit Sammy in the shoulder. He staggered back into the room and fell onto the bed.

"Go ahead, *kill* her," Ricard yelled as he lay in pain on the hallway floor. Isabelle's door was still closed and locked. Jefferson cautiously walked toward it.

A light sleeper ever since her tour of duty in Iraq as an Army officer, Isabelle had jolted out of bed hearing the two blasts from Sammy's gun. She grabbed her Glock model 26 from the nightstand and hurried to the side of her room's door. Crouching, she listened, then heard more shots and yelling in the hallway.

Raising up, Isabelle peered through the peephole. She saw the open door to Sammy's room. She could see Sammy lying on the bed holding his bloody shoulder. Then the figure of a man blocked her view. She saw him raise an arm and take aim at Sammy.

Isabelle wrenched open her door. "Police, drop your weapon!" she yelled.

The man was fast. He spun around and fired a round that flew by Isabelle's head. At the same time, Isabelle fired four times, each shot hitting him square in the body. Eddie Jefferson dropped like a rock, dead in front of her. She looked down the hallway and saw Ricard trying to pick up his .45 from the floor.

"Don't touch that weapon or I'll shoot!" she yelled. He stared into the barrel of her gun and raised his hands.

The elevator doors opened, and Nicole got out, gun in hand, pointing at the killer lying on the floor. She used her radio to call for backup and an ambulance. Then she holstered her weapon and handcuffed Ricard.

"Thank you!" Isabelle said, as she picked up Ricard's .45 for safekeeping. Just then, Special Agent Burt Warner ran from his room toward the scene with pistol drawn.

SAMMY WAS STILL CONSCIOUS AND HAD MANAGED TO SIT UP BY THE time Isabelle went to help him while Nicole and Burt Warner guarded the handcuffed shooter. She pulled off Sammy's shirt and saw the bullet had made a clean exit out the back of his shoulder. Using a bath towel, Isabelle wrapped it around the entry and exit wounds but wasn't happy with the solution because her training told her it was still easy to bleed out from poor bandaging when it didn't put enough pressure on the wound.

Within ten minutes, ambulances arrived and paramedics took over. They re-bandaged Sammy and rolled him down to an ambulance. As he passed by Nicole, Sammy said, "Thanks for the radio warning. I'd be dead if you hadn't called."

"That's what partners are for," she replied, smiling at him.

When NOPD backup arrived, Isabelle turned over both perps' guns and explained the situation while Nicole confirmed her story. Within thirty minutes the drama was over.

Sammy, the cop, and Ricard, the assassin, were now both at the hospital. Jefferson's body was taken to the morgue; Nicole was being treated for stress by a paramedic. Burt told Isabelle he would stand watch with another NOPD officer for the rest of the night.

When crime scene police officers arrived to bag shell casings, take photos, and ask Isabelle some questions, other guests on the floor who had come out to look after hearing the commotion, began returning to their rooms.

Finally, after everything was done, Isabelle tried opening her room door and found it had locked behind her. There she stood, gun in hand, wearing boxer shorts and a Houston Texans t-shirt stained with Sammy's blood. Burt took one look and laughed.

"I better call the front desk for a master key."

Chapter 27

After Action

Once back inside her room, Isabelle sat on the edge of her bed. Her hands were trembling a little. She walked to the small fridge and pulled out a mini bottle of scotch, poured half into a glass, and swallowed it down. Then she grabbed her cellphone from its charger and dialed Alex Boyd's cell.

"Hi, Alex, sorry to wake you up. Baptiste sent two gunmen to kill me at the hotel tonight. I shot and killed one of them and the NOPD cop stationed across the hall wounded a second one. That cop was wounded, himself, and is now in the hospital. I'm unhurt and Burt Warner and another cop are guarding my room now."

"Jesus Christ, Isabelle! I'm glad you're okay," Alex said. "Tell me everything." After she told all the details, Alex said, "Looks like my plan to smoke them out almost got you killed, Isabelle. I'm so sorry."

"It's not your fault, Alex; actually, the plan worked, just with more drama than we expected."

"You need to report the incident to the DS Command Center in Washington; they'll notify others in headquarters. I'm coming over to your hotel now. In a few hours, we'll move you and the other three agents to another hotel. Do you still have a weapon, or did NOPD confiscate it as part of their investigation?"

"I have it. They never asked for it, and I didn't volunteer to give it up."

"All right, I'll let Susan Witt know what happened. I'll also contact Sgt. Washington. We need to decide what to do next. Thank goodness you're unhurt. You did a great job tonight."

ISABELLE CALLED THE 24-HOUR LINE AT THE DIPLOMATIC SECURITY Command Center in Washington, DC. Five minutes later, she'd finished telling the story of the shootout. The Command Center confirmed they would handle notifications to DS senior management in Washington. Next, she called the home number of the special-agent-in-charge in Houston and repeated the story.

Now mentally drained from focusing on exact details during her calls, she walked over to the credenza on the other side of the room, unzipped her shoulder bag, and took out a loaded spare magazine for her Glock 26. She popped the existing magazine out of her pistol, now four rounds shy, and replaced it with a full magazine of ten rounds. After putting the gun on the bedside nightstand, she lay back on the bed, hoping she could sleep. It didn't work. She hadn't expected it would.

RACHEL HEARD THE ENTIRE CONVERSATION BECAUSE ALEX HAD PUT his cell phone on speaker when he had spoken to Isabelle.

"I'm glad she didn't get hurt," Rachel said. "I'm coming with you to her hotel to lend support."

"Yeah, I agree. Let's get dressed and go. But first, I need to call Jim Riley. I imagine the Command Center has already spoken with him, but he'll want some reassurance that we're on top of the situation."

He dialed Riley's home number and got him on the second ring. "Has the Command Center already called you?" Alex asked.

"They did. Was it a legitimate good shoot?"

"Yes." Alex described what happened and concluded with, "I believe it was justified. The assassin had already shot the cop on duty. Rachel and I are going to her hotel in a few minutes; we'll talk to Isabelle."

"Regarding the big picture, what are you going to do next, Alex?"

"One of the gunmen was only wounded, so NOPD will be able to interrogate him. Maybe he can tell us where to find Baptiste. Also, I want NOPD to haul in the bartenders from the three places Isabelle visited. They know something and I want to know what they know. We'll also start protection for the two witnesses from City Park, 'Moon Glow' and her buddy. I think our two DC agents, the US Marshal's service, and NOPD can handle that. I'd like Isabelle and Burt to work with me and Susan Witt on tracking down Baptiste. Can you tell the SAIC in Houston that we have a change of plan for their people?"

"Consider it done."

"And one other thing: We've had three shootouts in one week on this case . . ."

"I know what you're going to ask," Riley interrupted. "That I stop the State Department from sending down investigators to look into how everything has been handled?"

"Exactly. They'll just get in the way and slow us down. We can answer the bureaucratic questions later. If someone *must* come down here, the DS agents would be best. At least they've worked in the field, and I won't have to explain to some novice from the Inspector General's Office how the *real*-world works. Those guys are inexperienced and just plain terrible."

"I'll see what I can do. I'll speak to the Secretary of State tomorrow morning. By the way, Alex, how is Isabelle handling the incident?"

"I'll know more when I see her, Jim, but at least over the phone she seems to be doing fine."

"Please give her my personal regards and tell her that I'm glad she's okay."

"Will do." The two long-time friends hung up.

Then Alex called Susan Witt and Detective John Washington before getting dressed. He slipped his Glock pistol into the holster on his right hip, clipped two extra magazines onto his belt on the left side, after which he and Rachel walked over to the Marriott Hotel.

By the time they arrived, the lobby of the Marriott was chock-a-block full of people, the bulk of whom were checking out.

"I guess word spread about the shootout," Rachel said.

"I can't blame them for leaving. They're here to party, eat, and drink, not get shot." Alex looked around the lobby and spotted John Washington talking with someone at the reception desk whom he presumed to be the night manager.

"Let's go talk to John." They approached him and waited for him to finish speaking to the man behind the desk.

"Hey, Alex and Rachel," John said spotting them as he spun around to leave. "Close call tonight, huh?"

"Yeah, it was," Alex replied. "How is *your* guy doing?"

"He'll be fine. The bullet passed through the soft tissue in his shoulder. The docs are letting him go home tomorrow."

"What about the shooter who survived, is he talking?" Rachel asked.

Washington looked around before saying, "I'll tell you upstairs."

They rode the elevator up to the twelfth floor. Two uniformed officers were standing outside Isabelle's room. Both were dressed like they were from a tactical unit; helmet, grey urban pattern camouflage fatigues, each holding a 9mm submachine gun with a pistol on their belt.

"NOPD has turned out in force," Alex said to Washington.

"It's the least we can do. Isabelle saved the life of our cop. The guy she killed has a rap sheet longer than my arm. He was a bad dude. As far as NOPD is concerned, Isabelle is a rock star."

"I bet she's already up," Washington said to Alex and Rachel as he knocked on Isabelle's door.

To Alex's surprise, Susan Witt opened it with Isabelle and Burt standing behind her. Both women and Burt smiled as the three new arrivals entered. "Rachel just asked me if the injured shooter has been talking," Washington said after he stepped inside the room.

"The answer is, 'not yet,'"Washington said. "By the way, his name is Joseph Ricard. He's still in the hospital under armed custody. When the docs are finished, we'll book him for attempted murder. The court will assign him a public defender who might convince the guy to cut a deal with us."

"It might take a while for his lawyer to arrive," Susan replied. "I'm worried that Jules Baptiste will be long gone by then."

"I know," Washington said. "Do you guys have any other ideas?"

"What's the penalty in Louisiana for attempted murder?" Alex asked.

"It's between ten to fifty years in jail. But since Isabelle's job as a special agent will qualify her as a peace officer under state law, the penalty could be between twenty and fifty years. Why? What are you thinking?"

"First, I have to admit that I don't actually know what the penalty is for attempted murder under federal law," Alex replied. "We can look it up. But my point is that the gunman won't know either. Maybe we can frighten him into thinking that if he *doesn't* cooperate with NOPD, then he'll be prosecuted by the Feds and get the needle, or life in prison."

"Is that ethical?" Rachel asked.

"That depends; a US Attorney has to be precise and careful about what he says when negotiating an official plea deal with a defense attorney. But a cop can imply just about anything to the guy in custody."

"I hate to pour cold water on your idea," Susan said, "but I'm pretty sure that under U.S. Code 18, sections 1113 and 1114, the death penalty, or life in prison, only applies if the federal employee is *murdered.* For "attempted" murder, the penalty is not to exceed twenty years." Alex and Susan exchanged smiles.

"I had to learn that type of stuff when I was assigned to run the DS New Orleans office," Susan said.

"But maybe that doesn't change your strategy," Washington said. "I can still imply that the Feds might have the death penalty on the table. The guy won't know. Let's give it a try if I can question him before he gets a lawyer."

"Since you don't work for the Feds," Susan said, "I guess you can say whatever you like." No one disagreed.

"Isabelle, you need to change hotels," Alex said, while Washington agreed. "In fact, the Marriott has already asked that you checkout."

"Where should I go?"

"Before we walked over here," Rachel spoke, "I asked the receptionist at the Royal Sonesta if they had rooms available. The guy said they weren't fully booked since it was the end of the summer. How about if the entire DS team, all four of you, move to the Sonesta in a few hours? That way everyone can provide mutual support." Susan and Washington agreed it was a great idea.

"I'll tell the two other guys from the DC office about the new plan," Susan said.

"One more thing," Rachel said, "everyone should ask for a room facing the inner courtyard and swimming pool. It's a lot quieter than getting a room facing Bourbon Street, or any side streets for that matter."

"I'm going to the hospital now to see if I can talk to Ricard," Washington said. "I'll let you know if he's ready to spill the beans on Baptiste."

Chapter 28

Baby Steps

Sgt. John Washington drove to the University Medical Center on Canal Street. It was the only Level One trauma center in New Orleans.

He flashed his badge at the desk attendant seated inside the building's entrance for the emergency room. "I'm Sgt. John Washington with NOPD Homicide and need to question a man who was brought in this evening with a gunshot wound."

The attendant wore a set of scrubs and a nurse's ID badge from the hospital, She appeared middle-aged, and looked tired, perhaps from whatever trauma she had seen that evening, but seemed unfazed by his statement.

"You'll have to be more precise. We've got four new gunshot victims this evening. One was hit in a drive-by shooting on the I-10 near the Superdome around midnight, another took two bullets to his body in the 700 block of Bourbon Street an hour ago, a third guy was shot in the Marriot hotel, and a fourth . . ." she hesitated. "Sorry, I can't recall where the fourth one was shot." She sighed and shook her head. "*Shit,* I'm too old for this crap."

"I'm sorry," Washington half-smiled. "I know you have your hands full." She nodded at his appreciation and understanding tone.

"I hate to tell you, but it's just another normal night in the 'Murder Capital of America.'"

"My guy was shot at the Marriott. We believe his last name is Ricard."

"Oh, yeah, that one. He's out of surgery now and in the recovery room. I doubt he can speak to you for another few hours, though." She stared at Washington for a few seconds. "I think I've seen you here before."

"Yeah, when I'm not on the street investigating crime, I divide my time between the Medical Center and the morgue."

"I think maybe you should call back a little later. Your guy hasn't been assigned a room yet."

"Thanks. I'll just go to the recovery room now and talk to the cops guarding him."

"Is that because he can identify the shooter?"

"No, they're guarding Ricard, so he doesn't escape. He *is* the shooter from the Marriott; wounded a cop."

He was about to walk away when an ambulance pulled up to the emergency entrance and two paramedics wheeled in yet another injured man. He lay semi-conscious on a gurney; an oxygen mask covered the lower half of his face and a drip bag hung from a hook, feeding into an IV line running into his arm. Bloody bandages covered part of his chest. Washington stepped aside and watched them hurry toward the suites of operating rooms.

Being a cop in New Orleans is hard enough, but being on the medical side might be mentally tougher, he thought. Then he turned and thanked the nurse before walking to the recovery room. Two uniform officers were standing outside the area and he gave them an update on what had happened at the Marriott. In turn, they said Sammy, the wounded police officer had been operated on and already taken from the recovery room.

"He's probably sleeping in a regular room somewhere," one cop said. "A few other cops from his precinct have already stopped by."

With nothing more to be done, Washington decided to return home, take a shower, shave, and return to work before the sun rose over the Crescent City.

———

AT TEN O'CLOCK THE NEXT MORNING, ISABELLE, BURT, AND THE two D.C. special agents moved from the Marriott to the Royal Sonesta. The hotel was able to put them all on the third floor where Alex and Rachel's room was located; although no one's room was adjacent to another.

The seven-story hotel took up most of an entire city block, but had a unique configuration. The center of the hotel on the third floor, was filled with a courtyard, outdoor swimming pool, and bar. Guests could walk directly out from their rooms into the area.

For the past fifteen minutes, Susan Witt had been in Alex and Rachel's room. They were discussing the morning's article in the New Orleans Times-Picayune which described the $50,000 reward for information leading to the arrest of Jules Baptiste or Claude Toussaint.

"You know we'll get a lot of bullshit calls about this," Susan said.

"Always," Alex replied. "It comes with the business. Who's on duty now to receive calls?"

"I've got Pete Fong staying in the office until three o'clock, then Luis Torres will take over until nine o'clock. After that, any calls on the tip line will be routed to NOPD," Susan replied. Alex simply nodded.

When is Director Riley's interview with WDSU television going to be aired?" Rachel asked.

"There will be a special airing today at noontime. Then it'll be repeated for the regular news tonight at five and ten," Susan said.

Alex's cell phone rang. He recognized Washington's number and put it on speaker.

"Hi, John. Did you see the reward ad in the newspaper?"

"I did. It was eye-catching. I'm sure we'll get some tips from it."

"Jim Riley will be on television at noon to discuss the reward. Do you have anything else for us?"

"Yeah, I'm at the hospital now, and Ricard is awake. He might talk to us, but my guess is that he'd prefer to speak with the Feds."

"Okay. Either Susan or I will come over there now. What's happening with protection for Billy Whiteman and his girl, Moon Glow?"

"NOPD is ready to deploy. I'm not sure about the Marshall's Service. What about DS?"

"Our four special agents just moved into the Sonesta, so they're ready to start. Recall, I'm keeping Isabelle and Susan to work the homicide case. But you'll have three of our people to be bodyguards. Plus, Director Riley said he'd like to send more agents down here, either to work with NOPD investigating the case, or perhaps to help protect our two witnesses."

"Excellent. I'll call the Marshall's Service and set up a schedule to protect Whiteman and the girl. In the meantime, I'll see either you or Susan here at the hospital in a few minutes."

"Okay, bye," Alex replied.

Alex turned to Susan. "You should be the one to go to the hospital because when Ricard goes to trial, you'll still be here to testify, or give a statement; I'll be back in London."

"Makes sense to me," she said. "To recap: I'll tell him he may face a long term in prison, or worse, if he doesn't cooperate. I'll hint that prosecutors can be very tough on criminals who try to kill federal agents. But I won't make any promises."

"That's great, Susan. Just lay on your Oklahoma accent and charm, and don't let him know you're as smart as you look." Rachel chuckled from the other side of the room.

"First, I don't have an accent," Susan replied with a smile. "And second, I'll take that as a compliment. What are you going to do now?"

"I thought I'd stop by Moon Glow's tattoo parlor, discuss her personal security, and ask her where Billy Whiteman works."

"Sounds good."

He turned to Rachel. "You want to come with me to speak with Moon Glow? Maybe you can get a few tats while we're there."

"I'll come, but why would I mess with perfection?" Susan laughed, snorting a few times.

Alex looked at Rachel thoughtfully. "Hmmm, maybe Moon Glow could give you an 'Alex' tattoo on your inner thigh," he said. "That way no one else, but me, will see it."

"Maybe you shouldn't be so confident about that," Rachel said, a grin spreading across her face.

"What do you think, Susan? Did I deserve what she just said?"

"I think you're as smart as you look," Susan said. "You know the answer."

Chapter 29

Tattoos and Hospitals

Alex led the way on the short walk to Moon Glow's tattoo parlor. He noted that not many people were on the street this time of day since it wasn't even noon yet on a hot August morning. Those who *were* out looked "normal" . . . normal for the French Quarter, that is.

Alex wore shorts, boat shoes with no socks, and a purple and gold striped polo shirt he had purchased at the local Perlis clothing store on Decatur Street in the Quarter. He had locked up his pistol in the room safe, although he was carrying a folding Spyderco knife with a serrated blade. Rachel also wore shorts with a matching polo shirt and the same tennis shoes she had worn in the gym.

The tattoo parlor's window was filled with colorful designs on cardboard displays. Most were elaborate and some could cover a person's entire back or chest. Alex shuddered at the thought. He didn't like tats to begin but one covering an entire half of a body was even more unthinkable.

When he was in the Navy for four years, several men in his unit had tried to convince him to get one, but he had always refused. Then one day, the unit bully had badgered him for an hour about getting a tat, and when he called Alex a pussy for refusing, Alex took a swing at him. The next thing Alex knew, he was waking up in sick bay. He couldn't recall how he got hit, but the side of his face hurt like hell. Standing around his bed were members of his unit, all of whom had said it had been a bad idea for an intelligence officer to take a swing at a Navy SEAL. Nevertheless, they applauded his courage for standing up to the guy. No one ever bothered him again about getting a tattoo.

Now, before entering the parlor, Rachel said, "Don't ask me to get a tat, even a little one on my inner thigh."

"Okay, I'm sorry. I agree with you. I was just joking."

"Good. I thought so." She paused a few seconds. "Of course, I *could* get one on my butt, so when you get amorous and want to jump on my bones, I can say, 'kiss my ass.'"

She began laughing so hard at her own joke that she started choking. When she finally got herself under control, he asked, "Are all California girls that crude?"

"Only jocks like me."

Alex pushed the front door open and saw Moon Glow standing behind a counter writing on a piece of paper. When she looked up, he saw recognition in her eyes. "Hi. I remember you from the other day," she said.

"Yes," Alex replied, "We'd like to talk, if it's okay." His smile was a little forced.

Moon Glow looked across the room where a colleague was creating a masterpiece on someone's arm. "Let's go outside. We can get coffee across the street."

They settled around an outdoor table, and after ordering

coffee, Moon Glow asked, "Are you guys going to protect us, or what?"

"Yes, we are. The team is about to meet to divide up the task among a couple of agencies."

"Okay, sounds good. How will you do it? I don't want a bunch of uniformed guys blocking our front door."

"I understand," Alex replied. "Everyone will be in plain clothes and will blend in." He looked at Moon Glows multi-colored hair and nose ring. "Well, they'll *try* to blend in.

"I'm going to recommend we have someone sitting in one of your inside chairs, as if they're a client."

"Alex," Rachel said. "I think a cop can also sit here drinking coffee while they watch the front door of the tattoo parlor."

"Good idea," he replied. "Where does your boyfriend work?"

"Most of the time Billy works from home. He creates art on his computer and can do that anywhere."

"Okay, that's even better," Alex said. "If you don't mind, an officer can be inside your apartment, or he can sit in the lobby. Again, he won't be in uniform."

Moon Glow paused; her brow wrinkled in apparent contemplation. "I think the lobby would be better," she said.

"I understand."

"How long will this go on?"

"We're not sure. It will depend upon the perceived threat."

"All right, I have to get back to work now. Whoever comes first needs to talk to me, so I know he's a good guy."

"Got it."

As Moon Glow walked across the street to the parlor, Alex said, "Let's return to the hotel and call Susan. I want to find out what happened at the hospital."

THE CALL TO SUSAN WENT TO VOICEMAIL. ALEX ASSUMED SHE WAS still questioning Ricard. Rachel opened her laptop and logged into the unclassified U.S. Embassy London portal. After entering a passcode and placing a special encrypted key fob next to the computer, she was able to open her unclassified emails.

"Gosh, I've got about sixty emails here."

Sadly, as the embassy's political counselor, most of her cable traffic would be classified. She'd have to go to Susan's DS office to read those. "Alex, while we're waiting for Susan to contact us, I think I'll sit by the pool and read these messages."

"Maybe I'll join you after I watch the noon news. I want to see Riley's interview."

He watched as Rachel opened a dresser drawer, pulled out her two-piece, fuchsia-colored bikini and a shear white cover-up, then changed next to the bed. He kissed her on the lips and watched as she walked out through the French doors onto the pool patio with her laptop in-hand. He smiled and shook his head, fixated on her swaying hips, her erect posture, and her athletic physique.

She found a chair in the shade at one of the round metal tables, slipped off her cover-up, and started working. When she propped up her long, shapely legs on an adjoining chair, he wanted to rush to her side and put suntan lotion all over her body. But, just then, his erotic thoughts were interrupted by the noon special TV news story with Riley.

After the interview, he thought Riley had done an excellent job of describing the Rewards for Justice Program and giving out telephone numbers to call. His cell phone rang just as the news ended. It was Susan.

"Alex, Ricard didn't have much to offer. I'll tell you about it in person. We're going to need more sources."

"Okay, why don't you come back to our hotel room; we can talk."

"John Washington and I are going to grab some lunch first and review our interview with Ricard. I'll see you after that."

With a break in the day's events, Alex was about to join Rachel by the pool when the French doors opened, and she walked in carrying her computer in one hand and the white cover-up in the other.

"It was too bright out there to see my screen. So, I'm back. I'll look at emails here."

She stood with most of her weight on her right leg. The fuchsia bikini revealed her nice breasts, and hour-glass figure, with firm abs. As if this wasn't enough to excite him, her diamond-shaped calves and solidly muscled thighs whispered, *Let's play.*

"Susan is going to lunch with Sgt. Washington, so we have nothing on the agenda for a few hours," he said with a smile.

She grinned and winked. Putting her computer on the nearby table, she let her cover-up slip to the floor. She then undid her bikini top and tossed it on the computer. To tease him, she flexed her quad muscles. Rachel's smile grew wider. It was the invitation Alex was hoping for. He walked over to her, wrapped his strong arms around her waist and lifted her off the floor. His tongue played with her nipples, gently sucking on each one. She responded by rubbing herself against his body.

"Oh, god, *yes,*" she moaned, raising her legs around his waist. "Let's do it!"

He pivoted and lowered her onto the bed, then pulled off his clothes as she removed her bikini bottom. She lay there invitingly, her arms ready to hold him.

At that moment, Alex thought: *Life is too short and fraught with peril not to maximize pleasure with the woman you love.*

Chapter 30

Camille

Two hours later, Susan knocked on Alex and Rachel's hotel room door, interrupting Alex and Rachel's review of U.S. Embassy London unclassified emails on their laptops. Alex glanced at his watch; it was mid-afternoon.

"Gosh, I hope you guys haven't been hanging out here with nothing to do," Susan said.

"Oh, no, we had our hands full staying on top of the situation," Alex said with a sly grin. When Rachel laughed, Susan rolled her eyes.

We also talked with Moon Glow," Alex said. "She's ready for protection, as long as it's low key. Even better news is that Billy works from home. What did you find out from Ricard?"

"We don't think he knows exactly *where* to find Baptiste or Toussaint. He did mention a few general locations, such as New Orleans East or Algiers, across the river. One possible bit of useful information was that Baptiste has a fishing camp on the Pearl River."

"Where's that?" Alex asked.

"It's the lower Louisiana-Mississippi border."

"Can you search state or country property records to find this camp?"

"I doubt it's registered under his name. Most likely he pays some guy to rent it, but I can check."

"I know it's early," Rachel said, "but has anyone called the tip line yet for the reward?"

"I spoke with Fong before his shift ended. He said there were two calls which he passed on to NOPD, but he thought the callers sounded vague. Oh, I almost forgot. Bill Westbrook from the FBI called. He wanted to know if our agent was hurt in the shootout at the Marriott. I told him Isabelle was okay. I think he was genuinely relieved to hear that. My guess is he'd have to get involved if a federal agent had been shot."

"Hmm, seems uncharacteristic of the FBI *not* to want to take over an investigation," Alex replied.

"I know," Susan said. "I think the New Orleans office is short-handed because they had to send some officers up to D.C. Rumor has it that something fishy is going on with the background of several White House staffers."

"Really? Corruption?" Alex asked.

"More than that." There was a long pause.

"You mean *loyalty*? Like staffers working for the Chinese or Russians?"

"You shouldn't be surprised," Susan said. "You're the guy who unearthed two traitors last year in the State Department. But, so far, it's just gossip."

"What the hell is *wrong* with our country?" Rachel asked.

"You know that answer already," Alex replied. "For now, let's just focus on capturing Simone's killers. Oh, one more thing, did Westbrook ask any more questions?"

"Yeah, he wanted to know if we captured either of the shooters at the Marriott. I told him what happened." Alex was silent while staring at Susan.

"What?" Susan asked.

"Maybe nothing. I need to check something with John Washington." Alex's cell phone rang and he answered.

"Alex, its Papa Ed. I'm calling from Ochsner Medical Center. Camille has been admitted to the hospital."

"Did she have an accident?" Alex asked, quickly putting his phone on speaker.

"No. She tried to kill herself." Papa Ed's voice broke up as he said it. Alex closed his eyes and shook his head. Rachel moved closer and rested her hand on his shoulder.

"That's terrible, Papa Ed. How is she?"

"Camille's in a private room now. She's awake, but extremely depressed. Can you and Rachel come over?"

"Of course. We'll leave the hotel now."

Alex reached out and hugged Rachel. After a few seconds, he said, "Susan, can you come with us?"

"Of course." They used Susan's car because she knew where the Ochsner Medical Center was located.

On the drive, Alex wondered, *Well, now, how else can things get worse.*

AT THE FRONT DESK OF THE MEDICAL CENTER, THE THREE OF THEM were told Camille's room number. Riding up in the elevator, Alex took deep breaths. He nervously tapped his foot on the floor and licked his lips. While he respected medical professionals who worked in hospitals, the sights and smells brought back unpleasant memories of his own emergency operation in Cairo, Egypt. The surgeon had told him afterward that he had died twice on the operating table. *How is that even possible?* he wondered.

Looking over at Rachel, he saw her watching him and knew she understood what he was thinking. She reached out and took his hand. Susan, on the other hand, focused her attention on the digital display indicating each floor as they passed. At last, the elevator doors opened, and they walked down the hall to Camille's room.

As they entered, Papa Ed released Camille's hand, stood, and turned to embrace each of them. Rachel was the first to move to the bedside and stared into Camille's eyes. Rachel reached out to touch her shoulder. "What can I do to help?"

Camille looked away and appeared lethargic. She shook her head as tears dripped from her eyes. "I guess I made a mess of it. I realize now what I did was selfish. I didn't consider Ed's feelings. But it seemed my world had come to an end when I lost Simone. It's so hard to move on with life."

"I know, Camille," Rachel said soothingly. "Seek out your friends for strength. They all love you, they love Papa Ed, and they loved Simone. You're not alone. You are part of a group who want to support and comfort you."

Camille reached out with both arms. Rachel leaned over and embraced her. They stayed that way for several seconds.

Papa Ed spoke to Alex and Susan. "Any news of Simone's killers?"

"Let's talk in the hallway." Alex led the three of them out of the room. "We have confirmation that Jules Baptiste, himself, killed Simone. Two of his hitmen tried to kill one of our undercover DS agents last night at her hotel. One is dead and we captured the other but he doesn't know much. Did you see the TV news about the State Department's Rewards for Justice offer?"

"No, I've been at the hospital for a while."

Alex described the fifty grand offer for information leading to the arrest of Baptiste or Toussaint.

"Okay, that's good."

"I hate to be indelicate," Alex said, "but do you think Camille will be all right?"

"I'm not a shrink," Papa Ed said, "but I believe she understands that she made a mistake. In any event, when she comes home, I've hidden the sedatives she used. But you know she's a doctor, so I presume she can get new ones if she's determined." He took out a handkerchief and blew his nose.

"What's your plan going forward?" Alex asked.

"I'm not sure. I've never been in this kind of situation. At least, not personally. I doubt Camille will want to see other people if everyone wants to discuss the tragedy of Simone's death. That's too much sadness for her," He was silent a moment, then asked, "Do you have any suggestions, Alex?"

"Maybe a change of scenery. I mean just take short trips for the two of you. A time to meditate, to get your feet on the ground again. Quick trips for stability and renewal."

"I'll consider it once Baptiste has been caught. While that

can't bring back Simone, at least it will allow us to know justice will be done."

They re-entered Camille's room and stayed for another fifteen minutes. On their way out, four friends of Camille and Papa Ed arrived, as well as one of her doctors.

Alex felt she was in good hands for the moment, but would this be enough for her in the long run?

Chapter 31

Witness Protection

The knock on the apartment door startled Moon Glow. She looked at Billy. "Who the fuck can *that* be?" she asked, her eyes darted to the door. Ever since they had talked to the cops, she was nervous about their safety.

"Stay here," he replied, and went to the apartment door's peephole. He saw two men in the hallway, both wearing loose fitting short sleeve shirts not tucked into their pants. Each wore blue jeans. "Who are you?" Billy called through the closed door.

Both pulled out Diplomatic Security Badges and held them up for his inspection. The guy on the left said, "I'm Special Agent Adam Benzinger; this is my partner Special Agent Rob Peters."

Billy turned back to Moon Glow. "It's the feds." Then, he cautiously opened the door. "Let me see those IDs, again."

Each ID included a picture of the agent's face, their signature, and the director's signature. The credentials also had information stating their right to carry firearms and their powers of arrest. It also affirmed that each held Top Secret security clearance.

"Okay, I guess you can come in," Billy said as he stepped aside, opening the door wider.

"Thank you. We're from Diplomatic Security in the U.S. State Department." Benzinger reached out and shook Billy's hand. He offered his hand to Moon Glow who shook it with less intensity than Billy. "We're handling the first shift for your protection. We'll be on duty until midnight, then two officers from NOPD will replace us. After that, two US Marshals will guard you. That will begin a repeat rotation, and so on."

Benzinger's smile was infectious. It made Billy and Moon Glow relax a little. "We've never seen armed agents before," she said. "You have guns, right?"

"Yes, we do," Rob Peters replied.

"I don't see any guns," Billy said.

Both men lifted their shirts so Billy and Moon Glow could see their pistols in holsters on their belts.

"Whoa!" Moon Glow blurted out. "Have you done this kind of thing before?"

"Yes," Adam replied. "We've protected the Secretary of State, U.S. ambassadors in dangerous countries, congressmen when they travel to high threat areas abroad, and even FBI agents conducting counter-terrorism investigations overseas. We've also protected visiting VIPs like foreign secretaries of other countries visiting America. We think we can handle protecting you."

No one said anything for a few seconds, then Adam said. "You'll probably want us to stay outside your apartment."

"No, no. You guys are interesting," Moon Glow said. "Come

on in. I want to learn more about what you do, and where you've traveled."

"Thanks," Benzinger said. "That will be helpful because we need to establish some ground rules about how we interact with you. We'll need your complete cooperation as we provide protection and we intend to be as unobtrusive as possible."

Moon Glow thought: *Unobtrusive . . . great word.* She loved it, a big word just like Billy used.

"Okay, let's sit in the living room. Can I get you anything to drink?" she asked. "We have some herbal tea, or Elderberry wine.

Neither Moon Glow nor Billy had ever traveled abroad or been around VIPs and were enthralled with the conversation. But after an hour, they had exhausted their list of questions for Special Agents Benzinger and Peters.

They were, however, more confident than before that they would be well protected. Since the apartment was too small for the agents to hang out in the living room without impinging on privacy, all decided it was best for them station themselves either down the hall in the small lobby by the elevator, or downstairs in the building's entrance area.

Hours later, the next shift of two NOPD officers arrived and were briefed by the departing DS agents. Two miles away, two more NOPD plainclothes officers had just arrived across the street from Moon Glow's tattoo parlor and sat at an outdoor table at the café.

When the U.S. Marshalls assumed their shift, new introductions had to be made and relationships established all over again. It was a manpower intensive operation that would be re-evaluated in a week to determine if protection could be scaled back at that time.

For the next two days, Billy Whiteman only had three visitors at the apartment, all connected to his computer graphics business. As for Moon Glow, there was a stream of clients inquiring about tattoos. From time to time, one of the protection officers would enter the parlor, sit in a chair, and pretend to be considering a tattoo.

This ain't bad, Moon Glow decided. *I kinda like this protection stuff.*

IN NEW ORLEANS EAST, JULES BAPTISTE TOSSED THE NEWSPAPER ON the table. "God *damn* it," he yelled. He had just seen the ad in the New Orleans Times-Picayune offering a $50,000 reward for tips leading to his arrest.

"What the *crap,* man!"

Claude Toussaint was sitting nearby in Baptiste's living room. He had already seen the newspaper and knew there was also a reward on his head. "Them Feds got big money, Jules. What we gonna do about it?"

Baptiste rubbed a left hand over his bald head and closed his eyes. "At least, we got to find out what they know," he said. "They wouldn't be spending that much money unless they knew for sure what we done."

"How about we ask our snitch? He'll know something."

"Good idea, Claude." He picked up his cell phone and typed a text message: *Your dry cleaning is ready for pickup.* Then he hit the send button and put his phone down on the table. After ten minutes he had a reply: *I will pick it up tonight at 6:00 pm.*

Baptiste smiled. According to their pre-arranged code, the actual time was plus two hours. That meant the meeting was set for 8:00 p.m. The location had been agreed upon at their last meeting. The location changed every time but was now set for the top floor of the multi-story parking lot of the Hilton hotel at the end of Poydras street, across from Harrah's Casino.

Baptiste thought to himself, *This guy better have some good info because I'm paying him a lot of money for inside shit.* In the past, the bribes had been worthwhile because Baptiste had been tipped off about the raid in Chalmette, and numerous other drug busts. He turned back to Claude.

"We're on for tonight at 8:00 pm. I want you there as backup. Take one of the boys with you."

"You got it Jules. We'll blast anyone who tries to interfere."

Jules leaned back in his chair to think. He'd been paying this inside source for three years. It had been so easy. The guy had screwed one of his hookers in Haiti when he had traveled there on business, caught the clap, and went to see a doctor who reported it to Baptiste. After that, the guy was blackmailed into cooperating. Well, it wasn't exactly *blackmail*, because once he was confronted, and saw some cash, the guy was eager to exchange more information.

Toussaint and his fellow shooter arrived on the Hilton garage's top floor at 7:30 p.m. to observe the area. They had backed their dark blue Cadillac Escalade into a space near the down ramp. Each carried a 9mm pistol in a holster and Toussaint also had a compact Mac-10 9mm, sub-machine gun.

There were plenty of parking spaces available when Baptiste arrived at 8:00 p.m. in his black BMW. He drove around the garage floor one time and spotted Toussaint before he saw the guy he was meeting. He parked next to the guy's old Buick. The guy got out of his car and joined Baptiste in the BMW. They shook hands.

"What do you want to talk about?" the guy asked. He was in his mid-fifties, solidly built, and looked like he was law enforcement, which he was.

"Did you see the reward offered in the paper on me?"

"I sure did."

"Did you know they were going to do that?"

"Yes. They even had a TV interview with a senior State Department man about the reward."

"You should have told me."

"I guess you're right. Sorry. How can I help?"

"What do they know? *How* do they know?"

"The Ardoin woman told Diplomatic Security about you before you killed her. Also, your guy, who was captured at the Marriott Hotel, snitched on you to NOPD."

"What's 'Diplomatic Security'?"

"They handle law enforcement, passport and visa fraud, and counterterrorism for the State Department. They're stationed all around the world in embassies and consulates. By the way, the woman you wanted killed at the Marriott was a Diplomatic Security agent working undercover."

"*Shit.* Why didn't you warn me? That's two for two," he said in a menacing tone of voice.

"I didn't know until *afterward.* One last thing, there were two witnesses who saw you kill that Ardoin girl. They identified you."

"You *got* to be kidding me."

"Nope." He reached into his pocket and pulled out an envelope with photos of Moon Glow and Billy Whiteman from their driver licenses that had been shared with him, and handed it over. Baptiste opened it and stared at the photos. "I don't know them."

"But they know who *you* are. At any rate, you can see where they live. They've talked to the cops and to Diplomatic Security and they're willing to testify against you."

"Is that right . . . well, I'll take care of it."

"Be careful, they're being protected."

"Okay, thanks." Baptiste opened his center console and pulled out a packet containing $10,000, handing it to the guy, who stuffed it into his pocket. They shook hands and Baptiste watched him get out of the car and leave. *I'm glad he needs the money,* Baptiste sneered.

Chapter 32

Heating Up

When Baptiste returned to his place in New Orleans East, he spoke with Toussaint and Destiny, his girlfriend. "We need to move to another location because Joseph Ricard might know where we're staying."

"Who's Ricard?" Destiny asked.

"Babe, he's one of the men I sent to the Marriott to do some work, and now he's being interrogated by the cops. So, staying here just became a little risky." Destiny was unfazed with the move.

"Where we going, boss?" Toussaint asked.

"Let's go to our place in Algiers. We haven't been there in a while. Call the boys. Have them meet us there."

Claude made the call. Then everyone packed their stuff, got into the cars, and drove off.

ONCE SETTLED INTO THE OLD HOUSE IN ALGIERS, BAPTISTE FELT comfortable. Although it needed a good cleaning inside, a coat of paint, and some incense to mask the musty odor, he felt it was safe, at least for now. Gathered around him were Toussaint and the six men Toussaint had wanted to meet them at the house. Destiny was out of the room taking a shower.

"I have a job for y'all," Baptiste said. "There are two witnesses I want killed."

No one batted an eye. They often did this kind of thing as ordered. The most recent time was when they erased the three ex-cons who tried to find Baptiste. That was about a week ago. They had dumped the bodies on a public street in Algiers, just like garbage waiting for pick up.

"The problem," Baptiste said, "is that they're being protected by cops. That's why I'll pay each of you a bonus. I don't want *anyone* left to identify us."

"When, boss?" A thug asked.

"Tomorrow night. Late. I think both witnesses will be home late in the evening."

"Where?"

Baptiste pulled out the sheet of paper showing photos of Moon Glow and Billy on each one's driver's license. "You can see their address here."

"How many cops?"

"No idea. Just deal with them."

The six nodded in agreement.

———

THE NEXT DAY DRAGGED ON FOR ALEX AND THE OTHERS WITH NO success finding Baptiste. The Rewards for Justice offer had produced a few calls, but nothing had panned out so far. They had just finished a very late meal of burgers and fries that a cop had brought to the police station when Susan Witt looked at her watch.

"It's getting close to midnight and our DS agents will be off in thirty minutes. I'd like to swing by the Esplanade Apartments to ensure everything is going fine with the protective detail."

"I'll go with you," Alex said.

"I'll join you," Sgt. John Washington joined in. "What about you guys?" Sitting across the conference table were Rachel and DS Special Agents Isabelle Lewis and Burt Warner.

"I'm beat," Rachel said. "I think I'll go back to the Royal Sonesta."

"I can go," Burt said as he yawned.

Isabelle smiled. "Burt, maybe you need some shut eye. I'll go since I haven't seen the Esplanade yet."

As agreed, Susan drove Alex and Isabelle, while Washington went in his own vehicle. Because the city had blocked off some streets to repair sewers, the group had to make a detour and were caught in traffic. They didn't arrive at the apartment until a little after midnight when the shift change had already occurred. Both DS agents going off duty had left for the hotel. They had been replaced by two NOPD cops in plainclothes. One was now positioned in the building lobby while the other was on the third floor elevator landing, down the long hall from Billy and Moon Glow's apartment.

Susan parked in a visitor's space in front of the building. They entered the lobby and saw the cop, patrolman Jake Hartman, talking with the night concierge. Looking over as they entered, Hartman recognized John Washington and introductions were made to the others.

"Everything's quiet," Hartman reported.

"Where's your partner?" Washington asked.

"He's upstairs."

Alex looked at the concierge. "Has anyone called or visited, asking about Janet Ross or Billy Whiteman's apartment?" he asked.

"Janet Ross? Who's that?"

"Moon Glow."

The concierge laughed. "Oh yeah. The girl with all the tats and colored hair. No, no one has called or visited."

"Okay. Well, if anyone does inquire about them, tell the cop on duty immediately. We're going upstairs," Washington said. Alex, Susan, and Isabelle followed him over to the elevators.

When the doors opened on Billy and Moon Glow's floor, Sgt. Lemoine was standing on the landing staring at the sliding doors, knees partially bent; he was alert and ready. His gun was holstered, but his hand was resting on it. Then, recognizing the four figures as non-threatening, he removed his hand from the holster and casually stood erect as badges were flashed at him.

"Do you take turns between this floor and the downstairs lobby?" Susan asked.

"Yeah, it helps with the long hours. The witnesses are pretty nice, though. In fact, they just spoke to me a few minutes ago, so I know they're up, if you want to talk to them."

"I'd like to do that," Alex said. "Do they seem calm under the circumstances?"

"Not bad."

Alex walked down the hall with the others, leaving Sgt. Lemoine by the elevator. He knocked on Billy and Moon Glow's door and she answered.

"Thanks for all the protection," she said. "It helps."

"You're welcome," Alex replied. "How's it working out?"

"Come on in and I'll tell you."

They all found seats in the small living room as Billy confirmed that the protection personnel had been polite. "No bother at all."

"Yeah . . . everything's been pretty normal. Maybe we don't even need so much protection . . . " Moon Glow had just finished saying when John Washington's radio squawked.

"It's Hartman in the lobby. . . we have trouble. Two vehicles, four attackers. I'm engaging!"

Chapter 33

Death on the Doorstep

Two beat up old gangbanger cars screeched to a halt in front of the Esplanade Apartments. Each driver stayed behind the wheel while four gunmen ran toward the front doors of the building, weapons drawn.

Hartman had just pressed his radio transmit button to contact Lemoine and Washington upstairs and call: "It's Hartman in the lobby, we have trouble, two vehicles, four attackers, I'm engaging!"

The concierge dove behind the reception counter, eyes bulging and mouth agape, while patrolman Hartman dropped his cell phone onto the reception desk and fumbled while getting his pistol out of the holster.

In his frenzy, he fired five shots through the glass doors at the approaching attackers. The entire glass crashed to the floor while he missed with all five shots. It was either because the glass doors disrupted the path of his bullets, or because, frankly, he was a poor shot. But the attackers weren't.

The four gunmen returned fire, wounding Hartman in the arm and stomach. His undercover ballistic vest stopped two more rounds aimed at his chest. Now Hartman lay on the ground, out of the fight, while the gunmen ran through the opening, crunching broken glass under their shoes. Two of the four jumped into the elevator while the other two ran up the stairwell.

Upstairs, Sgt. Lemoine heard the radio call from Hartman followed by gunfire. He radioed for emergency backup from NOPD Dispatch and drew his pistol, but there was nowhere in the hallway to seek cover. As the elevator doors opened, Lemoine fired, as did two of the attackers. His shots zipped between them, but their return fire with Mac-10 automatic sub-machine guns cut him down.

Inside the apartment, Susan heard the gunfire and grabbed Billy and Moon Glow, pulling them into the bedroom. "Lock the door and get on the floor under the bed!" she yelled at them.

She returned to the living room just as Alex, gun in hand, opened the front door to the apartment. He spotted two gunmen by the elevators about 60 feet away, and Sgt. Lemoine as he lay on the hallway floor, dead. Alex popped back inside.

"Two gunmen by the elevators," he said to Susan and Washington.

It took a moment for the attackers to know which way to go in the hallway, but then they sprinted toward the apartment. Alex knew most residents would have heard the gunfire, and someone would be calling the police by now. *Good. Time is vital,* he thought.

As the attackers got within thirty feet, Alex raced across the hallway into the small front door alcove of another apartment. He fired at the gangsters as they sprinted toward him.

Washington knelt on one knee in the doorway of Moon Glow and Billy's apartment and fired as well; Isabelle stood over him partially protected by the doorframe and emptied her magazine into the killers. The massive volume of ear-splitting gunfire sounded like open warfare as bullets flew in both directions and cordite powder filled the air with its caustic smell.

In under ten seconds, it was over. Both gunmen were dead and no one else was injured.

Alex popped out his old magazine, letting it drop to the floor, and slammed in a fresh magazine while walking toward the two dead on the floor. But just as he approached their bodies, two more attackers ran out of the stairwell into the hallway.

Pausing for a second to get their bearings was all it took. Alex fired two quick shots first at one, and three at the second. Then, he fired another two at the first man. Washington also unloaded on them. Both gangsters dropped dead barely ten feet from Alex. Not missing a beat, both he and Washington popped out their magazines and slid in new ones.

Susan came through the scrum, accompanied by Isabelle, and they slowly walked down the hall, arms partially extended with handguns pointing ahead of themselves, ready to kill any more attackers.

Alex's heart was racing, sweat dripped from his forehead, and he realized that adrenalin was making his hands shake a little as he stood in the hallway. He tried getting his breathing under control as he provided backup to Susan and Isabelle just as they cleared the top of the stairwell.

OUTSIDE THE BUILDING POLICE CARS RACED TO THE SCENE AND surrounded the two remaining gangbanger drivers. They surrendered quickly, rather than risk a gun battle to the death.

A quick talk with the shaken concierge confirmed to police that there had only been four armed attackers inside the building.

"I don't know what happened upstairs," he said. "There was just a lot of shooting."

Once the cops spoke to Sgt. Washington on the radio, they confirmed the upstairs floor had been secured. Ambulances arrived and paramedics treated Hartman before taking him to the hospital. Sgt. Lemoine's body was placed in a body bag and taken to the morgue.

It wasn't long before NOPD Captain Jim Wells arrived on the scene with more backup officers. He went upstairs to find out what had happened. After Sgt. Washington gave his brief report, Alex grabbed Wells' bicep and pulled him off to the side. His eyes bore into Wells' own as he leaned toward the Captain, nose to nose.

"Captain Wells, there has to be one *goddamn serious leak* in your department! Billy Whiteman and Janet Ross haven't been mentioned in *any* news articles, and they haven't testified in court, yet. Someone *had* to have told Baptiste who they were, and where to find them. That information could *only* have come from law enforcement."

Alex was furious and looked ready to unleash hell on someone. Wells stared wordlessly back at him as tension began to build. Its grip was broken only when a policeman guided Billy and Moon Glow out of the bedroom and told them to sit on a living sofa. Once they were out of earshot, Wells gave an answer.

"I agree with you, but where to start looking?"

"There are potentially a lot of suspects," Alex replied. "NOPD, DS, U.S. Marshals, maybe even the District Attorney's office. This won't be easy."

"Let's talk in the morning at my office," Wells suggested.

"Right." Alex was not pleased. He looked across the room and saw Susan had joined Billy and Moon Glow, trying to calm them down.

"*God damn it*!" Billy said, "you told us we'd be *safe!*"

"We said you'd be *protected*, and you *were*," Susan replied.

"But we were *attacked*, and almost *killed*," Moon Glow yelled back.

Alex stepped into the conversation. "One cop was killed protecting you, and another was wounded. One gave his *life* for you, and the other risked his. Do you *understand?*"

"I didn't know a cop was killed," Billy said, beginning to calm down. "I'm sorry.

"How did this happen?" Moon Glow asked.

"We don't know yet, but we're going to figure it out. In the meantime, we'll move you elsewhere."

"I have an idea," Susan said. She took out her cell phone and called Vern Bordelon at DEA.

"Hello," Vern answered gruffly. "If this is a telemarketer calling me at this hour, I'm going to find your *ass!*"

Susan laughed at Vern sounding like he'd been in a deep sleep. He was in no mood to chit-chat.

"It's Susan Witt in DS, Vern, sorry to call you after midnight, but I need a big favor and it's an emergency."

There was a pause on the line and Susan guessed Vern was trying to wake up. Finally, he cleared his throat. "Okay, Susan. How can I help?"

"We had two material witnesses attacked tonight by four gunmen, six, if you count the guys who stayed in their vehicles. There was a fatal shootout at the witness's apartment while under our protection. Someone leaked their identities and where they live."

"Damn! Are you alright? Are the witnesses injured?"

"They're okay, but shaken. One NOPD officer was killed and another wounded. The four attackers were killed by us. But now we need to move our witnesses immediately. Do you have a safe house we can use until we make new arrangements?"

"Sure. Meet me at my office in an hour; I'll take you there."

"Thanks, Vern. I owe you big time. See you in an hour."

Chapter 34

Safe House

Alex trusted Sgt. John Washington not only because he had fought alongside him at the Esplanade Apartments, but also in Chalmette. As for the rest of NOPD in general, Alex felt their loyalty remained to be confirmed.

"John, we're going to move Moon Glow and Billy. I don't want you to tell *anyone* in NOPD where the new location will be."

"I get it, Alex. Every organization has bad apples," Washington said. "But if I can't tell my chain of command, how can we provide bodyguards for the two witnesses?"

"Good point, but *damn it*, we could have lost the witnesses tonight! It also could have gotten more of us killed. I'm not saying that a leak *came* from NOPD, but *someone* in the loop is talking to Baptiste. I'm going to demand D.C. send more agents down here. Then maybe we can take over most of the work."

"Well, if you can swing that, it would help a lot."

Alex turned to Billy and Moon Glow. "Pack a bag and anything you'll need for a few days. We're moving you in thirty minutes to a temporary location. Leave your cell phones here."

"What?! No way! I need it," Billy replied.

"Me, too," Moon Glow chimed in.

"Pretend you're on vacation and not making, or taking, calls. We'll get you burner phones, and that's final. I can't risk having you tracked because of calls you make on your own phones. You can bring your computers. Now, get packed."

As Alex walked out into the hallway for privacy, he saw NOPD forensic teams collecting evidence from the shootout. He turned back into the apartment and went into the bathroom, closing the door behind him.

The phone in the DS Command Center in Arlington, Virginia, rang only two times before a special agent picked up. Alex asked to be patched through to Director Jim Riley. He looked at his watch and remembered that D.C. was an hour ahead of New Orleans. *Shit,* he said to himself, *Riley will be an unhappy camper at this hour.*

"Alex, why the late call? Is there a major problem?" Riley asked.

"There *is* a major problem, Jim. We have a leak, and I need additional manpower." He told Riley about the assassination attempt on the witnesses and his suspicion of a leak to Baptiste.

"Who can you trust in New Orleans?" Riley asked.

"I'm not sure about the local cops, other than Detective Washington," Alex said. "The U.S. Marshals are probably okay, but I have no way of confirming that. DEA should be good. And, of course, *our* guys are fine. But just to be on the safe side I'd like to keep NOPD away from the witnesses until we capture Baptiste. It would be easier if DS handled the entire protection operation with only Washington as liaison to the cops."

"Agreed. I'll send two Mobile Deployment teams to you tomorrow," Riley said.

"Much appreciated, Jim. Have them dress in civilian clothes. Anything else you need to know tonight?"

"I don't think so. I guess you'll want to stay in New Orleans until this is resolved, right?"

"Afraid so. Can you square this with our boss in London?" Alex asked.

"I'll take care of it. But plan on stopping in D.C. when this is over. We need to talk about your future."

"Future? Rachel and I have two more years to go in London."

"Let's talk; stay safe. Regards to Rachel and Susan." Riley said then hung up.

Alex stared at his cell phone. *What the hell did he mean, talking about my future? I'll bet Riley still wants me to be his deputy. No thanks. D.C. is a cesspool for back stabbing SOBs and cover-your-ass types of men and women. Not that embassy leadership is without integrity issues, but going back to D.C. at this time? Forget it.*

ALEX PUT BILLY AND MOON GLOW IN DETECTIVE WASHINGTON'S car. Susan drove her office suburban as a follow car with Alex and Isabelle inside. They met Vern Bordelon at his office in Metairie, then followed him to the safe house in a residential neighborhood, also in Metairie.

It was a normal looking one-story house with a small front yard, similar to most of the other houses on the street: Under

2,000 square feet, and built out of red brick with a short driveway in front.

As the group entered the house, Alex watched Billy and Moon Glow's reactions. He thought they were still pouting about having to leave their cell phones behind. He was right.

"I need to talk to my friends about what's going on," Billy said to Moon Glow. "How long do you think we'll be here?" he asked Susan.

"At this moment, I don't know. But we'll know soon," she answered.

"Here's an update," Alex said. "Tomorrow, Diplomatic Security is sending a couple of four-man protection teams of officers to guard you. These guys are military Special Forces-trained and they'll have automatic rifles as well as pistols. The teams are on 24-hour stand-by to deploy anywhere in the world, so coming to New Orleans is a short trip for them."

"Are they cops like you?" Moon Glow asked.

"Yes, they're all federal special agents from Diplomatic Security," Alex replied. "I suggest you try to sleep now; we can work things out in the morning." Billy and Moon Glow walked into a bedroom and closed the door.

"Thanks, Alex, for the emergency manpower," Washington said.

"It's the least we can do. I'm sorry about the officer who was killed. I hope the wounded guy will be okay." Then Alex turned to Vern Bordelon. "Vern, thanks for the safe house."

"No problem. You can use it for at least a few weeks," he replied.

"I'll keep you all updated on my wounded guy's condition," Washington said. "What's the plan for tonight?"

Alex looked at Susan already on her cell phone calling the

two agents who had gone off-shift at midnight. She told them what happened and said she would pick them up the next morning at 10:00 a.m. to bring them to the new safe house location, not being able to give its address on the call.

"*We* need to protect this place tonight," Susan said.

"I'll stay," Alex volunteered.

"Me, too," Isabelle said. "I'll call Burt Warner and read him into the situation."

"Okay guys," Bordelon said. "I'll leave you here and we can talk tomorrow." The DEA chief left as the others settled in for what was left of the night.

Alex looked at Washington. "I hate to ask this again, John, but can you *not* tell anyone in NOPD about this safe house? Until we figure this out, anyone in New Orleans who may know Baptiste, has to be treated with caution."

Washington's eyes got a little squinty, his jaw tightened. "I understand. But this won't go down well with my bosses."

"I realize that," Alex replied. "Do you have a better idea?"

"No, I don't."

"Maybe this will help. I'll talk with Captain Wells and take the heat off you."

"Thanks, Alex, that should solve the problem."

After Washington left the safe house, Susan also prepared to leave but first gave Alex two of her spare Sig-Sauer magazines; she knew he had fired a lot of rounds earlier at the Esplanade Apartments and probably needed them more than she did.

Alex called Rachel at the hotel, updated her on what was happening, then he and Isabelle made a pot of coffee to keep them alert until the next shift arrived.

After the intense shootout earlier this evening, we're both lucky to be alive, he thought. *At least manpower is on the way. The question is can we find Baptiste or Toussaint before it's too late?*

Chapter 35

View From the Top

Jim Riley sat at his kitchen table eating breakfast with Caroline, his wife. Last night's call from Alex worried him. Even though Alex had acted properly and with good judgment, Riley anticipated he would have to defend Alex's actions to a few detractors still in the Foreign Service who voiced displeasure over the fact that the State Department had a law enforcement component.

As its director, Riley was aware of those who had never wanted DS to be part of the State Department. Some of the longest serving FSOs especially disliked the fact that DS agents carried firearms. They also questioned why the State Department needed a law enforcement element in the first place, objecting to resources that flowed to DS instead of to the rest of the service.

With the passage of time, those detractors have become fewer and far between as terrorism and criminality has kept growing, he thought. *After Diplomatic Service had effectively handled some deadly incidents overseas, it quieted a few of the loudest voices.*

But now, the body count was building in New Orleans.

His appetite wasn't very strong this morning, mostly because he was worried about the safety of his agents there. Not only was he ultimately responsible for their actions, but because of his personal relationships with Alex Boyd and Susan Witt.

He and Caroline had lived in Alexandria, Virginia, for twenty-five years. They always rented out their brick colonial style house whenever they, themselves, served overseas. Alex and Rachel had been to their home many times and Riley considered them close friends and great professionals.

"What do you think will happen this morning, Jim?" Caroline asked.

"I believe that once I brief Secretary Martin about last night, the pressure will grow to examine our actions in New Orleans."

"Like an accountability review board?"

"Perhaps, or someone will want the Inspector General to look into it. Llewellyn Andrews, the new deputy secretary, is a former foreign service officer who left to become an advisor for an investment bank. I'm thinking that he may approach the issue with some old biases against our security."

"When he was appointed, you said he previously had a sterling career at State."

"Yes, I did. His career was unblemished, and he rose to be an ambassador before he left the service early to seek out big bucks on Wall Street. But it's one thing to have keen political reporting and analytical skills on narrow, specific issues, and quite another thing to lead a complex organization with diverse functions. I guess I'll find out where he stands this morning."

Riley finished his breakfast, kissed Caroline goodbye, and drove to the office.

AN HOUR LATER, RILEY SAT IN SECRETARY OF STATE CHARLES Martin's office waiting for others to arrive. One by one, they entered: Deputy Secretary Llewellyn Andrews, Legal Advisor Jameson Henry, and Director General of the Foreign Service, Ambassador Margaret Townsend. Everyone took a seat around the conference table.

Secretary Martin opened the meeting. "I know you are aware of the murder of Foreign Service Officer Simone Ardoin in New Orleans. I have asked DS Director Riley to provide an update on what has occurred since this tragic event. Jim, please begin."

Over the next ten minutes, Riley provided the update, then closed by saying, "We are dealing with a violent Haitian gang lord. His network is linked to local criminal elements in Louisiana. The investigation continues to be led by the New Orleans police department with cooperation from DS, DEA, and other federal and local law enforcement agencies in the city and surrounding parishes."

"Thank you, Jim." Martin said. "Any questions?"

"Can't we leave this matter entirely to the New Orleans Police Department?" Llewellyn Andrews asked. "After all, they have more manpower than DS in New Orleans. Why should we get involved?"

"They *do* have more manpower," Riley replied, "but they are stretched thin due to several factors. They are dealing with such issues as the Defund-The-Police Movement and in the present hostile political environment they are also having trouble recruiting. Presently, their number of uniformed officer positions stands at about thirty percent unfilled. Equally important, since it was a Foreign Service officer who was murdered, I believe the State Department has an obligation to assist in capturing the killer of Simone Ardoin."

Sitting across from the deputy secretary, Ambassador Townsend listened to the exchange, then cleared her throat to speak. Having served as ambassador in several minor posts, most recently Trinidad and Botswana, her portfolio included oversight of State Department internal issues such as human resources, entrance examinations, and assignments. She reported to the under-secretary for management.

"I note from Special Agent Boyd's reports there have been several shootouts. The number seems rather high."

"Yes, there have been a number of shootouts, all initiated by the Haitian gang lord," Riley replied. "The first one was an attack on the St. Bernard Parish Sheriff's SWAT team when they were searching for one of the gang's lieutenants. DS was on the ground in support of that operation. The second was the attack on the causeway. The third shootout occurred when they tried to kill an uncover DS officer in a New Orleans hotel, and the fourth was last night's assassination attempt on two witnesses to the murder of Simone Ardoin. I should add that we suspect three more recent murders may be linked to Ardoin's father, a prominent and respected lawyer in the city. It is believed the victims were searching for Ardoin's killer at the time they were executed by gang members."

"This doesn't look good," Ambassador Townsend replied. Riley wasn't sure how to take her comment.

What didn't look good? he wondered.

"Could you elaborate, Margaret?" Secretary Martin asked, also perplexed.

"All the victims were black and I presume that law enforcement and DS officers are all white. How many deaths and injuries have occurred? Seven, eight? This could be seen as *carnage.*"

Riley took a deep breath. *This is all more 'woke' bullshit from Ambassador Townsend. It isn't my first interaction with her on this type of matter and it probably won't be my last,* he thought before responding.

"First," Riley said, "the gang members who were killed are not victims; they are vicious murderers. When you think of a victim, think of Simone Ardoin. Yes, she was black, and from an established New Orleans Creole family. Second, over *half* the New Orleans police force are black. Third, two of our DS special agents involved are women. One other agent, Pete Fong, is an American of Chinese heritage, and another agent, Luis Torres, is an American of Mexican origin. Three of the four were involved in the first shootout in St. Bernard Parish. They put themselves in harm's way to solve the murder of Simone Ardoin. No one is concerned with her race. She deserves justice. Furthermore, we don't control the race of any gang members."

Ambassador Townsend's eyes grew cold and hard; her jaw tightened and she raised her chin defiantly. Her anger was palpable as it became clear she was displeased with her political narrative being exploded in front of the Secretary of State. The room was quiet for a moment.

"Maybe we need to get out in front of this issue," Llewelyn Andrews said.

"There *is* no issue," Secretary Martin exclaimed. "Let's not try to spin a problem that doesn't exist." Then he looked at

Riley. "Jim, thank you for your briefing. What else should we be doing on this case?"

"I just dispatched eight more special agents to New Orleans to help protect the two witnesses of Simone Ardoin's murder," he said. "You've already authorized a reward for tips leading to the arrest of the gang leader, Jules Baptiste. I hope this is successful. For now, I believe we are doing everything possible. As I've said before, the local police are in the lead and we are *supporting* their efforts. I should mention one more thing: DEA has provided an emergency safe house for the witnesses."

"Isn't the FBI involved as well?" Andrews asked.

"Their New Orleans office is part of a crime taskforce providing general assistance."

The room was silent for a moment. Still pissed off at Ambassador Townsend, Jim Riley took deep breaths to calm himself; he slowly relaxed his neck and shoulder muscles.

"Again, Jim, please give my appreciation to your agents in New Orleans," Secretary Martin said. "Let's hope we can resolve this quickly."

Returning to his office, Riley felt confident that Martin had his back. *If I was a betting man, I'd wager that Martin is beginning to regret his selection of Andrews and Townsend for high office.*

Chapter 36

The Tip

By mid-morning, Alex and Isabelle had been replaced at the DEA safe house by the two D.C. based special agents who had flown into New Orleans earlier. Special Agent Scott Fellows from the New Orleans office joined the two coming on duty. Alex and Isabelle returned to the Royal Sonesta Hotel and crashed.

First, however, Alex explained to Rachel everything that had occurred the previous evening. She grilled him on how close he had come to getting shot at the Esplanade Apartment. To her credit, once she had the details, she calmed down and accepted the situation. Then Rachel let him sleep for a few hours before calling room service for a late lunch.

At mid-afternoon, Susan picked up the eight Mobile Security Deployment agents at the airport. Several wore khaki cargo pants; others wore blue jeans. All had on hiking boots and some type of lightweight jacket or vest to cover their sidearms. After they collected their duffle bags and rifles they had shipped in the cargo hold, she led them to the safe house to start around-the-clock protection of Billy and Moon Glow. The two witnesses were now going to be protected by two groups of agents who were used to working as a team. All were well-armed with pistols and M-4 carbines, along with state-of-the art communications.

Alex called Captain Wells to soften the blow about DS not sharing the location of the safe house, but Wells wasn't too concerned. Perhaps his experience told him Alex was doing the right thing, or perhaps it was his thirty-year friendship with Papa Ed Ardoin that made him cooperative. Either way, he wanted to focus on finding Baptiste and Toussaint.

At 4:17 p.m., Pete Fong was manning the tip line in the DS office when a caller said he had information about Jules Baptiste.

"I seen your advertisement in the paper 'bout a reward for the whereabouts of Jules Baptiste," the caller said.

"Yes," replied Fong. "That's our ad. Do you have something you'd like to tell us?"

"How I know you'll give me the $50,000?"

"That's a good question Mister . . . what should I call you?"

"You can call me, 'Willie.'"

"Okay, Willie. Once you give us your information, we'll check it out, and if we capture Baptiste as a result of what you tell us, then you'll get paid."

"I want it up front."

"Sorry, Willie, it doesn't work like that. Would you pay someone to do work for you based on a promise? No, you wouldn't. You'd want to see the goods first. Well, so do we."

"I guess you be right. But how long will it take to get da money?"

"I can tell that you really want the reward. We'll pay as soon as the information pans out, meaning *after* Baptiste is arrested, or killed."

"I guess I can live with dat. What you want to know about me?"

"Your full name would be a good start."

"I can give you dat later. How can I give you the information?"

"Willie, you can give it to me now, or we can meet to talk about it."

"I want to meet."

"Excellent. Would you like to come to our office?"

"No way. Let's meet someplace safe."

"Okay. When and where?"

"Tomorrow night at Sammy's bar in Gentilly. You know where dat be?"

"No, but I can find it." Fong looked at his phone's display and saw the incoming number. "Can I reach you at the number you're using?"

"You can see dat?"

"Yes. I hope that's not a problem. You can trust us. You *do* want the reward, right?"

"Well, I guess it be okay. Yeah, you can call me at this number."

"Alright, Willie. I'll call you back later and we can confirm the time for the meeting." After they hung up, Fong walked into Susan Witt's office for further guidance.

———

JUST AFTER SUSAN SPOKE WITH PETE FONG, HER CELL PHONE RANG. It was Vern Bordelon from DEA. "Hey Susan, how is it going with your two friends?"

"It's going great, Vern. I heard they like your place very much. I appreciate your help last night."

"Good. Listen, I just finished a meeting downtown and thought I'd stop by your office. Are you there now?"

"I am. I'd also like to pick your brain on something new that has just come up."

"Okay, I'll see you in a few minutes."

Susan was about to dial Alex's cell phone when he and Rachel walked into her office at that precise moment. "Good timing," Susan said. "Did you get any sleep?"

"Yeah, after I got back from the safe house, I managed to grab a few hours."

"How are you doing, Rachel?" Susan asked.

"Okay, but I'd like to contribute more."

"I appreciate that. But this is a law enforcement matter now, so your political expertise is not part of the solution. Besides, you don't even carry a gun."

Alex knew Susan was trying to lighten the conversation. He briefly thought about joking that Rachel's thighs were deadly weapons but figured it wouldn't be the smartest thing to say in this situation. Instead, he simply said, "She's right, Rachel, just having your advice is *very* helpful."

Susan asked Fong to explain the latest call on the tip line. Everyone knew the caller could be a scam artist, but they were obligated to pursue it. For the next ten minutes, they sat around drinking coffee and discussing possibilities. Fong and Rachel even had a short conversation in Chinese, although it was clear that Fong's linguistic skills did not match Rachel's, a little surprising given his heritage.

Then Vern Bordelon arrived. He had not met Fong. Susan

made introductions and after some chit chat, Susan came to the point.

"Vern, the caller wants to meet in a bar in Gentilly. That's not a great part of town, and frankly, I don't know that area very well. What about you?"

"We've done a number of drug raids there. Nothing major, but it's active. What's the name of the bar where this guy wants to meet?"

"It's called Sammy's," Fong said.

"I've heard of it," Vern said. "In my position, I don't work the streets, but I've got guys who do. Let me make a call." He was directed to a spare office cubicle, made a call, and spoke to some of his agents. Returning to the group, he reported his news.

"I have an agent who's worked undercover there several times. He said it's a hangout for low level drug dealers, an occasional pimp, and some wanna-be gang punks. He said he'd be glad to work with one of your DS agents to hook up with this caller. But there's a problem."

"What's that," Alex asked.

"I don't see anyone here who would fit in."

"Ah, you're saying the agent should be an African American," Alex replied.

"Yeah. My guy has worked the bar before, so *he'll* fit in, and he's known to some by his cover name."

"How about if he brings the guy *out* of the bar and drives him a short distance to meet with us?"

"He could. By the way, this operation will blow his cover. But you're in luck."

"Really? Why is that?" Alex asked.

"Because he's done working the streets in New Orleans. He's

going to transfer out next week to our Nashville office as a supervisor."

"Lucky us," Alex smiled.

"I have to call the tipster back with a time for the meeting," Pete Fong interrupted. "I suggest a late meeting, say about 11:00 p.m. That way the bar will be crowded, and it will be easier to leave without others noticing."

"Okay, how will the caller know who to approach?" Fong asked.

"Tell him our guy will be wearing a baseball cap with a Miami Dolphins logo on it. Plus that our guy is 6'3", very dark skinned, and muscular."

"Okay." Fong said, then walked into a separate office, closed the door, called Willie and set up the meeting.

Would this meeting be useful or bullshit? They were about to find out.

Chapter 37

Undercover

The fifty-year-old bar was still in business after hurricane Katrina because it was a brick structure on a slightly elevated piece of ground. The surrounding businesses and homes had been damaged years before by the water and wind of Hurricane Katrina. New construction, however, was visible on several nearby lots. There were two working pole-mounted streets lights on the block; all other lights had been shot out by vandals. The streets had potholes, while other sections of the road had buckled up, much like other parts of the city, all of which pre-dated Katrina. It wasn't a good part of town.

Hank Deavers, DEA undercover agent, sat in the bar's parking lot in his ten-year-old office SUV which he used for undercover work. With an assortment of dents and patches of rust, it was perfect for this type of work. Even though it was drizzling outside, he had the window cracked open because he was smoking a cigarette, one way he handled stress. Deavers realized he was nervous because, with his upcoming transfer, his mind had already adjusted to his new supervisory job in Nashville. Jumping back into street work at the last minute had jarred his mind back into the dangers of undercover work. He looked at his cheap watch. *It's time,* he thought.

He reached over to the passenger seat and grabbed his Miami Dolphins baseball cap, put it on, and got out of the car. He wore faded blue jeans and an untucked dark green polo shirt. His Sig-Sauer P365 handgun with ten rounds of ammunition was secured in an appendix-carry holster under the front of the shirt. In his right ear, he wore a concealed communications earpiece that also allowed him to transmit. Ready, he walked into the bar.

Alex Boyd and Isabelle Lewis were waiting in a rental car two blocks away. It had been decided that a male and female agent sitting in a vehicle would be less suspicious than two guys sitting together. If they drew unwanted attention, they could always pretend to be making out as part of their cover.. Each carried a Glock 19 9mm pistol. One block further on, two DEA agents were waiting in their vehicle. Also armed, they were prepared to help Hank Deavers in an emergency.

Deavers eyes adjusted to the low light in the bar and smoke-filled air, some from cigarettes, some from weed. He scanned the clientele as he walked over to grab a vacant stool at the long wooden bar. Deavers recognized a few faces from his prior undercover work. A few of them nodded as he passed by, but for the most part, he was ignored.

"I'll have a beer, whatever you've got on tap," he said to the barman. He'd take an occasional sip but would avoid drinking more than that. He felt a tap on his shoulder; when he turned, he saw a small-time thief he had met before.

"Hey, Randy, good to see you again," Deavers said. They fist-bumped.

"Yeah, man, I haven't seen you around lately."

"I know. I was out of town doing some construction in Gulfport," Deavers replied.

"Okay; nice to have you back in town."

"Good to be back."

Shit, the last thing I want is to be tied down with Randy. Deavers felt a tinge of nausea. Suddenly the room felt too warm. His eyes looked for the bar's emergency exit just in case he needed to make a quick getaway. He needed to meet "Willie" and that wasn't going to happen as long as he carried on this conversation. Looking around the room, he saw a guy watching him.

"Listen, Randy. I need to take a piss. It's been good seeing you, again. Let's talk later."

"Okay, man."

Deavers got up and walked toward the bathroom. He exchanged a glance with his mystery watcher. About twenty seconds after entering the men's room, the mystery guy came in. Deavers was ready to attack, if need be, and hoped he hadn't fallen into a trap.

"What's your name?" Deavers asked. He could barely keep his voice steady as his breathing became labored and sweat formed on his forehead.

"Willie. Are you Joe?"

"Yeah, I'm Joe. I'm with the people who want to speak with you."

"Not here."

"*Damn right*, not here. First, confirm to me who you want to talk about?"

"Baptiste," Willie replied.

"Okay, that's good. Willie, I'm going to leave the bar. Follow me a minute later. Turn left out of the front door; you'll see me. I'm going to walk another two blocks to a parked car. Got it?"

"Okay."

Deavers left and waited outside. Willie came out and followed him until he got to the parked vehicle. He opened the back door and Willie slid inside, followed by Deavers. Alex and Isabelle were already seated in front.

Willie looked nervous. "You guys the Feds with the ad in the paper?"

"We sure are," Alex replied. "You're safe with us, Willie. Now tell us what you know about Baptiste." In the side mirror, Alex saw the DEA vehicle pull up behind them and flash its lights. He returned his attention to Willie.

"Baptiste has this fishing camp right off da Pearl River on a side creek. It ain't big. I been there . . . maybe twice. But he goes there. He likes to fish."

Alex reached into the center console, rummaged through several maps, and pulled out a map of the river area, opened it, and asked Willie to show him on the map where the camp was sited.

"Man, I can't read no map. But I can *tell* ya' where it's at."

"Okay, tell me. I'm all ears," Deavers replied.

"You know where the dock is for tourist boats?"

"Yeah, I do."

"Well, you get on da' river and head right for about ten minutes."

"How fast are you going?" Alex asked.

"I don't know, man. We just go pretty quick. Right after you pass an old destroyed camp house on the left, you look for the creek on the right. You can see Baptiste's fishing camp right away."

"Can you be more specific?" Deavers said. "There are several destroyed camps on the Pearl River."

Willie thought for a moment. "Yeah, when you're at the creek, you also see the raised I-10 highway in the distance. That how I know when to turn."

Deavers gave Alex and Isabelle a thumbs up, but Alex wanted more info. "What does the camp look like from the outside?"

"Whadda ya' mean?" Willie replied. "It look like a camp."

"Is there a porch or a raised deck?" Alex asked.

"Yeah, a raised deck. And a small satellite dish on the roof."

"What about a boat dock?"

"There be a boat dock. You climb a ladder to reach da porch."

Then Deavers asked, "Can you get to the camp by road?"

"I don't think so. I ain't never seen no road."

"Anything else?" Deavers asked everyone.

"Do you know if he's there now?" Isabelle asked.

"I don't know. But he goes there every few weeks to fish. Sometimes, he just hides out there, if he be in trouble."

"Okay, Willie," Alex said. "You've been a big help. If we catch him there, you'll get the reward. We'll call you."

"Yeah, I can sure use it, man." Willie slithered out of the car.

Alex looked at the others. "If there's a satellite dish, Baptiste might be on record as having purchased it. And if so, maybe the cable company will tell us when he uses their service. We should also check property records; although, I doubt he'll be listed as the buyer."

"Good idea," Deavers said. "Sorry, but I need to pack out for

Nashville, so I'll be tied up for a few days. I'll pass on your ideas."

"You've been a great help. Thank you, Hank,"

"Glad I could help." Deavers walked back to the bar's parking lot and drove off in his vehicle.

Alex was lost in thought. *If he's not already there, how can we force Baptiste to visit his camp?*

Chapter 38

Next Moves

Claude Toussaint sat in the Algiers safe house and counted on his fingers. "We've lost a lot of men," he said. "I think around ten. Maybe we need some guys from Miami." He meant gang members who controlled the Miami area known as "Little Haiti."

"I know," Jules Baptiste replied. "I've thought about that. But this operation is going in the wrong direction. Maybe it's time to shut it down for a while, and get out of town."

Toussaint didn't like the idea. He was born and raised in New Orleans, and didn't want to follow Baptiste to some other city. "If you shut it down, where you go?" he asked.

"I haven't decided. Besides, it wouldn't be permanent. We could go to Miami until it cools down. Or, maybe Port-au-Prince."

"I don't speak Haitian Creole."

Baptiste shrugged his shoulders, "I know. Guess that *would* be a problem."

If Baptiste goes to Haiti, Toussaint **thought,** *I'm making other plans.* Not only didn't he speak Haitian Creole, he didn't speak *any* foreign language. Even his ability to read English was limited because he had dropped out of school at age fifteen.

He'd been pushed from one grade to the next every year without grasping the fundamentals of each level of education. If it hadn't been for the abysmal standards of the New Orleans public school system at the time, he would normally have been held back year after year. He was never going to graduate, so he left.

Where Toussaint *did* excel was in street smarts. He was good at detecting liars. He had a sixth sense when something didn't appear right, such as people behaving out-of-character. While he had been arrested several times, his intuition had saved him from even more arrests. As for surviving the mean streets of New Orleans East at night, he was like a Ph.D. grad. His street smarts had saved his life on several occasions.

Sitting in NOPD headquarters in the Central Business District, Alex looked at his watch. It was 11:00 a.m. and a small group had assembled in a conference room at the chief's office to discuss the noontime press briefing on the shootout at the Esplanade Apartment building. Present were representatives from DEA, the U.S. Marshal's Service, and a handful of NOPD officials. Susan Witt and Rachel were with him.

"Are the hitmen's drivers cooperating?" the chief of police asked, "You know, the ones captured at the Esplanade."

Sgt. John Washington answered, "No, they're not, even

though they've been told they'll be charged with 'accessory to murder.' They've refused to tell us anything."

"Have these guys done time before?" the chief asked.

"Yes, sir," replied Washington. "They have long rap sheets."

"Okay, well, we need to find a way to smoke out Baptiste," Captain Wells spoke up. "Maybe the DA's office can offer the drivers a deal in exchange for information."

"Also talk to the U.S. Attorney's office," Alex said. "Murder of a federally commissioned officer, in this case, Simone Ardoin, is also a federal crime."

"We *should* have invited a rep from the US Attorney's office," the NOPD public relations guy said.

"Speaking of reps, where's the FBI agent-in-charge? the chief asked.

"We invited Bill Westbrook," Captain Wells replied. "I'm surprised he's not here."

Tired of the conversation non-starters, Susan Witt said, "Can we get back to smoking out Baptiste? Right now, we don't know *where* he's hiding, but we do have a solid lead on his fishing camp on the Pearl River. He may be there, but if he isn't, how can we make him panic and go to the camp?"

"Good question," Wells replied.

"I have an idea," Rachel said. Her question drew attention to her presence.

"Excuse me," the chief spoke. "*Who* are you?"

"I'm Rachel Smith with the U.S. State Department. Simone Ardoin worked for me in Washington D.C. We were invited to New Orleans by Miss Ardoin. My expertise is in both press and political affairs."

"Okay, Miss Smith, please speak your mind," the chief replied.

"Thank you. Although the two drivers under arrest have refused to speak, Baptiste won't know that. At the noon press conference, what if NOPD *implies* that the two are cooperating? I believe we can assume the two know where Baptiste is located. My further assumption is that Baptiste is not *yet* at his fishing camp. But once he thinks the drivers *are* talking, he may decide to move to a safer place."

"I don't like lying to the press," the NOPD press officer said. "In the future they won't trust us."

"So, don't *lie*," Rachel replied. "Merely demonstrate optimism that your interrogations will result in *complete* and *total* cooperation. That's enough to infer you've already gotten some level of cooperation."

"I suppose that's okay," the NOPD press officer replied.

The chief noticed most people in the room nodding in agreement. "Is everyone okay with this strategy?" he asked. No one objected.

"Then the next step will be to surveil the fishing camp," Alex said.

"Agreed again," the chief replied. "Let's discuss how later."

There was a knock on the conference room door. The chief's secretary leaned into the room. "Special Agent Bill Westbrook is here." Westbrook entered and took a seat.

"Sorry I'm late. I had an important call from D.C. that I had to take."

"Glad you came, Bill," the chief replied. "Although we've almost wrapped this up, we're about to announce at the noon press conference that both drivers under arrest will cooperate."

Again, there was a knock on the door and the chief's secretary entered. "Chief, the mayor would like you to call him *immediately*."

"Thank you," he replied. "Well, everyone, I think we've achieved a lot this morning," he said to the group as he rose to leave. "I appreciate all of you attending." Then, as the chief left the room, everyone figured the meeting was over.

Bill Westbrook walked over to Alex and Rachel. "Are you free for lunch? It's not often I get downtown for a meal."

"Sure, Bill. Where do you have in mind?"

"One of my favorite spots is Mandina's up on Canal Street, not far from here."

"Sounds good, let's go."

Baptiste looked at his watch and saw it was noon. "Claude, turn on the TV, I want to catch the news." Claude found the remote, pressed the button and tuned to the correct channel. The lead story was a follow-up on the shootout at the Esplanade Apartment building a few days before.

"We seen this news already," Claude said.

"*Quiet*, they could have more info."

". . . both surviving hitmen are likely to fully cooperate with police," the NOPD press spokesman just finished saying. Baptiste was glued to the screen, jaw clenched, neck muscles strained.

"Those *fucking bastards!*" he yelled. "I've taken care of them for *years* and now they're *turning* on me."

"I'm surprised they'll talk," Toussaint said. "I figured they be tougher than that."

Baptiste rubbed his shaved head with both hands and looked down at the floor for a moment. *"Shit!* We just moved here. But we better get out of town. Those guys know about this Algiers safe house."

"To where?" Toussaint asked.

"Let me think."

Chapter 39

A Chat With the FBI

Susan drove Alex and Rachel to Mandina's and parked the Suburban on the street. "Rach, I was impressed with your suggestion to publicly imply the hitmen would cooperate. It was well received by the group," Alex said as they exited the vehicle.

"Thanks. It's what I do for a living. I mean, having big thoughts and thinking up great ideas." She smiled at him.

"Okay, let's not get carried away," he replied.

"Not everyone needs a gun to be effective and dangerous," Rachel replied.

"You're right, Rach," Alex replied. "You have a variety of weapons in your repertoire."

"I think I should meet you guys inside the restaurant," Susan said, "before this discussion gets any hotter."

"No, no. You can walk with us," Rachel said with a grin. "I'm just glad that the big man here is aware of my superior range of skills."

Alex laughed as Susan walked on ahead of them. He squeezed Rachel's ass. She turned and whispered in Alex's ear, "At least you didn't make a crude remark about my muscular legs."

"Who, me? I'd never say anything like that. After all, I fell in love with your personality and intellect. I didn't even *notice* your legs when we first met."

"Oh yeah, so it was just a coincidence back then when you kept feeling-up my thighs? In fact, you still do."

"I plead the fifth." They both chuckled. After they were seated, Bill Westbrook joined them a few minutes later at their table.

"Sounds like I didn't miss much at the meeting," Westbrook said.

"We were almost done when you arrived," Susan said.

"Bill, if you don't mind my asking, where else have you been assigned?" Alex asked.

"A lot of places, actually, like the field offices in D.C., Cleveland, Chicago, and Miami."

"Ever serve overseas?"

"Yeah, in the Miami field office, we covered the Caribbean. I had a few temporary gigs in the islands."

"Ah, paradise, palm trees, beaches, and rum," Alex replied.

"There was some of that. But it wasn't all paradise. Jamaica had serious gang violence, and Haiti was a dump. What about you and Rachel, where have you served?"

"I was in Argentina and Tunisia before I met Rachel in Pakistan. Then we served together in Italy, now in the UK."

Rachel added, "Before Pakistan, I served in Hong Kong and Beijing. And just briefly in Italy."

"Actually, that sounds fascinating," Bill replied.

"I have another question, Bill," Alex said. "You mentioned when we began this murder investigation that the FBI was comfortable with NOPD and DS handling matters. Has there been any pressure from headquarters for you to take over the case?"

"We've talked about it. If you capture Baptiste, I'll discuss federal charges with the U.S. Attorney's office, but so far, we're content with the status of the investigation."

Alex shot a quick glance at Susan, who briefly raised her eyebrows. He surmised she was surprised over the lack of FBI direct involvement.

"Okay, well, let's order," Alex said.

EVENTUALLY, THE WAITRESS BROUGHT THEIR ORDERS WHICH WAS Italian sausage with anise and spaghetti for Alex. Rachel ordered soft shell crab with fries, Bill had an oyster po-boy, and Susan ate a muffaletta.

"I've noticed there are a lot of Italian restaurants in the city," Alex said. "This is our first time here. I hadn't realized that."

"Oh, gosh, yes," Bill replied. "Starting around the 1890's, Sicilians flooded into New Orleans. They operated warehouses in the French Quarter where they mostly lived until they moved into the suburbs; many, however, still kept their businesses in the Quarter. There are loads of Sicilian-based restaurants and food stores in New Orleans. Think of Central Grocery, Liuzza's, and even Commander's Palace. They all can trace their heritage back to Sicilian immigrants. The Tourist Board created the myth surrounding a dominant *French* heritage of the city, but, in fact, the city is a true mix of cultures."

"I know in the past there was a strong Sicilian mafia presence here," Alex said.

"Yeah, that's true. The FBI office has always been busy with mafia cases. But there is a lot more organized crime today than just with the mafia."

After finishing their meal of New Orleans' basic food groups, they parted ways. It had been a pleasant gathering.

BACK AT THE DS OFFICE, RACHEL ASKED, "I SAW YOU AND SUSAN exchange a glance at the lunch table. What's up?"

"My, my, what sharp little eyes you have," Alex said.

"Enough games. I mean it, what's up?"

"We think it's strange the FBI doesn't appear ready to take the lead in the murder of a federally commissioned officer," Susan replied.

"Why is that?" Rachel asked.

"I'm not sure. What about you, Alex?"

Alex didn't answer the question for a moment. Then he said, "Did you notice Westbrook had a temporary assignment in Haiti?"

"I sure did," Susan said.

"Really?" Rachel commented. "I didn't pick up on that. Are you thinking there's a link to Simone's case?" she asked.

"I'm saying we need to find out if there *is* a link." Alex replied.

"I'm going to call the RSO in Port-au-Prince and see what he might know," Susan said. "There's more to discover here."

Chapter 40

Turning Over Stones

Back in her office, Susan looked up the number for the RSO's secure voice landline and used her encrypted secure telephone to call him. Alex and Rachel sat across from her.

"RSO. Port-au-Prince. Tommy Rogers speaking."

"Hey, Tommy, it's Susan Witt in New Orleans. Alex Boyd is with me, so is Rachel Smith, who was Simone Ardoin's former boss."

"Oh hi, Susan, Alex, Rachel. Have you guys captured Baptiste yet?"

"No, afraid not; I'm calling on the secure voice because I have a sensitive question for you.

"How can I help?"

"We spoke over lunch with the agent-in-charge of the New Orleans FBI office, Bill Westbrook. He mentioned he had temporarily served in Haiti while he had been assigned to the

Miami field office. I'm not sure *when* this happened. Have you ever heard of him?"

"The name is familiar, but I don't think in the two years I've been here we've met. Maybe I saw his name on an old investigative report. Hold on a minute while I dig into my files."

The secure phone didn't have a speaker function, so while Susan waited, she told Alex and Rachel what Tommy Rogers had said. Their wait turned into ten minutes.

He came back on the phone with a little pep in his voice. "Okay, I found something. Westbrook was here for about two months, but that was three years ago. He was part of a team doing liaison with the Haitian police over a narcotics and human smuggling ring."

"Anything more in detail about Westbrook?"

"Not in this file. It's just a standard report. Why? Do you have suspicions about him?"

"Let's just say we're being cautious. Our murder case is about two weeks old, and he's only just now casually mentioning that he had been in Haiti. Also, the FBI hasn't exercised its right to take over the case. We think that's a little odd. Plus, we believe someone in law enforcement is leaking information to Baptiste."

"Okay, I see your concern."

"Is there anything you can do to dig deeper into who may have links in New Orleans to Baptiste?"

"I'll try to find out something."

"All right, thanks, Tommy. Do what you can. Let's stay in touch." Susan hung up and recapped the conversation for Alex and Rachel.

"As I recall," Alex said, "At today's meeting with the Chief of NOPD, Westbrook didn't arrive until *after* we talked about the fishing camp."

Susan thought for a moment, "I'm not sure."

"I'm sure," Rachel said. "I recall the conversation had already moved on when he arrived. Are you thinking if Westbrook is dirty, he wouldn't know we're aware of the fishing camp?"

"That's right," Alex replied. "You know Rach, your intuition and logic are *so* good, you should change your job in the Foreign Service and become a DS special agent."

"No way, because then I'd be *under* you instead of a co-equal."

"That's funny, you didn't complain about that the other night."

Susan saw both of them smile. "Hey, guys. Remember me? I can *hear* you. Let's stick to discussing the investigation."

"Sorry," Rachel said. "But my husband is showing his adolescent humor again."

"How about we explore with Vern Bordelon any possible links between law enforcement, and Baptiste?" Susan suggested.

"Good idea," Alex replied. "Let's give him a call."

Susan called Bordelon at his DEA office, but he was out at a meeting, so she left a message. She looked at Alex. "What now?"

"I just remembered we never decided which unit would surveil the fishing camp," he said.

"You're right! NOPD has a marine patrol unit, but their jurisdiction may not extend to the Pearl River."

"If not, which Parish has jurisdiction?"

"I guess it would be St. Tammany Parish. We could speak to Sheriff Billy Landry and ask his guys to do it. You remember Sheriff Landry from when we went across Lake Pontchartrain, right?"

"Yeah, he was a nice guy and seemed competent," Alex said.

"Let's give him a call and set up an appointment. I don't want to discuss this on an unsecure line," Susan said. "After that, I'm going to drive by the Metairie safe house and see how protection is going for Billy and Moon Glow."

"I'd like to come along," Alex said.

"Count me in as well," Rachel declared.

On her call to Sheriff Landry, Susan was surprised to learn that he would be in New Orleans for a meeting early the next morning. "I can see you right after that," he said. They set a time, and Susan asked if he could also bring the head of his marine patrol unit with him.

"I can and I will," he agreed.

AS THE THREE OF THEM DROVE TO METAIRIE TO CHECK ON BILLY and Moon Glow, Susan got an unexpected call on her mobile from the DS career manager, who handled assignments. Despite his official title, most agents called him the "career *mangler*." She put the call on speaker so she could drive without holding the phone, but also so the Alex and Rachel could hear.

"Susan, I'm calling about where you'd like to go after your New Orleans assignment."

"I'd like to be an RSO overseas."

"We were thinking the same thing."

"Great, send me a list of options."

"I think we've moved beyond that stage."

"Who's *we*?"

"Just the people in the assignment's office."

"All right. In that case, where do you have in mind to send me?"

"How does Costa Rica sound?"

Susan looked at Alex, who shook his head negatively.

"Can I get back to you? I'm driving right now."

"Sure, let us know this week. We'd need to first assign you to twenty weeks of Spanish language training.

"Cool, thanks for calling. I appreciate the opportunity." She hung up and looked at Alex. "What's wrong with Costa Rica? A lot of Americans retire there."

He smiled. "Why do you think the place has appeal for retirees?"

"*Ahhh*, I get it. It's safe."

"Exactly. It's *so* safe that you'd be bored out of your mind as an RSO. I recommend going to a more challenging embassy, or perhaps a country that's wonderful to live in."

"I don't think I have a choice."

"Let me call our old boss from Islamabad and see what he thinks. I believe you've done a terrific job here in New Orleans; it should be rewarded."

"Thanks. Do you think he'd get involved?"

"As the Director of DS, Jim Riley has the final say on *all* assignments. He likes to reward excellence."

Susan's grin spread across her face.

Rachel was sitting in the back seat. She reached forward and placed her hand on his shoulder. "You're a good man, Alex."

Chapter 41

Witnesses and Assignments

A lex called Director Riley in Washington, DC., while Susan and Rachel were listening to his call.

"Alex! How's it going in the 'Big Easy?'"

"Well, not so 'easy,' Jim, but we're working with the local cops and DEA to make progress."

"Glad to hear it. What's up?"

"First, thanks for sending the MSD teams to New Orleans. Knowing the witnesses are protected means we can focus on the investigation. But there is one other thing I'd appreciate your help with."

"Tell me."

"Susan got a call earlier today from the DS career manager and he told her they would like to send her to Costa Rica as the RSO for her next assignment."

"Hmm."

"Sounds like you understand, Jim. Although Costa Rica is pleasant, it's not a busy place. Susan can handle a post far more demanding. She's already managing a medium-sized office here with three other agents, and she handles liaison with the rest of the law enforcement community. She's demonstrated skill and guts in confronting threats.

"If there isn't a good match from a threat perspective for her next assignment, could she, at least, be assigned to a cultural post to balance out her time in Pakistan and as an agent-in-charge of the New Orleans office?"

"I agree. Let me look at future openings and get back to you, or Susan."

"That would be great, Jim." Alex paused as Susan gave him a double thumbs up. "One other thing, has the FBI been talking to you about our case?"

"Not to me. Maybe they've spoken to Nat, our chief of investigations here at DS, but he hasn't mentioned anything. Why do you ask?"

"The local agent-in-charge just seems a little passive on the case. His name is Bill Westbrook. Ever heard of him?"

"Nope."

"Okay. That's all I've got. Thanks for looking into Susan's next assignment."

———

LATER, AFTER ARRIVING AT THE DEA METAIRIE SAFE HOUSE, SUSAN parked down the street. It looked like any other house on the block, which was the idea, and why it was secure. She, Alex, and Rachel walked to the front door; it was opened by Ray, one of the four DS special agents on duty. Susan had already met all four of the agents, but Alex and Rachel had not, so introductions were made.

"How long have you guys been in Mobile Security Deployment?" Alex asked.

"Two of us have been there for three years; Jonas and Fred for only one," Ray replied.

"Where have you deployed?"

"We just got back from Cairo two weeks ago; before that, we were in Kabul and Baghdad."

Alex was satisfied the team had been to enough high threat posts to know their business. While they were talking Billy Whiteman and Moon Glow came out of the kitchen.

"How's it going?" Susan asked.

"Not bad," Billy replied. "I've been able to work remotely on my computer."

"I called the tattoo parlor and told them I was sick and needed a few days off," Moon Glow said.

Susan turned to one of the agents and asked, "Were you able to find the local grocery store?"

"Yeah, one of us went to Dorignacs on Veterans Blvd. They had everything we needed."

"How's the security here?" Alex asked.

Ray took the question. "All the windows and doors have hard-wire alarms, and there are four cameras outside that we monitor over here." He pointed to a computer screen in the corner of the living room. There's also an emergency alarm button next to the computer. DEA told us it will wake up the entire block."

Alex saw each of the four agents wearing their pistol, a Sig-Sauer 9mm. Each had extra magazines on his belt. Their M-4 carbines were visible in several locations in either the living or dining rooms. He liked what he saw.

All these MSD agents could move on to being an RSO once their

279

tour of duty in MSD is completed., he thought. For DS, this meant an increasing number of agents around the world who had gotten MSD special training and knowledge would help them protect U.S. embassy personnel around the globe. *That'll be useful knowledge for training embassy Marines and local guard forces they'll need to do.* He was pleased.

"Is there anything you guys need from us?" Susan asked.

I hope we haven't missed something important, Alex thought. *But you never know.*

"I think we have everything covered," Ray replied as the three said their goodbyes; returning to their vehicle, they drove back to the office.

Susan's secure voice phone rang. It was Vern Bordelon from DEA."Hi, Susan. You called me earlier?"

"Yeah, we were wondering if you've had time to think about who in New Orleans might have had prior contact with Jules Baptiste, because someone tipped him off about our witnesses."

"Sorry, I haven't thought about it much. Headquarters has me crashing on end of fiscal year spending and budgets. But off the top of my head, I'd say look at NOPD because their salaries are low. That's always a recipe for taking bribes."

"You may be right, Vern. That's all we wanted to talk about.

"Excellent, since I have to take an incoming call from D.C."

"So long, Vern, and thanks."

Susan turned to Alex and Rachel, "Well, what do you guys think?"

Alex replied, "Sounds like Vern hates bureaucracy and balancing budgets as much as I do." He turned to Rachel.

"You're lucky, Rach. All you have to do is think 'great thoughts and have big ideas.' The rest of us are slaves to the number crunchers in D.C."

Susan laughed. Rachel smiled. "*Someone* has to operate on a higher plane. I guess I'm just built for that."

"You're built for a *lot* of things," he replied.

"Geez, guys, when is your high school graduation coming up?"

"See what I have to put up with," Rachel said. "I'm sure listening to his humor must be some form of human rights violation."

Alex chuckled as he walked across the office to get a cup of coffee. He stopped at Pete Fong's desk. "Any new calls on the Rewards for Justice tip line?"

"About a dozen today, but they all seemed like bullshit."

"I guess we'll have to hope the fishing camp lead works out," Alex said.

Chapter 42

Sheriff Landry Cooperates

Before dinner, Alex and Rachel returned to the New Orleans Athletic Club to workout. Neither wanted to put on weight from the extraordinary local food they were devouring, so they used the treadmills and free weights as they had last time. After showering, they grabbed a 'light' supper at the Desire Oyster Bar: seafood gumbo plus a dozen chargrilled oysters each.

Back in the hotel room, Alex said, "You know, oysters are supposed to be an aphrodisiac because of their high zinc content."

"Uh, oh. I know where you're going with this," she replied. "Do you feel your dopamine levels rising from all that zinc?"

"Not, yet. But who knows what will happen in a few minutes?"

"Well, let me know when you 'rise' to the occasion. In the meantime, I'm going to read my book." She chuckled at her own joke and returned to her reading.

Alex stripped down naked, stood by the bed, and coughed a few times to get her attention. Then he climbed into bed and slid under the sheet. He smiled and stared at her. His ploy didn't take as long as he had anticipated before she joined him.

THE NEXT MORNING, THEY WENT INTO THE DS OFFICE. BOTH logged onto classified computers and accessed their emails from Embassy London. At 10:00 a.m, Sheriff Billy Landry arrived with the head of his marine unit. Susan asked everyone to take a seat at the office conference table.

"Thanks for swinging by, Sheriff," Susan said.

"My pleasure. Were any of you folks injured in the shootout at the Esplanade Apartments?"

"No, only the hitmen were killed," Susan replied. "Thanks for asking. We have a potential lead on where Jules Baptiste may go next, and we think you may be able to help us."

"Sure, whatever I can do. I saw there's an updated arrest warrant out for him and his buddy, Claude Toussaint. Do you think they're in St. Tammany Parish?"

One of the office phones rang, breaking into the conversation; Agent Scott Fellows answered it. "Susan, it's Director Riley coming on the line for you."

"Sorry, Sheriff, I have to take this call." She walked into her office and closed the door. The others continued talking.

"Sheriff, we think Baptiste uses a fishing camp on the Pearl River," Alex said. "It's in your Parish."

"You want us to observe the camp?"

"Yes, we do. He doesn't seem to *own* it, so there may be

others who use it as well. But we'd like you to keep a watch over it and let us know when he's there."

Alex pulled out a map and pointed to the area described by Willie, the tipster, who had spoken with Hank Deavers, the undercover DEA agent. Alex described the camp, using the detailed info that Willie had mentioned.

"The good news is that this area is used all the time by the swamp tour companies," Sheriff Landry's marine unit chief said. "That means we can blend in and use our civilian-looking craft instead of sailing by every time in a marked police marine vessel. It may take a few trips to nail down the location of his camp with certainty, but the place you noted on the map is a great start. Also, I don't have the manpower to put on 24-hour surveillance, but we can go by this place a few times a day, if that would be helpful."

"That would be *great*," Alex replied.

"Do you have any idea how many thugs Baptiste has left in his gang?" Landry asked.

"I don't," Alex replied, "but maybe Captain Wells or Sgt. Washington have an idea. I think the problem will be that Baptiste has a lot of money, so he can pay new thugs to work for him."

"That sounds about right."

Susan rejoined the group. "Sorry for the interruption, Sheriff, but when the big boss from D.C. calls, you have to take it. What did I miss?"

"We went over the map of the Pearl River and the Sheriff committed to sending his officers by the camp a few times a day," Alex said.

Landry looked at his watch. "We need to go now. I'm making a presentation to the St. Tammany School Board about our emergency response plan for this coming fall. It's been nice talking with you about Baptiste. We'll start the marine patrols this evening." Everyone shook hands and Landry departed with his marine unit chief.

Susan pointed her head in the direction of her private office, Alex and Rachel followed her inside. She closed the door, not wanting Scott Fellows or Pete Fong to hear the conversation.

"Riley just offered me two options instead of Costa Rica. Both are solo RSO jobs. The first is in Colombo, Sri Lanka; the second is in Copenhagen, Denmark."

"Fantastic!" Rachel replied. "Which one appeals to you?"

"I haven't decided, yet. Alex, what do you think?"

"I've not been to Colombo, but I think the work will be very good. They used to have an indigenous terrorist group, called the 'Tamil Tigers,' but I don't know if they're still active. As for Copenhagen, it's a beautiful city, loaded with culture and history. And it's easy to travel throughout Europe from there."

"Gosh, this is a tough decision. My family roots are from northern Germany, so maybe if I did some research, I could find some ancestral links to distant relatives in either Germany or Denmark. That would be fun, plus the culture has to be amazing. On the other hand, I want to work where security is important."

"When did Riley say you had to make a decision?" Rachel asked.

"He wasn't specific and I don't want to appear indecisive, but I don't want to make a mistake either."

"Look at it this way," Alex said. "One option offers the opportunity of eating great fire-hot curries in a tropical climate, maybe fighting off terrorists, and battening down the hatches against annual typhoons, while the other option offers sophisticated dining, world-class museums, but with a slow pace at the office. However, there is chance of finding a muscular Viking boyfriend." Everyone laughed.

"Somehow your humor cuts to the heart of the matter," Susan said. "I think I have a few days before Riley needs my answer.

"Now, let's get back to finding Baptiste," Susan said.

Chapter 43

Time to Reflect

Alex envied Susan's situation. Not her dilemma per se, but the fact that she was still at an early stage in her career. All her options *would* seem exciting, so many cultures to explore and adventures to pursue. By mid-point of many RSOs careers, they had already become jaded and frustrated with the bureaucracy, or they had refocused their attention on family matters. When that happened, the job was, well, only a paycheck.

Alex still saw the job as an adventure. He was grateful to DS for the places he had served, and while he wouldn't wish tragedy on anyone, he had to admit that when danger or threats arose, he wanted to be on the front line dealing with it. Confronting exciting challenges was nearly as important as the end results. He believed Rachel felt the same way.

Their decision years ago not to have children still seemed like the right choice. Perhaps one day he might regret it, but so far, it had worked out. They had seen so many kids in foreign service families who had turned into nightmares---drug users, discipline problems, or just out of control. It was hard enough for parents to deal with these issues while living an ordinary life in the states, but to confront such problems while serving overseas just wasn't something he or Rachel cared to deal with.

He knew of two families who had been ordered by their ambassadors to cut short their tours of duty and return to Washington because of child-related extreme bad behavior. After that, those employees had to convince the State Department why they should ever be assigned abroad again. Kids could be a career-killer.

No, thanks, he thought. *If I can't live overseas with the State Department, I'll work for someone else.* Alex's introspection was cut short when Rachel asked him what he was thinking.

"I was just reflecting on our life in the foreign service and how lucky we've been."

"Where'd that thought come from?"

"Oh, Susan's dilemma just got me thinking, that's all."

"We're fortunate we met each other in Pakistan," she said.

"That's for sure; I can't imagine anyone being a better match." *She's an extraordinary woman,* he thought, *one who enjoys intellectual challenges and, if necessary, physical battles. She gains satisfaction from overcoming adversity, and I like that.*

"Ah, that's sweet."

"Of course, I always *hoped* to find someone tall, gorgeous, and athletic, but we can't have everything in life."

"You *creep!*" Then, she laughed, knowing she ticked all those boxes. "You forget to mention that *you're* the lucky one because I can appreciate your warped sense of humor. I'll bet in high school you were voted 'most likely to be a failed comedian' when you grew up."

Alex smiled. "Oh, you heard about that?" They both laughed easily.

"On a serious note," he said, "how about if we go see either Papa Ed or Camille? It's been a while since we gave them an update on the case."

"Good idea; please make the call."

Alex spoke to Papa Ed, who suggested he and Rachel join them for lunch at their home.

BY NOONTIME, THEY WERE DRIVING DOWN ST. CHARLES AVENUE; the temperature hovered around ninety degrees. While sunny, the mid-day weather report indicated a tropical storm in the Gulf of Mexico would make landfall near the Louisiana-Mississippi border. Alex expected clouds would roll in and drench the city with rain within the next two days.

They arrived at the Ardoin's uptown home and everyone embraced in greeting. Camille's hugs lasted a longer time than usual. They sat in the living room, sipped iced tea, and chatted about recent developments in the case. Alex wasn't about to mention the latest tip regarding the fishing camp but he did tell them there had been confirmation that Baptiste *was* the shooter.

"We're making progress on finding him," Alex said, hoping it would be enough to lift their spirits.

"Thanks for the update, Alex," Papa Ed said. "We're grateful that DS has sent an additional eight agents down here to help protect witnesses and work the case."

"Has Captain Wells been in touch with you?" Alex asked.

"He has. And like you, he has been circumspect in describing specific leads."

'I hope you understand why."

"Of course. I would do the same thing in your position."

"Camille, is there anything more we can do to help?" Rachel asked.

"No, but thank you. Both of you have been strong shoulders to cry on. I appreciate your support and friendship."

Alex wanted to ask Camille how she was coping following her recent suicide attempt but felt it best not to mention the sensitive subject. Besides, the fact they were having lunch together, and discussing the investigation, probably meant she was able to to handle things better now.

"Alex, I know the State Department and NOPD are in the lead in finding Baptiste, but are other agencies supporting you?" Papa Ed asked.

"The St. Tammany Parish Sheriff's office and DEA are doing a great job, and St. Bernard Parish jumped in when we asked them to raid a house where we thought Claude Toussaint was staying."

"I noticed you didn't mention the FBI."

"They've been helpful as well. But so far, they're just content to support us and NOPD."

"Okay," Papa Ed simply said. He offered no further thoughts.

I hope he's not going to try something like last time we talked. After our conversation, he sent men out to search and now we have three dead bodies, Alex thought. *I'm going to bring it up, but I wonder what he's really thinking.*

Then the conversation switched to other topics, for which Alex was grateful.

After chatting moments longer, Camille said they could move into the dining room. She apologized for not cooking something from scratch but noted that her friends were still bringing over dishes they had prepared to relieve the burden from Camille. The food had to be eaten before it all went bad, or she could freeze some. The food had been warming in the kitchen during their chat. Now it only took a minute or two more to bring it out and serve.

When they finished their sausage jambalaya, and red beans and rice, Alex once again asked Papa Ed if he could see some of the photos in his office. They walked down the hall while Camille and Rachel continued talking in the dining room.

"What did you want to see, Alex?"

"I really wanted to ask you a question, and I didn't want to talk about it in front of Camille."

"I see. What's on your mind?"

"It's about the three guys who were murdered in Algiers a week ago. You had represented all of them in court at different times. I assume they were looking for Simone's killer at your behest."

Papa Ed's expression was unchanged. Alex wasn't surprised. As a successful defense attorney, he knew that Papa ED would not show his hand until he was certain of the outcome.

"Has NOPD talked to you about these guys?" Alex asked.

"Yes, Captain Wells spoke to me. We agreed it was an unfortunate coincidence that I had been their lawyer."

"So, you have nothing to worry about from NOPD."

"Correct, Alex."

"I'm glad. Off-the-record, and speaking hypothetically, I

would have done the same thing in your position." Papa Ed relaxed his shoulders and Alex noticed a small uptick of his lips, an almost imperceptible smile.

"I think it's time for us to leave now. Rachel and I are going on to the DS office. I'll let you know if anything develops." As Alex turned to leave, Papa Ed touched his shoulder to get his attention. Their handshake was as strong as their bond.

Chapter 44

Shocking Developments

The secure phone rang in Susan Witt's office; it was Tommy Rogers, RSO at the American Embassy in Port-au-Prince calling from Haiti.

"Susan, I have breaking news. I met with our embassy law enforcement crew about who in New Orleans might have contacts in Haiti, and here's what I found: You already knew about Bill Westbrook's temporary assignment in Haiti three years ago. But around the same period, Vern Bordelon of DEA was *also* here for several weeks. He spearheaded a team that reached an agreement with the Haitian police to share intelligence about criminal gangs and drug smuggling."

"That's incredible," Susan said. "Did someone in the embassy DEA office remember him?"

"There's no one here in the embassy now who was here three years ago, but the bilateral agreement is important, and forms the basis for *who* shared intelligence. Moreover, the embassy DEA office *still* speaks with Bordelon, or one of his staff, on the phone *every month*. And they still exchange classified messages on possible smuggling routes along the US Gulf Coast on a regular basis."

"That's like a highway of information being shared," Susan said.

"I assume Bordelon never mentioned he'd been here?"

"No, he sure didn't. Of course, to be effective in his job, he'd *have* to have these regular contacts.

"Anyway, that's all I've got, Susan."

"Which agencies attended the meeting?" she asked.

"Homeland Security, which includes guys who deal with both customs and immigration, DEA, and the Coast Guard. I also met with the Consul General, the CIA, and I met with a Department of Justice lawyer working on judicial system reform here in Haiti."

"Sounds like you've been busy. I really appreciate this, Tommy. I assume you *didn't* tell them about our concern over leaked intelligence."

"Of course not. I said we hoped to find someone who had Haitian experience to help with an investigation."

"Excellent. You've been a big help, Tommy, thanks for this news." After they hung up, she told Alex and Rachel about the development.

"Bordelon!" Alex exclaimed. "I thought the guy was all right. *Shit*, he's been helpful all along. But I don't *ever* recall him saying he'd been to Haiti even though he *knew* that was our focus."

"What's the next step?" Rachel asked.

"We need to be cautious," Alex replied, "because both Bordelon and Westbrook have extensive contacts throughout law enforcement. If they get wind of our inquiries, they'll cover their tracks. If they're innocent, and get pissed off, they might end their cooperation with Susan's office."

"Can't we just bug their phones?" Rachel asked.

"We'd have to know what number they're using or calling, and we'd have to get a judge's approval if we were to target them specifically. Moreover, I'm sure they would never use their office phone. They wouldn't be that *naïve*."

"Getting a judge's approval could be problematic in Louisiana," Susan said. At first, Rachel looked confused at her comment, then a light bulb turned on.

"Oh, you mean you're worried about corruption."

"We might have a better chance if we went to a federal judge," Alex said.

"Yeah, I'll bet, however, Bordelon or Westbrook have friends working as clerks for the judges, too," Susan pointed out.

"Yes, indeed," Alex said. "besides, so far, we only know both of them travelled to Haiti on US Government business. That's not evidence of corruption. No one in the U.S. Attorney's office will support a search warrant without more substantial evidence. Plus, it's equally probable someone in NOPD could be Baptiste's informant.

"I have an idea," Alex continued. "I'm going to call Jim Riley and ask him to set up a meeting. It'll involve a road trip." He caught Rachel's eye. ". . . for me."

THE NEXT MORNING ALEX'S FLIGHT LANDED AT REAGAN NATIONAL Airport in Arlington, Virginia. He was met by DS Special Agent Indira Chakrabarti, who Riley had told him worked in the Office of Criminal Investigations, when the two men had spoken by phone the previous evening. Alex hadn't met her before, so Riley gave him the agent's name and a brief description.

Now, as he saw her standing by the arrival gate, she met Riley's description perfectly: tall, slender, olive complexion, and straight jet-black hair.

"Indira Chakrabarti?" Alex asked.

"Yes. And you are Alex Boyd?"

They shook hands.

"We have a slight change of plans," she said. "Director Riley has asked me to drive you to Ft. Meade, instead of stopping by his office. He'll meet us there."

"Fine. I had hoped to talk to him on the drive, but if he's tied up, I'll have the pleasure of your company instead." As she smiled, perfect gleaming white teeth captured his attention. They walked to her vehicle in the parking lot.

"How long have you been with DS?" Alex asked.

"Almost two years."

"I'm surprised you're not in a field office, or on the Secretary's protective detail."

"I started in the Washington Field Office but was transferred following a complex fraud investigation I helped close."

"Was that the case of the State Department civil service guy who worked in the procurement office and channeled millions into his private accounts?"

"Yeah, that's the one. He pleaded guilty in court."

"I read the highlights of the case. Congratulations on a job well done."

"Thanks." She gave him another brilliant smile. As they drove on the Baltimore-Washington Parkway toward the National Security Agency's headquarters, they chatted. She hadn't served in an American Embassy yet, but had traveled widely abroad prior to joining DS.

"What did you do before joining DS?" he asked.

"I was a sort of bank examiner for one of the major accounting companies." She elaborated in more detail as she drove. Based on how she described her past, he liked her self-confidence and maturity.

"I don't believe I've met anyone else in DS with that background."

"Yeah, I've also found that out. But after a few years in the accounting firm, I realized I'd rather deal with *people* than numbers, which is strange because I majored in mathematics and accounting in college. Besides, I also wanted to live abroad from time to time. I had heard about criminal cases DS handled, and about overseas embassy assignments; so I took the tests, and passed."

As they continued driving, Alex learned that her grandfather had immigrated to America from India and eventually became an engineering professor at Purdue. Her parents were both accountants, and Indira graduated from the University of Chicago, later getting an MBA from Indiana University.

Impressive, to say the least, he thought.

They pulled into NSA's parking lot and found a visitor's space. Alex had been there several times in the past, but this was Indira's first venture into the world of communications espionage and counterespionage.

He hoped the NSA meeting would be fruitful, otherwise he'd have to solve the New Orleans case the old-fashioned way . . . with boots on the ground.

Chapter 45

Technology is Your Friend

T
he NSA conference room had bare white walls and no windows. Alex and Indira made small talk with an NSA escort officer while waiting for the others to arrive. Fifteen minutes later, Jim Riley came into the room and apologized for being late.

Alex and Riley warmly shook hands with broad smiles on their faces, the mark of true friends seeing each other again. Having first served together in Islamabad, Pakistan, Alex had later been Riley's Special Projects officer in Washington, a unique position established for Alex as he healed from serious battle wounds inflicted when he was serving in Cairo. The two men had known each other for years.

As three more people from NSA arrived, Alex recognized Alan Pickett, director of security, but the others were unknown to him.

"Alex, you know Alan," Riley said, "but let me introduce you to Irene Grossman, from NSA's Office of Legal Affairs, and Sherman Lampert, Assistant Deputy Director of Operations."

In turn, Alex introduced DS Special Agent Indira Chakrabarti to the group. Then they all settled around the conference table.

"How can we help you, Jim?" Lampert asked.

"I'll let Alex Boyd explain the situation," Riley replied.

"In New Orleans, we're investigating the murder of Simone Ardoin, a foreign service officer. She had worked for my wife in Washington, D.C. We were also friends with Simone and happened to be visiting her in New Orleans, her hometown, at the time she was murdered.

"Witnesses have confirmed the killer is Jules Baptiste, leader of a Haitian gang dealing in drugs and human trafficking there. He has a close criminal associate named Claude Toussaint who the victim was supposed to meet on the evening she was murdered.

"Both men are now hiding somewhere in the greater New Orleans area and arrest warrants have been issued for them. We know Baptiste has regular telephone conversations with members of his gang in Port-au-Prince, Haiti. We also suspect someone in law enforcement in New Orleans is leaking information to Baptiste because his hitmen attacked federally protected witnesses that no one outside of law enforcement knew about.

"In addition, his smugglers have had *remarkable* success avoiding DEA and Coast Guard efforts to stop their operations. We believe this could only have happened by them receiving insider information.

"One last thing," Alex said. "Baptiste's gunmen have also killed a New Orleans policeman and wounded another." He assumed everyone around the table knew what was coming next.

Sherman Lampert said, "I presume you'd like NSA to intercept calls between Baptiste and Haiti."

Before Alex could respond, Irene Grossman spoke up. "Is this Jules Baptiste a U.S. citizen?"

"No, he's a Haitian citizen," Alex replied. "Furthermore, he's in the United States illegally. If we can identify who he called in Haiti, and the phone numbers he's calling *from* in New Orleans, we'll have a better chance of locating him." Alex passed a file to Lampert.

"Here is a file with the numbers we know he has used in the past," Alex said. "However, I doubt he still makes his calls from the same cell phones."

Irene Grossman spoke again. "Are you asking only to see metadata, or to hear actual conversations?"

Alex looked at Riley, who waved for him to continue. "Preferably both, but metadata will do."

"Just to be clear," Grossman said, "you are *only* requesting information on calls between Baptiste and Haiti?"

Alex knew this was a sticky point, but he didn't want to lie to NSA. Throughout his career, DS and NSA had been good allies and he didn't want to drop them into a pile of legal shit.

"To be honest, if you identify Baptiste's calls," Alex replied, "you may also come across domestic calls he's making, or receiving, from one or more U.S. citizens in New Orleans."

"Which might be *to* or *from* the leaker of law enforcement information?" Grossman asked.

"Yes."

"Who almost certainly will be a U.S. citizen in federal or local law enforcement," Grossman said. This was the sticky point – not being legally permitted to monitor American citizens' private conversations.

Riley jumped back into the conversation. "Since Jules Baptiste, the target, is a *foreign* citizen, if you happen to overhear his conversations with an *American* citizen, I believe that would still be within the law."

"Technically, you are correct," Grossman replied. "The law permits collateral collection. But as you well know, Congress has become concerned with our operations as it affects the privacy of the average U.S. citizen."

Alex responded, "We agree with the congressional privacy concern. The target, however, is a *Haitian* citizen. If he is receiving sensitive U.S. law enforcement information from someone, that someone is not your 'average' U.S. citizen. He or she is a criminal and part of a conspiracy to commit murder and smuggle drugs and illegals into the country."

Sherman Lampert said, "I think you've made some very effective points. We'll get back to you after further internal discussion."

I wish Alan Pickett, the NSA security director, had weighed into the debate. Alex thought, *but then, maybe he sees the DS request as both an operational and legal matter, not security per se.*

"One last question," Lampert asked. "Do you have new specific telephone numbers for us to track?"

"We do not," Alex replied. "But perhaps his old numbers will prove useful after all. Since Baptiste uses burner cell phones, once the NSA's mathematical algorithms identify a pattern of calls, the computers will also need to search for key words that Baptiste might use."

"Easier said than done," Lampert replied.

"Excuse me; may I say something?" Indira Chakrabarti asked. Lampert nodded.

"I presume your NSA algorithms are based on quantum mathematical formulas that can analyze data from infinitesimal measurements, therefore, they can confirm linkages that older computers would take much longer to link. I feel you're being modest Mr. Lampert."

"Well, yes, that's true about using quantum mathematics, Miss Chakrabarti. You did say earlier you work for DS, but have you worked for *us* in the past?"

"I do work for DS, and I have never worked for NSA. Perhaps my mathematics degree from the University of Chicago has helped me understand this stuff." Indira smiled.

"You seem to have an intuitive feel for this so-called 'stuff.' By the way, do you speak other languages?"

"Just Hindi. And, oh yes, some Urdu and Farsi," her megawatt smile was blinding. There was a slight pause.

"Okay, Jim, it was nice to see you again," Lampert said. "Mr. Boyd and Miss Chakrabarti, it was nice to have met you both. Someone will get back to you."

He rose from his chair, a clear signal the meeting was over.

I'm not sure whether NSA will agree to the DS request for assistance, but it's clear they're gun-shy after getting beaten up by Congress in the past over spying on Americans, Alex thought.

There was a fine line between protecting America from terrorists and criminals and invading the personal privacy of U.S. citizens.

I know the FBI had exceeded its authority under the law many times in recent years and has lied to both Congress and the American people while it engaged in partisan domestic politics, Alex thought.

As for the intelligence community, including the NSA, I know they have acted without legal authority in their surveillance programs, too. But I want justice for Simone Ardoin . . . and I want Baptiste captured or . . . whatever. There's got to be a way for us to do something under existing laws.

IN THE PARKING LOT, RILEY SPOKE TO INDIRA. "THANKS FOR picking up Alex at the airport and driving him here. I enjoyed your comments to Lampert. I need to speak with Alex before he returns to New Orleans, so he'll ride back with me." She nodded her understanding and turned to bid Alex goodbye.

"I've also enjoyed our conversation," he said. "Indira, when you request your first overseas assignment as an assistant RSO, think about bidding on London. The embassy has employees from many different agencies; I believe you'll have an opportunity to learn a lot and I would welcome your contribution to my office, if I'm still there."

Her smile was broad and warm. They shook hands and Alex joined Jim Riley in his car for the drive back to D.C.

"My, my, when did you become the DS Human Resources manager?" Riley asked as they drove out of the parking lot. He looked at the smile on Alex's face.

"Boss, I wouldn't be doing my job if I didn't try to get the best people to work for me. You know her work. Is she as good as I think she is?"

"You bet she is," Riley replied. "We moved her from the field office to criminal investigations because her mind grasps complex situations quickly, and her written reports are excellent."

"Terrific. I hope she contacts me when she has to submit her next assignment preferences."

"Speaking of next assignments, I want to chat with you about just that point," Riley said.

Alex had dreaded this moment. While most officers welcomed a reassignment to a big job in D.C., he wanted to stay abroad, and besides, Rachel's career was booming in London. Not only was she the political counselor for the American Embassy, but she had been acting deputy chief of mission on and off for several months during their first year at post. This was not the time to return to DC.

"I thought you might want to twist my arm," Alex replied.

"You'll recall I've wanted you to be my deputy in D.C. for a while now. But we had to fill that job last year because you had just arrived in London. Moreover, there isn't anything coming up that's worthy of your talents."

"What a pity."

They locked eyes and Riley said, "Yeah, sure. Wiseass! So, I've been contemplating how else I can use your talents beyond your current RSO job in London."

"Such as?"

"For starters, the director of NATO's security has always been a DS position. Next year, that may be open. This Brussels-based job has an international staff who would work for you. Since you speak French, Spanish, and Italian, you'd be a natural fit."

"That's interesting, Jim. If there's a job for Rachel as well, then an assignment to Brussels has real appeal."

"I need someone who is prepared to commit to the job for a several years. Lately, the DS officers we've sent there retired after just one year in Brussels, often for better paying corporate positions. That didn't sit too well with the NATO political hierarchy."

"Yeah, no surprise there. You know, since Rachel and I are a team, if she also has a senior position in Brussels, there would be no reason to leave early. Besides, I'm not old enough to retire."

"In this case, that's great. Just file this idea away until next year. Plus, there are some other thoughts I have about domestic assignments for you."

"I thought you said there was 'nothing suitable.'"

"That's true. I meant *within* DS. But here's what I'm thinking: Although we already have mid-ranked DS officers assigned to counterterrorism fusion centers at the FBI and CIA, I've been considering some type of liaison position at the highest level."

"Have you talked with the FBI and CIA about this?"

"Not yet. I'd welcome your ideas."

"I'm not clear what this 'senior liaison officer' would do that isn't already being handled. It seems like an end-run around your existing senior managers within DS. What would be the real work for the position? That point seems vague."

Riley remained silent.

They drove another minute before Alex turned to him. "You're trying to do an end run, but not around senior DS offices; you're trying to do an end run around other *bureaus* in the State Department."

Riley smirked. Alex continued, "I think that would be a bad business model, Jim. Once the other bureaus realize you were by-passing them, the lack of trust would take *years* to overcome. You'd be better off insisting the FBI and CIA always share the same relevant information with DS as they are sharing with other State Department bureaus.

"Why not provide some type of incentive for sharing? Look,

I have the same doubts about foreign service officers as you do, although in fairness, *most* are dedicated and competent. The judgment of a few is sometimes flawed, but if the interagency agreements aren't working because of sneaky individuals in the other bureaus, then hash it out with the Secretary of State. Besides, I don't trust the FBI, they've gone to the political dark side. Knowing that, I wouldn't want to work within their sphere."

"What about the CIA?"

Alex thought for a moment. "They're a lot better. Both their case officers overseas and their analysts in D.C. are smart, talented, and experienced. But it depends on *who's* running the organization. Let's just say that at present, I believe things are not good. They're involving themselves too much in our domestic politics, which is off-limits according to their charter *and* the law. Some might even consider these domestic political operations in the U.S. by both the FBI and the CIA akin to treason."

"I'm glad we spoke. You've clarified some of my concerns."

Thirty minutes later, as they approached Reagan National Airport, Alex said, "Let me know what the NSA is prepared to do about our New Orleans situation. We can use their technical support."

"Will do. Good to see you, as always."

LATER, WALKING INTO THE TERMINAL, ALEX FELT THE conversation with Jim had reinforced his view that staying abroad was the best thing for Rachel and himself. Washington, in general, and the State Department in particular, was a snake pit he wanted to avoid.

Chapter 46

Back in New Orleans

Alex took a taxi at the New Orleans airport for the trip into town. He knew both Susan and Rachel would want a detailed report on his meeting with the NSA, but later, he would only tell Rachel about Riley's thoughts on his own future assignment.

The taxi dropped him off on Canal Street; he walked into the building and rode the elevator up to the DS office on the eleventh floor.

"Welcome back," Susan said in greeting. "How did the meeting go?"

"It went well. Now we'll wait and see if they can deliver the goods."

Even though Susan stood next to Detective Sgt. John Washington, Alex couldn't go into detail about NSA's electronic capabilities because Washington did not have a security clearance. Nevertheless, it was essential for him to know the investigation might benefit from NSA's intercept capabilities. He figured Washington was smart enough to figure out *how* that would happen on his own.

"Let's go into the conference room," Susan said.

Just then, Rachel walked through the office front door, winked at Alex, and joined them for the meeting. It didn't take him long to explain what he hoped NSA would do. When he finished, Washington said the St. Tammany Parish marine unit had started their discrete surveillance of the fishing camp on the Pearl River.

"But so far, it appears that no one is there," he said.

When the meeting ended, Alex asked who wanted to join him and Rachel for dinner, John said he would eat with his wife; Susan said a male friend had asked her out. So, Alex and Rachel decided they'd return to the Royal Sonesta Hotel where he could shower, then they'd go to Mr. B's Bistro in the Quarter.

As they walked out of the conference room, Susan grabbed Alex's arm. "I've thought all day about Jim Riley's offer of either Denmark or Sri Lanka for my next tour."

"And the winner is . . . ?" Alex paused with bated breath.

"Sri Lanka. I just can't pass up the dynamic work environment of a South Asian posting."

"Career-wise, I think you made the right decision."

"So says the man who is assigned to *London*, and has also served in Rome."

He laughed. "Touché. If it helps confirm your decision, you can always take R&R to London and stay with us to balance out your hardship tour in Sri Lanka."

"Thanks," she smiled. "I appreciate how you went to bat for me with Riley."

"You're welcome. Enjoy your evening with your boyfriend."

"He's not a serious boyfriend. He isn't even a Danish Viking, but he'll do for tonight."

Alex smiled. "See you tomorrow morning."

Alex and Rachel walked back to the hotel in the pleasant afternoon weather. He told her about Riley's thoughts on the NATO position in Brussels for the following year. She was intrigued. But Alex couldn't shake the feeling there was something she wasn't revealing.

SEATED IN MR. B'S BISTRO FOR DINNER, ALEX AND RACHEL EACH sipped a glass of *Pouilly Fuisse,* a chardonnay from the Maconnais sub-region of Burgundy. They talked while waiting for their main dishes of roasted garlic chicken for him and Bluefin tuna for her. Neither was a classic New Orleans delicacy, but they needed a change of pace.

"I have something to tell you," she said.

Aha! he thought. *There was something unspoken.* Aloud, he said: "I assume it's about Brussels and the job offer you received."

She had an astonished look on her face. "How did you know about that?"

"Am I not the world's greatest detective?"

She laughed. "Listen, Poirot, you're good, but still, that informal offer was only made today around noon. In fact, at *this* point, it's just a suggestion. *Nobody* was supposed to know about it. So, big guy, how *did* you know?"

"I watched your body language when I mentioned Riley's thoughts about the NATO job. Also, when you said it was intriguing, I felt you were thinking of something related."

She leaned back as the waiter brought their meals and placed them on the table.

"Bon appetite," the waiter said and left.

As he cut into his chicken, he was aware Rachel was still staring at him. He put down his knife and fork, reached over, grabbed her hand, "Honestly, it was just a guess. I assume I was right on the mark. So, what's up?"

"You're scary smart sometimes," she said.

"Only *some*times?"

"Okay, *all* the time. Here's what's up: Archie called me after lunch and said his Deputy Chief of Mission was transferring next summer." Rachel referred to Archibald Watson, the new U.S Ambassador to NATO and outgoing Assistant Secretary of European Affairs with whom both she and Alex were good friends.

"He wanted to know if I'd be interested in replacing his DCM in June. He also said he's been following Embassy London's political reporting and felt my analysis on NATO issues was excellent."

"Of course, it has been."

She shook her head and chuckled. "Stop buttering me up. I'm just repeating what Archie said on the phone. So, if *you* get the job as head of security, which reports to the Director General of NATO, and *I'm* the DCM for the U.S. Mission, we can work there for perhaps four years."

A moment of silence ensued as they looked at each other, thinking of all the possibilities,

"We'll have to cut short our London tour after only two years," Alex replied.

"Is that so bad? Bainbridge Wellington leaves in a month,

and our new DCM is Porter Franklin. I've heard he's disagreeable."

"Yeah, I've heard the same from RSOs who worked for him. They say he's old-school in the worst way."

"Plus, the NATO positions are at higher grade levels, so they'll be great for our careers," she said.

"How do you feel about *moules*?" he asked.

"What are you talking about?"

"Moules. You know, it's the French word for mussels; it's a big part of the Belgium diet, along with *frites*."

"I know what *moules* are. Why are they important to this conversation? I think you're trying to make a joke because you agree with me about going to Brussels next year."

Alex raised his wine of glass for a toast. "Here's to you, the smartest officer in the foreign service." After they sipped, he took her hand and kissed it. "I meant what I said about you being the smartest . . . and a whole lot more as well."

Rachel's green eyes moistened and her lips quivered for a moment. She put her hand on his and squeezed.

They finished their meal without talking further about Brussels.

Jules Baptiste is still on the loose and needs to be found, Alex thought, trying to recenter his thinking. He hoped NSA would agree to contribute to the law enforcement effort. *Between modern technology and good old gumshoe work, I'm confident Baptiste won't be around much longer.*

Chapter 47

Down the Pearl River

When Alex and Rachel arrived at the DS office the following morning, Susan told them the St. Tammany sheriff's office had offered them a reconnaissance trip on the Pearl River to introduce them to the area where Baptiste might be located. It took only a microsecond for them to agree.

"Okay, then," Susan said. "You should meet them at the boat dock. It's where some of the commercial swamp tours leave."

"What time?" Alex asked.

"Eleven-thirty this morning. Here's a map with the address. You can put it into your GPS."

As Alex and Rachel were studying the map, Isabelle Lewis and Burt Warner walked into the office. They were coming from the safe house where Moon Glow and Billy were being protected. Since the MSD teams had arrived, Isabelle and Burt had been splitting their time between protection duties and being on call to assist Susan and Alex with the investigation.

"Anything we can do to help?" Isabelle asked Susan.

"There is," Susan replied. "For the past few days, Pete Fong and Luis Torres have been taking turns manning the tip line for the Rewards for Justice offer. They could use a break and get back to their other investigations."

"Consider it done," Isabelle replied. "Burt, which shift do you want?"

"I can take over now; you can relieve me this afternoon." She nodded.

Luis Torres gave them a short briefing update and showed them how to link incoming calls to the NOPD call center.

"Are you coming with us to the Pearl River?" Alex asked Susan.

"I don't think so. I've been there many times, so I'll stay in town and get some paperwork done."

ALEX AND RACHEL DROVE TO THE DESIGNATED BOAT DOCK WHERE they met St. Tammany Parish Deputy Vinnie Fiore, who wore a short-sleeve uniform shirt and Cammie pants with cargo pockets. Everyone shook hands. Vinnie was Alex's height, good-looking, and had incredibly muscular biceps the size of tree trunks.

As Vinnie led the way onto the 21-foot craft, Rachel nudged Alex and whispered, "You should hit the gym more often." He smiled.

"Don't be so shallow. I have my positive traits, as you may recall from the other night."

She chuckled. "Still . . ." she said and rolled her eyes.

They both climbed into the boat that was indicated to

them. It had a small wheelhouse with open areas at the bow and stern. Vinnie unwrapped the rope from the cleat on the dock, got onboard and backed the boat away from the dock. As they moved down the river at a slow pace, he said, "We have a couple of these 21-foot-long boats and some more that are 12-feet-long which we use in very shallow water."

"Do you support the Parish's SWAT team?" Alex asked.

"We do. Every year we assist them with several raids. A lot of the Parish is covered by water, so we're always busy, mostly with routine water rescue or some type of emergency."

They passed a lot of semi-dilapidated wooden houses on the river. Most were raised a few feet off the water; some had a TV antenna on the metal roof, and all had a boat slip for a small craft. Early in the journey, above an embankment, Alex saw a few substantial houses with roads nearby.

"How often are the small fishing camps used?" Alex asked.

"That depends," Deputy Fiore replied. "Some owners are here most weekends, but other camps are almost never occupied. Let me give you a tour of the overall area."

He turned the boat into a narrow channel which was surrounded by cypress trees with their trunks exposed above the water line. There were numerous cypress knees sticking out of the water and fallen dead trees in the distance. Alex could hear the chatter of birds in the nearby trees. The entire wildlife refuge was rich with flora and fauna, fish, turtles, alligators, and snakes of various kinds. Some trees had moss hanging from branches; the area, although beautiful, almost looked prehistoric.

"Keep your hands in the boat," Vinnie said. "You don't want to lose an arm to an alligator." As if on cue, Alex saw a medium size gator raise his head out of the water about thirty feet in front of the boat and seemed to be staring at them.

"I heard they taste like chicken," Rachel said.

"Funny, that's what the gators think about humans," Vinnie replied.

Rachel looked nervous, but Alex laughed. Vinnie turned the craft around and they motored back onto the Pearl River. A commercial swamp-tour boat passed by and everyone waved.

"What kind of fish are in the river?" Alex asked.

"Largemouth bass, drum, catfish, a few other types," Vinnie replied. "They're all great for cooking on the grill."

"How long is the river?"

"Starting north of here, it meanders about 400 miles before it drains into Lake Borgne, then into the Gulf of Mexico."

"So, if Jules Baptiste wanted to escape the area, he could go all the way to the Gulf and get on a bigger ship?" Alex clarified.

"Yeah. It wouldn't be difficult."

They motored for another twenty minutes, stopping on occasion to view the dense vegetation, or a particular camp.

"Okay, we're almost there," Deputy Fiore said. "At least, this is the area you asked us to keep an eye on. Coming up on the right is a tributary where we think Baptiste has his fishing camp. I won't go down there because it would be too obvious in this marked police boat. But it's the only house in sight, about 100 yards from the main river."

As they passed the entrance to the tributary, Alex saw the fishing camp as described by Willie, the DEA source from the bar. The camp, an old wooden shack, was raised off the ground on stilts and had a boat dock at the bottom of the raised deck. A ladder allowed someone to get from the boat to the upper deck. There were no boats present.

"How deep is that tributary?" Rachel asked.

"I guess about eight feet, max," Vinnie replied.

As they proceeded at slow speed, a giant alligator left the bank and swam into the water.

"Holy *shit*," Rachel said. "Did you see that big one?" She looked at Alex.

"Yeah. He'd make a nice handbag for you."

She pushed him in the arm. "How old is he?"

"We're not sure," Vinnie replied. "My guess is at least a few decades. He even has a name. We call him 'Big Beau.'"

"Why that name?" she asked.

"Rumor has it that twenty years ago that gator devoured a local fisherman named Beau Guidry. They say he was bit in half, and his upper torso floated in the water until the gator wanted dessert."

Alex and Rachel looked at each other at the same time. She mouthed the words, *what the fuck.* Then she turned her eyes back to the gator and watched him disappear underwater. She didn't smile.

"Do you know what type of boat Baptiste has?" Vinnie asked.

"Sorry, haven't a clue," Alex replied.

"Okay, we'll just keep patrolling twice a day. We'll also use the smaller 12-foot boats that aren't marked as 'Marine Police.'"

"Do the gators ever attack small boats?" Rachel asked Vinnie.

"Only if they have women onboard. They like the scent of perfume. And you should know that women tend to be tastier and tenderer."

Alex laughed at the joke. Still, he was glad they were on the larger patrol boat. When they returned to the dock, Alex and Rachel thanked Vinnie for the tour and shook hands.

"I have to ask," Rachel said looking at his huge biceps. "How often do you work out?"

Vinnie grinned. "Six days a week. Why? Do you want to touch 'em?" He flexed his biceps. Alex saw her blush.

"Wow, they're really big," she said. "But, no thanks, I'll pass."

"Okay. By the way, I've got the biggest biceps on the force."

"I have no doubt."

Walking back to the car, Alex said, "You can touch *my* biceps if you'd like."

"I'm sorry. I shouldn't have asked him that. It's just that it's been a while since I've seen arms *that* huge and muscular."

"Seen? Or felt?"

"You're jealous, aren't you?"

"Perhaps a little."

"Oh, Alex, you shouldn't be. You're more than enough man for me. You have *great* biceps."

"Nice of you to say so."

"Yeah," she paused. "For a State Department diplomat, they're *great* biceps."

"You know there'll be payback later for that sarcastic remark."

"God, I'm counting on it."

They laughed and got into the car. While the swamp trip had been informative, Alex hoped he wouldn't have to return to the waterway for the capture of Baptiste. While beautiful, the area was also creepy, and not without danger.

Chapter 48

The Snitch

The boat ride and fresh air gave Alex and Rachel an appetite, so they stopped at a Popeye's on the way back to the office. It was just a quick snack of spicy fried chicken breasts with sides of red beans and rice, and a biscuit on the side.

"Hmm, this tastes just like alligator," Alex remarked. Rachel looked skeptical.

"Have you ever *had* alligator?"

"No, but I think what Vinnie implied is right on."

"What do you mean?"

"Well, if we think alligators taste like chicken, and they think humans taste like chicken, too, then I agree with them. They do. But you taste even better than both." He wiggled his eyebrows.

She shook her head with a hint of a smile. "I think you should keep your day job, because although you're charming, you make a lousy food critic, and an even worse comedienne."

Without more comments, they finished their meals and drove back to the office.

I still think I'm right, Alex thought with a smile.

"HOW WAS THE RIVER TRIP? SUSAN ASKED.

"Terrific," Rachel replied. "Beautiful, but a little scary. Anything new on Simone's case?"

"Not yet. The shooters who were arrested from the attacks at the Esplanade Apartment, and at the Marriott Hotel, aren't telling us anything useful. Also, the police grilled the three bartenders from the places Simone, and later Isabelle, visited in the Quarter. One of the bartenders provided a cell phone number he used to contact Baptiste. The other two guys gave us nothing."

"One phone number is something, at least," Alex replied. "If NSA agrees to support us, we need to give them that new number."

Susan's secure phone sitting next to her desk rang at that moment. She answered, listened for about a minute, and asked the caller to hold on.

"Guys, you'd better take a seat," Susan said, shaking her head. She hit the desk lightly with her fist. "This is a special assistant in Director Riley's office." She pointed to the still active handset she was holding. "This morning, NSA agreed to support our investigation. There were two calls of interest that caught the attention of NSA analysts. One was made to a cell phone number you gave them for Baptiste, and the other was a return call from Baptiste to that incoming number."

"Do they know who Baptiste was speaking to?" Alex asked.

"Yes."

There was a long pause as Susan looked down at her desk and blew out a breath of air. She was in total disbelief.

"I'm sorry to say that during his conversation, Baptiste called the man 'Bordelon.' When NSA triangulated the call, it seems to have been made from a burner phone located near, or at, Vern Bordelon's home in Metairie."

Alex was stunned, as if he had been hit in the chest by a sledgehammer. "Son of a *bitch!* Vern Bordelon, the regional head of DEA!"

Susan returned to the call and spoke again on the secure line. "Does NSA know where Baptiste's phone was located during the call?" She listened, then thanked the caller before hanging up.

"The call was made from the Algiers neighborhood here in New Orleans. But Baptiste must have been on the move because the signal wasn't stationary. The special assistant will email us the streets used during the call and follow up with the text of the conversations."

"What should we do?" Rachel asked.

"We'd better alert NOPD and the FBI," Alex replied. "Shit, I never would have believed *Bordelon* was Baptiste's source."

"Now it's all coming together," Susan said. "Baptiste knew where the DEA and the Coast Guard had patrols in the Gulf, so his smugglers just avoided those areas."

"And that's how Baptiste got tipped off about the raid on Toussaint's house in Chalmette," Alex said.

"Then, why did Bordelon offer us the DEA safe house in Metairie?" Rachel asked. ". . .and are Billy and Moon Glow still safe there?"

Susan raised her shoulders and shook her head. "Damned if I know."

"I guess Bordelon must have figured that once the attack at their apartment failed, and Susan asked for his help, he decided it was better to know where the witnesses were being relocated and when. That way, he could keep an eye on them and inform Baptiste at a later time, if they still needed to be killed."

Susan's cell phone beeped; she looked at the message. It was a text from Riley's special assistant listing the streets used by Baptiste while he spoke with Bordelon.

"I'll call Bill Westbook at the FBI and John Washington at NOPD," she said.

WESTBROOK USED A SECURE GOVERNMENT PHONE, SO SUSAN WAS able to give him details about the calls between Bordelon and Baptiste. He confirmed the FBI would initiate a case of corruption against Bordelon and notify headquarters. Susan knew once they started investigating there might be additional charges.

Detective Washington did not have a secure phone, so he agreed to come to Susan's office to be briefed. Alex called Jim Riley in D.C. and told him the FBI would assume the lead in investigating Bordelon, while the NOPD still had the lead in Simone Ardoin's murder case.

WHEN WASHINGTON ARRIVED AT THE DS OFFICE, SUSAN AND ALEX briefed him in detail.

"I can't believe it," Washington said. "Although I don't work directly with Bordelon because our drug squad is his main point of contact, I always assumed he was a straight shooter. I guess you never know someone as well as you think. Do you believe he did it just for the money? And how much would motivate somebody to turn traitor?"

"All good questions," Alex replied. "I don't have any answers. Once he's arrested, the FBI will give him an opportunity to tell all. I imagine there will be several reasons behind his corruption."

Washington decided NOPD needed to stakeout the Algiers neighborhood in hopes of capturing Baptiste. Using Susan's secure office phone, he called Westbrook and told him what he intended to do. That's when the pissing contest started.

"We don't want you spooking Baptiste before we can put surveillance on Bordelon," Westbrook said on the phone."

"Baptiste is a vicious killer. This is the best lead we've had on him so far. But the information is perishable," Washington spat back. "He could leave Algiers at any minute."

"I'm not just *asking* you to hold off, Washington, I'm *telling* you not to flood Algiers with your people!" Westbrook said.

"Listen Bill, unless I get a specific order from City Hall to stand down, we're searching for Baptiste. His people killed a *cop* and wounded another. Not to mention they *killed* Ardoin. We'll do whatever is necessary to get him."

Westbrook was silent for a moment. "I understand your anger at Baptiste. But we'd like to establish a rock-solid link between him and Bordelon. That requires planning and may take time. I'm sure you don't want to jeopardize a federal case against Bordelon."

Washington shook his head in disgust. Alex watched, and

guessed John was thinking what most law enforcement agencies thought, that the FBI worked too slowly in the name of caution and was only focused on making its own case.

"If we capture Baptiste," Washington said, "you can squeeze him for info about Bordelon. But if he escapes, you'll have nothing at all."

"You make a good point," Westbrook said. "Let's compromise. I'm okay with NOPD using undercover officers in the Algiers area. Let us know if you spot him. I'd like to see a more substantial link between Baptiste and Bordelon."

"Okay, Bill, you have a deal."

John turned to the others and filled everyone in on the conversation. "I need to return to City Hall and get the ball rolling on putting undercover cops into the Algiers area. Thanks for your cooperation, Susan," he dipped his head in her direction, then at Alex, as he left.

"I've seen tension between State and the FBI before," Rachel said, "but is there always a strained relationship between the FBI and local law enforcement?"

"Sometimes," Alex replied. "It depends on who the players are. It's unfortunate, but the FBI has a penchant for demanding total control, at least from the headquarters level. In the old days, under Hoover, they always took credit for everything. They're better now and realize their prior strategy to maximize their PR image at the expense of other agencies was counterproductive."

"Let's hope Westbrook is a team player," Susan said.

"Yeah," Alex said, "but the question is, whose team is he playing on?"

Chapter 49

Surveillance

L ater that evening, NOPD put undercover officers on the streets of Algiers to look for Baptiste and Toussaint. Some sat in unmarked cars; others hung out in local bars and restaurants. A few walked the streets and chatted with passers-by. All these locations were set around the neighborhood where Baptiste had used his cell phone to talk with Bordelon.

As expected, it took the FBI longer to start their surveillance because FBI headquarters in Washington had to approve the operation. That entailed having to go to a judge who would grant search warrants for Bordelon's phones, bank, and credit card records. After eighteen hours, the New Orleans FBI office finally had full approval from D.C. for their activity. Then, in the middle of the night, they surreptitiously placed trackers on Bordelon's personal and official vehicles and began monitoring his calls 24/7. However, much to their disappointment, Bordelon's financial transactions appeared routine; but of course, if he was using cash from Baptiste's bribes, then many purchases would not appear on any record.

One bright young female FBI agent noticed the minivan parked in Bordelon's home driveway had a wheelchair attachment on back; it was one of two personal vehicles parked there. She suggested perhaps Bordelon had a handicapped family member who needed special medical treatment. Within 24 hours, the FBI had accessed Bordelon's government insurance records and established that his twelve-year-old son had been receiving cancer treatment for several years.

"Apparently, he's been treated at both Ochsner Hospital in New Orleans, and MD Anderson Cancer Center in Houston," an agent reported. "Of more importance, Bordelon has submitted claims for an extremely expensive regime of cancer-fighting medicines. Some are new and not covered by his insurance."

Further investigation with area pharmacies revealed Bordelon had paid for the non-covered medicines with large amounts of cash.

A DAY AFTER THE FBI OPENED ITS CASE ON BORDELON, ALEX WAS sitting in Susan Witt's office and calling Bill Westbrook.

"Hi, Bill, it's Alex Boyd. Just checking if you've been able to develop any leads on Vern Bordelon and his link to Jules Baptiste."

"No new links, yet, but we may have uncovered Bordelon's *motivation* for taking bribes. There may be additional reasons, but this one really stands out." He described the medical situation for Bordelon's son.

After another few minutes talk, Alex thanked him for the update and hung up. He looked at Susan and Rachel.

"At least we know the FBI field office is working hard on the case. Too bad I had to call to get a report. The fact they didn't volunteer to share their results is troubling. But I believe our primary concern should be to find Baptiste for Simone's murder. The FBI can handle the Bordelon corruption case by themselves. Besides, they're good at that type of investigation."

"Yeah, I agree," Susan replied. She tapped her fingers on her desk and stared at the wall.

"What are you thinking?" Rachel asked.

"We're doing a good job of being reactive to what's happening, but maybe we need to provoke Baptiste into panicking, so he'll leave his lair."

"*Lair*?" Alex said. "Have you started reading Shakespeare?"

Susan smiled. "Hey, I went to college, too. On a more serious note, if Baptiste doesn't start moving, we may not be able to find him."

"I know," Alex replied. "But Westbrook asked NOPD not to be too aggressive in searching because they didn't want Baptiste to get spooked and flee before they could make their case against Bordelon. Catching them together would make prosecution easier."

"But at this point, I think Baptiste will do whatever is necessary *not* to be caught," Susan replied. "So, the chance of them meeting while under surveillance is almost nil."

"Well, thanks to NSA, the FBI can use the monitored conversation between Baptiste and Bordelon as evidence; I imagine the FBI will also find more records of Bordelon using cash that he won't be able to explain away."

Rachel weighed in. "So the best hope of capturing Baptiste,

and helping the FBI make their case against Bordelon, is to flush out Baptiste?"

"We think so," Alex replied. Susan's cell phone rang; the caller ID showed Sgt. Washington's name. She put the call on speaker.

"Hi, John. What's up?" Susan asked.

"Some good news for us, but Westbrook won't be happy. Captain Wells convinced the chief and the mayor that we need to go all out to find Baptiste. Therefore, we're starting active patrols in Algiers at noontime."

"How active?" Susan asked.

"Black and whites driving all around. Uniformed patrolmen on foot stopping passers-by and asking about Baptiste and Toussaint."

"John, it's Alex Boyd," he said speaking up so he could be heard.

"Hi, Alex."

"Is someone going to notify Westbrook about the new tactic?"

"Yeah. The chief is calling him now."

"Excellent. We support you one hundred percent."

"Thanks, Alex. That's all, so I guess we'll talk again soon." The call ended.

Susan tapped her fingers on her desktop. "You know, I stopped by the safe house this morning. I wonder if we should move the witnesses again since Bordelon has turned out to be the snitch."

"I think that might tip him off that he's under investigation," Alex replied. "Besides, where would we move them?"

"Actually, I may have taken care of that yesterday afternoon. I received a funding cite from DS to rent a furnished corporate apartment in town, and just found a place in the Central Business District."

"I'm impressed with your initiative," Alex replied.

"Thanks. I learned from the best."

Alex thought she referred to his mentoring her in Islamabad, Pakistan, when he said, "That's kind of you to say so."

"Oh, I was referring to the U.S. Army when I served in the Middle East."

Rachel laughed. Alex tried to repress a smile.

"I see. Not bad humor for a girl from Oklahoma."

The three continued talking since there was nothing more to do but wait and see if Baptiste was spotted, so they could pounce.

What law enforcement didn't know was that Baptiste had already decided to move to the fishing camp. He was no longer in the Algiers neighborhood.

Chapter 50

The Kidnapping

Jules Baptiste was furious that he had been forced to become defensive in his fight with law enforcement. It wasn't in his nature to be in that position and it was intolerable to him.

Now he paced the large room in his fishing camp on the Pearl River. Claude Toussaint and Destiny watched him storm back and forth, observing his anger at the situation.

"Why don't you sit down, honey?" asked Destiny.

"I can't, I'm thinking."

"About what?"

"I need to grab the upper hand. I need to regain power over the cops."

Claude listened to the exchange. "How can we do that, boss? Do you have something in mind?"

"We need to snatch at least one of the two witnesses, hold them hostage, just in case we need to cut a deal with the cops."

"But they're protected. We already tried to kill them at their apartment. It was a disaster."

"I know," Baptiste replied. "We need to smoke them out. Hit them when and where they aren't expecting it."

"I don't think we can attack their new safe house," Claude said.

"No kidding. Maybe we can get that girl to come to her tattoo parlor."

"I have an idea," Claude replied. "Let's get the owner to call the girl and say it's important for her to come to the shop. We'll just make up an excuse. Then we grab her when she's there. Maybe her boyfriend will be with her and we'll get 'em both."

"I like that idea. Of course, they'll be protected, but if we can surprise them, it could work out," Baptiste said. "Claude, make the plan and call our men to get the job done."

FOUR OF BAPTISTE'S MEN SURVEILLED THE SHOP FOR TEN MINUTES, before descending on the tattoo parlor, The fact no cops were around made perfect sense since Moon Glow and Billy weren't allowed to leave their safe house in the Metairie suburbs

When the men arrived, luck was on their side; it was empty of customers. They entered and quickly turned the sign around on the door. It now read: "Closed." One of them drew the shade while the others surrounded the owner and a second tattoo artist.

It took only a few minutes of implied torture to convince the owner to call Moon Glow. With a gun pointed at her head, the owner used the new cell phone number Moon Glow had secretly texted to her.

"Hey, Moon Glow, it's me. Good to hear your voice," the owner said on the phone. "But we have a serious problem. A guy just came in that you did recently. You put a dragon tattoo on his arm, remember? Well, his arm is bleeding. Plus, the tattoo is looking a little rough around the edges. He says he'll sue us, if we can't fix it. I need you to come down here now and take a look. You gotta come now."

"Holy *shit*, how can that be?" Moon Glow replied. "It was a *perfect* tat when he left the shop."

"I know, but I'm looking at it right now, and it's bleeding. If he sues us, I'll be out of business. I can't afford an attorney to fight this."

"Okay, okay. Let me see if I can convince my cops to drive me there. I'll call you back one way or the other," Moon Glow said and quickly hung up.

THE REGULAR TEAM OF DS SPECIAL AGENTS PROTECTING MOON Glow and Billy were off duty now, sleeping at their hotel, when the tattoo parlor owner called. They had worked through the night and would return to duty later in the evening.

The daytime shift at the safe house was being handled by three NOPD officers. There was supposed to be a fourth officer, but he had been delayed by working a private detail in the Garden District and his detail was running overtime.

After hearing Moon Glow's pleas, the cops reluctantly agreed to drive Moon Glow to the French Quarter, but only if she stayed for no more than fifteen minutes; then they would return her to the safe house.

The plan was for one cop to stay at the house with Billy

while the other two escorted Moon Glow to the parlor. They figured fifteen minutes wouldn't hurt anything.

Finding no place to park in front of the tattoo parlor, the driver parked further down the street; the second cop walked Moon Glow into the shop. Once inside, Baptiste's men immediately disarmed the cop and using his own equipment, the cop was handcuffed to a pipe in the toilet room.

The other cop waited fifteen minutes in the car, then drove back to the shop, surprised his partner and Moon Glow weren't already waiting outside. Double parking out front, he entered, and was shocked to find his partner handcuffed . . . and Moon Glow gone.

Reluctantly, he called in the situation to NOPD headquarters, knowing his career was now toast, and the key witness in the case might already be dead.

Baptiste's thugs had skillfully driven Moon Glow out of the French Quarter moments before. They were headed for the fishing camp on the Pearl River where Baptiste would decide her fate.

Chapter 51

The Sighting

S t. Tammany Parish deputies Gardner and Treadwell drifted along the Pearl River in their unmarked twelve-foot skiff, fishing rods in hand. Their lines reached into the water, pretending to catch dinner. Both were dressed in casual khaki shorts and nylon short-sleeved, cream-colored shirts with extra pockets for gear. Their Harley-Davidson baseball caps helped mask their faces.

The weather was spoiling with heavy, dark clouds rolling in from the Gulf of Mexico. As they floated by the channel where Baptiste had been reported to have a camp, they saw two boats tied up at the camp's dock. Each boat had an enclosed cabin and appeared to be no longer than thirty feet. On the dock, below the raised deck, were two shirtless, muscular black men who wore blue jeans and tennis shoes. It appeared they were loading jerry-cans of fuel or water onto the back end of each boat.

Gardner took out his cell phone and snapped a few pictures. They observed the area for another five minutes, then returned to their launch point and reported their discovery to St. Tammany Parish Sheriff's headquarters.

Sheriff Landry's office called Sgt. John Washington's office in NOPD with the news. Washington spoke to Captain Wells, who initiated a three-way call to Bill Westbrook and Susan Witt. Alex and Rachel were still in Susan's office at the time and listened in to the conversation.

"Hello, Bill and Susan. This is Captain Jim Wells. We just received a report from the St. Tammany Parish Sheriff's office that two boats are docked at Baptiste's fishing camp. Our concern is that the boats may have extra fuel in jerry-cans onboard. My guess is they're preparing to leave town."

"How far can they travel?" Westbrook asked.

"I'm not sure. But if they go to the mouth of the Pearl River and enter nearby Lake Borgne, they'll be at the Gulf in no time. There they can transfer to a bigger ship with far greater range and be gone for good."

"Hold on a second," Captain Wells told the group on the speaker phone meeting. Alex heard voices in the background, then he heard Wells explode with anger at someone. After more chatter, Wells rejoined the phone conversation.

"I have terrible news. Stupidly, my men brought Moon Glow Ross to her tattoo parlor for some business. It was a set-up and she was kidnapped. Since she wasn't killed immediately, I believe she's been taken to Baptiste.

"We should raid the camp," Susan said.

"I agree," Captain Wells replied.

"I can have the FBI's hostage rescue team down here by tomorrow," Westbrook said.

"That'll be too late," Wells said. "I think we need to raid tonight. We should also call the Coast Guard to send a cutter into Lake Borgne just in case Baptiste gets by us. I have photos of the two boats now loading at his dock. I'll text them to you both in a moment."

"We have two Mobile Security Deployment teams in New Orleans at this time," Susan said. "They're all former military and well-trained. They can help with the raid."

"Good. I'm going to coordinate this with Sheriff Landry," Wells said. "We have enough combined law enforcement to do the job, if we don't trip over one another. I'll get back to you, Bill. Trust me, I'll ensure every agency has a role to play."

As they hung up, Susan turned to Alex. "What do you think?"

"I think this raid will either be great, or a huge cluster-fuck. But so far, I'm impressed with Captain Wells; let's see what he can arrange."

"What's the problem with everyone participating?" Rachel asked.

"The problem is they haven't trained together as a unit," Alex replied. "If assumptions are made that prove wrong, people could get hurt, even killed by friendly fire. It's like too many cooks in a kitchen with everybody doing their own thing."

"That's why you do so many drills with the marines in our embassies, isn't it," Rachel said.

"Exactly. Everyone should be on the same page when it comes to tactics and overall objectives; that takes practiced coordination. We don't have that in this situation."

"Susan, if you want to get MSD involved, how about contacting them at either the safe house or at their hotel. Maybe we can keep one team of four guarding Billy and the other team available for the raid."

"I'll do that now," she said.

OVER THE NEXT TWO HOURS, CAPTAIN WELLS WAS ON THE PHONE coordinating a plan of action to raid the fishing camp on the Pearl River: Using two boats, SWAT teams from NOPD and St. Tammany Parish Sheriff would assault the camp. Two other boats would block the river headed toward Lake Borgne manned by a team from St. Tammany Parish in one and the MSD team from Diplomatic Security in the other, using an NOPD boat. The US Coast Guard would have an eighty-seven-foot-long cutter on Lake Borgne in case Baptiste, or his men, evaded everyone else. The cutter had a complement of ten sailors, and carried two .50 caliber machine guns, plus small arms for each man or woman on board. Its top speed was about twenty-five knots.

Detective John Washington and a squad of NOPD officers would remain at the dock where the boats launched to take Baptiste and his men into custody after they were handed over by the SWAT teams. The killers would then be taken back to New Orleans and charged with both the murders of Simone Ardoin and the NOPD officer at the Esplanade Apartment building. Other felony charges would most certainly follow.

Bill Westbrook and a few FBI agents would be at the dock as observers, but once Baptiste was in custody, the FBI would squeeze him to testify against Vern Bordelon for accepting bribes.

Drug charges would be brought against Baptiste after Bordelon was in custody. Susan Witt and Alex Boyd would remain at the dock, also as observers. If, however, the raid found fake passports or phony US visas for Baptiste, then, upon return to the city, DS would ask the US Attorney's office to charge him with passport/visa fraud. That alone could bring ten years in jail and a fine $250,000. While these were lesser charges than murder, they could play a crucial role in keeping Baptiste and his men in jail until the murder trial.

Everyone was now in agreement on the plan. It was a good plan if it worked.

All Susan's New Orleans-based DS officers were now sitting in her office with Alex and Rachel along with the four MSD agents who would be part of the operation.

Alex watched the MSD agents put on their brown and green camouflage pants and jackets they had brought with them from D.C. Each wore lite-weight military style combat boots. For weapons, each carried a Glock 9mm pistol and an M-4 carbine in 5.56mm caliber. Just before getting on the river, the MSD agents would don their ballistic vests.

As for Alex's own attire, he only had what he brought to New Orleans for vacation - blue jeans, a short-sleeved black polo shirt, and black running shoes. The office lent him a dark blue jacket with the words "Federal Agent, Diplomatic Security," on the back. The jacket's front had a large emblem of the DS badge. He would carry the Glock Model 19 with extra magazines that Susan had given him after he had first arrived in town. His attire and equipment were fine with him because he and Susan were only supposed to be observers.

All units agreed it would *have been* best to make the raid late at night, or in the early morning while still dark, but Baptiste's boats had been spotted taking extra fuel on board. It was assumed Baptiste was not planning to hang around for long.

Therefore, the raid had been moved up to begin at nine that

evening. This would allow all tour boats to finish their travel on the river. It would also allow time for the St. Tammany Parish and NOPD marine units to get their equipment to the river and in place.

Alex looked at his watch. *It's 7:00 pm. Time to leave the office*, he noted. Then, he hugged Rachel and gave her a big kiss. She would stay in the office with a couple of Susan's agents who weren't participating in the raid.

"Come back safe, Alex," she said.

"Sure thing. I'll be surrounded by cops. This will be a no risk operation for me."

"Sure. That's what you said in Cairo, remember? Just before you were shot."

"Hey, don't worry, sweetheart, Cairo was different. I was part of the bodyguard team then. Now, Susan and I will be waiting on the boat dock for the SWAT teams to return."

He stared into her eyes and knew she wasn't happy with his story. He kissed her again and all the DS agents went down to the garage to drive to the Pearl River.

She's right, you know, he thought, as he climbed into his assigned vehicle.

Chapter 52

Swamp Assault

At a little past 9:00 p.m., two twenty-one-foot patrol boats were the first to take up position on the Pearl River, between Baptiste's fishing camp and Lake Borgne. In one boat, six SWAT team members from the sheriff's office were onboard; on the other, four DS Mobile Security Deployment agents, one NOPD SWAT officer, and a pilot from NOPD were present and ready.

All motors were muffled as part of a routine noise reduction package installed when the crafts were built.

Once their position was confirmed by radio, two more twenty-one-foot boats left the pier and headed for the fishing camp. This was the assault force comprised of officers from NOPD-SWAT and St. Tammany Parish SWAT teams.

The plan was for the St. Tammany sheriff's boat to unload first at Baptiste's dock, followed by the NOPD team. All were experienced cops who had been in violent shootouts in the past. Some had seen prior military action in Iraq or Afghanistan while serving in the Army or Marines. All were currently heavily armed.

For Alex, Susan, and John Washington waiting back at the pier for reports, time seemed to stand still. Alex wanted to be much closer to the action, evaluate the situation, and, if necessary, take decisive action. Sheriff Billy Landry was also on the pier with a few supporting officers along with Bill Westbrook and three more FBI agents from the New Orleans office.

Alex was reluctant to form an opinion on men he had never met, but he couldn't help but notice how uncomfortable the three FBI agents with Westbrook seemed to be. They were fidgeting and moving their feet.

Probably nerves, he thought. *There's no other reason unless I misjudge them. Could they really want to be on the raid? No, it's probably nerves, or maybe the swamp really terrifies them.*

Washington and Sheriff Landry were monitoring progress on their radios while Alex and Susan listened in. As they stood, waiting for reports, the heavens opened up and hard rain pelted them without mercy. Alex, Susan and Washington pulled out baseball caps and turned up the collars of their jackets. The FBI agents popped open small umbrellas.

"Alpha One, we're approaching the channel to the camp," a voice came over the radio.

"*What the hell?*" someone in the background yelled.

"Alpha One here. Two boats just left the camp at high speed, heading toward Lake Borgne. We are in pursuit."

"Bravo One, we copy and are ready to intercept." Bravo One was positioned to block the mouth of the Pearl River.

Thirty seconds later two boats rounded a bend at high speed from the direction of the fishing camp, the boat wakes flooding the docks of nearby fishing locations. Both waiting police boats turned on powerful spotlights, blinding those in the escaping boats.

"*POLICE!* Heave to, and arms in the air!" a blasting announcement came from Bravo One's loud hailer.

Men on both Baptiste's boats opened fire. Bullets ricocheted off the side of the police cruisers; sparks flew everywhere. Without hesitation, the cops and DS agents all returned a barrage of firepower. All police and DS agents had M-4 carbines with night-vision optics mounted on their weapons making it easy to zero in on their targets with great accuracy.

The fleeing boat closest to the DS craft immediately lost power after it took numerous hits from the DS marksmen's gunfire. Without an operational engine, the boat was virtually dead in the water and drifted ever closer to the agents. The agents saw a few dead bodies sprawled on top of the deck; belching smoke billowed from the engine. Two wounded thugs were quickly taken into custody and handcuffed while the bodies of the dead remained onboard as the boat caught fire.

The second gangster boat nearest to the cops fared no better. It had tried to veer around the cops but with its engine still roaring at high speed, the boat ran aground and launched everyone overboard.

The pilot from the St. Tammany Parish police boat swung his searchlight onto the boat's wreckage. Two bodies were floating lifeless in the water and three more were flopping around in the shallow water apparently injured. Without resistance, they were hauled into the police boat, and handcuffed. It was all over in minutes.

Everyone back at the pier heard gunfire. Sheriff Landry

waited a few seconds, then called on the radio: "Landry to Alpha and Bravo, what's happening?"

There was a ten second delay, then an officer replied, "All okay!" He proceeded to give an update on the shootout and subsequent arrests.

Alex walked up to Landry. "Ask them if they have Baptiste?"

"Do you have Baptiste?" Landry called into the radio.

"Negative," was the surprise response.

Alex punched one fist into the palm of his other hand in frustration. Then he spotted one remaining twenty-one-foot boat at the pier. Turning to Deputy Vinnie Fiore, he yelled, "Let's go!"

Fiore looked over at Landry who nodded as Alex, Susan, and Washington leaped onto the boat. Alex called over to Westbrook, "Want your agents to come?"

"I think we're good here," Westbrook called back with a wave of his hand.

"Hit the gas!" Alex yelled to Vinnie. The boat accelerated and tore down the river toward Baptiste's camp. Wind and rain smashed into their faces; Susan shuffled next to Alex.

"Did you *really* want the FBI to come with us?" she asked.

"Are you kidding? *Hell* no! But at least, I made the offer. Maybe the FBI's Hostage Rescue team guys would have joined us if they'd been here. But the guys on the dock now from the field office? They're probably afraid of getting wet if their umbrellas turned inside out." Susan chuckled in understanding.

Vinnie's boat had a small wheelhouse, so everyone moved inside, out of the pouring rain. Minutes later, they were approaching the channel where Baptiste's fishing camp was located.

"Vinnie, slow down," Alex said, "Let's observe the camp before we leave the boat."

Vinnie pulled back on the throttle and the boat went forward at only a knot or two. Alex grabbed binoculars hanging on the wall and stepped outside onto the deck. The rain pelleted his face in the total darkness. No movement was visible in the direction of the camp, although it was hard to see through the rain and thick trees.

Then he heard the sound of a low-powered motor. As Susan joined him on deck, he put a finger to his lips. They listened for seconds, then she touched his arm and pointed down river to the opposite bank from the fishing camp.

Through the binoculars, he watched a small boat about one hundred yards away moving slowly toward the camp, Apparently, it was leaving a small shack on the other bank. He barely made out three figures aboard the boat which wasn't much larger than a canoe. But it was too dark to identify any individuals.

Vinnie also spotted the boat. "I don't think they can see us; let's wait for them to enter the channel, then follow."

"What do you think is happening?" Washington asked Alex.

"I think Baptiste is either in that boat or waiting to be picked up at the camp."

When the small boat disappeared into the channel, heading toward the fishing camp, Vinnie picked up speed. What no one saw was Big Beau, the humongous alligator, also tracking the small boat; it was well past his feeding time.

Alex's thoughts were only on the man they were tracking. He touched the pistol in his holster, *Baptiste, this is for Simone Ardoin. You're a dead man.*

Chapter 53

Best Laid Plans

A loud thunderclap destroyed the silence of the night as two lightning bolts struck nearby. Through his binoculars, Alex could see the outline of the camp in spite of the pouring rain. He could make out the features of the shack, the raised deck, and its lower dock, exactly as Willie the Snitch had described. The small boat they had quietly followed was now docked on the near side of the landing. He could also see a man bent over, doing something on the far side.

As Vinnie let the police boat drift silently closer to the camp, he saw a second dock where the man was removing camouflage netting from a larger boat, perhaps a 25-footer.

The heavy rain helped mask their approach as Vinnie's boat drifted closer with the motor off, then gently bumped into the dock. Washington leaped off the boat onto the wood planking. The unknown man spun around just as Washington connected with a powerful punch to his jaw. He staggered back, fell off the dock, hitting his head on the stern of the 25-footer as he landed in the water.

Within seconds, Big Beau's mouth opened wide before clamping down on the man's head and dragging him underwater. Dinner had been served.

Everyone froze in place and looked up the ladder at the raised deck above until they realized no one had been alerted by the man's splash into the water.

As Vinnie tied his boat line to a cleat on the dock, Alex climbed the ladder followed by Washington, then Susan.

Once he reached the top, Alex drew his pistol. To his left, toward the end of the raised deck, were pieces of deck furniture and storage cabinets anyone could hide behind. To the right was the shack. He went left as Washington climbed to the top of the ladder and went right. Susan held her position at the ladder.

Alex cleared the end of the raised deck and joined Washington now at the left side of the shack's door. Susan slid to the right-hand side. Washington turned the door handle, then pushed it open to make a dynamic entry into the room.

He hadn't counted on Claude Toussaint standing right in front of him. It was pure bad luck. Toussaint grabbed Washington's gun hand and they wrestled to the floor. Washington kicked him several times with his knees, then used his left elbow to smash Toussaint's face which gave him the edge to overpower Toussaint.

Alex had rushed in close behind Washington with eyes focused on both men when Baptiste hit Alex's wrist with a beer bottle, knocking the gun out of his hand.

Baptiste was taller than Alex with lots of lean muscle, so Alex had his hands full. Baptiste nailed him twice with punches to the head, but Alex was quick to counterstrike with powerful straight right and left punches to Baptiste's lower ribs. When Baptiste tried another haymaker with his right hand, Alex side-stepped and locked Baptiste's extended arm between his own bicep and forearm, then with maximum upward pressure, he snapped Baptiste's humerus bone above the elbow.

Baptiste howled in enormous pain. Again, Alex lifted Baptiste's broken arm in a painful hold. But Baptiste drove his other hand hard into Alex's face and freed his trapped, injured arm. He ran out onto the deck in the pouring rain and turned to face his nemesis. But Alex was emotionally fueled with the desire to kill this man and nailed Baptiste with two powerful straight kicks to the balls. Baptiste staggered backward into the railing of the raised deck which shattered under his weight and he fell off the platform.

As the men were fighting, Baptiste's girlfriend, Destiny, came out of the bathroom, saw the fights going on, and reached for a shotgun resting against a wall in the corner of the room. Susan sprinted across the room and collided with her in a perfect tackle. They landed on the adjoining bedroom floor where Susan got the upper hand, punched Destiny twice in the head, then used flex-ties to handcuff her.

In the downpour, Alex stood up on deck, sucked in some deep breaths, and touched the side of his face where he'd been hit. Then he walked over to end of the deck expecting to see Baptiste floating in the water.

Surprised, he saw Baptiste precariously hanging below on a rail support with his good hand, his body dangling just above the water.

A motion in the water to his right caught Alex's attention. Big Beau was directly below Baptiste. The Haitian looked down, following Alex's gaze, and saw the hungry gator being joined by two others swimming toward them. Big Beau raised himself out of the water but was unable to reach Baptiste's dangling legs.

Alex smiled. *Must be dessert time.*

"Help me!" Baptiste cried out. He followed his plea with something in Creole French, but another thunderclap and the sound of the rain drowned out his words. A close by lightning strike again lit up the sky. Alex flinched at the sound, but his eyes remained focused on Baptiste.

I wonder how long Baptiste's strength will last? he thought. *Just how long can any man hold on with just one hand?* But Alex had no patience to wait. He placed one foot on Baptiste's fingers and debated sending the bastard to his death.

At that moment, Vinnie arrived. He reached down around Alex's leg and pulled Baptiste onto the deck with his muscular arms as if the injured man was a child.

"I guess you were just keeping him from falling," Vinnie said to Alex.

"Something like that."

Then Alex looked back toward the shack and saw Washington and Susan escorting the handcuffed Toussaint and Destiny out the door. Walking behind them was Moon Glow, who had been held in the bathroom. It didn't seem she had been roughed up in any way. Seeing Alex, Moon Glow reached him and gave a big hug.

Susan came up to Alex and handed him back his gun. "Try to hold onto to this, will you? It's in my office inventory and I have to account for all weapons." Alex smirked, appreciating the humor.

Searchlights roamed the water from all four returning police boats and illuminated the fishing camp. As they docked, several officers man-handled Baptiste, Toussaint, and Destiny down the ladder and onto several of the patrol boats. Moon Glow was escorted onto another one of the boats.

Alex and his team stayed back at the shack to search for evidence of Baptiste's crimes. Using small flashlights, they found a bag filled with equipment and documents to forge U.S. visas, as well as another bag stuffed with $200,000 cash. There was an opened box in the corner of the room with some drugs that appeared to be cocaine, but the wrappings were torn.

I'm sure the main stash was already transferred to the escape boats, Alex thought. *They were so close to leaving and I'm not sure they were planning on taking Moon Glow with them. At this point, she was just a liability. Glad we got here in time.*

One last item they uncovered was a ledger with notations for dates and amounts of money. Next to some of the notations were the initials "V.B." Alex assumed that implicated Vern Bordelon. Written in pen on a separate piece of paper was a list of telephone numbers, some with the country code for Haiti. Alex would share this list with the NSA.

He was about to carry the bag down to Vinnie's boat when he realized there was a second, smaller bag within the first. Opening it, he saw a dozen grainy photos of Vern Bordelon humping a naked woman. He turned over each photo to read handwriting on the back. The photos were three years old and taken in a Port-au-Prince hotel room. Bordelon may have needed money to pay for his son's expensive cancer medications, but there was little doubt he had been blackmailed with these photos.

Alex hauled everything in the bags down the ladder to Vinnie's boat. They motored back to their starting point at the pier. Moon Glow was already being led away to a police car by an NOPD officer. She would be in safe hands now as the NOPD and DS decided how best to protect her and Billy.

Alex handed the ledger, $200,000, and photos to Bill Westbrook.

From her vehicle, Susan retrieved a document for chain of custody, and a large evidence bag. She filled out the document, signed it, and handed it to Westbrook who countersigned.

Alex took the opportunity to ask him, "Bill, I want to hold onto the passport and visa fraud equipment to help with our separate criminal case against Baptiste," Alex said.

"Sure, no problem, Alex," Westbrook said.

Then, turning to Sheriff Landry, he said, "Thanks for all your support, Sheriff. We couldn't have done this without the St. Tammany Parish Sheriff's office."

"It was a pleasure to work with you, Alex. I need to learn more about Diplomatic Security."

"Just tell Susan if you ever want to visit D.C. I'm sure Director Riley will roll out the red carpet for you."

"Are you going back to London, now?" Landry asked.

"In a few days; we've got some things to wrap up in New Orleans, then we'll stop in D.C. on our way back overseas."

By the time everyone shook hands and departed the pier, the rain had stopped. It hadn't been the vacation trip Alex and Rachel had bargained for, but at least they were able to capture the murderer of Simone Ardoin and bring a small bit of closure to Papa Ed and Camille.

Perhaps the best part for Alex and Rachel now would be to personally tell the Ardoins how justice would be meted out.

Yes, they would enjoy that most of all.

Epilogue

Papa Ed and Camille Ardoin found solace and support among their many friends in New Orleans. As a group, they decided to honor Simone's memory in perpetuity by establishing a fully funded mentoring program for disadvantaged youth with an emphasis upon recruiting male mentors to guide troubled boys. The Ardoins also felt a need to better understand Simone's journey through her short, yet successful career with the State Department. In her honor, they planned to travel to cities where she had been assigned such as Rome, Milan, and Port-au-Prince. Because Simone had also worked in Washington, D.C., Rachel arranged a special tour of the State Department including a visit to several offices in which Simone had worked and an opportunity to speak with her former colleagues.

Jules Baptiste and **Claude Toussaint** would stand trial for murder, drug smuggling, visa fraud, kidnapping, and conspiracy to murder federal agents, along with a host of other crimes. In exchange for their cooperation to testify against Vern Bordelon of DEA, the death penalty would be removed from consideration. However, if convicted, both would face life imprisonment.

Vern Bordelon, DEA, would stand trial for bribery, conspiracy to smuggle drugs, and conspiracy to murder. He confessed to being blackmailed over his relationship with prostitutes in Haiti the three years prior but claimed he had been distraught over the recent diagnosis of his son's cancer. He also confessed to accepting bribes to fund his purchase of cancer medications for his son.

Sgt. John Washington, NOPD, received an award for his outstanding work in bringing Baptiste and Toussaint to justice. He is currently on the short-list for promotion to Lieutenant. Future plans include visiting Alex and Rachel in London; Alex has promised a special tour of Scotland Yard during the visit.

Susan Witt received several State Department awards for her work on the Simone Ardoin case. Her future assignment to Colombo, Sri Lanka, has been confirmed.

Willie, the Snitch, received $50,000 for providing information leading to the arrest and conviction of Baptiste at his fishing camp. Willie immediately purchased a new Cadillac to drive and a gold tooth for the front of his mouth. As he drove around his 9th Ward neighborhood in his new Caddy, he was carjacked and punched so hard in the mouth that his gold tooth was knocked out and stolen. The car was never recovered.

Moon Glow Ross and **Billy Whiteman** had never technically been entitled to reward money, but Alex convinced Director Jim Riley that they never would have known where to begin searching if the two hadn't identified Baptiste as the killer of Simone Ardoin. Riley persuaded the State Department to award the couple $25,000. Billy used the money to buy new computer graphic programs and hardware, and Moon Glow added tattoos to her body.

Nicole, the heavy-set NOPD cop assigned to the Marriott hotel to protect undercover DS agent Isabelle Lewis, received plaudits for notifying her partner on the radio that two gangsters were on their way up in the elevator. She was embarrassed, however, that she could not have moved faster in leaving the restaurant table to confront the gangsters. As a result, she vowed to lose weight and eat a healthier diet. To date, she has already lost twenty pounds.

Alex Boyd and **Rachel Smith** had one last meal with Papa Ed and Camile at the Dooky Chase restaurant in New Orleans. It was a tearful goodbye, but the Ardoins promised to visit them in London following their trip to Rome and Milan. As for future assignments, it appears after another year in London, Alex may become the next Security Director for NATO in Brussels, and Rachel may become the next Deputy Chief of Mission at the U.S. Mission in Brussels, reuniting with her former State Department boss, Ambassador Archibald Watson. Rachel is also working with the State Department to create and fund the Simone Ardoin Foreign Affairs Fellowship at Tulane University.

Sgt. Vinnie Fiore, St. Tammany Parish Sheriff's office, sent Rachel a photo of himself in uniform, showing his huge muscular biceps. He signed it with the inscription: "Work out or die." After sharing the photo with Alex, she noticed that shortly afterward, he began each day doing twice as many push-ups as before. He is now also lifting heavier weights at the gym and looks fantastic.

Acknowledgments

There are many people who helped me write this novel. First, my wife, Irene Harrison, who deserves a great deal of praise. Born in New Orleans, Irene attended three years at Tulane University, lived in the French Quarter, and was a resident there before graduating from the American University and joining the Foreign Service. Her instinctive knowledge of the city, the people, and culture was of immense help in my research.

I also asked two friends in New Orleans to be my beta readers. Allison Raynor and Sandra Dartus both looked at my manuscript and gave sound advice. I met Allison in the 1980s when working at the World Trade Center of New Orleans when I was on loan from the U.S. State Department.

Although Allison was not born in the city, she has adopted it as her hometown and to this day has a wonderful understanding of its culture and people.

Sandra, who I met in the early 2000s, is a legend in the New Orleans area where she was born and raised. She is the former head of the French Quarter Festival and continues to be very active in civic and social events. Many thanks to you both.

A few years ago, Diann Schindler asked me, as a favor, to be a beta reader for her new book. She is an excellent writer and I enjoyed doing the project for her. She has since moved from Florida to Portugal, yet still offered to return the favor by using her keen eye which helped to improve my manuscript. As a former English professor and college president, Diann's suggestions were right on the mark. Thank you, Diann.

Finally, Paula Howard is my editor for this book, as well as for my previous five Alex Boyd action thrillers. Again, I thank her for her expert knowledge of character development, story arcs, perceptual pacing, and dialogue. She has done a terrific job on my series, and I am very grateful for our partnership, and friendship.

Thanks to all!

Award Winning Author of the
Alex Boyd Thriller Series

About the Author

During Mel Harrison's twenty-eight year career with the U.S. Department of State, he won both the Department's Award for Valor and the worldwide Regional Security Officer of the Year award.

Serving most of his career in the Diplomatic Security Service, Mel was assigned to embassies in Saigon, Quito, Rome, London, Seoul, and Islamabad. Prior to joining the Foreign Service, he graduated from the University of Maryland with a degree in Economics, and completed post-graduate work at The American University. The Department of State assigned him to the NATO Defense College in Rome for political-military studies.

Following government retirement, Mel spent ten years in corporate security or consulting work, with assignments often taking him throughout Latin America and the Middle East.

Other Novels by Mel Harrison
The Alex Boyd Thriller Series

Death in Pakistan

The Ambassador is Missing

Moving Target

Terror in Cairo

Spies Among Us

Review: Death in Pakistan

Book One

In the early 1990s, America changed course and supported military and economic assistance to India at Pakistan's expense.

As a result, Alex Boyd, deputy regional security officer at the US Embassy in Islamabad, Pakistan, must defend the Embassy, employees and a visiting U.S. Senate delegation against vicious, heavily armed, fanatical terrorists who are supported by a rogue element within Pakistan's military intelligence service (ISI).

Because of this, Alex and his team fight for their lives.

Complicating the situation, Alex must overcome the staid traditionalists within the Foreign Service, itself, who believe nothing should be done to aggravate the locals even in self-defense. The new Embassy press officer, Rachel Smith, an accomplished athlete and intellectual powerhouse, intimately bonds with Alex. She eventually battles the terrorist leader in ferocious hand-to-hand combat during the attack at the Embassy compound.

When you go to Pakistan, no one promises you'll return alive.

REVIEWS ON BOOK ONE

...An excellent story and well worth the reader's time...

The author is a veteran of the State Department and how it operates; the setting is our Embassy in Pakistan. His attention to detail of how embassies work is right on the mark. I should know as I retired from State after 40+ years of service, Seventy-five percent of my time was abroad at embassies around the world. He describes how his office (Diplomatic Security) fits in with the rest of the Embassy staff.

The story also describes how embassy security officers and the Marine Security Guards defend the Embassy when it is attacked by terrorists. This is an excellent story and well worth the readers time to devour it.

J. D.

...Can't put it down...

Death in Pakistan is a fact-based account of the working configuration of staff...top to bottom...in Islamabad during a crisis, well written by a retired Security Officer.

Tom Clancy's Jack Ryan's and Vince Flynn;s Mitch Rapp

need to make room for Mel Harrison's Alex Boyd! It is truly a "can't put it down story."

C.D.

...heart-pumping...

One of the most exciting novels I have ever read. Anyone that wants to know anything about the US Foreign Service or what the ambassadors and their staff do while stationed in a foreign country will come away with a real knowledge that sometimes the cushy jobs can be more dangerous than you think they could ever be.

If reading this story doesn't get your heart pumping, nothing will.

B. P.

Review: The Ambassador is Missing

Book Two

In the sequel to Death in Pakistan, Regional Security Officer Alex Boyd arrives in Rome expecting a comfortable assignment after the terrorist violence in Pakistan where he nearly lost his life.

On his first day in Italy, he is caught in the crossfire during a bank robbery where he saves the life of a grateful Italian VIP.

However, complicating his assignment, Alex's new embassy boss despises him for an old grievance, and his girlfriend, Rachel, is running hot and cold.

However, when terrorists kidnap the American ambassador and his wife, Alex swings into full-on action. He must maneuver through a maze of State Department bureaucratic incompetence and interference from the FBI, dodge bullets during police raids, and confront lying officials within the embassy staff.

Meanwhile, after two weeks of being held in a filthy basement, the ambassador is ill and running out of lifesaving medicine. With the FBI and State Department arguing with the Italians over how to deal with the crisis, Alex leads the way with the Italian police in a bold attempt to rescue the ambassador and his wife while they are still alive.

REVIEWS ON BOOK TWO

...a fast-paced thriller...

The Ambassador is Missing, is a great follow-on to Death in Pakistan. Mel Harrison's descriptions of life working in an embassy are rich with detail and his characters are well drawn and interesting. *The Ambassador is Missing* is an especially fast-paced thriller that is hard to put down. The growing romance between Regional Security Officer Alex and Public Affairs Officer Rachel Smith is a plus, as we follow these two talented and like-able characters on their professional and personal journeys.

Looking forward to the next! *E. E.*

...ENTERTAINS WHILE GIVING UNIQUE INSIGHTS...

Another thriller in the Alex Boyd series, can't put it down until finished. Having served in an Embassy and worked in security for many years, author Mel Harrison, I found it entertains while giving unique insights on embassy workings and their unique cultures. *D. W. CDR (Intelligence), USNR (Ret.).*

. . .

...COULDN'T PUT IT DOWN...

Another great book and can't wait for the next one. I told my wife and now she's getting into these books. I stayed up later than usual because I couldn't put it down. Fun to read but also very interesting as to the goings on of the state department.

T. W.

...even better than the first...

The second Alex Boyd thriller is even better than the first. This book brought me right back to Italy and inside the embassy. Not usually a fan of nonfiction, I had to keep reminding myself this *was* a work of fiction. All around this was a great read. I finished the last page and downloaded the next book

- L.

Review: Moving Target

Book Three

Alex Boyd, restless at a desk job in Washington, D.C., hates bureaucracy and misses the excitement of an overseas assignment. When unexpected opportunities arise, he and Rachel Smith, his new wife, jump at the chance to work in Paris. But nothing goes as planned.

Soon their lives are at risk from a vicious Sicilian Mafia leader; their new bosses, Henri and Giselle Ducat, have disappeared. Were they kidnapped? Or did they run?

Moving Target is the third book in Mel Harrison's Alex Boyd thriller series after Death in Pakistan and The Ambassador is Missing. The Thrill continues!

. . .

REVIEWS ON BOOK THREE
...tough to put the book down...

Just when you think Alex Boyd and his beloved Rachel Smith are settling in to long U.S. Government careers, they take a turn to the private sector with Paris as a background and working among the very wealthy. Mel captures the essence of greed in "Moving Target" that makes humans do foolish things that cost lives and destroy relationships.

Mel obviously has high profile, private sector experience to be able to depict the characters so realistically that the reader finds himself guessing what danger or action lies around the corner. Mel also portrays the network of contacts that he made and maintained in his exemplary Department of State career through Alex.

Again, it is very tough to put the book down. Congratulations to Mr. Harrison.

D.D. M.

...his best book yet...

I was totally amazed at how the author put all the information together to make this storyline. His other books which I also have read were good and given 5 stars so I wish I could give this one SIX Stars!

B.P.

...a pleasure to enjoy his intelligent stories...

Mel has brought us into the international financial world

with this well written book. My sister who was trapped at home in the blizzard with no power was delighted to have this book. We both enjoy Mel's writing, he brings us into the world international intrigue and it's a pleasure to enjoy his intelligent stories.

H. D. B.

...so much fun...

This book is so much fun, a page turner as they say. When I finish each book written by Mel Harrison, my first thought is when is the next one going to come out? For now, I'll just wait but I highly recommend Moving Target.

T. M.

Review: Terror in Cairo

Book Four

Egyptian Islamic Jihad, (EIJ) a vicious terrorist organization determined to thwart peace with Israel, attacks an important Middle East Peace Conference in Cairo attempting to stop any chance of a successful conference outcome.

As special agent with the State Department Diplomatic Security Service (DS), Alex is responsible for the overall protection of U.S. delegates, including the Secretary of State and several senior senators and congressmen attending the conference.

When it appears the peace conference may be resurrected, the terrorists seek to inflict a mortal wound against America with an unprecedented target. With superb Arabic language skills and military experience, Alex is tasked with identifying the leaders of EIJ before they strike again. A team of U.S. Navy SEALs leads the way into the harsh desert of Libya to terminate them.

Alex takes charge of Embassy security. Rachel Smith, now his wife, has assumed the role of Embassy Press Officer, risking her own life in the line of duty. Questions remain whether Alex, and his colleagues, can win this life and death struggle. Even more important, who is arming the terrorists?

REVIEWS ON BOOK FOUR

...gripping, fast-paced...

From the very first page, this story is gripping and fast-paced... Anyone interested in embassy life will enjoy reading these books. Thanks to Mel for his service and for writing these enjoyable thrillers. O. P.

...very accurate in his descriptions of the city. . .

The story line from start to finish was presented in such a way that it was hard to put the book down once I started it. You could just picture the sights and sounds of Cairo as the story unfolded. The author was very accurate in his descriptions of the city, the people, the traffic and the food. I lived and worked at the embassy in Cairo so I can attest to the authenticity of his descriptions. Hats off to Mel for another great book. Can't wait for the next one!

P. C. B.

...romance and humorous banter...

Fast paced and suffused not only with harrowing events and twisty plot elements but also with romance and humorous banter, the story pulls you in and keeps you there through the very end. What will Alex and Rachel get themselves involved in next time? I can't wait to find out.

E.E.

Review: Spies Among Us

Book Five

Assigned to London, Alex Boyd and his wife Rachel Smith, a political officer for the Department of State, step into a spider's web of intrigue at the U.S. Embassy.

But as stories appear inconsistent and anomalies occur, Alex and Rachel begin to suspect an insider is responsible for passing on highly classified information to a deep cover Russian spy. With the help of the Embassy, CIA Station Chief Anna Battles, Scotland Yard's Special Branch, and British Intelligence Services, they work closely together to sort out the lies.

But the Russians have more than one ace up their sleeve. Alex and Rachel soon realize American secrets are still being lost to the other side and that it will take the combined efforts of the CIA and the FBI to figure out who else is trading secrets before the damage is beyond repair. Will they be able to find the spy among them?

REVIEWS ON BOOK FIVE

...great picture of mystery and intrigue ...

Just finished reading "Spies Among Us" by my favorite author, Mel Harrison . . . paints a great picture of mystery and intrigue. I found the story to be believable and well written. The characters all seemed real, and it felt like you were actually there as everything was happening.

Personally, I would like to see the Alex Boyd books turned into a mini-series on TV. I believe it could be just as good as Tom Clancy's "Jack Ryan". I can't wait for the next Alex Boyd thriller. Keep up the good work Mel!

P.C.B.

...easy reading and was hard to put down...

I have read all five of Mel Harrison's books with Alex Boyd as the main character. Was completely shocked to realize how little I know about foreign embassy work and how dangerous the jobs can be. His latest book, "Spies Among Us" inserts us into the thrilling world of espionage. The book is easy reading and was hard to put down. Enjoyed it immensely!

J.

...Great story and well written...

Great story and well-written. . . good insight into the world of diplomatic security.

P.S.

...intrigue kept me reading into the night.

My first book by Mel Harrison, I expected a thriller but instead was treated to a complex mystery within the the international world of espionage. The complexity and intrigue kept me reading into the night.

T.Z.

www.ingramcontent.com/pod-product-compliance
Lightning Source LLC
Chambersburg PA
CBHW071648260626
47170CB00001B/278